BALTHAZAR'S CASKET

To Trish
Who loves adventure stories!

With best wishes,

Cheryl O'Brien

READER REVIEWS OF BALTHAZAR'S CASKET

'Congratulations on your amazing story – what a read! I was enthralled from beginning to end. It is very well written and of course the research you have obviously done showed from the beginning, so much so that the story could all be true. It is certainly a riveting tale and the reader wants to keep reading as long as possible. I do hope that you protect the film rights so that it can become a motion picture.'

Conor, The O'Briain (Chief of the O'Brien Clan),
Earl of Inchiquin, Ireland

'I think you really have a hit! The concept was great: it really made one think. Raised as a Catholic, but not practicing, I felt a certain kinship to Sam and her thoughts on religion. I cannot say enough how enjoyable it was. The detail is amazing - I have no idea how you put together all of those facts, but such great background and a good blend of truth and fiction. I go back to the descriptions; these really allowed my imagination to visualise certain scenes. I also liked how you went from present to past to give the reader the history of the casket. I liked the pace and how the stories from the past tied into the present. I just wanted to say how much I enjoyed your novel – quite the treat!'

Cheri Beatty, Chicago, USA

BALTHAZAR'S CASKET

CHERYL O'BRIEN

This is a work of fiction. Names, characters, places, and incidents either are the product of the author's imagination or are used fictitiously. Any resemblance to actual persons, living or dead, events, or locales is entirely coincidental.

Copyright © 2023 by Cheryl O'Brien
Tigerlily Press

All rights reserved. No part of this book may be reproduced or used in any manner without written permission of the copyright owner except for the use of quotations in a book review.

First paperback edition 2023

ISBNs
Paperback: 978-1-80541-157-4
Hardcover: 978-1-80541-156-7
eBook: 978-1-80541-155-0

www.cheryl-obrien-author.co.uk

Instagram: @Cherylobrienbooks
Twitter: @Cherylobrien_
Linkedin: Cheryl O'Brien Books
Facebook: Cheryl O'Brien Books

For more information, contact: cheryl@cheryl-obrien-author.co.uk

DEDICATIONS

Originally, this novel was to have been co-written with my inestimable writer friend, Steve Sands. We met as members of Nottingham Writers' Club in the late 1970's and instantly took a grievous dislike to one another. Steve termed me a bossy, over-educated young woman who would never become a 'proper' writer and I disparaged Steve as an argumentative, hairy-arsed git. To put it succinctly, we were poles apart. Funny thing was, our loathing incited us to spar verbally – largely after club meetings and almost always in the nearest pub. And the magical inevitable happened. We became acquainted and, in so doing, both realised that our initial assessments had been way off the mark. From loathing we graduated to tolerance, then liking and ultimately to becoming literary soulmates (and the deepest of life-long friends).

We both wrote, in small ways, in between earning our livings – and even succeeded in occasionally winning competitions and seeing some of our creative works published (poetry and short stories), but neither of us found the time to write a full-length novel. For years we tossed around ideas for plots, but the dictates of life, as for the vast majority of people, kept getting in the way of serious literary accomplishment. Steve had a passionate interest in history and militaria, while my bents focused on fantasy, magic and twists in the tale. Consequently, our combination plot concepts generally proved too bizarre and discordant to be realistic, even though we'd agreed we would love to co-write a novel. Just as a potentially feasible plot was at its nascent stage, Steve was unexpectedly diagnosed with terminal cancer - and within weeks he was gone. All I had time for was to promise him that I would work out the plot properly and write the novel – for both of us.

Steve, if you're looking on from the other side, my dearest hairy-arsed friend (and the brother I never had), you'll know that

I've finally managed to keep my promise. I just wish you were here to share the moment.

Being married (to a different sort of soulmate), I know that my husband, James, paid me the greatest compliment imaginable in granting me the time and space to write this novel, which took a year to research and another year to write, in between all the other complexities of everyday life. He never complained that I was neglecting him; never criticized my late-night stints on the PC; forgave my absent-mindedness whilst temporarily mentally in Biblical times, the medieval crusades or the 15th century era of Richard III - and even tolerated my poor temper when some element of the modern-day plot just wasn't gelling. He proffered coffee, left me to my work and was always there, close by, whenever I needed him. How truly fortunate I am to have been blessed with such a partner in life. Thank you, James. I loved you from first sight and will love you to my last breath.

CONTENTS

Dedications v
Prologue ix

Chapter 1	Finders Keepers	1
Chapter 2	A Star in the East	14
Chapter 3	Grave News	31
Chapter 4	The Oldest Legend on Earth	43
Chapter 5	Two Kings and Three Gifts	57
Chapter 6	A Lost Treasure	73
Chapter 7	Raising the Dead	88
Chapter 8	Holy Orders	106
Chapter 9	A City or A Crown	120
Chapter 10	A Creep in the Crypt	128
Chapter 11	Double-Edged Gifts	139
Chapter 12	How Big is a Nuclear Bomb?	148
Chapter 13	Two Princes Too Many	165
Chapter 14	Half a Clue	179
Chapter 15	A Dilemma and A Deed	188
Chapter 16	Prayers for Success	209
Chapter 17	A Life Saved Twice; a Map Lost Once	226
Chapter 18	A Mercurial Massacre	244
Chapter 19	Reaching the Promised Land	258
Chapter 20	An Inspirational Salutation	268
Chapter 21	Playing 'Follow My Leader'	280
Chapter 22	Lost in the Labyrinth	290
Chapter 23	Let There Be Light	306
Chapter 24	The Chamber of the Casket	315
Chapter 25	To the Manor Born	337

Epilogue 343
Postscript 345
Biography 347

PROLOGUE

Mount Quasioun; Damascus, Syria, 12 June, 2016 AD

Inside existed a microcosm of darkness and constant temperature - outside, a world of towering cliffs and ravines, distant jet trails and the merciless noonday heat of the Syrian Desert.

An insistent metallic scraping sound disturbed the silence and needle-thin rays of light ravaged the sable void as a steel pick pierced the seal of the rough-hewn chamber in several places. Following repeated thumping noises, a section of mud-brick wall crumbled forwards and a triumphant shout echoed round the ancient sandstone walls.

Moments later, a tall, muscular figure ducked through the jagged hole.

'*Enfin*! Finally!' His boots crunching on the clay debris, Doctor Alain Rousseau straightened up and revolved slowly, his flashlight dancing around the rock sepulchre. Addressing the young Syrian peering through the hole from the access tunnel, he gave orders. 'Tell Alim and Umarah to bring up lights and tools.'

Bashir's head inclined in assent before vanishing from view as he scrambled away down the low stone passage towards the blinding sunlight.

Dabbing suddenly cold sweat from his brow with one sleeve, the French archaeologist estimated the chamber's size at roughly fifty feet square by eight high. Its stale air was dry on his throat. On one side, a flat slab projected from the sandstone wall and on this rested a sarcophagus-like limestone coffin. Small boxes constructed of baked clay - ossuaries, perhaps - were dotted in niches around the sides of the chamber, but it was the imposing coffin that captured his gaze.

'Greco-Roman, I'd say. Nice find,' he murmured. Running his fingers along the overhanging lip of its lid, he resisted the urge to try and lever it off. The right tools would be needed to avoid damage. Ranging his flashlight along the side of the coffin, he glimpsed an indistinct inscription carved into the stone. Eager to reveal the epitaph, he took a small brush from his pocket and began to sweep away the dust of eons with light, soft strokes.

Rousseau's concentration was broken only when Bashir reappeared, clambering through the uneven hole and turning to manhandle the aluminium tool cases and solar lamps his compatriots proceeded to pass in. Their task complete, Alim and Umarah promptly squatted in the narrow passageway, conserving their energy.

Rousseau issued abrupt commands. *'Alors*, set the lights, *comme* ça.' His arms described a semi-circle. Bashir's teeth gleamed in the semi-dark as he complied. Soon, harsh beams illuminated the coffin and Rousseau stood back to view the inscription his brush had revealed.

As he mouthed the Latin words, his mind reeled.

HIC REQUIETUM CORPUS YESHUA - NUNTIUS CRUCIFIXUS - CARUS FILIUS MARIUM ET YOSEPHA
Vox pyus pyxidis servo vos insquequo unus adveho quisnam mos addo lux lucis quod vita ut omnia.

Below the epitaph was a deeply incised emblem - a sunburst, with symbols spiralling to its centre in a language unknown to him.

'Doctor? Is good, yes?' Rousseau's shocked expression had not escaped the observant Bashir.

'*Oui*,' responded Rousseau, thinking fast. 'Tell your men I won't need them again.' He reached for his wallet. 'Here's double pay for their work today. Oh, and tell them to stay quiet about this dig. Understand?' As he spoke, he counted out cash, thrusting the wad at Bashir.

The young Syrian's face was a blank page. Crouching by the hole, he spoke rapidly in Arabic to the men in the tunnel, who muttered at the summary dismissal, but obediently took their money and left.

Returning to Rousseau, who was now taking photographs, Bashir ventured another question. 'Doctor, please - you know what the words say?'

'More or less.' Rousseau recited the translation aloud.

'Here rests the body of Yeshua of Nazareth, crucified Messiah - beloved son of Mary and Joseph.'

He paused for a reaction, but Bashir's expression remained unreadable.

'Is all?' queried the Syrian.

Rousseau glanced at the olive-skinned face; at the curls of black hair escaping the white gutrah and the simple, ankle-length didashah of a man he judged had only taken on this temporary work because he was fit enough to perform physical labour in heat that would floor the un-acclimatised and because he needed the cash - not because he had any serious interest in Syria's archaeological heritage.

'No; there's more. *'May the power of the tomb - or box – or, maybe, casket, protect you until the one comes who will bring light and life to all.'* I am not certain about that one word,' he said, shaking his head in irritation.

Bashir blinked, then pointed at the emblem, his dark eyes flicking over it as if memorising it. 'Nice picture.'

Rousseau scratched his stubble. 'Probably just decoration.'

'Is good thing, find this?'

The Frenchman stared at Bashir. 'Don't you realise what we've got, here?' *Only the biggest archaeological coup of all time!* His voice rose. 'Unless I'm crazy, we're standing just inches away from the mortal remains of Jesus Christ!'

The young man shrugged. 'Jesus? His name Isa in Arabic. The Sunni say Isa is prophet from long time past. My faith, Alawi, not Sunni. My God, Ali ibn-Talib.'

'Prophet or Messiah, once this goes public, it'll become a worldwide theological and political time bomb on a very short fuse. If I had any sense I'd bring the roof down on this place - seal it forever.'

Bashir looked confused and then grinned. 'You want me put time bomb in tunnel? Go boom! *Then* is good thing?"

'No,' Rousseau laughed in amused despair. 'Quiet, now, while I think.'

Frowning, he ran his fingers over the arcane sunburst and its strange symbols. *Your presence here intrigues me, Jesus. What you're doing so far from Jerusalem I can't imagine.* His attention moving to the lower case inscription, he pursed his lips. *And what is it that protects you, I wonder? Is it the power of God - or something else?*

Composing himself, Rousseau climbed up onto the stone base slab. 'Open the tool kit and pass it up,' he told Bashir. 'We have much to do.'

Arbitrarily picking one corner of the ancient coffin lid, he selected a fine chisel and began chipping away the dried mortar of the seal. Bashir busied himself sweeping up the chippings as Rousseau worked. When the lid was free, they stopped to quench their thirst. Screwing the top back on his canteen, Rousseau flexed gritty fingers and said, 'Help me slide it off.' He mimed the actions he was describing. 'We will lower it, so - and prop it against the far side - slowly, without dropping it.'

A dull, grating noise resonated round the solid walls as the two men inched the thick limestone cover sideways and lowered it painstakingly to the floor, grunting with the effort. Rousseau coughed as fine dust billowed, carrying with it the musty odour of ancient death. Not a pious man, at this moment he felt like praying.

There must be a body!

Peering into the tomb, his heart leapt to see the shrouded form within. Unaccountably, he felt impelled to reach down and touch the ancient linen, as if only the visceral fact of it, rough against his fingertips, could make him believe he had truly found Christ. Lightly, he pinched a scrap of grave-cloth between his thumb and forefinger, but it cracked like a wafer at his touch.

'Jesus!' he exclaimed, flinching back from the fragile material and uttering a nervous bark at the irony of his outburst.

One truth, at least, was undeniable - he could progress no further without expert assistance. 'I'll be back in a minute,' he told Bashir,

Prologue

jumping off the slab. 'Wait here. Don't touch anything.' Ducking through the hole, he made his way along the short tunnel into the blistering desert heat. At the base of the mountain, Damascus lay glittering under its heat haze like a veiled and sequinned whore.

Alone, Bashir licked dry lips and reached inside the coffin. His questing hand chancing upon an object, he grasped it and lifted it out. Once, it had lain inside a small pouch, but now only a coating of dessicated filaments remained. Placing his prize on the sandstone slab, he squatted to brush away the fibrous material, disclosing a three-quarter-inch thick piece of rusty iron, eight inches long, tapered to a point at one end, hammered flat at the other and pitted with age. Wrapping the ancient crucifixion nail in a soft cloth, he pushed it through his cord belt and smiled.

In the stifling oven of his hired Toyota Tacoma, parked on the dirt road that wound through the ravine fifty feet below the cave tomb's entrance, Rousseau rummaged in the glove compartment for his i-phone. He had to get a message to Doctor Jean Desselle, a colleague in the Archaeology Department at the Pantheon Sorbonne in Paris. Rousseau's co-worker, Doctor Henri Laurent, was already due to join him tomorrow, but, for this find, Desselle's unparalleled anthropological expertise would be vital - and a couple of sturdy post-graduates would be far more suitable than these local labourers. Composing a brief overview of the find, including its location and a plea for help from Desselle, he attached photos of the coffin, copied the message to Laurent - and hit *send*.

The iphone stowed away, he quit the truck and strolled to the edge of the gorge for a view of war-ravaged Damascus. If any city ever needed redemption, he contemplated, it's this one. His reverie ended abruptly when a dark hand snaked over his mouth from behind, brutally jerking his head backwards.

Bashir closed in fast, plunging his curved Khangar dagger into the Frenchman's exposed throat, puncturing his larynx and splitting the jugular. Soundlessly, Rousseau dropped to his knees, clutching at the ivory handle of the dagger as his life blood spurted out, turning his green shirt into a meadow of poppies. Toppling sideways, his body lay still, his uncomprehending eyes remaining fixed on his killer until they glazed over.

The young Syrian squatted to retrieve his blade, gazing briefly into the lifeless eyes. 'You were right, Doctor,' he said calmly, wiping his Khangar clean on the infidel's chinos. 'We *do* have much to do.'

Rising, he called Alim and Umarah, who rose from the concealing shade of a cliff overhang. Together they manhandled Rousseau's corpse into the back of the Tacoma and covered it with a tarpaulin. 'Camouflage the tunnel entrance and cover up all this blood,' ordered Bashir, scuffing dirt over the nearest blood spatter with his shoe. 'Then take the truck and the body to Karam. He must dispose of both.'

'...That Sunni hashish-head?' Umarah complained. 'Why him?'

'Because he asks no questions - and because I need to show this to the *Dhu Samawi* immediately.' Bashir tapped the wrapped object at his belt.

'And what is it that the Lord of Heaven will want to see, so damn fast?'

'Your tongue cut out if you keep wagging it. Do as I say,' snapped Bashir, already heading for their vehicle, a battered old Sham saloon parked behind the Tacoma.

An hour later, the tunnel entrance lay obscured behind a fresh heap of rock debris and dirt covered the bloodstains on the unpaved road. Once again there was darkness and silence within the sepulchre and, outside, just the relentless heat of the desert and a few tyre tracks in the dust.

CHAPTER 1

FINDERS KEEPERS

Chaumont Hall, Derbyshire, England, 16 June, 2016 AD

A shaft of sun slanted through the mullioned windows and blazed light across the papers heaped on her late father's desk. The oak-panelled library walls remained dark under the weight of centuries of books.

Lady Samantha Dexter surveyed the desk and scowled.

Death and taxes were supposed to be the only certainties in life; no-one ever mentioned the administration that invariably followed death. Wasn't it enough to become an orphan at twenty-nine, last of the Chaumont line and now unexpectedly responsible for Chaumont Hall and its eighteen thousand acres, without having to wade through this lot? Her father had apparently kept every blasted horse-vet's bill and letter he'd ever received. Worse still, all these irrelevancies were jumbled up with the useful stuff she would need in order to run the place.

Her irritability was a facet of her grief. She knew this, just as she knew she had to persevere with the paper-pushing. Sam had been raised to persevere. One was expected to keep going, even while mourning the sudden accidental death of one's beloved father. *He was only fifty six, goddammit!* The Earls of Chaumont had not survived the wars, politics and social upheavals of half a millennium by taking to their beds or throwing tantrums when disaster struck. *Damn them all.*

Armageddon had been reduced to a set of tidy stacks, with today's post on top: a large brown envelope from the family solicitors.

Sighing, Sam tore it open and drew out the contents - a letter, some inheritance tax forms for signature and a small, sealed cream envelope. God knows what that is, she thought.

She rapidly scanned the letter, signed by the senior partner, Edgar Sherringham. There was a lengthy preamble and then, *'...having covered matters connected with the late Lord Dexter's estate, I draw to your attention the enclosed sealed note he left in my keeping, to pass to you in the event of his death. Assuring you of my best intentions, I remain yours...'*

Flipping over the small envelope, she murmured aloud the four words her father had penned in his unmistakeable, looping script: 'To the next Keeper'. The assignation puzzled her. Laying aside the rest of the correspondence, she reached for the antique dagger that lay on the desk. Habitually employed as a letter-knife, its blade was double-edged and its pommel, a white bone in the shape of a boar's head, was inscribed with the words *'Loyaulte me lie'*. Using this potentially lethal implement, Sam slit open the enigmatic envelope, removed the single sheet it contained and began to read her father's final message.

'My dear Samantha,

'If you are reading this, it means I am no longer around to explain everything, so this must serve to reveal to you a vital family knowledge that will shape your destiny, as it has shaped the lives of all the Dexters and their ancestors back through long ages.

'Certain members of our line inherit a unique responsibility, the understanding of which is passed on to them at age thirty, because it is at that age that a Keeper seems to develop an instinctive awareness of - let's say – being 'different'. But for you, this familial responsibility begins as of this moment.

'I was blessed with only one child, so it must be fate that you bear the same mark as me, the one that signifies a true Keeper - the small, star-shaped mark over your heart.'

Instinctively, Sam's hand went to the site of her rather unusual birthmark, her fist crumpling the pleats of her linen blouse. She had not known that her father bore the same blemish.

'Understanding the documents to which I shall direct you will be only your first challenge. Rise to it with determination and dedication, for it is the key to the greatest secret of all the ages. It is your duty and destiny to guard this secret and to attempt to fulfil its mission. I know this will be hard for you, who have shunned things spiritual up to this point - but all must now change, for you are obliged by blood to become the Keeper of a Power that can only be described as having a spiritual basis.

Oh, please, no, thought Sam.

'One day, a Keeper will prove to be - or will discover - The One we have sought down the ages - The One possessing the ability to use The Power without limit. I like to think this will usher in something resembling the fabled Day of Judgement, the very concept of which may have its basis in the lost writings of the Ancients who had knowledge of The Power.

'This must seem arcane to you, not to mention cryptic. It's hard to condense extraordinary concepts into an ordinary letter. But I assure you, I am not crazy, nor am I going to ask of you anything you can't handle. You will find that, despite your secular inclinations, you will develop an undeniable urge to adopt the Keeper's mantle - and that you will prove fit for the task. But heed this warning: many have died to protect The Power and more have died through its glamour. Neither share

your secret, save with the next Keeper, nor trust in the shallow friendship of men.

'Now it is time to fetch the documents that will set you on the path. Look in the library, within the cupboard hidden behind the Dexter Coat of Arms. Good luck, darling girl. And always remember that I love you.
Daddy.'

The letter bore her father's seal, with his full name and title: Lord Alexander Augustus Dexter, Earl of Chaumont, along with the family motto, '*Custodiae Lux Lucis*' - 'Guardians of the Light' - which Sam had always presumed was of Christian origin. Now, she was not so sure.

Blinking away the tears that had welled at his last few words, she turned to the long wall and there was the oak-carved Coat of Arms, a decorative centrepiece in the floor-to-ceiling bookcase. Did it really hide a cupboard?

As if sleepwalking, she traversed the Persian rug to stand in front of the heraldic crest, yet despite examining every square inch of the carved oak with her fingertips, she discovered nothing resembling a door latch. At length, frustrated, she thumped the escutcheon's central fess point with the ball of her fist. It gave to the blow and the carved panel sprang forward with a click, revealing a bevelled indent down one side. Curling her fingers into the hollow, Sam tugged - and a hinged door swung wide.

Dismissing the heaped papers on the desk from her mind, she reached into the dark recess, grasping the slim file that her questing fingers found.

As morning turned to afternoon, she began to wish she had inherited less sense of duty. The file may have been slim, but its single sheet listed numerous locations within Chaumont Hall where further documents were squirreled away. Sam retrieved them all - from places as likely as the secret drawer in the bureau, which she had known about since she was a child, to places as unlikely as the inside of a hollow brass curtain rail in her mother's old dressing room. Some of the papers she found were no more than clues directing her elsewhere. Her rambling quest led to rooms no-one had used for years and corridors where the patina of dust on the oak floors spoke of long neglect.

Her hunt even took her to places she had not known existed, including a Priest Hole on the second floor of the east wing. Probably dating from the era of Queen Elizabeth's persecution of the Catholics, it was artfully concealed and accessible only via secret stairs squeezed between the oak panelling of the east wing rooms and the thickness of the outer walls of the Hall. Squeezing into its cramped confines, Sam levered up floorboards to locate a cache of rolled parchments, sealed in tubes of crumbling leather. Cringing back from a spider, she banged her head on a cross beam and muttered crossly, 'Why am I doing this? What's it all for?'

Finally, the subterranean mustiness of the cellars yielded a slip of paper which led her to some photos tucked inside a Royal Crown Derby porcelain teapot, one of a collection of over a hundred pieces of valuable antique porcelain in the huge display cabinet housed on the east wall of the grand dining room.

Daylight was fading fast. Sluicing away the grime of the day under a hot shower and dressing in clean clothes, Sam decided to press on and evaluate the finds she had left strewn on the refectory table in the kitchen. The material was daunting, not to mention dusty.

Nursing a mug of coffee, she pulled up a kitchen stool and began sifting through the documents. Some looked very old and were hand-written in cramped, foreign scripts. Sam had qualified in business management, ready for the day when she would take over the estate, little knowing how soon that day would arrive. She was neither an historian nor a linguist, so could make no sense of the foreign language texts. Included in the material were photographs taken by her father - and probably her grandfather too - ranging from moody black and white studies of some nameless Middle Eastern city to snaps of several ancestral family portraits; oils that had been gathering dust on the walls of Chaumont Hall for centuries.

The earliest such painting was a study of the first Earl, a knight who had fought in the War of the Roses and was honoured for services to the crown. It was a grateful Richard III, in the late fifteenth century, who had granted Simon Dexter an Earldom, along with the lands and dwellings that formed Chaumont Hall and estate. In his portrait, Simon was depicted standing in front of the huge granite fireplace in Chaumont's great hall, one hand on the hilt of his sword, the other resting lightly on an ornament gracing the mantle. His cloak dripped with ermine and his lips were curled in a haughty sneer suggesting the contented vanity of a man enjoying his new-found aristocratic status. Sam had never cared much for that sneer.

Wrinkling her nose at the sly, swarthy face, she realised she had strayed from her purpose. How these photos fitted the puzzle she couldn't say. Turning her attention to a printed document dated 2015 - only a year old - she found it to be an historical account of the family, from the first Earl down to the sixteenth; her father. On one page was a family tree. Sneering Simon had sired twin sons, Godwin and Grimbald. Godwin must have been the elder, as he had inherited the Earldom and Chaumont. Nothing further was noted concerning Grimbald and it appeared that subsequent Earls had each sired only one son, although an occasional daughter was listed and instantly dismissed.

We've never been the most fecund of families, so perhaps it's not surprising that the line has finally petered out in me.

Sam had always resented the fact that under the laws of promigeniture, only males could inherit an Earldom. Why couldn't she have been born a man, to secure the title for future generations?

But no dynasty lasted for ever and that was a fact.

It was six and there should be a busy clattering of pots and pans in the kitchen; muted strains of a violin concerto emanating from her father's den; the housekeeper humming as she polished the brasses in the scullery... but, instead, there was silence. Sam had given most of the staff two weeks' leave. It was a sad and uncertain time for them all and Sam could not bring herself to dissemble in front of people who now depended on her. It would be irresponsible to tell everyone that their jobs were secure before she had grasped the true financial picture - and she was not expecting it to be good.

Listlessly, she rose and prepared a snack. Seated again and selecting another document at random, her sandwich in one hand, she blinked in surprise. It was written in a language she did not even recognise. She turned its pages and all were full of the same mysterious script, except for the foot of the final page, where a complex emblem appeared, consisting of a sun-like orb with twelve wavy rays, inside which a concentric spiral full of nameless symbols ran from rim to centre. Sam could not think where she might have seen it before, yet it held a haunting familiarity.

Leaning back, she rubbed tired eyes. What was she dealing with, here - some secret cult? Would she spend precious hours deciphering her father's apocryphal secret only to find it was just a pile of religious claptrap cooked up by superstitious minds? Then again, why was she holding a document written in an unknown language?

I've got to have help. Daddy wanted me to work this out, but I can't!

It was after midnight when she retired, but sleep eluded her as her mind replayed the last time she had seen her father alive. From her bedroom window, on that fateful June morning two weeks ago, she had glimpsed his black-coated figure disappearing into the woods surrounding the lake. Weekly, over the nine years since her death, he had visited the family crypt to pay his respects to his beloved wife, Charlotte. When, after two hours, he failed to return, Sam grew worried and raised an alarm.

The fourteen steps leading down to the burial vault were steep and worn. Her father's body was discovered slumped at the foot of them. No witnesses stepped forward and the police could discern no evidence of foul play. Quite simply, the Earl must have tripped, fallen headlong down the steps and staved in his skull: the coroner's verdict was death by misadventure.

Scrolls and priest holes and cryptic symbols crammed her mind as she tossed and turned, over-warm. At last she threw back the duvet and her fingers found the source of her discomfort, the slightly raised birthmark on her chest. It pulsed with an unnatural heat as if intent on burning a path to her heart.

What does it mean?

For the first time in her life Sam felt close to panic, alone in the great edifice that was Chaumont Hall. When the heat at last faded away, she fell into an uneasy doze.

At nine the next morning she phoned the solicitor.

'Edgar Sherringham, please. Yes, I'll hold.' Sam drummed her fingers on the marble-topped console table that hugged the vestibule wall.

Sherringham came on the line. 'Good morning, Lady Dexter. Did you sign the inheritance tax papers I sent over? I'd like to crack on as soon as possible.'

Obnoxious man...

'I haven't had time to attend to them yet, Edgar, but that's not my reason for calling.'

'I see.' Sherringham sounded disappointed.

Sam continued quickly. 'I've come across some foreign language material of my father's. Do you know anyone who could help with translation - a professional linguist, perhaps?' She paused. '...Better yet, someone expert in old or rare languages; that kind of thing?'

'Let me cogitate for a moment.' Sherringham thumbed ferociously through the contents of his in-tray. Only last week he'd had reason to call on the services of someone who specialised in medieval and antiquarian texts and lost languages. He knew he hadn't filed the correspondence. Ah! There it was.

He cleared his throat. 'Fortuitously, I can assist you, Lady Dexter. I recommend you try Professor Oliver Kaye. He's a codicologist - I'll spell that for you - and first rate on the rare language front. Works freelance sometimes. Got a pen handy...?'

As soon as she had extricated herself from Sherringham's persistent pleas for signatures, Sam dialled again, tapping in Kaye's number. The phone rang on unanswered. On the point of hanging up, she heard a click and a well modulated voice said, 'Kaye speaking. Can I help you?'

'I do hope so,' replied Sam politely, introducing herself. 'I need some rather unusual old documents translating and I'm told you're an expert in codicology - is that right?'

'Well, I like to think I hold some grasp of the subject, yes. Tell me more,' he prompted.

She explained the essentials. '...So I would appreciate it if you would come and look at them, as suits, of course.' She bit her lip. 'But it is very urgent....so today would be good.'

Kaye gave an engaging laugh. 'I see it's a case of Hobson's choice. Let me check my frantic schedule.' After barely a pause, he said, 'Guess what, I'm free today and it's only twenty miles from my paltry nook to your stately spires. Give me half an hour.'

'I didn't intend to be... demanding.'

'Yes you did, but that's okay. I can't abide women of weak conviction.'

'Oh!'

After he had hung up, several minutes elapsed before she realised she had forgotten to ask about his fees.

Stamping her heels into her green wellies, Sam headed for the stables and spent a few minutes reassuring Digby that she was managing, except for being buried in paperwork. 'So I won't have time to ride this week,' she told him.

The old groom leant stolidly on his hay fork. 'Aye, well... I'll make sure the beasts aren't neglected; don't take on, lass...' Faltering, his weathered cheeks reddened in embarrassment. 'Beg pardon,' he apologised. 'I should be callin' thee m'Lady, shouldn't I? I'm that brain-addled just now.'

Sam patted his liver-spotted hand. She'd rather be called 'lass', if truth be known. 'I'm expecting a visitor at any moment,' she continued. 'If you notice a car coming up the main drive, would you please point the gentleman to the conservatory door?'

'Aye – that I can do.' Digby said nothing more, waiting until his mistress had passed from view before raising a hand to brush wetness from the corner of one rheumy eye.

In the kitchen, Sam prepared coffee, idly switching on the wall-mounted television, with the sound muted. Turning to the documents scattered over the refectory table, she hastily shuffled the majority into a loose pile, covering them with her unread morning paper. The documents she selected for Kaye's initial inspection included the one in the unknown language and a single, yellowed sheet in a squiggly script that she thought might be Arabic.

Someone rapped on the conservatory door. That airy space offered an unrivalled panorama of the formal gardens, beyond which lay the extensive rolling Derbyshire meadows comprising the southern part of the estate. Tucking her blouse into her black jeans and composing herself, she went to greet her visitor.

Peering through the glass, Kaye waved politely. He was much younger than she'd expected; around thirty two, she guessed, his bookish good looks accentuated by a shock of corn silk hair... was he really a professor? He wasn't dressed like one - no cords, brogues or pipes in sight. Unexpectedly, he stood tall and square-shouldered in tailored slacks and a crisp, cream shirt accented by a Windsor knotted tie, with polished brown leather shoes and a sports jacket over one arm.

Opening the door to his arresting blue eyes, Sam shook hands and said, 'Professor Kaye? You must have a fast car! Do come in.' Ushering him into the kitchen, she added, mischievously, 'Clearly you realised how much we demanding women appreciate promptness.'

'Naturally, I did.' Kaye's eyes twinkled as he followed her. 'I can see we're going to get along swimmingly.'

'Do pull up a stool, Professor - coffee?'

'Coffee would be great – but please call me Oliver. Even my postgrads use my first name. How should I address you, though? I'm not entirely conversant with aristocratic protocol.'

'Never mind protocol. Just call me Sam.' Sam gestured at the refectory table. 'While I pour the coffee could you please cast an eye over these two documents for me?'

Kaye nodded. 'By all means - Sam.' He sat down and pulled a small notepad from his jacket pocket, followed by a pair of white linen gloves; a magnifying glass, a small digital camera and the stub of a pencil. 'Now, what are we looking at, here?' he queried rhetorically, resting his jacket over his knees and drawing the nearest piece of paper towards him.

Bearing full mugs, Sam came and perched alongside him. 'All I can tell you is that my late father left me a puzzle to work out and these form part of it. I think the one you're looking at may be in Arabic, but I'm not sure.'

Kaye tapped a finger on the faded script. 'It is Arabic, you're right, but medieval, not modern. I should be able to make sense of it.' He began to read, his lips silently mouthing each syllable. Sam sipped her coffee while he worked, glad he hadn't commented on the fact that her father was 'late'. She didn't need the meaningless platitudes that strangers were likely to gush.

'Fascinating,' he sighed at last, looking up. 'What you have here is a twelfth century letter to a spy. This isn't an original, I'm afraid - someone's copied it from an earlier document. I'll give you the gist of the thing. With a few minor breaks while he searched his brain for the most appropriate word in English, Kaye translated.

> *'Al-Malik al-Adil Sayf al-Dīn Abu-Bakr, Governor of Damascus, sends greetings in the name of Allah on behalf of Al Aziz Uthman ibn-Ayyūb, Sultan of Egypt and Syria, to his servant Abdul Hamid and demands that you now provide to Al Aziz Uthman that which was promised to the late beloved Salāh al-Dīn Yūsuf ibn-Ayyūb as a condition of your freedom to travel with the mystic treasure gifted to the English King. The Lord Al-Adil reminds you that the new Sultan's patience has limits and that his supreme power lends him long arms.*
>
> *If you fail to fulfil your oath, those arms will reach you, though you hide beneath the surcoat of Richard himself. What is Richard's intent, now he is released from captivity and has returned to his Kingdom? Does Christendom prepare once again for battle? Send full intelligence to the Citadel in*

Jerusalem, with your personal seal upon it, before winter turns to spring. In Allah's name, do not delay.'

Sam blinked. 'Long names, haven't they? The recipient of the letter is this Abdul, yes? But who are Al-Malik, Al-Aziz and Salāh?'

Kaye smiled. 'You might know Salāh al-Dīn better as the famous Saladin. He died in 1193 and, after some argy-bargy, his brother, Al Aziz, took power. Al-Malik is usually referred to as Al-Adil. He was another of Saladin's brothers and became Sultan after Al-Aziz. At some point during the crusades - we're talking Richard the Lionheart - it seems Saladin must have given his enemy, Richard, a gift - this 'mystic treasure', as it's referred to in the letter. Why this Abdul Hamid accompanied the gift to England, who knows, but I imagine the intent was for him to act as a Saracen spy, because this letter is a fairly threatening demand from Al-Adil to Abdul Hamid to provide intelligence to Al-Aziz, the new Sultan, concerning King Richard's plans - I wonder if he did?' Kaye shook his head. 'You've got yourself a fine little piece of medieval espionage, recorded there. I'd love to know its provenance and how your family came by it.'

'I wish I knew,' said Sam. 'Could you jot down the translation for me? I don't know where this fits into my puzzle, but I might need it later.'

This done, Kaye reached for the other document and gave a disbelieving whoop. 'How did this get here?'

Sam's eyebrows shot up. 'Why? What is it?'

Kaye's excitement was palpable. 'No idea, yet, but it's written in *Vedic Sanskrit*! I've spent *years* studying Sanskrit, but the last place on earth I'd expect to find an example is in rural Derbyshire. It originates from the Indian sub-continent.' Replacing the document on the table, he laid his hand over the top page, his fingers splayed almost reverently. 'I'd expect any work written in this language to be very, very old - thousands of years old, in fact.' He rubbed a corner of the top sheet of the document between his thumb and forefinger and glanced at Sam. 'But this foolscap is contemporary, so either it's been copied from an earlier piece - or the writer was fluent in a dead language.'

Sam squinted at the text. 'It might be by my father's hand, but if he was familiar with Sanskrit, he certainly never told me,' she replied, nonplussed. 'How long will it take to translate?'

Kaye rifled through the pages. 'Let's see - it's quite large script. An hour or two's scribbling should do it. Will that suit you?' As he spoke he was already twirling his pencil between his long, slim fingers, keen to get started.

'Absolutely,' replied Sam with an outward calm that belied her rising concern. Supported by a fresh dose of caffeine, she left him to focus on his work, went outside and paced restlessly round the formal garden.

Horses were no trouble: she *understood* horses. And the land and its continuity under the aegis of sixteen generations of Dexters - she had a pretty good grasp on that. She had thought she understood her father, too. Wasn't he just a typical aristocrat dedicated to propping up the family pile in an increasingly hostile world that generally saw the landed gentry as toffee-nosed anachronisms left over from long-gone days of conquest and empire - reminders that a few still had it better (and thought themselves better) than the rest? That was a palatable, if pitiable, scenario, yet from the instant she had read her father's strange letter, her conception of his - and consequently her own - niche in the world had started to run like mercury over marble.

If he wasn't the man I thought he was, then... who on earth am I?

Her once well-ordered, predictable world had suited her. Uncomfortable ideas like *Keeper* and *spiritual* and *Power* - not to mention a father who apparently led a double life and might be able to write in some archaic Indian language - didn't fit in at all.

What the devil was going on?

CHAPTER 2

A STAR IN THE EAST

Bharukachcha, North West India, early May, the Year after Christ's Birth (6 BCE)

Heeding its call, he had always followed the star.

The star, notwithstanding its scythe-sharp rays, was symbolic of the beneficent orb of the sun and, in appropriate parallel, the sun god, Surya, was the focus of his vocation as a Maga Brahmin, a religious and scholarly calling encompassing the multiple skills of priest, astrologer and ayurvedic healer. But the star cared nothing for the Brahmin faith. The star's sole purpose was to remind him that he was bound in blood and secrecy to an infinitely more archaic creed; that of *The Power* - for *The Power* was *of* the sun, wrested from that inexhaustible source of life-giving energy by his ancestors, the Ancients, long, long ago.

And he was its current Keeper.

That grey morning, it was the star which drew him down to Bharuch, the shallow sea port of the bustling city of Bharukachcha, capital and trade centre of the North West Indian Saka Empire. His steps were laced with urgency because the star was pulsing again, a roseate brand directly over his heart. It was not the first occasion upon which he had felt its throb, but this time the burning agony had racked his body throughout the night. His birthmark and birthright, its call was a physical imperative: procrastination was not an option. All he knew was that he must take ship as soon as possible and travel westwards; to distant Parthia first, but perhaps further.

Ignoring the wails of filthy beggars thrusting out wooden bowls in hope of alms and sidestepping the persistent hands of pitiful street orphans, Balthazar wrinkled his nose and raised the skirts of his white cotton dhoti to step over the flowing effluent of a particularly pungent gutter as he hurried along the lively market thoroughfare culminating at the harbour. Like all the detritus of the teeming city, this foul rivulet would go to swell the rolling yellow-brown waters of the Narmada's estuary.

A major outlet for the monsoon rain waters that poured off the fertile inland plains, the Narmada disgorged copious quantities of land-leached mud and silt into Bharuch's narrow sea gulf, restricting access to the port. In consequence, manned by fishermen in the king's service, several sturdy tappaga and cotymba boats were invariably stationed at the port entrance, ready to pilot arriving and departing ships between the treacherous shoals. Two bleached hulks that lay weathering on half-submerged mud banks gave silent testament to the common sense of waiting for high tide before attempting to navigate a larger vessel into or out of the port.

Fortunately for him, reflected the Maga, as a final gale of flapping shawls and waving arms laden with cheap silver bangles swirled him out of the street to deposit him into the equally frantic hubbub that crowded the docks and wharfs, the call of the star had come at the optimal time for travel. Inland, the floods were high and the rain-swollen river barrelled relentlessly to the sea, its undulating eddies and whorls carving huge, slow bites from its soft, red, clay banks. For the duration of May and June, the north east monsoon winds blew constantly and trade ships took advantage of them to sail along the Makran coast, then on to one of the many trading ports in the Gulf or Red Sea.

Balthazar was confident there would be west-bound ships aplenty in port. To India they brought gold, silver and slaves from the Roman Empire, dancing girls and fine woven fabrics from Persia and rare ointments, frankincense and myrrh from Arabia. Returning westwards, they went laden with the pearls favoured by Roman matriarchs; cinnamon; cedar, teak and that most prized of commodities - the silk of the Orient. These sea routes were the favoured choice of merchants wishing to avoid the banditry rife on the silk roads leading west through the Parthian mountains and Balthazar would take passage with that floating procession of bales and bolts as they made their way across the breadth of the known world.

The star had spoken.

Obedient to its demands over his thirty five years, the Maga had wandered widely within his own country, but now it was the will of Surya that he depart to distant lands. Gazing at the forest of masts in front of him, he bowed his head in a moment of humble prayer, chin to chest, his oiled beard dark against the whiteness of his dhoti. Would his astronomical observations and calculations help him locate exactly where *The One* might be found? Could he succeed where all previous Keepers of *The Power* had failed? Only time - and *The Power* - would answer those questions, but of one thing Balthazar was already certain - this would be the greatest journey of his life.

The Arab dhow would sail with the tide. It was rigged with a settee sail, the best type for the difficult waters of the Red Sea, or so the captain informed him. As he had never before set foot on an ocean-going vessel, Balthazar felt unequipped to comment. He decided he would entrust his maritime safety more to Surya than to the protestations of this Arab sea dog. His ears perked, however, during the captain's effusive praise of his own vessel, which, he declared to be indestructible, having been built to the same design as that of Noah's Ark - following the pattern set by the five stars in the constellation of Ursa Major.

Balthazar had no idea that this was, in fact, the design upon which most dhows were based.

In his chambers, a cool dampness from the rains refreshed him as he packed the chests that his porters would take by donkey to the dhow. Surya had been kind to him: he was a wealthy man. Those who sought the astrological and healing services of a Maga Brahmin tended to be of the highest caste and he had been called upon by lords and princes to recite the Vedic scriptures passed down through generations of the priesthood by word of mouth. These verses were revered for their spiritual power, particularly in times of crisis, grief or joy, or, indeed, when commencing endeavours dependent on the favour of the gods. Princes, in particular, were always generous - it would be foolish to insult the gods by disrespecting their mouthpieces. Prophecies also paid well, especially if fulfilled with alacrity.

Having locked and bound his chests, he poured a jug of thrice-boiled water into a large deodar bowl. Himalayan cedar, as well as releasing restorative oils that were relaxing, had significant medicinal properties, including stimulation of the digestive system and the removal of toxins from the bowel. Balthazar let the water steep in the bowl before he drank of it, using the remainder to wash his face and body. At least he would begin his journey well - though he had little confidence that even a healthy gut would help him if he ran out of supplies and was obliged to partake of the Arab crew's fare.

Now his travel plans were set, his birthmark had ceased its torment. Quiescent, the star was blush-pink, raised slightly upon the smooth, brown skin of his chest. He passed his hand over it but felt no throb or pull, a reassurance that he must be pursuing the right course of action.

Donning the clean white dhoti and blue, star-embroidered robe that he had laid to one side, he oiled his curly black beard and wound a fresh turban cloth round his head. At his waist he clasped a sturdy goats' leather belt, from which depended a number of small bags and gourds containing gold coins and personal items, along with various dried goods - the herbs, spices and natural products he used for ayurvedic healing procedures. Also from the belt hung a filigree-silver-worked leather scabbard containing his Kukri. Although only a knife, it was substantial enough to use as a short sword should the need arise. Even a holy man would not be fool enough to travel unarmed.

Finally, he went to a cupboard set into a recess in the stone wall of the chamber, drawing back the curtain that hid it from prying eyes. Taking the key that he kept on a gold chain round his neck, he unlocked the cupboard to reveal an object wrapped in oiled linen. Reverently, he withdrew this and set it on a nearby table, where he unwrapped its protective covering to display the mystery that gleamed within.

The casket of the Ancients...

Few eyes had ever gazed upon this precious object - for it contained a thirteen-thousand-year-old secret more jealously concealed from the world than the tombs and burial treasures of the greatest Egyptian pharaohs, a secret with implications so huge that, until *The One* with the unique ability to use its powers limitlessly had been found, only its Keepers would lay eyes upon the housing that held its secret secure. Small, but crafted of pure gold, it was heavy enough to require two hands to bear it. Having un-wrapped this glory, Balthazar regarded it.

Here were its four corners, the cylindrical pillars of strength and endurance, topped with pointed turrets, the whole being finely engraved with symbols in the lost language of the Ancients - symbols, his father had opined, undoubtedly placed there with a purpose. After all, the Ancients had captured the heart of a star and imprisoned it inside this tiny space forever. What arcane bewitchments they had used to accomplish this feat, no Keeper knew, for the knowledge had been lost in the veils of over ten thousand years of Keeping.

Here were its four deeply tooled and worked sides, the front bearing the great seal of the Ancients - a star, like the one on Balthazar's breast, with twelve sharply pointed, wavy rays and, at its centre, an orb containing further symbols of un-guessable meaning.

Here was the domed lid, embossed with intricate, intertwining designs seeming to draw the eye to a summit holding a thumb-tip-sized hollow. Balthazar would not place his own thumb there without compelling reason, knowing that, like any Keeper of the line of Baal, he would be able to call upon *The Power* only once in his lifetime.

The longer he observed the casket, the deeper it drew him into its patterned complexities. On the great seal, the symbols circled ever more minutely to a centre that held his eyes - until his mind began spiralling into a far infinity where galaxies of stars rotated on pinheads.

'Enough!' he gasped.

Dragging his eyes from the glamour of *The Power*, he deftly re-wrapped the casket in its windings, clinching the whole with leather thongs and securing it in his personal pack, which he would have about him constantly. Once ashore in Parthia, he proposed to acquire an ox wagon, mules and bodyguards and join a caravan to Seleucia, which a trader had once described to him as Hellenistic in style - a marble city by the banks of the river Tigris. That would be something to see! If the star led him on westwards, he would reach Dura Europos, high on a cliff above the river Euphrates. Then, Surya permitting, he would hazard the crossing of the great Arabian desert to Palmyra and thence Damascus. And after that...? He could turn north towards Cappadocia, south towards Palestine or take ship again, this time across the Mediterranean. He shook his head. Even his powers of prediction could not tell him what the future held beyond Damascus.

From habit, he closed the shutters of the chamber window against the recommencing rain. A typical monsoon downpour, its susurration quietened the clatter of the streets, most of Bharukachcha's townsfolk seeking refuge indoors. Only his indomitably patient donkeys stood waiting in the rain, their heads down. Fresh rainwater bucketed along the city's gutters, sluicing away the odours of humanity for a short while. It was time to go and, typically, Surya was going to make sure that a good drenching would dowse his pride sufficiently to make him glad of whatever shelter the Arab dhow had to offer.

Dura Europos, Parthia, September, the Year after Christ's Birth (6 BCE)

Controlled by a tolerant Macedonian aristocracy, Dura Europos enjoyed a cosmopolitan culture, allowing Balthazar to secure suitable lodgings for himself and his entourage without interrogation. Entering the walled and towered city through its newly completed Palmyrene Gate, an imposing edifice well suited to the ambitions of this progressive trading city, the Maga had murmured thanks to Surya for another stage of his journey completed without misadventure. Of course, having an armed bodyguard of six men had undoubtedly assisted in deterring strangers from attempting to investigate the packs and chests loaded on his small caravan of mules.

Here, he must visit the camel market to equip his trek across the desert. Here, also, he hoped for corroboration of what some eastbound traveller had related to him concerning the birth in Palestine of a boy child of the royal line of Judah, last mid-September. When Balthazar sought provenance for the tale, the man had replied, 'I was in the temple in Jerusalem when the whole family came in to make the birth sacrifices. Doves, it was, if I remember right. His father held the swaddled infant up to the altar of the Holy of Holies, named him Yeshua in the eyes of Yahweh and went on to declaim the boy's lineage. I heard every word, I tell you. He rattled off those ancestors - bang, bang, bang - all the way back to King David. That babe is a true Prince of Judah, make no mistake!'

Sitting cross-legged on a tasselled cushion he had placed on the stone-flagged floor of his quarters, the Maga rested his elbows on his knees and opened his hands palms upwards in an attitude of meditation. Closing his eyes, he remained still until his mind was empty and calm, then, murmuring a prayer for guidance, he began to consider how best to further his quest.

Later that night, straining his eyes in the glimmer cast by a few oil lamps, he pored over planetary charts and scribbled astronomical calculations on scraps of parchment. Next, he consulted his Kundli, an astrological chart designed to assist in predicting the horoscopes of individuals based on their birth dates. If the royal child had been born on September the fifteenth of the previous year, as the traveller claimed, Balthazar found that the birth would have coincided with a rare conjunction of Jupiter, Mars and Saturn, hinting that it was of great significance – and, from the Kundli, he was able to predict that the child would become a man of peace and healing; a holy visionary and a great leader, though with a clouded destiny. That sounded promising.

Next morning, donning formal robes and, setting two bodyguards to watch his rooms and the rest to guard his caravan, he made his way to the great Temple of Bel, a white marble structure dominated by rows of tall columns surrounding a central building. It stood at the edge of the high escarpment on which the city was built and, from its steps, devotees could look down eight hundred cubits to the river Euphrates below, currently glistening in the early morning sun. Fronting the temple was a spacious courtyard where people strolled and contemplated until the noon sun scorched the spiritual enthusiasm of all but the most zealous. Here, it seemed likely he might find a traveller who, like himself, was taking a moment of considered repose - someone who might carry news from the west. Seating himself on a stone bench and arranging his robes comfortably, the Maga waited, watching the scene.

Several passers-by acknowledged him politely, inclining their heads, but did not stop to converse. Eventually, a man aged around fifty years came out of the temple, attracting Balthazar's attention because of his cultured and priestly bearing. His clothing, of Persian style, consisted of a pleated and embroidered white robe cinched tightly at the waist with a woven lambs' wool belt, topped by a brown, fringed cloak. He wore soft leather boots turned up at the toes and a double-peaked tall black felt hat with flaps that covered his cheeks to the chin. A sprig of myrtle leaves adorned this extraordinary headdress. Two men of soldierly build, clad in linen tunics, breast armour and conical helmets wrapped in twisted cloths, rose from the temple steps and resumed their place behind him as he strode into the courtyard. Armed with curved blades, these personal guards maintained a hawk-like awareness as they shadowed their master.

Rising, Balthazar bowed deeply as the three approached. Learned as he was, his Parthian was imperfect despite several months of practice, but he ventured to speak in hopes of being understood. 'I am your servant, sir - Balthazar by name, a Maga Brahmin - you might prefer the Persian word 'Magus' - and a man of standing in my own country. Bound westwards, I desire knowledge of Palestine, so if you have travelled from that region will you graciously share any news you may carry, particularly concerning any known or rumoured royal birth?'

Surprised, the priestly man halted before gracing Balthazar with a slight bow, unable to deepen it for fear of toppling his tall hat. 'Greetings in the name of the great Ahura Mazda,' he said in heavily accented Parthian. 'I am Gaspar of Istakhr.' He hesitated. 'Perhaps our meeting is ordained, for I am bound in the same direction as you, having travelled north from Persia - and, by extraordinary coincidence, I also seek confirmation of the birth you mention. You see, I am also a Magus - a Zoroastrian - and have heard the same rumour.'

'I am blessed to meet you!' exclaimed Balthazar, now better understanding Gaspar's initial surprise and beaming with pleasure, for the Brahmin and Zoroastrian faiths held very close links and to meet another Maga - no, Magus - he corrected himself, mentally, was a boon beyond expectation.

'Let's find some shade,' suggested Gaspar, as, with evident relief, he removed his tall headdress, beneath which a delicately embroidered white wool cap cupped his dark curls. 'Pardon my informality, but this is too warm to wear for long in the sun,' he apologised.

Balthazar gladly acceded to Gaspar's proposal and accompanied his new friend to the side of the temple, where a stand of Cypresses offered dappled haven and the sibilant chirrup of cicadas was the only distraction. Here they sat on a low step, admiring the Euphrates far below, while Gaspar's guards settled on a higher step with unobstructed views of the vicinity.

After exchanging pleasantries, Balthazar returned to his interest in the line of Judah. 'So, what do you know of events in Palestine?' he asked, 'And have you performed divinations that encouraged your journey?'

'My original intent was solely to visit the leading Zoroastrian Magi here,' Gaspar told him. 'But my hosts apprised me of the rumoured royal birth, so I consulted the skies using my charts and an astrolabe, a tool gifted to me by a Magus of the Nabataeans, the mentor of my youth. The planetary conjunctions proved quite unprecedented and my astrological interpretation was that a birth of major political significance had indeed taken place. This brought to mind the prophecy of Daniel, passed down amongst Zoroastrians these several hundred years: '...*A star will come out of Jacob; a sceptre will rise out of Israel...*' - foretelling the coming of the Messiah of the

Jews. The elder Magus of Parthia tasked me to discover the truth concerning this birth - although whether it took place in Jerusalem or some other place, I cannot say. I travel west to find out.'

'What would a Judaean royal birth mean to the Magi here?' asked Balthazar.

No man save I can be seeking The One, this is certain.

'...An excellent question. Coming from afar, you may be unaware of royal politics in Asia Minor. In the Parthian Empire, the senior Magi have far greater influence than you can imagine - even to the raising and deposing of regional kings, should the need arise - so news of any potential change in the royal order, especially in a Roman province, will cause their ears to twitch mightily and their brains to contort in consideration of how that might impact upon their own power base.'

'So, would the Parthian Magi greet a royal birth of the line of Judah with celebration or with concern?'

'In the camel market, yesterday, I met a slave trader from Damascus,' replied Gaspar obliquely. 'When I enquired of the stability of Palestine's throne, he snorted that Herod was an untrustworthy tyrant dancing to the drums of the Roman Empire - which, of course, holds Palestine as a Province, with a Roman Governor to render justice and collect taxes.' Gaspar lowered his voice. 'Herod is almost seventy now and desires that his son, Archelaus, succeed him. The Roman Senate could cast Herod down as easily as it raised him up and his own subjects, discontent under the Roman yoke, could rally to a Prince of Judah if they thought he might win them their freedom.'

'This birth could herald war, then?'

Gaspar shrugged. 'Hard to say, but a Palestine free of Roman subjugation - and of the Roman army - might present a target for annexation by another power - and Parthia is certainly ambitious. Still; conjecture on its consequences cannot help us prove this birth. And besides, the Jews are unpredictable people – none know which way they'll turn.'

'There may be more certain news in Damascus,' murmured Balthazar. 'Are you leaving with the next caravan?'

'With the help of Ahura Mazda, yes,' confirmed the Zoroastrian.

'In that case,' proposed Balthazar, 'Shall we combine trains and travel together for added safety? I have six men at arms and will be acquiring a string of camels later today.'

Gaspar smiled. 'That makes good sense and will give us the pleasure of each others' company on the wearisome trek across the desert, which has only the questionable relief of Palmyra to break its monotony - though at least that city has not fallen under the dominion of the Romans, yet.'

'I heard Palmyra is a pleasant oasis,' offered Balthazar, 'And that the great Temple of Ba'al there is very fine - with taller columns than this one and a colonnade extending from the temple all the way to the city proper.'

'You won't mention Ba'al to any Jews you happen to meet, will you?' laughed Gaspar. 'They consider his cult a huge threat to the exclusive worship of their god, Yahweh. Some of them call Ba'al by another name – 'Ba'al Zebub', meaning Lord of the Flies – a derogatory designation for a false god.'

'I had no idea!' admitted Balthazar, mortified. 'One must always try not to offend the beliefs that others hold sacred. Thank you for saving me from that guilty act.'

Gaspar's brown eyes twinkled. 'I am your servant in all such matters. I do suggest, though, that you may find it more apt to visit Palmyra's Temple of Malak-bel.'

'Oh?'

'That's their local name for the sun god.'

Damascus, City State of the Decapolis, December, the Year after Christ's Birth (6BCE)

'Will these abominable saddle sores never heal?' the Magus grumbled as he eased himself onto a cushioned couch in the villa he and Gaspar had rented near the Cardo Maximus, the Roman road that traversed the city centre of Damascus, a member city state of the Decapolis. This loosely-knit group of ten city-states was an enclave of Greco-Roman culture to which Rome permitted an autonomy not enjoyed by Semitic cities in its annexed provinces. Damascus even minted its own coins. Moreover, the trade routes from southern Arabia, Palmyra, Petra and the silk routes from China all converged there, satisfying Rome's demand for Eastern luxuries.

There was much to be said, reflected Balthazar, wincing as pain flared anew under the pressure of his weight, for the pleasures this city afforded well-heeled travellers - the Roman baths from which he had just returned being one fine example. He just prayed that the unguents he had mixed and applied to his bruised dignity would work their magic quickly. Both sages had endured an arduous journey to reach this civilised haven. Balthazar feared he would retain a hatred of sand for the rest of his life. Nothing had prepared him for the desert's cruel vicissitudes.

He recalled the day their camels had been plodding along as usual, in the middle of a line of over fifty beasts, the Magi rocking incessantly on their ungainly steeds, their chins bowed almost to their chests, their turban cloths swaddling their faces - all but the eyes - and those eyes dulled by the monotony of endless sand. Within a heartbeat, that ordered progression was destroyed by the mad, mindless violence of a sandstorm, the discomfort of chafed flesh instantly forgotten in the pure fight for survival that the maelstrom thrust upon them.

Albeit unwittingly, his camel had probably saved his life, reflected Balthazar. With the unerring instinct of the desert-bred, the animal reacted to the whirling, stinging blasts of grit by dropping to its knees and lying down with its head turned away from the furious onslaught. Falling from its back, he blindly crushed himself into the hollow of its flank, his face pressed to the stinking sweat of the animal's harsh coat. His whole world became compressed into a second by second battle to breathe without choking on hair or sand. Losing all concept of the passage of time, he experienced only fleeting thoughts of the fate of his fellow travellers - whatever their condition, he could do nothing to help them, for only a madman would attempt to stand up in the face of that pure force of nature.

Although the experience seemed to last an eternity, in truth, the sandstorm blew itself out within the hour. When, at last, the vortex released him from its terrifying grip and he cautiously raised his head, rubbing a crust of sweat-compacted sand from his eyelids and blinking light back into the world, all he could see were dozens and dozens of loosely scattered, camel-sized dunes behind and ahead of his own. Apparently, all the beasts had done the same thing - lain down - and the blown sand had covered them, part burying, part sheltering both beasts and riders. As Balthazar staggered to his feet, showering the ground with his own mini-dune, other travellers also began to rise, sand-dazed, to shake piles of loose silica off their robes, cloaks, turbans, goods and animals.

Panic struck him at that moment - *what of the casket?* Scrabbling crazily at the sand heaped over his own camel, his shaking hands finally found what they sought - his pack - still secured by palm twine to the back of the saddle. Sinking to his knees in relief, he mouthed gritty thanks to Surya and made obeisance to *The Power* - for which he had endured much and would, no doubt, endure more.

Despite his best efforts, he never quite managed to rid his clothing of sand until they reached Palmyra, an annoyance that contributed substantially to the itchy torment of the latter part of the trek.

Now, the Magus relaxed back on his Damascene cushions and sighed, letting the accumulated stress of past trials slip away from him, calm in the knowledge that the casket lay behind locked doors in guarded quarters, here in a city where sandstorms were merely adventurers' tales.

Gaspar, despite his own aches and pains, had ventured forth to explore, being minded to walk the banks of the city's great river, the Barada. He said his eyes had been too long starved of the sight of flowing water. His companion's return roused Balthazar from a noontide nap.

Pouring himself a cup of watered wine from a clay flask on the table, Gaspar drained it in one thirsty gulp and turned to his sleep-bemused friend with a look that bespoke exciting news. 'I've been to the Temple of Jupiter,' he announced.

'...That gigantic pile at the end of the Decumanus Maximus? By Surya, you took a long walk!'

Gaspar nodded ruefully. 'My feet agree with you - but pilgrims come from all over to see it, you know. And my own visit was truly blessed, for as I passed through the market in the outer court, I spied, against all expectation, a most dear friend.' Gaspar's eyes betrayed emotion, but he forged on. 'Remember the astrolabe, that precious gift from my mentor? I never thought to see its giver again after parting from him these twenty years past, but by all that's holy, there he was, resting peaceably next to the propylaeum, the temple's Eastern gateway. He's grown so old his beard's turned white and he supports his infirmities with a staff - but I knew him instantly for Melchior.'

'I give thanks for your reunion,' said Balthazar warmly.

'You'll be even better pleased when you hear what he imparted to me. But, no, let him tell you himself - he wants us to join him at repast this evening. He's sending litters to bring us to his house.'

This is no house - it's a palace, thought Balthazar, drawing the privacy curtain aside as the four slaves bearing his litter halted at an imposing door, its portico supported by ornate marble columns. As he and Gaspar stepped out of their litters, a well-dressed slave opened the main door and admitted them to the front atrium, a paved courtyard with a large central fountain, on either side of which the main public rooms of the building were arranged. This layout was typical of the modern Greco-Roman style preferred by wealthy city-dwellers. Beyond the atrium was a tabulinium, an open air alcove for summer dining and beyond that, a wide doorway leading to the peristylum, a mosaic-tiled courtyard housing a sunken pool. Skirting its edge, marble columns supported a three-sided, covered colonnade which gave access to private family rooms.

The slave guided them politely to a large room set for dining in the Roman style, with couches ranged around the low central table upon which culinary delicacies would shortly be laid out to delight them. With sumptuous cushions and embroidered throws to add to their comfort, the lamp-lit setting was most appealing.

With some difficulty, the venerable Melchior rose to greet them, leaning heavily on his staff. Gaspar and Balthazar were glad they had dressed formally, for their host was similarly attired, his white beard highly oiled and plaited with thin silver wire. Despite his taste in architecture, his dress was not in the Roman fashion. Nabataeans tended towards the Greek style and Melchior wore a long, white, pleated linen chiton with embroidered borders. Like Gaspar's, his belt was the white lambs' wool Kusti belt of a Zoroastrian and on his long locks rested a white wool cap with a sprig of myrtle pinned at one side.

This white wizard raised his free hand, saying, 'By the grace of Ahura Mazda, you are welcome here.' Gesturing for them to be seated, he nodded to a slave who immediately disappeared through a side curtain to arrange the serving of the meal. Gauging, from his expression, that Balthazar was particularly impressed with the surroundings in which he found himself, Melchior smiled graciously and said, 'I am fortunate in my declining years of semi-retirement. My lord the King of Nabataea has seen fit to bless me with a measure of comfort in return for the many years of my skills that he and his rose red city of Petra enjoyed. Now, I humbly beg of you to delight in the fruits of my labours as my honoured guests. Be at ease, for we are all Magi and may speak freely from our hearts to one another.'

While the sages conversed, slaves passed in and out of the room bearing trays of food - flatbreads, spicy sausages, fried dormice rolled in honey and poppy seeds, green and black olives and a delicious paste of sesame and eggplant, the main dish comprising a sturgeon stuffed with herbs and almonds and smothered in a rich garum sauce. They continued with cheeses, dates and sweetmeats contrived from thin pastry, nuts, honey, rosewater and cinnamon. As the evening grew late, a tray of tiny honey cakes completed the meal. Balthazar had never eaten better.

'If you are replete, brethren,' said Melchior, pouring sweet wine, 'May we address matters of concern? I have already spoken something of this to you, Gaspar, but I will review the issue in more depth now that Balthazar is with us. Having built many links over time to inform my work, I have it on reliable authority that a boy child of the royal line of Judah - a direct descendant of King David of old - is indeed born to Israel, although you should not be surprised to find him in lowly estate, for the sons of David have been long without a throne. Marvellously, it seems that planetary confluence has coincided with an apparent fulfilment of Semitic prophecy, which foretells that a king of David's line shall arise to be their Messiah, the saviour of his people in their time of greatest need - and never can they have needed one as much as they do now, after more than sixty years under the fist of Rome. Let's hope news of this child has not reached the ears of Emperor Tiberius.

'I understand that you, Gaspar, are charged with bringing evidence of the child - and his likely destiny, I imagine - to your fellow Magi and their rulers in Parthia, who will trust only in a first-hand account of the babe, hmmm? A prudent commission, I dare say. Is it already thirty five years since the Parthians last invaded Palestine?' He raised a meaningful eyebrow at Gaspar. 'Meanwhile, young Balthazar, no doubt, also has good reason for his interest in the matter...' and here Melchior paused, as if to allow the subject of his comment to pass comment of his own, but Balthazar remained silent, so the old sage cleared his throat and carried on.

'...and my interests are those of Nabataea, namely to garner intelligence of any changes in the great game of power in struggling Palestine, particularly if it might affect trade - or promote war within the near East or with Rome herself. In view of this, I was already planning a journey to Jerusalem, but now I would embrace the opportunity to combine my star of passage with yours, not least because it occurs to me that the mighty Herod will be more inclined to receive us if we arrive as one party - in a caravan designed to impress.'

Gaspar turned to Balthazar. 'This sounds an excellent strategy! What do you say?'

Balthazar placed a deferential hand over his heart and murmured, 'It would be an honour... I say yes!' Under his robe, he felt his star emit a tiny throb, as if in acquiescence.

'Does Herod know of this child and where he can be found?' Gaspar asked his mentor.

Melchior shook his head, the silver in his beard glittering in the lamplight. 'This is what we go to discover. But, if he has no knowledge of the prince, that in itself will tell us much.' Under their bushy white brows, his eyes flashed like diamonds as he added, 'One word of caution; be very careful what you divulge to this Judean king. His mother was a wealthy Nabataean noble's daughter and his father, an Edomite Arab from Southern Judea who courted the Romans most successfully, so he is only as Jewish as he must be, if you understand me - and certainly lacks the royal provenance of a child of David's line. He may be ageing and plagued with diminishing health, but he came to power through a bloodbath, has kept his puppet throne for thirty odd years and, by all accounts, is still liable to have your head on a plate if he takes the whim.'

CHAPTER 3

GRAVE NEWS

Paris, France, 12 June, 2016 AD

In his office at the Pantheon Sorbonne, anthropologist Doctor Jean Desselle was checking his emails, between lectures. Ah, good, news from the front, he thought, opening an email from his friend and colleague, Alain Rousseau. Quickly scanning the message, he clicked on the attachment to view the photos Rousseau had sent and immediately dialled the extension for Doctor Henri Laurent, whom he knew was about to join Rousseau in Syria.

'Henri?'

'Jean; what can I do for you?' Laurent's rich, genial tones boomed down the phone. 'Those undergraduates of yours must be giving you hell if you're too exhausted to walk the length of the corridor to see me.'

'Don't they always?' laughed Desselle. 'But phoning was quicker than walking - and this is urgent.'

'Fire away, then.'

'Have you received an email from Alain today?'

'No idea, because my computer went pop yesterday and I'm still waiting for tech support.'

'When are you off to Damascus?'

'Tomorrow: why?'

'I need a seat on the same plane. Alain has asked for my help - and some postgraduates too, if you have any half-decent ones. Let me explain...'

Minutes later, Desselle was phoning the departmental secretary concerning his travel requirements, while Laurent, who had hot-footed it up the corridor, was clicking through Rousseau's photos on Desselle's laptop. 'This is *huge*!' he exclaimed, clutching his thick mop of brown hair in excitement.

'No kidding? Just wait until the media get their hands on it,' cautioned Desselle wryly. 'Those jackals always twist the truth and this is going to be a religious bombshell. Alain's right about that. His research grant was for medieval rock tombs, wasn't it? Who'd have thought he would uncover something like this? It's a whole new ball game now.'

Beneath his bushy brows, Laurent's hazel eyes sparkled in anticipatory delight. 'Don't I know it? I'll phone to let him know we're coming out in force.' He dialled Rousseau's mobile but it rang out to answerphone. 'Unavailable,' he told Desselle. 'If he's inside the tomb, of course, he won't get a signal. I'll try again later.'

Damascus, Syria, 12 June, 2016 AD

Descending Quasioun in the Sham, Bashir took the road's switchback curves with practiced ease. The dead Frenchman's i-phone lay on the seat beside him - he had used it to make just one call, arranging a place and time to meet the *Dhu Samawi*. It was a pity he'd have to dump the gadget, but it might be traceable. On cue, it began to ring, making him start. He ignored the sound until it stopped of its own accord, then tossed it through the open window into the depths of the gorge.

Gaining the outskirts of Damascus, he became entangled in crawling, honking traffic as he made for Wurud, an Alawite enclave within the shabby Sunni suburb of Qudsaya. There the Sham disappeared into a maze of narrow streets.

Members of his covert group, the Brotherhood of the Sabaeans, continued to live here to remain inconspicuous. Considered heretics, the Alawis had always been the butt of bigotry in a predominantly Sunni Muslim nation. Nevertheless, in the mid twentieth century, these despised mountain peasants had infiltrated the army and gained a power base within the progressive Ba'ath Party, culminating in a coup that gave rise to an Alawi presidency in nineteen seventy.

At the turn of the millennium, President Hafez al-Assad was succeeded by his son, Bashar al-Assad, whose hold on power was being severely tested by an extended and particularly bloody civil war. Violence was commonplace in a capital city torn by persistent rebel attacks. Islamic fundamentalists funded and fuelled the struggle, amused by the West's ineffectual posturing. Apparently, the US and its allies did not understand that ousting Assad could bring about the accession to power of those whose sole aim was Islamic world domination - making intervention likely to prove antithetical to the Christian world's best interests. What was even more amusing to the Islamists was that the west was covertly funding some of the anti-Assad rebels – but then, the west never had understood the Arab world.

Considered an extremist sect, Alawis were secretive about their religious beliefs - a habit born of a thousand years of persecution and repression. They gathered in private homes to worship, their faith comprising a mixture of pagan, Gnostic, Christian and Islamic beliefs whose earliest origins stemmed from the Sabaean sun-worshippers of upper Mesopotamia. Alawi prayers were still made facing the sun rather than Mecca. Their Qudass ceremony involved the consecration of bread and wine - the latter being termed 'The Servant of Light' - and considered to be the transubstantiated essence of their Trinitarian Godhead.

Bashir loved the way his faith echoed his own Sabaean origins and blended with his commitment to *The Power*, which he saw as the distilled essence of the sun's holy, life-giving light. God was the Sun; the Sun was the Light; the Light was *The Power*; *The Power* was God.

With these thoughts running through his mind, he parked the Sham and hurried to the house of the *Dhu Samawi*, who was also the senior officiate – the Khassar – of the local Alawi congregation. Entering the well-paved courtyard, Bashir climbed the steps to the main entrance and let himself into the imposing residence. The Khassah enjoyed the privileged lifestyle of a wealthy man, not because of his religious duties, but because his father, an army officer and senior member of the Ba'ath Party, had performed services for those who had, in that cleverly executed turnaround of Alawite fortunes, effected the Presidential coup almost fifty years earlier.

The *Dhu Samawi* was kneeling in his prayer room, having just completed some private devotions. Silently, Bashir knelt at his side. The thin, ascetic face turned inside the cowl of its gutrah and acknowledged the younger man. 'Tell me all,' commanded the low voice of the Lord of Heaven.

The title of its leader reflected the Brotherhood's origins, dating back some eighteen hundred years. The story handed down was that five brothers had been denied their rightful inheritance by their father, a Keeper of *The Power*, who bestowed that birthright only on their sixth and youngest brother, Adeeb. The five split away, vowing revenge and the restoration of *The Power* into their hands. From a distance, they watched Adeeb and plotted how to regain the golden casket he held. But Adeeb made a fool of them all by placing the casket beyond their reach, under the aegis of the Christian Church in Jerusalem, who locked it away in an underground crypt.

Thwarted, the five brothers, whose mother was a descendant of the Sabaeans, founded the Brotherhood of the Sabaeans, its name reflecting their love of their blameless dam. The eldest brother became its first leader, naming himself after an ancient Sabaean god - *Dhu Samawi*, the Lord of Heaven - a name to reflect the godlike power that he felt should have been his.

The modern Brotherhood - limited to those men of direct paternal descent from its founders – maintained the same creed and aim as their founding fathers. Over time, it became accepted that when restoration of the casket into their hands was finally achieved, the *Dhu Samawi* at that time would prove to be *The One*. Unfortunately the casket's whereabouts had been unknown to them for almost a thousand years. Any information on that score was infinitely precious. Consequently, Bashir respectfully related his story to the *Dhu Samawi*, who did not interrupt until the younger man pulled the cloth-wrapped object from his belt and uncovered the ancient crucifixion nail he had taken from the coffin in the mountain.

Then the Lord of Heaven spoke. 'This evidence is compelling! I believe you *have* found the tomb of Isa, on which our ancestor, Balthazar, has engraved the seal of the casket as witness and proof. This bears out our blessèd scrolls, which state that Balthazar bore great love for Isa and taught him many arts. Now we must discover what else he may have left in Isa's tomb - without delay - for despite your quick thinking in silencing the French unbeliever, others may come across the tomb at any time. How well its entrance has been obscured, I cannot know. Any information relating to the casket must come to our eyes alone. I will consult with brothers Zikar and Hafiz and instruct you further - be ready.'

'I'm always ready, day or night,' declared Bashir fervently.

'You are a young hothead and must learn patience. Nevertheless, you have done well. You may go, while I shall now perform the five great prayers, *Ali, Fatimah, Hassan, Hussain* and *Muhsin*, to ask for guidance.' He bent forward until the crown of his head touched the floor, with his elbows bent and his palms flat on the Persian rug. Obediently, Bashir stood and padded out in silence, leaving him to his holy prayers.

Police Headquarters, Damascus, Syria, 13 June, 2016 AD

From the airport, a cab had taken Laurent, Desselle and their postgraduate team to the hotel where Rousseau was registered, only to have the manager inform them that the police wished to speak to them urgently in connection with their colleague. Laurent asked what the problem was, but the hotel manager shrugged – he knew no more. Leaving the students to unpack, they immediately caught another cab - to the grey, fortified police headquarters on Khaled bin al-Walid Avenue in the central Qanawat district.

Neither of them spoke more than a few words of Arabic, which made matters hard to grasp. An interpreter was eventually produced and the shocking facts emerged. They were escorted to the morgue to identify Alain, desperately hoping that someone had made a terrible error. Sadly, that was not the case. Haltingly, they asked whatever questions occurred to them. It seemed that Rousseau's body had been discovered in a culvert in an area they felt sure he should have had no reason to visit, out on the eastern edge of the city. The police thought he might have been killed elsewhere and the body dumped, but they had no leads and could suggest no motive.

Desselle glanced at Laurent when the word motive was mentioned and said slowly, 'I think we should tell them what Alain found on Mount Quasioun – it could be linked to his murder.'

Laurent nodded, his usually jovial features drawn. 'You're absolutely right, of course. We also have to break the news to his wife. I suppose I should do that. Josette will want to fly out and take him home. The university will have to be notified, too. What a tragic mess. I can't believe it.'

'Take your time, Henri. Why don't you handle the home front while I sort out the field implications?' suggested Desselle, kindly. 'I'll have to break it to the postgrads gently. Alain was well liked by the student body.' He blew out a long breath. 'And we'd better secure the tomb as soon as we can. If there are murderous tomb robbers about, we'll need to display a strong enough presence to send them packing. We have to protect Alain's find, but not at the expense of our own lives, so I suggest we ask for a round-the-clock police guard. When we explain everything, I think they'll understand why.'

Eventually, they did.

The Alawi Quarter, Damascus, Syria, 14 June, 2016 AD

'The filthy *shurta* found the Frenchman. Karam failed us, the son of a whore!'

'Calm down, Umarah. And don't swear.'

'Don't tell me to calm down! My fingerprints must be all over that truck!'

'The police found the truck as well?' Gripping the phone, Bashir's palm felt suddenly damp. 'Don't tell me Karam left the body inside it!'

Umarah sniffed in disgust. 'No, he moved the body, but hid it poorly. Maybe he should have left it in the damn truck, because the *shurta* haven't found that - yet. Karam promised to drive it into the desert and burn it. That would get rid of fingerprints, wouldn't it?'

'Of course... Be brave, like the lion you are. Ali and *The Power* will protect you.'

Umarah sniffed again, somewhat mollified. '...Any news from the *Dhu Samawi*?'

'Yes: we go tomorrow. Get some sleep. I'll be with you at seven.'

Ending the call, Bashir sighed and sprawled back on his mattress, closing his eyes against the mean sum of his possessions - a narrow wardrobe, a tallboy with a small TV on top of it, a noisy but inefficient air conditioning unit high on one side wall and a single hard wooden chair. The floor was plain white ceramic tile. At the rear was a cramped bathroom containing basic essentials. To cook, he went out into the courtyard with his portable stove. It wasn't much, but at least he had a roof over his head, he reflected - unlike the liquorice drink sellers and the shoeshine boys.

When he found the casket, life would be very different...

Then our Brotherhood will own the world! All the newspapers will want our pictures and they'll pay to interview us. I'll get a brand new Mercedes and the Sunnis will grovel as I drive past. They'll be the heretics, not us! And if the infidels want to benefit from The Power channelled through The One, they can beg for it on their knees, mouths to the ground, eating the dirt as they speak. They'll eat dirt... and I'll eat pistachio-stuffed lamb with honey sauce... Yes...and slender, sloe-eyed women will swoon when they see me and vie for the honour of washing my feet... anyone who dares to put a hand on the casket will die... it is ours alone...

His disjointed thoughts deepened, at last, into fitful slumber.

Mount Quasioun, Damascus, Syria 15 June, 2016 AD

On arrival in the gorge, they had found no obvious tomb entrance at the location Rousseau had described. It had taken the sharp eyes of one of the students to pick out an anomaly on the steep bluffs above; a patch of loose-looking boulders. When they climbed to the spot, they saw how the rocks had apparently been hastily - and very recently - piled into a low tunnel to block and disguise it.

Two armed militia men stood guard while the archaeological team cleared the tunnel, grateful that it was early evening before they had commenced this labour, having not yet acclimatised to the searing heat of a Syrian June. The guards remained overnight, replaced by a fresh pair the following morning.

Next day, having purchased supplies and equipment, the team set up a makeshift but adequate camp – it was more convenient than commuting from the city centre. The day was spent taking photographs, bagging up samples for analysis and making extensive notes and measurements.

Today, Desselle would commence work on the remains in the coffin, while Laurent's sad task was to drive to the airport to meet Josette and assist her in claiming her husband's body. It was agreed that if, after thorough examination of the ancient corpse, Desselle was satisfied as to its provenance, he should break the news to the world press immediately, on behalf of the team.

And that's when the shit will hit the proverbial fan, thought Desselle. Nodding to the stone-faced guards, he disappeared into the tunnel, followed by the two postgraduates carrying the specialist equipment needed for their anthropological investigations.

Bashir, Alim and Umarah drove part way up the mountain, where they parked and camouflaged the Sham, off-road, in a patch of brush. Extreme caution had been advised by the Lord of Heaven, so they would walk from here, picking their way over stony ground to avoid telltale footprints. Nearing the location of the tomb, Bashir sent Umarah - the youngest amongst them at just twenty years of age - to scramble up the crags and find a good spot overlooking the tomb.

Bashir and Alim sat on convenient boulders and sipped from their water bottles while they waited, occasionally craning their necks to scan the heights above, but never glimpsing Umarah.

'If we can't see him,' Bashir observed, 'No-one else can, even if anyone is looking. He's a snake in the grass.'

'I see no grass, either,' said Alim, attempting levity.

Bashir was unamused. 'You should have trained in a Libyan camp like I did. Then you'd know the difference between an adventure hike and man's work.'

After over an hour waiting in a place where shade was just a concept, loose gravel and small stones suddenly began to patter down on their heads and Umarah reappeared, clambering down the steep bluffs. Reaching his brethren, he crouched and took a long pull from his water bottle before speaking. 'Bad news,' he muttered finally, spitting the last half mouthful of water disgustedly onto the rocks at his feet. 'It's like the Damascus Film Festival down there. We're too late.'

'Give me a full report,' demanded Bashir.

'Maybe the Frenchman phoned or texted someone before you dealt with him; who knows? But anyway, the place is swarming. There are at least three foreigners with the same sort of equipment he had, only they have more cameras and bigger lights and they've already cleared the way in. They've set up camp down by the track on that wide bend.'

'...Only three, you say?' Bashir pinched his nose thoughtfully. 'Good odds, if we surprise them one by one as they're ducking out of the tunnel...'

Umarah put up a staying hand. 'No. They have pistols, plus there are at least two armed militia guarding the place. With only our Khangars, we wouldn't stand a chance.'

Bashir swore. 'We'll have to go back, pick up a load of gear - guns, too - and come back prepared to camp out for as long as it takes.' His dark eyes narrowed. 'Only Ali is perfect. Sooner or later they'll make a mistake - and we'll be ready.'

The Tomb, Mount Quasioun, Damascus, Syria, 16 June, 2016 AD

Local Syrian news correspondents were the first to arrive, followed by newsmen from CNN and Al Jazeera, then a BBC Middle East news correspondent with a cameraman and driver in tow. The narrow dirt road through the gorge became clogged with vehicles - those of the academics and the militia eclipsed by the eclectic variety of press vehicles. Laurent left it to Desselle to give statements and interviews.

Desselle responded simply and practically to the questions fired at him, remaining calm and stressing that much work remained to be done before they could categorically confirm that Jesus Christ was buried in this lonely spot. He avoided conjecture as to why and how Christ's body might have ended up here, restricting his comment to scientific evidence and providing photographs, since they could permit no-one into the tomb until the scientific studies had been completed. Making one exception, he allowed one BBC cameraman brief access to assure independent evidence of the inscription on the tomb - the team wanted no later accusations of fraud to mar their professional reputations.

The BBC correspondent gave a live report to camera from the road below the tomb and, afterwards, passing Desselle his business card, asked to be contacted if there were any major developments. 'If my mobile's off, just phone the office and ask for Darren Carmichael,' he said. Opening his car door, he added, 'Thanks for your co-operation - makes my job much easier. I'm glad I'm not in your shoes, though.'

'How do you mean?' enquired the academic.

'Well, it's going to be a three ring circus, isn't it? And you'll probably have a hard time defending your right to conduct the full analysis - I wouldn't be surprised if you don't end up piggy-in-the-middle between all the factions likely to claim possession of the body.'

'Such as..?'

'Well; let's see - the Syrian authorities; the Vatican; the Israelis; the Islamists - oh, every Tom, Dick and Harry with a vested interest, I'd imagine.'

Desselle flexed his fingers through his salt and pepper hair. 'We'll have to cross those bridges when we come to them, I suppose. Personally, I don't think this discovery belongs to any one nation or faith - it belongs to the whole world. I'd like to see everyone co-operating to determine the truth, whatever their religious stance. What outcome would you like to see?'

Carmichael chuckled as he got into his car. 'Me? I couldn't give a monkey's - I'm an atheist.'

Mount Quasioun, Damascus, Syria, 17 June, 2016 AD

The three young Sabaeans returned under cover of darkness, setting up their own camp in an adjacent ravine. From there they hiked to a vantage point where they could lie concealed and watch everything that was going on. Two rifles now lay at their side.

There was plenty of activity to observe, consisting mostly of newsmen coming and going, but a visitor of a different ilk arrived in the early afternoon. Dressed in a well-tailored Italian suit, he had a clerical cast about him and was admitted to the sepulchre. Before ducking into the tunnel, he made the sign of the cross.

'Catholic,' hissed Alim.

'Nice suit, though,' noted Umarah, whose cotton didashah was dusty, crumpled and making him itch.

'Quiet,' growled Bashir.

The Italian was a Papal Emissary, who announced that he had come only to take photographs and make notes that would inform the Pope accurately on the nature of this interesting discovery. 'His Holiness is being asked to give a press conference on the implications of this find to the Church and wants to make sure that he is in advance possession of the facts,' the Emissary explained. The French team could not very well refuse his reasonable request, so in he went - and, ten minutes later, re-emerged, looking faintly worried and seemingly in somewhat of a hurry to return to Damascus and file his report with the Holy See.

'Everyone seems to know about this place, now,' spat Bashir resentfully, sweat running down the nape of his neck in the blistering heat.

His was the pick that had broken the seal on the tomb. *He* should have been the one receiving all the attention, the limelight and the glory for the discovery. *He* should have been the one finding the casket and becoming a hero in the eyes of his Brethren and the Lord of Heaven. And when the casket was in his hands? Well, the blessèd scrolls might say the *Dhu Samawi* was destined to be *The One* - but who knew, really? The scrolls could be wrong. It was blasphemy to think it but...

I am of the blood as much as he is... I could be The One!

The whole glorious sequence of events he had imagined was dissolving before his eyes as unbelievers swarmed over his discovery. Everything he deserved was being stolen from under his nose - and as this bitter thought crossed his mind, he equated the injustice committed on his ancient forebears by Adeeb with the injustice he was now suffering and it stoked the furnace of his anger to a white hot fury.

CHAPTER 4

THE OLDEST LEGEND ON EARTH

Chaumont Hall, Derbyshire, England, 16 June, 2016 AD

Kaye scribbled down the last sentence, stuck his pencil stub behind one ear and reached for his coffee mug. Even if this was the old Earl's handwriting, he had copied the material from an older source, of that Kaye had no doubt. How many times had this masterpiece been transcribed to preserve it, he wondered? Engrossed in the tale that the Vedic Sanskrit told, he had forgotten his drink and grimaced, now, as he sipped the bitter, cold liquid. *Never mind; what lies in front of me more than compensates - a thousand times more. They'll have to sit up and take notice when I publish on this.*

His call from the conservatory door brought Sam in, eager for answers. 'Sit and prepare to be amazed,' he commanded, grinning, all sense of etiquette lost in his enthusiasm to share his discovery. 'I'm going to read you a story that might just be the oldest legend on Earth!'

The incongruous combination of his child-like excitement and professorial delivery amused Sam. 'Do stop pacing, Oliver. It's exhausting to watch you.'

'Oh, sorry,' he replied distractedly and settled onto his stool. 'The thing is that the document in your possession is just the latest in a long line of copies of an old legend originating in India - and to the best of my knowledge it's a totally *unknown* legend. I've translated it in keeping with its age and subject matter, so it might sound frightfully quaint...'

'Hang on,' interposed Sam. 'How old is this legend, exactly?'

'About four thousand years old,' replied Kaye deliberately, a small smile hovering on his lips. 'But the story it tells could well date from thousands of years earlier than that - passed down by word of mouth before the written word was invented.' Sam stared at him, giddy at the thought of a story that old surviving until now - and at the possibility that only the two of them knew about it.

'Ready?' he enquired and began to read aloud.

'Hearken to the star whence cometh The Power. For The Power is the firstborn of the last and greatest battle of the time of heroes, the battle marking the end of the time of the Ancients, when silver-white vimanas embraced the heavens like vast flocks of cranes circling the floodplains before choosing a place to alight.
'And it came to pass that the supreme Lord Ashar, ruler of the Ancients, built a glittering net of light and directed his army to fly their vimanas high - higher than the tallest eagle's stoop; higher than the mountain's crest; higher even than the white cloud's mantle - and to cast that net amongst the heavens.'

'Sorry to interrupt you,' apologised Sam, 'But what's a vimana? ...Some kind of bird?'

Kaye laughed. 'Not exactly - chariots of the gods, more like. Ancient myths from India, called 'Vedas', talk of vimanas, some of which are described in great detail. This is the word in Sanskrit...' He pointed it out to Sam: विमान. 'One literal translation of the word is 'traverse', suggesting a moving vehicle of some kind. In the ancient mythical stories, these are flying machines that the gods and heroes use - for example, in one story, the sun god is transported in a flying, chariot-like vimana. Some idiots use these myths to claim that we were visited by aliens in spaceships at the dawn of civilisation - pure bunkum, of course. Anyway, shall I go on?'

Sam nodded.

'And they caught the embryo – part of the life-force of the sun - in the net, like a huge golden carp thrashing its agony. And the lightning of its anger filled the firmament and was wont

to burn the earth to a cinder. Then stood forth Baal, bravest warrior Mage of the Ancients and he challenged Ashar, who had trapped this terrible force, yet now seemed powerless to harness its power and halt the immolation of the home of men. And the army was divided, half remaining loyal to the commander and half in accord with his challenger. Thus began the final battle.

'And at its peak, Baal captured control of the net holding The Power of the sun. And he concentrated his mind on subduing The Power. Long he laboured, near losing his life many times, until the sweat of his effort sprang so freely from his brow that it formed a river and flowed to the southern sea, there spreading to form a vast delta that steamed night and day from the heat of the fires that consumed the land. And while he laboured, The Power countered him by issuing streams of lightning bolts that split the skies like vipers' tongues until every last vimana was rent asunder and scattered to the ground in flames and molten doom.

'And at last Baal forced The Power to his mighty will, compressing its boundless strength into the small space between his outstretched hands, imprisoning it in gold and there binding it with spells and arts now lost in the mists of time.

'And in return for this victory he gave of his blood to be forever bound to The Power and, with its lightning, The Power marked him upon his breast with the symbol of its origin - a star - and he became the First Keeper of The Power.'

Sam blanched. ...A star on his breast - like hers?

'And it came to pass that, after the battle, of all the Ancients there were but two survivors - Baal, the First Keeper and Ashar, the Lord. And they bowed their heads in shame and

sorrow as they looked upon the utter destruction that was the fruit of their overweening arrogance.

Renouncing the fabulous artifices that men had conceived and wrought, to their ultimate destruction, Ashar donned a simple loincloth, took a wife from amongst the few lowly peasants left alive and, in the delta formed from the sweat of Baal, began his atonement - the long task of planting rice to renew the land. And Baal donned a cowled mantle and belt, to which he cinched a bag to hold and hide the golden box that housed The Power, for it was his duty to keep its secret safe until the day when The One would be found with sufficient purity of heart and spirit to use it to benefit all men. And Baal departed to wander the earth, he and his descendants, ever guarding The Power; ever seeking The One.

'And The Power is absolute and may be guarded only by its Keepers, descended from the First Keeper.

'And The Power is bound by the blood of the Ancients and can be quickened only by that blood.

'And The Power may be quickened by any Keeper only once in a lifetime, until the day when The One is found who is pure enough to use The Power without limit.

'And the Keepers and The One shall use The Power only to redeem death, never to cause it.'

Kaye finished his oration and tabled his notebook with a small flourish. A moment of silence hung between them, like the hush preceding an expected round of applause. Even though Sam wasn't an antiquarian by profession, thought Kaye, she was intelligent, well-educated and, he was sure, capable of realising the huge significance to antiquarians and archaeologists of a find like this. He was delighted he had been the means of bringing it to light - she must be as thrilled as he was.

Having presumed her positive reaction, his shock was absolute when Sam's lower lip began to quiver and she dissolved into horrified tears. She couldn't help herself. It had taken a few moments for the full impact to hit her, but when it did, it proved an emotional bombshell. This impossibly ancient story reinforced her father's message in the most terrifying way. It could be no coincidence that its core theme encompassed *The Power*, its *Keepers* and *The One*. Kaye had called it a legend, but Sam had a sinking feeling that it was much, much more.

This is nothing less than the foundation for a complete spiritual belief system...

So it was all true. Her father had secretly followed a faith that had somehow survived for at least four thousand years - making it twice as old as Christianity and perhaps much older than that. And she was supposed to take responsibility for its continued survival. How bitter a pill was this, for an impious daughter to be obliged to become the exponent of her father's ridiculous, anachronistic creed?

Ridiculous, is it? Then explain the star-shaped birthmark over your heart.

'What on earth...?' The dismayed Kaye pulled a handkerchief out of his pocket and proffered it.

Sam accepted it and held it to her face. 'Dreadfully sorry,' she sniffed, her voice muffled behind the white cotton. 'Don't know what got into me.' Forcing herself under control, she wondered how to rationalise her outburst. 'Everything suddenly got on top of me,' she told him, wiping her eyes. 'My father's funeral was only last Saturday and it hasn't been easy.'

'Quite understandable,' Kaye assured her, with genuine concern. 'Should I come back another day when you're feeling better..?'

She shook her head. 'No. I'll be fine, honestly.' And she would be, after a fashion. Dexters were nothing if not resilient. She sniffed again. 'I'll just take a short break before we carry on, if you don't mind.'

Kaye had no objections.

Glancing at the kitchen television, Sam noticed the BBC lunchtime news had just begun and thumbed up the volume to catch the headlines. She needed time to think.

Rather more interested in the material on the kitchen table than in the Prime Minister's latest initiative to lower unemployment figures, Kaye gave only half his attention to the news, devoting the rest to the unusual emblem at the bottom of the Sanskrit document. He had been dazzled by the script, but the emblem was equally stunning. Absently, he drew his pencil from its ear-rest and began copying the individual symbols that wound spirally to the centre of the sunburst.

After the headlines, the female newsreader, Melissa, announced a late-breaking newsflash. 'Here's Darren Carmichael, our Middle East correspondent in Damascus, on the controversial discovery of a two thousand year old tomb that archaeologists claim is that of Jesus Christ.'

Now that *is* interesting, thought Kaye, looking up from his notes.

Sam appeared to be watching the television, but her unfocused eyes told a different tale - they were fathomless pools. On the screen, a reporter in a short-sleeved shirt stood in bright sunshine in a landscape of barren sandstone crags. High on a ledge behind him, surrounded by the detritus of an archaeological dig, was a square black hole.

'Darren,' said Melissa's voice. 'The tomb of Christ - we've heard claims like this before, but they've always been repudiated. What's your take on this new discovery?'

'Yes, Melissa, there have been unsubstantiated claims before. Only a few years ago, a duo of tombs excavated on the outskirts of Jerusalem were found to have the names 'Jesus' and 'Joseph' inscribed on them. Sadly, those names were common in the time of Christ, making it impossible to ascribe the graves to any particular individuals. However, despite the unlikely location of the tomb here on Mount Quasioun - I say unlikely because it's hard to imagine why Christ's mortal remains should have ended up so far from his home - it does look as if the archaeologists might have got it right this time.'

'You're at the excavation site. What evidence have you seen that this is the genuine tomb of Christ?'

'There's an inscription on the side of the tomb in Latin. I'm told it translates as *'Here rests the Body of Yeshua of Nazareth, Crucified Messiah - Beloved Son of Marium and Yosepha.'* 'Yeshua' is the way they would have written Jesus's name two thousand years ago. That's a pretty convincing epitaph - but we shouldn't jump to conclusions. The world needs to step back and give the archaeologists time to complete this excavation and analyse all the evidence.'

'If Christ is in this tomb, it will be significant to Christians, Jews and Muslims. How are people reacting at the moment and is this discovery likely to affect stability in the Middle East?'

'That's hard to say - Syria's deep in the throes of civil war and volatile local conditions may impact adversely on attempts to shed light on this find. This is still breaking news and most of the world's press have yet to arrive. There's some way to go before we can be sure if Christ is indeed buried here, but this tomb certainly poses a question the whole world will be holding its breath to see answered.'

'Thank you, Darren. Now we're linking to His Eminence Cardinal O'Donnell, head of the Roman Catholic Church in England, for his comment. Good afternoon, Your Eminence. What is the Catholic Church's reaction to the discovery of Christ's tomb in Damascus?'

'Well, first and foremost, it's important that people don't become over-excited. Our understanding is that the tomb in question has only just been found and it's too early to say whose remains are buried there. I understand that a Papal Emissary is en route from the Vatican as I speak, looking forward to examining the evidence...'

'Can you comment on whether this discovery poses a threat to Catholicism - and other branches of Christianity? If this *is* the tomb of Christ, how will the Church handle the discovery of physical evidence so contrary to its doctrines?'

'Ah, well; I believe you will find that the Church is likely to be quite flexible on the issue. There has always been healthy debate exploring our understanding of the mysteries of the resurrection and ascension of our Lord, so even if mortal remains are confirmed to exist, I doubt that it will cause more than a ripple in the placid waters of Catholicism. Faith is all about believing what we *cannot* see or touch.' The Cardinal bestowed a benevolent smile to camera.

'Thank you, Your Eminence.'

The screen returned to Melissa, seated at the news desk. She looked into camera and said, 'Here's a summary of the headlines.' Her rapid overviews were accompanied by relevant still shots. When she got to '...archaeologists may have found the tomb of Jesus Christ..,' a close-shot of the tomb flashed up.

Screwing up his eyes in an effort to make out the inscription carved on it, Kaye glimpsed a complex symbol below the text. He caught his breath, but before he could be sure, the photo was gone. 'Sam, have you got any of today's morning papers, by any chance?' he asked casually. They were sure to have made this a major headline feature. There might be more photos...

'The Times is there. Help yourself.' Her thoughts still miles away, Sam flapped a hand in the direction of the folded newspaper covering the majority of her documents. Her stomach jolted as she belatedly realised her error, but by then it was too late.

'I see it.' Kaye reached across the table and dragged the newspaper towards him. Sam winced inwardly as the documents The Times had obscured became apparent. 'Oh, what are these?' he asked inquisitively, making to pick them up. 'More treasures for me to check out?'

Sam bit her lip. 'No. Don't touch them,' she said. 'I'll need to go over them first. Just leave them for now.' Her nervous, clipped tone suggested Kaye should not press the matter, so he politely withdrew his hand.

Instead, he shook open the newspaper and didn't have to look far for a close-up of the inscribed side of the Damascus tomb. Low-lit and grainy, the picture quality was too poor for Kaye to make out more than a few words of the inscription, but the emblem was clear enough.

Sam turned off the television and came to stand behind him, looking curiously over his shoulder. And it was she who, seconds later, corroborated exactly what Kaye had been thinking when she exclaimed, 'Hey!' and stabbed a finger at the tomb emblem in the Times photograph. 'Isn't that the same as the one on my Sanskrit document?'

'Let's see, shall we?' Kaye juxtaposed the document and the newspaper until the two emblems were adjacent. He and Sam gazed from one to the other and back again.

There was no doubt about it. The two were identical.

'Which leads us to the obvious question, Sam,' he murmured, unable to look away from the twin sunburst seals. 'What does a four thousand year old Indian legend have to do with a two thousand year old Syrian tomb? And what links them both to you?'

Good question.

Sam sighed. It was time she made a decision. Could she open up to this man? He did seem the trustworthy type. He was also very perceptive and was already putting two and two together to make five. What harm could come of him knowing a bit more about her peculiar old family secret? It might be confusing - even weird - but surely not dangerous? What about this *Power* business, though? Despite the morning's revelations and with all due respect to her father, she genuinely doubted that his spiritual legacy would alter her life. Besides, she decided, her hand unconsciously patting the spot on her blouse which overlaid her birthmark, she didn't have to tell Kaye everything.

'Would you like to help me find the answer to that question?' she asked him, her head tilting slightly.

Kaye searched her face intently, unsure whether she was serious. 'I'd love to,' he admitted. 'It's a fascinating mystery and I confess I'm completely intrigued. And as it happens, I'm on sabbatical at the moment, so I could put myself at your disposal - well, for a few weeks at least. So if you want me, count me in.'

'What about fees?'

Kaye considered. 'Tell you what; I'll settle for incidental expenses, permission to publish on anything of historical or linguistic significance and twenty percent of any profits arising from anything relating to your puzzle. How does that sound?'

'Providing I have the final say on what can and can't be published, it's a deal,' she agreed, giving him the first real smile he had seen from her. It transformed her strained yet elegant face into timeless beauty and made her cool, green eyes sparkle with an unexpected warmth.

Kaye smiled back. 'Does this mean I get to eyeball all those documents you were hiding?' he enquired innocently.

'I expect so,' conceded Sam, adding, 'I honestly haven't been through the bulk of them yet, so I'll do that after lunch and then they're all yours.'

'Lunch, you say? Sounds like a plan.'

As Sam busied herself preparing cold cuts and salad, she was acutely aware of the star on her breast. It throbbed with vague warmth, while her father's note of caution echoed in her mind: '... *many have died to protect The Power and more have died because of its glamour. Do not reveal to anyone your knowledge of it or trust in the shallow friendship of men.*'

After lunch, she skimmed through the rest of the documents. It was fast apparent that she might as well hand over the whole bunch. Only one was in English and from a rapid scan of the first page it looked unimportant, consisting merely of notes about a visit her grandfather had made to Israel in 1959. Shrugging apologetically at Kaye, who had been doodling symbols again while he waited, she nudged the pile in his direction.

'Now it's your turn to be patient,' he told her.

First, he made a rapid assessment of the material; where necessary, drawing scrolled items very carefully out of their leather tubes and unrolling them gradually, with a light and experienced touch. Then he opened his notebook to a clean page and catalogued the seven key documents in chronological order, including the ones he had already translated that morning, reading the results aloud to Sam:

'We start with the Vedic Sanskrit script with its emblem: it's a modern copy, but the earliest original could date from as far back as 2000 BC.

'Next, in Medieval Arabic script, is the Al-Adil/Al Aziz/Saladin letter, a copy dating to somewhere between 1850 and 1900. The original, I would say, was written in 1194, the year Richard returned to his throne in England. He was on his way home from the crusades late in 1192 when he was taken captive by Duke Leopold of Austria, who only released him on payment of a huge ransom... but I digress.

'Third is a Medieval English script which seems to be an original, untitled genealogy on thin vellum, requiring urgent restoration, by the way, if you don't want it to disintegrate. It has very crabbed writing in more than one hand. The first entry, dated 1215, is an illegible name beginning Hal..., all the other names end in your surname and the final entry, dated 1451, is the name 'Simon Dexter' - so this is probably a record of the first Earl's ancestry back to his earliest known forebear. I assume the document was finalised between 1451 and 1483, since no aristocratic prefix is shown for Simon, who was granted his Earldom in 1483.

'Then there's a Latin script, an original on parchment, again requiring preservative treatment, signed by Lord Simon Dexter and dated 1485.

'Fifth is another Latin script: an original on paper of the era, signed by Lord George Dexter, the ninth Earl, dated 1739.

'Sixth is an English script: an original on paper. This, you said, was an account of your grandfather's trip to the Holy Land in 1959, so I didn't read it, just checked the signature at the end - and can confirm it to be that of Lord Kai Dexter, dated 1962.

'Finally we have an English text, typed on contemporary paper; a genealogy of the Earls of Chaumont, written by your father, Lord Alexander Dexter, the sixteenth Earl.'

'There are also some birth and death certificates relating to holders of the Chaumont title and a rather odd, hand drawn map of some sort, with various annotations scribbled on it - plus a selection of photos. That's the lot.'

Collecting together the certificates, Kaye handed them to Sam. 'There's no work to do on these, so I'd suggest you put them somewhere safe. You might want to consider storing them with your solicitor. They have no commercial value but would be hard to replace.'

'Solicitors are the bane of my life,' said Sam, with feeling, 'Especially the one my father picked as his executor.'

'Then you might appreciate this,' grinned Kaye. 'What's it called when a ship with hundreds of lawyers on board goes down in a storm?'

'I don't know. What is it called?' she responded in time-honoured fashion.

'...A good start.'

She gave a brief laugh. Kaye couldn't remember the last time one of his corny jokes had raised mirth. 'Getting back to business, which of these delectable Latin manuscripts should I tackle first?' he asked.

'...The earlier one, perhaps?' A vaguely preoccupied expression clouding her face, Sam picked up the sheaf of certificates. 'I'd better file these, so I'll leave you to it.'

As she reached the portrait-lined gallery leading to the library, Sam thought of her father's photographs. Which portraits had he photographed - and why had he bothered, since all the originals hung right here in Chaumont? She began to take more notice of what was on the walls around her, whilst at the same time trying to recollect the photos. One snap was definitely of the first Earl - sneering Simon - she couldn't forget him. Then she remembered something else. Pandering to his vanity, Simon had commissioned several quite similar portraits during his lifetime - so why only photograph one? And which one was it? It was no use, she'd have to go and get the photos to be sure of identifying the right oils. Glad to have something useful to do, she retraced her steps to the kitchen.

There were, in fact, just three photos of ancestral portraits. First, there was sneering Simon in his ermine-trimmed doublet. Second, there was George, the ninth Earl, or 'galloping' George as Sam liked to call him, because the portrait of him she had loved best as a child depicted him on a frisky bay hunter, racing across Chaumont's meadows with his hounds. The photo her father had taken, however, placed him indoors in formal pose. The third photo highlighted the only painting she knew that included her grandfather, Kai. Painted when he was a child, it was more a study of Kai's mother - Sam's great grandmother, Alice.

Kaye was absorbed in a burst of scribbling. Without disturbing him, Sam pocketed the snaps and trotted off to locate the corresponding oils. She found George and Simon suspended from the west wall of the grand dining room, while her father's den housed great grandma Alice, standing with her lace-gloved hands on the shoulders of a very young Kai, seated on a wooden chair in front of her. From its style, the portrait must have been painted close to a hundred years ago.

Sam balanced on tip-toes on a chair to unhook Great Grandma Alice and lugged her to the dining room, setting her directly below sneering Simon and the not-galloping George, on the basis that looking at all three portraits simultaneously might help her work out why they had been photographed. Did they share some feature that set them apart from all the other family portraits? Sam's eyes ranged from one brown-eyed Earl to another: George – Kai – Simon – Kai – George. Come on, chaps, she thought, help me out, here. Simon's sneer seemed to be mocking her for missing the obvious. He was right to mock, for whatever her father meant to signify through these paintings continued to elude her.

Perhaps I'm looking at them in the wrong way, she thought. If I'm missing the obvious, maybe I should look at what *is* obvious. Let's see: they're all pictures of Dexters and each depicts an Earl. What else? Each is set in a room recognisable as being within Chaumont Hall - but there are plenty of other ancestral portraits with Chaumont backgrounds, so that can't be relevant. Or can it? What if the commonality is not the background, but something that forms part of it? And in a flash, the answer leapt out at her - three times over.

The young Kai sat with his knees together and his back straight. Alice's long lace shawl was draped elegantly over her arms and one fretted end lay in rumples on the little boy's lap, partially obscuring what he held between his hands. Only half of the ornate gold box was visible, but it was enough for Sam to be sure that it matched the one on the granite mantle on which Simon was resting his imperious hand. The identical box was again evident in the third picture, unobtrusively decorating an occasional table in the far corner of the drawing room in which George stood to attention in the full military regalia of his era.

The most detailed example lay under Simon's hand. Sam grabbed the nearest Queen Anne chair and set it directly below his portrait, climbing up to get a closer look at Simon's treasure. She almost fell off the chair in shock, for in rendering the likeness of the front of the golden object - a spectacularly worked, dome-lidded casket - the artist had taken pains to paint an excellent facsimile of the raised decorative emblem that formed its centrepiece - an emblem Sam recognised in the blink of an eye.

'So that's where I've seen it before!' she exclaimed. In fact, she had probably seen it a thousand times but never consciously noticed it, because it was just one more inconsequential ornament amongst many in the backgrounds of paintings that were so familiar that they had become virtually invisible to her.

'What does a four thousand year old Indian legend have to do with a two thousand year old Syrian tomb? And what links them both to you?'

She had discovered the link - it was this arcane sunburst on a golden casket.

...But why?

CHAPTER 5

TWO KINGS AND THREE GIFTS

Jerusalem, Judea, March, 5 BCE

They passed through Caesarea Philippi, Capernum and Scythopolis, following the banks of the River Jordan south for some distance before turning south west towards Jerusalem. It took time, because the caravan was considerable in size and, although currently dressed for travel, they had been obliged to bring with them all the trappings appropriate to the grandeur of a royal audience, as well as suitably magnificent gifts, which of themselves required a veritable cohort of armed men to ensure their safety. Added to this was the requirement for a string of camels, mules and donkeys bearing goods and provisions, sufficient slaves to attend to the menial matters and all the commensurate baggage that such a venture entailed.

Melchior favoured a stylish covered carriage pulled by two massive oxen, whilst Balthazar and Gaspar bestrode Arabian horses, procured in Damascus and liveried in the style of Persian royalty. Those they passed on the road marvelled to see the stately, measured prance of these thoroughbred steeds with their crimson-jaspered leather saddles, high silver pommels, cushioned seats and wide leather leg flaps. The saddles rested on flared saddle rugs of the finest silk and wool mix, woven in designs of intricately intertwined, stylised flora and cinched around the horses' bellies with broad, crimson silk bands. Elegant plumes of crimson-dyed feathers decorated their heads and their reins flashed and chimed incessantly due to the scores of slender silver pipes that fringed them. Fortunately, Melchior's personal wealth had no difficulty absorbing the cost of this extravagant display.

Their extended train raising a cloud of dust that must have been visible from its towering walls, at last the three Magi approached the great city that was their goal.

Once through the Eastern city gate, they wove their way through the cramped alleys of the Lower City, catching tantalising glimpses, to the north, of a massive building gleaming with liberal embellishments of gold, high on a rise known as Temple Mount. Herod, King of the Jews as the Roman Senate had proclaimed him, or Basileus, as he preferred to be addressed, had used his mother's Nabataean wealth - and the Judean taxes he had not been obliged to forward to Rome - to restore Jerusalem and raise it to a level of eminence it had never before enjoyed. As its crowning glory, he had commissioned the Temple of Solomon, the largest of its kind, to be built. This was the landmark awing the Magi.

They processed into the Upper City through a covered archway, from which point the streets became wider and the caravan made faster progress, finally halting close to the main entrance to Herod's newly constructed palace on the Upper City's western edge. Surrounded on all four sides by high defensive walls and fortified by three towers, it looked starkly impregnable. Inside, by contrast, all was elegant, refined and ostentatiously beautiful, the palace's two large, widely spaced buildings being connected by an enchanting water garden whose limpid canals and pools were lined with rows of bronze statues interspersed with delicately plashing fountains. Nothing of this was yet visible to the new arrivals.

Guided by Melchior, rather than attempting to enter the palace directly, they despatched a finely dressed emissary, accompanied by four slaves, to bear gifts to the king in announcement of their arrival.

Being already well informed of the size and pomp of the caravan that stood outside his doors and with his curiosity considerably aroused, Herod chose to receive the emissary in the state formality of his sumptuous throne room. Modelled on that of Solomon, its ceiling was timbered in heavily carved cedar wood supported by rows of cedar pillars, the royal throne occupying a high dais at the far end of the room. To reach the throne room, the emissary had to pass first through a magnificent courtyard, then a grand pillared porch, richly carved and painted. The throne room walls themselves were of stone overlaid with frescoed plaster and decorated with carved ivory reliefs inset with semi-precious stones including lapis lazuli, turquoise and cornelian.

On being admitted to the royal presence, the splendidly robed emissary bowed low, while his accompanying slaves knelt deferentially to place two gold-inlaid Lebanese cedar chests on the patterned mosaic floor in front of the King. Seated on his throne, fashioned of wood overlaid with panels of exquisitely carved, gold-inlaid ivory, Herod rested his palms on its golden lions' head arm pommels and leaned forward with interest.

'My Lord Basileus,' commenced the emissary, 'I thank you for the honour you do my masters by receiving their petition. I bear greetings - along with such small gifts as may provide some token of the deep esteem in which they hold your Majesty - from the three revered Magi - Melchior, Gaspar and Balthazar - great princes and wise men of the East who have travelled far and who, this very day, stand before your palace in hope of an audience with you on matters of international consequence.'

Although Herod was clearly paying attention to the emissary's words, his eyes darted repeatedly to the chests. Noticing this, the emissary gestured to the slaves, who proceeded to open and tip the chests forward. Out of the first rolled dozens of bolts of the finest silk, whilst from the other, smaller, chest tumbled a glittering heap of Damascene gold coins interleaved with muslin bags full of gleaming pearls. The slaves then withdrew to wait in the courtyard.

Herod leaned back, pursing his narrow, Arabic lips and stroking his full, grey beard thoughtfully before replying. 'Magi princes, you say? Can I assume that by 'matters of international consequence' you mean 'politically significant news'?'

The emissary nodded gravely.

'If these matters are relevant to Judea, it might interest us to discuss them.' Herod made his decision. 'You may convey to your masters that we are well pleased with their gifts and will extend our royal patronage to their party. Suitable accommodation will be provided within the palace complex for themselves and their personal servants - and within the city for their caravan and beasts of burden. Once they have refreshed themselves they may await our summons.'

Thanking him profusely and making low obeisance, the emissary departed and hastened to deliver the King's message to the Magi.

Each attired in his finest gown, over-gown and headdress, their dignity unassailable and their gravitas considerable - aided in no small measure by the sedate pace of their group due to the hobbling gait of Melchior with his gold-topped staff - the three Magi entered King Herod's throne room. They bowed in unison to the Lord Basileus, who had the grace to notice the infirmity of the eldest sage and, after formal introductions had been made, called for chairs to be brought so that all might be seated for the duration of their discussion.

Once issues of provenance had been settled and their origins better understood, Herod encouraged them to speak their minds.

Melchior began. Trying to keep his explanation simple and understandable, he said, 'We were guided here by the stars. In our home nations, the same stars can be seen as you observe in the night sky over Judea - and we have all independently consulted the heavens and the mystical charts of our calling. We severally conclude that a most prestigious event has taken place in your kingdom; an event coinciding with a rare planetary confluence that took place on the fifteenth of September last year. Combining this understanding with the prophecies of your prophets, we believe that this date marks the birth of a royal prince - perhaps the fabled Messiah of your people...'

'The *Messiah*?' interrupted Herod, his voice rising. 'Impossible! It is prophesied that the Messiah will arise from the line of David - and no prince of the line of Judah has ruled since Jehoiachin brought Jeremiah's curse down upon himself and his seed, all of five hundred years ago.'

Balthazar ventured a question. 'My Lord King, forgive my ignorance, but what, exactly, is conveyed by the word 'Messiah' in the histories and minds of your people?'

This gently spoken request went some way to restore Herod's humour and he barked, 'Ha! Has it come to pass that a King must give a priest a lesson in religion? In brief, Magus, from our holy scrolls we learn that Yahweh - the one true God - made a covenant with King David that David's descendants would rule Judah for as long as the people worshipped only Him. When King Jehoiachin let fall Jerusalem to the Babylonians, who were followers of false gods, many, including Jehoiachin himself, were enslaved in exile. This brought down Jeremiah's curse upon him, that neither he nor his seed would ever rule again - and indeed they have not. Yahweh's covenant was consequently deemed broken, although, in principle, His promise remains valid. The prophets say that He will honour that promise one day - when the people deserve it - and restore the seed of David to power. This long prophesied but so far elusive ruler will be the Messiah, also known as the Christ - the royally anointed one - and it is foretold that he will save his people by delivering them from their enemies, to reign forever after. It is right and good that the common man, in his weakness, should trust to the prophets, but a king must weigh the value of such hopes against a plainer reality. Besides, if this legendary saviour is born to Israel, why has no word of it assailed *our* ears?'

'Great King,' said Balthazar humbly, 'No man, not even a king as wise and powerful as you, my Lord, can be all-knowing and all-seeing. Is it perhaps possible that the Messiah has arrived but is yet to make himself known?'

Herod frowned down from his throne, suspicion suddenly clouding his mind. 'Why are you here - so far from your homes - asking these questions?' he growled. 'What is your agenda in this matter?'

Melchior quickly answered, 'We seek only to confirm the truth or otherwise of a royal birth so that if the stars have not misled us, we may view the child, pay homage and carry the glad news of him back to the kings of our own countries. That is all, Lord King.'

Herod thought about this before making any reply. 'We have misjudged you. Those seem fair and equitable aims,' he answered slowly, his mind still busy turning over all the possibilities.

What if some fool able to trace his male line back to David has whelped a son and harbours the ill-conceived pretension that his child is the Messiah?

This seemed more likely than the unpalatable alternative of the birth of the true Messiah – but, conversely, could he afford to ignore the combined weight of the words of the prophets and of wise men who could read the stars to foretell events? Either way, the issue, he began to realise, had the potential to constitute a very real threat to the stability of his throne. Word of this Messiah, whether he be true or false, would likely spread faster than the stench from a midden and could easily foment insurgency amongst those viewing Roman governance as an oppressor's yoke about their necks - and he was well aware that there were many such. The last thing he needed was an uprising. The Romans would probably react by massacring thousands, deposing him and... no, he refused to let his mind complete that train of thought.

How should he handle this?

'If it be the will of Yahweh that the true Christ is come amongst us, We will anoint him with our own hand,' he said. 'Go forth, good sages and, with Our blessing, seek diligently for this royal child. We shall provide a grant of passage; that you may travel throughout Judea about Our royal business, without hinderance. All We ask is that, should you find him, you return to Us with the knowledge of his place and situation, so that We may, in turn, pay homage and raise him up to his estate.'

Let them spend *their* gold discovering that which Basileus has need to know, he thought, gratified with his own cunning - and smiled beneficently at the Magi.

Nazareth, Galilee, July, 5 BCE

Before quitting Jerusalem, they pared down the caravan for speed of travel, selling unwanted chattels, beasts and slaves in the city's bustling market.

First, they made a short detour south in response to comments from a Rabbi they met at the Temple of Solomon. He had remarked that the Holy Scriptures prophesied that the Christ would come out of David's city, which proved to be a modest village called Bethlehem, only five miles south of Jerusalem. On horseback, it took little more than an hour to reach it. But no-one in Bethlehem knew of any local royal birth occurring within living memory, never mind less than two years ago. One avaricious innkeeper, assessing the splendour of the sages' bearing, pushed his own snot-nosed two-year-old in front of them in vain hopes of passing him off as the child they sought. They laughed at his impertinence, the hooves of their stallions kicking dust in his crestfallen face as they turned away.

Having subsequently worked their way northwards over three months, asking at every town and village for news of a son of David who would be a child now approaching two years of age, they were still no closer to success.

Weary after a long day in the highest temperatures the Summer had yet seen and with one of the wheels of Melchior's ox-carriage creaking ominously at every rut, it was almost dusk when they sighted Nazareth, an unremarkable but extensive cluster of stone houses and modest public buildings on the edge of the foothills flanking the plain of Esdralon in northern Galilee. Sepphoris, the capital of Galilee, was over the hills to the north-west and would have been a preferable overnight destination, but it was clear that the carriage needed urgent repairs and, on hailing a shepherd who passed by, driving his bleating flock to fresh pasture, he advised that Nazareth boasted an excellent carpenter.

'Ask at the guesthouse; they'll direct you to Joseph's lodgings,' said the herdsman. 'He enjoys a good reputation in the area around here. You'll soon have that wheel repaired and oiled, my lords.'

Kicking his heels into the flanks of his tired horse as it stumbled up the sloped track to the town, Gaspar sighed and muttered under his breath, 'Oh, please, not another night of flea-ridden straw mattresses in some shabby provincial inn...damn that wheel!'

Balthazar, conversely, approved the change of plan, for the instant he set eyes on Nazareth he felt heat swell in his chest and his star began to throb in a rising crescendo. Its urgent pull was upwards - which suggested he was very close to the culmination of his quest. 'Surya be praised', he whispered to himself, welcoming the pain because of what it meant.

After all these long months without guidance... at last The Power calls to me! Am I a madman - or could this lowly town truly be the birthplace of The One?

There were, of course, fleas at the inn; Gaspar was not a happy man. But there was also room for the ox-carriage in the alley outside, a large stable with hay for their beasts, enough rooms to accommodate them and their small retinue - and a wholesome meal of fresh-baked bread, olives, goats' cheese and pomegranates, capped with an agreeable pigeon and leek stew flavoured with garlic and mallow. No-one made mention of the Zoroastrian prohibition against the consumption of wild birds; it was more pleasantly convenient to believe that their host kept a supply of domesticated fowl. Picking a small bone shard from between his teeth, Gaspar called for more wine. Looking up at the swarthy, beaming Jew who brought them a fresh jug of spiced tirosh from his store, he tossed a few bronze prutahs onto the rough wooden table and asked for directions to the carpenter's abode.

Next morning, they sent a servant to fetch Joseph to deal with the troublesome wheel. Balthazar undertook to oversee the tradesman, since, being at unaccustomed leisure, his companions wished to engage in certain devotional ceremonies it was difficult to accomplish whilst travelling. On arrival, the carpenter proved to be a young man of perhaps twenty five years, industrious and well skilled at his craft. While he began the repairs, Balthazar, seated on a stool, struck up a conversation in an attempt to take his mind off the pulsing pain in his chest. Naturally quick with languages, his Hebrew had become quite passable.

'Have you and your family always lived in Nazareth, Joseph?' he enquired.

'Yes, my lord.'

'A large family, is it?'

'Yes, my lord. On both my side and Mary's - that's my wife.'

'And, if I may ask, have you been blessed with children yet? You don't have to keep calling me lord, by the way.'

'One son, so far, named Yeshua.' Saying this, Joseph smiled for the first time, his serious young face lighting up.

Balthazar's heart leapt at the name, but he remained outwardly calm. 'That's a fine name. What is its meaning?'

'It's not uncommon round here. It means 'deliverer' - a name given if one wishes to encourage a boy's altruistic side or favours him becoming a healer or priest when he reaches manhood.'

'I see. And what age is Yeshua?'

'He will reach two years this mid-September, Yahweh willing.'

So, Yeshua is not an uncommon name - but the birth date matches with the planetary conjunction...

Balthazar phrased his next question carefully. 'I am always interested to learn of customs in countries far from my own, for I come from the distant east. How do your people celebrate a birth?'

Joseph paused from his labours to answer. 'By holy law we make sacrificial thanks to Yahweh and name our children before his altar. As soon as Mary was fit to travel, we made a special journey to Jerusalem - combining our sacrifice with visits to relatives - so my son could be named in the great Temple of Solomon there - a proud moment! But it was important to us to give Yeshua the very best start, because he's so special.'

'All sons are special to their parents,' concurred Balthazar, smiling.

Joseph smiled back. 'True. But mine is also special in another way. It won't mean anything to you, my lord, but, through my ancestral line, my son will be blessed with the title of 'prince in waiting', following after me.'

Balthazar raised his eyebrows politely, not wishing to stem Joseph's willingness to say more.

'My distant forefathers were the kings of this land,' Joseph explained. 'You might have heard of the line of Judah? Even after half a millennium, that royal heritage still strengthens our family pride - and lends a measure of local prestige. I - and thence my firstborn - can prove direct Davidic descent, so we are 'princes in waiting', since Yahweh has promised to restore the kingship to David's seed, one day.' Here, Joseph gave a typical Semitic shrug. 'Times being what they are, of course, with Herod on the throne and the Roman legions to back him, I don't trumpet my heritage too loudly.'

Balthazar let out a protracted sigh of fulfilment.

It is this child!

'When you've finished that wheel,' he said, 'I have something rather important to tell you.'

Gaspar and Melchior had just completed their devotions and the lingering, aromatic scent of incense assailed Balthazar's nose as he strode purposefully through the door of the low-beamed chamber.

'My lords,' he declared, 'Prepare for celebration! Your ardent prayers are answered all at once. The child we seek is found at last - and rests within a stone's throw!'

'By Ahura Mazda!' cried Gaspar, jumping up from his chair in high excitement. 'Is it possible? How can one come to such knowledge through the repair of a humble wheel? I always knew you were a dark star - I said as much to Melchior - did I not, Melchior?'

'Cease your babble, Gaspar,' murmured the seated Melchior, his fierce eyes fastening on Balthazar. 'It has long been obvious that there is more to this young Magus than an expert priesthood and an enquiring mind.' He raised his voice commandingly. 'Admit, now, Balthazar; is it some powerful sixth sense you have, or arcane magic spells you work by night, whilst we dream on?' Then he uttered a deep, throaty chuckle at Balthazar's evident discomfiture. 'I jest,' he reassured him. 'Your diffidence and intelligent curiosity have borne far riper fruit than all our alchemy. However you came to conquer the truth, it is most admirably done. When we are recovered from our amazement, no doubt you will inform us fully.'

'It was wholly chance that led me to your undeserved praise, as you will soon perceive,' protested Balthazar and proceeded to relate the thread of his conversation with Joseph.

'I am well persuaded,' acknowledged Melchior when Balthazar had finished. 'Come, since you have prepared the way for our formal presentation to the House of Judah later this day, let us each consider and select a gift appropriate to a prince of men - it would be unfitting to pay empty-handed homage to the one we believe to be the Messiah of the Jews - even if his sire yet doubts it. Let us also dress for pomp and ceremony, making our visit the more likely to be remembered in later years by those who guide this future king in his choice of national allies.'

'Joseph! Joseph! Look! Those foreign priests are coming up the street. Oh, Yahweh, help me - look at their clothes!' cried Mary, round-eyed in disbelief, as she peeped through the half-open window shutters. Turning, she scolded her husband roundly. 'You should have told me these Magi of yours were princes - well, as rich as princes, anyway! 'What were you thinking, to invite them here before I've even had time to tidy up the place?' Panicking, she glanced wildly round their living area. 'What a mess. I shall be shamed in their eyes.' The thought of such embarrassment brought her close to tears.

'Hush, now, Mary. What if they are as rich as princes? The one I spoke to seemed human enough and anyway,' - Joseph drew himself up proudly - 'I'm a prince too and so is young Yeshua, so it will be a meeting of equals.'

'A fine prince you make,' she answered back angrily, rummaging in a box for her choicest jewellery and slipping a good pair of sandals on her bare feet. Critically, she looked down at her plain brown homespun robe. 'Quick; fetch me my best over-robe, the blue-grey wool one with the hood and the wild flowers embroidered on it. I can't fix the house but at least I can make myself appear like a respectable wife and mother. Hurry - they'll be here any moment!'

By the time Melchior's servant rapped on the wooden door of the stone and mud-brick house, Mary was dressed, bejewelled and seated demurely on the rug-covered bench that lined the back wall of the living area, with Yeshua fidgeting on her lap. Freshly lit spatulate lamps sputtered on the low table on which she had placed a carved olive wood dish containing unleavened loaves baked that morning, a small amphora of olive oil, a jug of local wine and a set of pretty pottery wine cups that had been a wedding gift. It was always polite to break bread with guests.

Joseph opened the door and ushered the Magi in, bowing respectfully to each in turn and bidding them welcome. Deferring to Melchior's seniority, his companions let him enter first. Ducking at the lintel because of his tall black headdress, Gaspar followed Melchior, with Balthazar bringing up the rear. As he passed across the threshold, the star pierced his heart with a fiery sword of pain and then, in the manner of a wet-snuffed wick, the burning fizzled out quite suddenly.

The wriggling Yeshua fell still, gazing under long, black lashes at the fabulous strangers in layered robes and outlandish hats. But shyness overcame him and he buried his face in the folds of his mother's robe, leaving only his dark, shining curls to be seen. Joseph formally introduced his wife and ruffled his son's hair as she, in turn, apologised for Yeshua's abashment.

'It is of no concern,' Melchior assured her. 'We are here to honour, not judge him.' Mary gazed at him, thinking his words kind, if somewhat puzzling. The old sage approached, using his staff to lower himself onto one arthritic knee. At this, Yeshua peeped round, his curiosity overcoming his fear. In a flash, he extended his chubby fist to grab Melchior's long white beard, fascinated by the bright silver threads running through its plait. The sight of the babe pulling on the old man's beard utterly banished the aura of dignified formality and after a moment, when Melchior's chuckle made it clear that he was delighted rather than offended, everyone else laughed too.

Gently freeing his beard from Yeshua's grasp, Melchior raised his eyes briefly to the wooden plaque adorning the wall behind Mary, which had a simple Star of David painted on it. He smiled at Yeshua and pointed to the Star, saying, 'See that? We've followed that star for half the world's breadth to find you, my Lord.'

'You've come all that way - just to see our Yeshua? I don't understand,' blurted out Mary, astonished. 'And why do you call him Lord?'

Melchior replied to her, 'We have his lineage from his father. Plainly, he is the one we have long sought - a legitimate prince of Judah; the seed of David and, I might add, bearing a given name entirely appropriate to his royal destiny, as we will clarify.'

Gaspar stepped forward and knelt. 'The stars have spoken and the stars do not lie. As Magi, you may trust our wisdom in matters of the heavens and that which they foretell, the study of which leads us to understand that one day your son will be anointed King over all Judea. This is why we are here - to pay homage...'

Mary looked at Joseph, open-mouthed.

And Balthazar knelt to complete Gaspar's words '...to he who shall be called the deliverer, the great redeemer - the Christ and long-awaited Messiah of your people!'

'...Messiah?' Mary and Joseph gasped in unison.

And, if he is also The One, he will redeem not just the Jews, but all men - and death shall be no more...

Several hours had passed since the revelation of Yeshua's messianic destiny and dusk was gathering in the eaves of the thick ceiling rafters. Much explanation, argument and rebuttal had marked the intervening time, but at last Joseph, followed grudgingly by Mary, had come to accept the Magi's certitude regarding their son.

Joseph sighed heavily. 'Accepting all you say, I still think we have to keep this secret, for now at least. He's not even two yet - far too young to understand the perils attendant on his situation. But I know them only too well - better than you possibly could - because I live here every day and I'm aware of what could happen to us if the wrong person gets hold of this knowledge. We suffer an uneasy peace, here in Galilee. We're a long way north of Judea, with Samaria a buffer between us and the centre of government in Jerusalem. People here have always retained their independent spirits - some might call it their rebellious natures - and this in spite of the Roman garrison just up the road in Sepphoris. But wherever there is a hint of disaffection, there are also informers - and the snake's tongue is a long one, as we say. People have been known to simply disappear overnight. Not my boy, Messiah or no Messiah. Not us. I simply won't risk it happening.'

Balthazar said, 'We understand. And this I promise, none of us will return to Herod and endanger you, but you cannot hide forever. You must also consider this: Yeshua will require an education suited to his kingly role. He needs a mentor who is knowledgeable, erudite and has only his best interests at heart.'

'You're right,' acknowledged Joseph, scratching his nose nervously. 'But how could such as we find a suitable and trustworthy teacher, or pay for his services?'

Gaspar sighed. 'There could be no better choice than one of us, but I cannot commit to the task. I am bound under my promise to return to Parthia with all due speed now that the truth is unveiled.'

'And I am similarly obliged to journey to my Nabataean homeland and make report, but will procrastinate in Damascus until guilt overcomes me,' promised Melchior, absently chucking a sleepy Yeshua under the chin as he dandled the child on his creaking knees.

'And so it falls to me,' said Balthazar, 'And I accept the task with gladness. In fact, I had already formed a desire to linger here in Galilee, to learn the language, the culture and the people better. I find it fitting that I should choose to stay where I am also needed.'

'You have a kindly soul,' Gaspar told him. 'I thank Ahura Mazda that the young king will benefit of it.'

'And you will enjoy an open welcome in Damascus should you care to visit me, or have need to flee Galilee, one day,' said Melchior. 'My house is yours; never doubt it.'

Deeply touched, Balthazar thanked them. 'I will divine the future as best I may and act accordingly,' he said. 'One plan I already have in mind is to take the young Messiah, in due course, on the same journey - in reverse - that I have already made. I think he would learn much along the way and there are many priests and princes in my homeland from whom he could gain great insights.'

Gently returning her sleeping child to his mother, Melchior arched his aching back and rose, limping to the door of the house. Outside, their guards sat cross-legged in the dying light, playing dice for bronze prutahs. 'You have been patient,' he praised them. 'Now, one of you, attend us with the gifts we brought and the rest, prepare, for we shall soon depart.' The men scrambled up and shook the dust from their cloaks, stooping to gather up their dice. One lifted the chest that lay by his feet and carried it into the house where he set it on the floor before returning to his fellows.

Opening the wooden box, Melchior reached in and drew out a carved ivory flask, sealed with wax, passing it to Gaspar. Next, he brought out Balthazar's larger package, exclaiming at its weight. Finally he clasped his own gift, an amphora made of blackware, wood-corked and sealed over with hard resin.

Mary, having settled the nodding Yeshua in the sleeping area that lay behind a homespun drape at one end of the room, hurried back to stand by Joseph for the formal presentation of these unexpected gifts.

Gaspar addressed them first, saying, 'I am honoured to pay homage to Lord Yeshua and present this gift, which I trust is worthy. It is myrrh from my country, Persia. Save it, sealed, and it will last for many years. It is an incense spice that we believe assists with the development of the inner light of the spirit. May the Messiah's inner light burn all the brighter for it!' He presented the ivory flask to Joseph.

'A thousand thanks,' murmured the astonished carpenter.

Melchior now spoke. 'Behold, in royal homage I present this gift of frankincense, the finest opaque resin that can be procured in the spice markets of Damascus. Even in the smallest quantities, it will promote the sense of calm, clear-headedness and well-being that a kingly mind will value when there are weighty decisions to be made. May Lord Yeshua's inner peace, his clarity of thought and health be all the greater for its balm!' He gave over the amphora to Mary.

'Your generosity overwhelms me - thank you,' she replied softly, lowering her eyes.

Leaving his mysterious package on the floor, Balthazar stepped forward empty-handed. 'The first part of my gift to the Messiah is my humble self,' he said, stretching out his arms in a giving gesture. 'I will retain the second part in trust until satisfied he is ready to receive it into his own hands. Encased in precious gold from ancient India, it was wrought in a way we cannot emulate today. More than that I will not say, except to assure you that it is a priceless and most suitable treasure that will bring him, Surya willing - or as you would say, Yahweh willing - to the peak of both his earthly and his spiritual powers.'

Joseph clasped one of Balthazar's outstretched hands and said, thickly, 'Truly, a man can give no greater or more precious gift than his own heart and mind. I'm sure my boy will be the better for your caring mentorship. Thank you.' He looked around the room in general. 'Thank you all.'

CHAPTER 6

A LOST TREASURE

Chaumont Hall, Derbyshire, England, 16 June, 2016 AD

'You *must* come and see!' Sam announced breathlessly the moment she reached the kitchen, where Kaye sat propped on his elbows, his pencil waggling between his fingers in time with the Latin syllables he was mouthing to himself. Startled, he dropped the pencil as his blond head came up. Before he could utter a word, Sam grabbed him by the hand, pulling him bodily off his stool and away through the sprawling maze of the medieval fortified manor that was Chaumont, until they stumbled to an abrupt halt in the grand dining room.

'What's this all about?' gasped Kaye, his brain whirling after his unplanned dash along faded oriental runners alternating with slippery parquet floors - past tables and cabinets crammed with delicate Ming vases, writhing bronze lions, fancy ormolu clocks, sweetly smiling marble cherubs and goodness knows what else. The place was a maze.

'Look!' Sam pointed upwards at a large and extremely old oil painting. Kaye did not consider himself to be particularly knowledgeable about art, but the style of the picture she was indicating suggested it was very early; perhaps fifteenth century.

'Which Earl is that?' he asked.

'It's sneering Simon - I mean, the first Earl - but that doesn't matter. Look what he's got under his right hand!'

Kaye squinted upwards. 'Ah,' he said.

'Ah? Is that all you can say?'

Kaye scratched his ear. It felt naked without the pencil tucked there. 'What am I supposed to say? It's just a fancy little gold box.

I would have thought 'ah' was about all it warranted. Have I missed something?'

Sam's expression spoke volumes. 'Get up on the chair and have a closer look.'

'But that's a Queen Anne,' objected Kaye, appalled. 'I can't stand on that. It's antique.'

'Yes you can. I did. This isn't a museum, you know; it's my home.'

'Of course it is. Sorry.'

Still hesitating to use the beautiful chair as a mere stepladder, Kaye slipped his shoes off before hopping up onto its padded seat. Being taller than Sam, his eyes were now almost on a level with Simon's fancy doublet and he could easily see every detail of the finely worked casket under the first Earl's hand.

'Oh my!' he breathed. 'That's the same...'

'...Emblem. Precisely!'

Carefully dismounting the chair, Kaye turned and, notwithstanding its antiquity, sat down on it to put his shoes back on while his analytical mind considered the mystery. Sam studied him with interest, wondering if he was thinking the same as she was; namely, that if they wanted to know what else was inscribed on that Syrian tomb they'd have to book flights to Damascus.

Thoughtfully, Kaye tapped his fingertips on his knees. After a short pause, he said, 'Before leaping to conclusions, it would be prudent to show you the English translations of the pieces I've been working on while you were busy making this exciting discovery.' He broke off and smiled disarmingly. 'That is, if you would be kind enough to guide me back to the kitchen. I've absolutely no idea where I am.'

'Chaumont does ramble a bit,' agreed Sam, amused. 'Then again, I wouldn't exactly class you as the world's most observant soul, based on your recent performance over that casket. Remind me never to have to rely on you to find the way round any mansion, maze or mausoleum, or, indeed, anywhere with more than one corridor and a clearly signposted exit!'

'I say, that's a bit harsh,' deprecated Kaye amiably as Sam escorted him back to the kitchen.

'You can read this for yourself,' he told her, back at the beech table that dominated the centre of the big country kitchen, passing Sam his translation of the older Latin scroll by the simple process of ripping out the relevant scribbled page from his notebook. 'It seems that your illustrious ancestor, sneering Simon, as you call him - quite aptly I'd say, by the way - wanted to set down for posterity his acquisition of Chaumont along with his and his heirs' rights to hold on to it for good. Makes you wonder who was turfed out to make room for Simon, doesn't it? Anyway, as you'll see, he goes on about having power and holding on to that too. I suppose might was right in those days. Still is, come to think of it.'

Sam shook her head. 'Not really,' she demurred. 'Most of this country's titled landowners have no real power any more - and they're generally far too busy trying to scrape together enough cash to keep their huge old houses up to the required listed building standards to be worried about what's slipped through their fingers somewhere along the way.' She sat down to read the scribbled translation while Kaye, regretting his thoughtless comment, concentrated on finishing off the second Latin piece.

Simon's text read:

I, Simon, of the House of Dexter, Earl of Chaumont by the grace of His Majesty, the late King Richard III, do proclaim that the royal grant of the holdings and lands comprising the property of Chaumont, entire and whole, makes it rightfully mine without let or hindrance and rightfully the inheritance of my heirs in perpetuity, as confirmed by the pledge and dragon token of King Henry VII, our glorious Monarch now reigning.

Furthermore, I vow that now the House of Dexter holds the power, it shall hold it in perpetuity. I lay a geas upon my chosen heir, Godwin and upon his heir and thence all heirs of the House of Dexter, to the uttermost of our line, to protect, preserve and keep the power. For so long as a Dexter draws breath, the power must never leave us, but remain close under our hand, now and down the ages, until the day of days when the One comes who shall release our house of its guardianship, that we may rest at last.

On this 18th day of October, in the Year of our Lord 1485, my seal upon this parchment affirms each word written upon it to be true and proper, set here by my own hand this day. This parchment shall now be kept safe in Chaumont, bound in waxed leather to stave off the ravages of time. May my vow, herein, prove righteous and may each Dexter that keeps the power keep also this same vow.

Promising herself that she would avoid the trap of preconception, Sam read everything several times over and still, try as she might, she could not help settling on an interpretation that was entirely at odds with Kaye's. Oh dear, she thought. I can see why he takes the text literally and assumes it's just old Simon crowing about his new estate and the power and prestige that the Hall, lands and Earldom brought to the family name, but of course, he hasn't seen my father's letter.

Simon is instructing his heirs that they must "keep the power" - as in being *Keepers*? That reminds me of Daddy's letter, saying the same thing. Then there's Simon's remark: '*The power must... remain close under our hand*', which I think means Simon had - or at least believed he had - *The Power* in his possession. Was that the selfsame power as the power mentioned in the Sanskrit legend? I think it was.

A further idea struck her. Talking of taking things literally, what was literally under Simon's hand in his portrait? The casket! Perhaps Simon meant that the casket had to stay at Chaumont, because he believed that *The Power* was connected with the casket? Then, there's that sentence about the 'day of days'. No doubt the professor would tell me that was just Simon's way of saying 'till the end of time when God will redeem us all', but I don't think Simon means God when he refers to *One*. I think he means the same *One* that Baal and his descendants were looking for in the Sanskrit story. She glanced at the last section of the translation of the Sanskrit text, which lay on the table next to her.

'...for it was his duty to keep its secret safe until the day when One would be found able to use it to benefit all men. And Baal departed to wander the earth, he and his descendants, ever guarding The Power; ever seeking The One.'

Yes, she decided, I think both documents are talking about the same *One*. I'm not sure about the nature of this *One* - the usual redeemer, I suppose: total hooey, of course, but what about *The Power*? That needn't be religious hooey. All my ancestors certainly appear to have believed there was - is - a hugely important, actual *Power* that must be protected and kept secret.

What if there really is such a Power and what if it's inside the casket?

Sam's eyes wandered to another passage from the Sanskrit document:

'...And at last Baal forced The Power to his mighty will, compressing its boundless strength into the small space between his outstretched hands, encasing it in gold and there binding it with spells and arts now lost to us in the mists of time.'

No, she thought. That's unimaginable. Yet there was a body of evidence beginning to build and she found herself wondering... could this casket be the very object that Baal fashioned and into which he compressed *The Power*, oh, many, many thousands of years ago - so long ago that only the legend had survived the passage of time? And what if he did that, not by magic, but using the science of a high-tech civilisation that once existed and was utterly destroyed by its own technology?

This idea appealed to Sam's romantic streak and she certainly felt more comfortable attributing the origins of *The Power* to science rather than religion. But even if her train of thought had merit, she realized, it offered no explanation as to why the sunburst, which she was coming to think of as signifying *The Power*, or at least its belief system, should be emblazoned on a tomb that might house the remains of Jesus Christ. The only link she could think of was the loose one of religion, but Christ had been born a Jew and from Christ stemmed Christianity - a far cry from *The Power*.

Or was it?

What had the Sanskrit said? *'And the Keepers and The One shall use The Power only to redeem death...'* Did that mean it was supposed to redeem men spiritually, in the same way as Christ - or could it actually bring the dead back to life? The Bible said Jesus brought Lazarus back to life... The ability to perform godlike miracles...? Who wouldn't want to be the Keeper of that kind of power?

A sobering thought broke in to shatter her daydreams.

There's just one problem. Where, exactly, is this casket?

'Finished,' said Kaye, dotting the last full stop and automatically sliding his pencil back into its special spot behind his ear.

'Yes, I think we might be,' replied Sam, reflecting that without the casket, she'd never find out the truth. Fortunately, her comment was sufficiently ambiguous to pass unremarked by Kaye.

'You'll find it a bit of a sad story, this one,' he said. 'Your ninth Earl, George, poor fellow, lost his son to what I'm pretty sure was smallpox. I won't say any more. You look at it and tell me what you think.' He pushed his notebook at Sam. Thanking him, she took it and tried to clear her mind enough to take in yet more information.

> *'Oh, Balthazar, forgive us that it should have come to this! Woe to Chaumont, stronghold of the power! Woe to its keeper, for what purpose has a guard without a key? Yea and woe to my firstborn, who lies full dead in his mother's grieving arms: he had yet to attain his third year and he did bear the mark that would assure continuance and a tenth Earl of the line. First the cattle sickened and died; then fever gripped my child and the telltale red pustules appeared all over his tiny body. And now, despite all our ministrations and all the praying of the priests, I have lost my sole heir.*
>
> *My bitterness is complete. I curse my distant forebears who let slip away the knowledge that lately was my sole need. In their*

carelessness was lost to us the key that might have saved the House of Dexter. Never have I borne such agony of the soul as the last days have wrought upon me.

That fateful night, I kept vigil with her through the long dark, beating my fists upon the casket and tearing at it with my blunt soldier's fingers, even to the point of bloodying my nails, yet all to no avail, while poor Mathilde lay on the damask coverlet, ever holding Jasper's wan, racked frame close upon her heaving breast. By turns she rocked and cradled him. By turns, she wept and laughed hysterically and, all the while, most piteously did she beg of me to find the key or force the lid and use my power to lay a healing hand upon his cold, white brow. And I tried - how I tried! But I could not. He had slipped away before my eyes and, God help me, I could not bring him back.

Plagued with misfortune and disaster, our star is waning and I can only pray that Mathilde will yet prove able to bear another son. I could vent my anger upon the evil vapours of the pox, were it not for the fact that I know I am not blameless in this tragedy. I should have married sooner or taken a younger wife. Mathilde miscarried twice before quickening with Jasper and he was a child ever delicate and pale.

I pray to God that she is not so weakened by this fresh grief that she proves barren at the last. For, even though my heart is broke and there could be none to take his place, my dear, sweet boy has outrun me in the race to Paradise and I am left to do one thing before I die. I must beget a thriving son who bears the mark!'

He means the star-shaped birthmark, thought Sam resignedly. George's graphic prose was the final nail in the coffin lid of Sam's disbelief. She needed no further evidence to support her conviction that her ancestors clearly thought they had the secret of all the ages

- the power to redeem death - stored inside a small gold casket. And perhaps they did, she thought. But even if I had that casket in my hands, which I don't, it seems we've lost the key that opens the damn lid, so whatever it contains can't be accessed. Poor George; I'm sure he must have turned to *The Power* as a last resort in extremis. And who could blame him? What parent wouldn't do their utmost to grab back their precious baby from the arms of death?

But why did George beg forgiveness of Balthazar? That name was familiar to her as one of the three wise men from the East who followed a star to Bethlehem in order to pay homage to the newborn Christ, a baby in a manger. It was the old nativity story, but she had never heard of anyone revering the wise men. Understandably, Mary had been elevated by Christianity, but the shepherds and the wise men were - well - just hangers on, weren't they? Come to think of it, the wise men were only mentioned in one of the four gospels, as far as she could recollect.

She must have looked puzzled, because Kaye, who had been observing her while she read the piece, said, 'It's a strange story isn't it? What do you make of it?'

Sam wondered how much of what she had pieced together Kaye himself might have concluded, independently. She answered tentatively. 'I'm not sure I fully understand it. I think you're right about the smallpox, though. It was quite prevalent in those days, wasn't it? And you could catch it from cows that contracted cowpox.'

Kaye probed further. 'What about the part where his wife begs him to revive their already dead child?'

Sam shrugged. 'A mother in grief - I imagine she was distraught, grasping at any straw in her desperation. Of course, poor George could do nothing.' She gave a nervous laugh. 'I mean, no-one can bring the dead back to life!'

Not wishing to meet his eyes at that moment, she glanced out of the conservatory windows at the gentle summer dusk settling on Chaumont. In the formal garden, the shadow face of the marble Aphrodite had stolen across the lawn to bestow a goodnight kiss on the lips of her marble lover, Adonis, in a conspiracy reminding Sam that myth and magic were only ever a breath away from the rational world. She turned back to Kaye.

'What I did find odd was George's apology to Balthazar at the start of his tirade,' she admitted. 'Why would one of the Magi be relevant?'

'I think we can assume he did mean the Biblical Magus, since it's certainly not a name with which anyone would baptise a child in the eighteenth century,' replied Kaye. He paused. 'Of course, accepting that we may only have tenuous links to go on in this emblem business, then Balthazar *is* linked to Jesus, whose - supposed - tomb bears the emblem.'

'That's true,' said Sam. 'But Balthazar was only present at the nativity, wasn't he, not the crucifixion?'

'And what did he do at the nativity?' prompted Kaye, a step ahead of Sam.

She frowned. 'Gave a gift to the baby Jesus; that's all, I think - and departed Israel without going back to see Herod again.'

'And the gift was...?'

It was starting to feel like a scripture lesson to Sam. 'Well, let's see; it was gold, frankincense or possibly myrrh; the Bible doesn't specify which of the Magi gave which gift, does it?'

'No, it doesn't. Nor does it say how many there were, where they were from, or give their names.'

'So what's your point?' asked Sam.

Kaye looked at her. 'It's obvious.'

'Not to me!'

Adopting the demeanour of a lecturer, patiently nurturing a particularly dim-witted student along the path to enlightenment, he said, 'Well, we have an emblem that dates back thousands of years. It first appears on a Sanskrit text; it reappears on a tomb linked to Jesus and, finally, it pops up again on a gold casket belonging to your family. Now, let's look at the casket. You've told me it appears in three family portraits, including George's - and it's George who mentions Balthazar and then, almost in the next breath, he mentions a casket. My best guess is that it's the selfsame casket that appears in the portraits. And it's *gold*. What might we infer from all this?'

Sam's eyes grew round. 'That the casket was the gold gift that Balthazar gave to Jesus? Of course...'

Kaye was pleased she'd worked it out, but there were still a lot more mysteries to solve. He ran his fingers through his fair hair. 'What still bothers me is how a seal from a four thousand year old legend got onto a two thousand year old object belonging to Balthazar. And why was the seal so significant that someone went to the trouble of carving it on the tomb of Jesus? I wonder if the inscriptions on the tomb itself would provide an answer.'

'That's all you can't grasp? What about how the casket came into my family's possession? That's what I can't get my head around.'

Kaye nodded. 'Yes, that is peculiar. But if we're right, then it's at least two thousand years old and who knows what path a precious object like that might have traced through the hands of men over the centuries? People are greedy for gold. It wouldn't surprise me if such a prize had been the cause of more than one murder. The Middle East has always been a hotbed of trouble, so a golden treasure like that probably exchanged hands many times, perhaps even as war booty. It's a wonderful serendipity that it ended up here. You do realise that even without provenance it's worth a fortune, but if we could prove it was Balthazar's gift to Jesus, it would be virtually priceless! I'd love to examine it. Where have you got it displayed?'

Sam's face dropped dramatically. 'I haven't.'

'Stashed away at the bank, is it?'

'I'm afraid not.'

'Where is it, then?'

'I wish to God I knew. My grandfather has it in his hands in that portrait of him as a child. But my father never once mentioned it and I've certainly never seen that casket in my life.' She gave Kaye a forlorn shrug. 'It's as if it's simply vanished.'

For a moment Kaye fell silent. Rearranging the papers on the table, he asked, suddenly, 'How can you be sure?'

'Sure of what?'

'That it's vanished; that it isn't cached away somewhere in Chaumont Hall? The fact that you've never seen it might not mean that it isn't here somewhere.'

Sam thought that unlikely. 'If he'd hidden it here, I think my father would have told me or left clear instructions regarding its whereabouts.'

Kaye looked glum. 'Assuming he knew about it. Then again, the casket could have been hidden or removed before he was even born.'

Oh, he knew about it, alright, thought Sam, but I don't think I want to tell you that.

Opening the Sanskrit document at its last page, Kaye began scrutinising the seal with his magnifying glass and, discarding his earlier doodles, made a proper note of the sequence of symbols that spiralled to the sunburst's centre. After several minutes of working in silence he looked up and said pensively, 'I wish I could see the inscriptions on that tomb.'

I knew it, thought Sam. We are going to have to go to Damascus. She glanced up at the kitchen clock and said, 'Back in a minute.' On her return, an unexpected smile dimpled her cheeks. Before Kaye could query the cause, she accounted for it. 'If the tomb was all over the lunchtime news then you can bet it'll be headlined on Newsnight. So I'm recording the programme and if the engravings appear on-screen, we can freeze-frame them on playback and you can translate them at your leisure.'

Kaye nodded approvingly before turning his attention back to the sunburst with its strange symbols. 'Is this the key, I wonder?' he murmured.

Sam came round the table to look over his shoulder. '...The key to what?'

Kaye answered hesitantly, 'I'm not sure - maybe to a door we haven't found yet. These seem similar to Vedic Sanskrit letters, but they're barely visible, as well as being connected to this spiral line, making it hard to identify where one symbol ends and another begins. I'd like to make sense of them, assuming they represent one or more words, in case it helps us in some way.'

Sam looked dubious. 'I commend your thoroughness,' she said, 'but Balthazar died about two thousand years ago, so one thing's for sure - he couldn't have incorporated a useful clue into that seal as to the location of the casket, because he didn't know where it was going to end up in the twenty first century.'

'True.' They both laughed briefly, but Kaye's next comment dampened their levity. 'I don't think we need the astronomical or astrological knowledge of the Magi to predict that wherever that casket is, whoever hid it doesn't want it easily found.' Discouraged by that thought, for a time there was silence between them.

Sam spoke first. 'Let's check the programme. It's probably finished recording, now.' Retiring to the nearby day room, they soon found what they needed, but Sam had difficulty freezing a suitable frame. 'That shot comes and goes so fast, you could be forgiven for thinking they don't want anyone to get a good look at it,' she complained.

Kaye inspected the grainy frame on which they finally settled. Only the first part of the inscription was readable. Copying the Latin quickly, he sighed. 'That will have to do. I think you'd have to kneel in front of the tomb itself to see the whole text.'

I'll let you do the kneeling if it's a dusty, dirty old hole, thought Sam. I've seen enough of those in the last twenty four hours to last me for a while. I wonder if you need a visa to get into Syria? What should I pack?

Back in the kitchen, Kaye translated the text. 'What does it say?' pressed Sam, impatient for any kind of progress, no matter how small.

Kaye spun the pad round for Sam to see.

'Here rests the body of Yeshua of Nazareth, crucified Messiah, beloved son of Marium and Yosepha.'

'So the reporter in Damascus got it right.' Sam sat down heavily on the stool. 'Do you think it really *is* the tomb of Jesus? I mean, *the* Biblical Jesus?' Before Kaye could reply, a second question popped out of her mouth. 'Why is the epitaph in Latin? Jesus was Jewish, not Roman.'

Kaye thought for a moment before answering and chose to disregard her first question. 'In Palestine, two thousand years ago, there were actually four main languages in use: Greek, Hebrew, Latin, and Aramaic. Most people spoke at least two of those languages to some extent, even if it was just sufficient to hold basic conversations for trading purposes. One might speculate that whoever carved these inscriptions used the language he judged most likely to stand the test of time. But the short answer to your query is - I don't know. All we do know is that the Vedic legend, the tomb and the casket all bear the same seal - and that the casket is missing.' He stopped, then said abruptly, 'All things considered, are you sure that you really want to go looking for it?'

The question took Sam by surprise. 'Of course I do. Why wouldn't I? I'm even more intrigued than you; after all, the casket was in my family for centuries. Why would you even ask me that?'

Kaye lapsed into silence again, deep in thought. Eventually he said, 'When I came out here this morning I never expected to walk into something so potentially explosive.'

'Explosive? Isn't that a bit melodramatic?'

'No.' Kaye contradicted quickly. 'Those news bulletins today will already have set in motion a complex chain of events over which you and I have no control."

'I can't imagine…'

He broke in. 'In this rural idyll, all is green and peaceful. But out there in the wider world the wolves will already be circling. The tomb of Christ…? The Catholic Church isn't going to take that lying down, nor will any other religion whose faith is based on the premise of resurrection. I was raised Catholic, myself, so the idea of Jesus being buried *anywhere* doesn't exactly sit well with me, so imagine how those leading the faith of millions are going to react. Trust me; they'll stop at nothing to preserve the status quo. Conspiracy theorists will start popping out of the woodwork to stir the pot. And let's not forget the radical sects who'll want to discredit anything in the tomb, or turn themselves into martyrs. Besides, anyone might realise that the seal represents more than just a pretty decoration. At that point, treasure hunters and mercenaries will get in on the act. The list is endless!'

'I hadn't considered any of that,' admitted Sam pensively. 'So, you think it'll be risky to go looking for the casket?'

'Damn right, it will. We'll be obliged to interact with people in order to make progress; people who may have hidden agendas or vested interests at odds with ours. To start with, we'll need to consult the Vatican's secret archives. You'd be surprised at the extent of their material and they keep some of it well hidden, especially anything contradicting the Bible or the established precepts of the faith. Does anyone besides you and I have any knowledge of this casket? We don't know. At the least, our enquiries would place us at the heart of what Catholicism will likely see as a fight-to-the-death controversy, whatever calming platitudes their spokesmen might mouth for the benefit of the BBC. Worse, still, what if we give away sufficient information for someone else to try and beat us to the prize? Think hard, Sam. This whole tomb and casket business could get dangerous. Are you ready to take on the role of...' He cast about for the right analogy: '...Some kind of real-life Lara Croft?'

With family honour at stake, there could be only one response.

'I am,' affirmed Sam adamantly. 'A Dexter never backs down!' She looked Oliver in the eye. 'What about you?'

Kaye smiled expansively. 'I wouldn't miss it for the world.'

It was after ten and fully dark. Sam became suddenly practical. 'I'd better book flights to Rome for tomorrow.'

'...Tomorrow?'

'Why delay?' She paused, thinking. 'And we'll take Ghulam along with us,' she added.

'Ghulam?'

'My chauffeur-cum-factotum; the guru of practical common sense and problem solving. He's good with gadgets, too. He listens more than he speaks, but there are no flies on Ghulam and he's extremely perceptive. Noticing and anticipating are the skills that make a first-rate factotum.'

'Superman personified, then. Just one small thing... considering the stakes, do you trust him?'

'Implicitly.'

And in the event that we do manage to find the casket, if there's one man alive who can work out how to get the lid open - it's Ghulam.

CHAPTER 7

RAISING THE DEAD

Bethany, near Jerusalem, Judea, March, 29 AD

'Give me the casket, Balthazar, I *beg* you. You always said I'd know when the time was right. In truth, it was right when I was ten and my heart was breaking with grief for my father after the Romans sacked Sepphoris. Hour upon hour we searched for his corpse in that burned and broken city, to no avail - and without his body I could do nothing! I remember you holding me while I sobbed. You said that life was often cruel, but that when I grew up, I'd create a world of peace and love where people didn't die any more - and you said that, in any case, I was too young to have tried to save him. But now I'm thirty four, Balthazar - not, perhaps, the man you hoped for, but certainly the man you helped to mould. The time spent in India changed me, didn't it?

'You've made me a man committed to peace and to the love of my fellow man, so if I'm ever going to succeed, it will have to be done peacefully; through persuasion, not battle. It's not easy, though. If Yahweh picked me to be the Messiah, why did he send me at the hardest time? It's not as if I can just turn up at the gates of Jerusalem and expect the people to strew palm leaves in my path as I stroll up to the Temple of Solomon for my royal coronation! Can *you* see Tiberius's Procurator, Pontius Pilate - the man who keeps our High Priest's vestments locked up in the Antonia Tower and only lets him wear them three times a year - bowing down before me and dusting off the throne of David for the better comfort of my royal backside? No; nor can I.

'I'm doing what I can - the hard way. And maybe I'm naive, or overconfident, but I think I'm gaining ground. I have to convince the common people first, don't I? I'm relying on them to spread the word that the Messiah has come and is calling on them to rise up and follow him. I've developed good support in Galilee and my disciples are all people I can trust - at least I hope I can. I want to make more inroads in Judea but you know how the Sanhedrin is stifling me. You'd think priests would be the easiest to convince, but they're so stuck in their ways they wouldn't recognise Yahweh if he appeared in front of them with the prophets' promises written in fire on his forehead. At least Nicodemus and Joseph of Arimathea are loyal to me. If only they had more than two votes in the Sanhedrin...

'I don't mean to sound ungrateful. Without your huge fund of knowledge, your patience, your guidance - and all the ways you've taught me of appealing to the minds, hopes and dreams of men - I'd still be sitting in my mother's house, whittling wood. And those extraordinary mind skills the Rajagrihan Brahmins taught me are helping enormously, like the one that made the crowd at Bethsaida think they'd enjoyed a good feast when we only had a few barley loaves and a couple of fish to share out. The levitation at the Sea of Galilee went well too, although, on reflection, I should have done it earlier in the day, because the only ones who saw it were already believers.

'The ultimate miracle - the one that would convince even the deepest sceptic that I am the true Messiah - has got to be raising the dead. If I can do that, even once, they'll flock to the fold. All these years, you've been preparing me for two roles, remember, not just one, although I think they're linked, in any case. You've taught me that only someone of the blood of the Ancients can use *The Power*. At first I thought I should have had a birthmark like yours to prove my bloodline, but now I know that Keepers have stars because they are all descended from Baal, whereas those of Ashar's line are never Keepers, so no descendant of Ashar will ever bear a Keeper's mark. But until I try and use *The Power*, we won't know if I have the blood of Ashar in me, or, even if I have, whether I am *The One* as well as the Messiah. The star drew you to me and that makes you confident that the blood of the Ancients must have called to it - but we won't know for sure until I place my thumb in that hollow.

'I curse the fates that stopped us from coming here the moment Martha and Mary's brother fell ill. They're such close friends and I loved Lazarus so dearly that I would have given anything to be here to comfort them through this crisis. It wasn't to be - and now we've finally arrived, we find the poor man died four days ago. Four *days*! And I feel so guilty - and so terribly sad. The way Mary looked at me when she told me; it's more than I can bear. I have to try, Balthazar, for Mary and Martha's sake - and for Lazarus's sake. I know this is an all or nothing outcome. No-one will ever take me seriously again if I fail. But I still want to do it!

'What do I have to say to persuade you?

'Surely I'm ready, now?'

They advised Lazarus' friends and kinsfolk to remain outside the crypt on the basis that, after four days, the stink would be enough to make them gag. While Yeshua closed the heavy crypt door behind them, Balthazar took the casket from the bag he had secreted under his cloak, placing it reverently on top of the tomb.

Breathing in deeply - then wishing he had refrained, because the stench of putrescence in the cramped space really was sufficient to sour the sturdiest stomach - Yeshua placed his thumb firmly in the small hollow at the casket's crown.

'What's supposed to happen?' he whispered through gritted teeth.

'I have never seen the ceremony performed - how can I know?' whispered Balthazar in return. '*The Power* will reveal itself if you are of the blood. That's all I can tell you.'

The crowd outside the crypt conversed in muted tones out of respect for the newly dead. A tense, expectant atmosphere was building. Could any man, even the Messiah, actually resurrect a man from the dead, as Yeshua had claimed he would? Martha, haggard from grief, turned from her sister to glance at the still-closed door of the crypt, only to scream in terror and throw her cloak over her face as multiple rays of fierce, bright light lanced out through the narrow gap between the crypt's door and its frame. Cries and exhortations to Yahweh were audible from within the crypt, but not a soul amongst the shocked onlookers reached out to open its door: they stood rooted to the ground in fear and wonder. After the space of a few heartbeats the inexplicable light rays vanished and there followed a protracted silence from inside the crypt.

Just as those outside began to mutter with concern, the crypt door creaked open and, quickly composing himself, Yeshua stepped outside.

Opening his arms to everyone present, he sucked in a lungful of blessedly fresh air and said in a gentle but commanding voice, 'Did I not tell you that I am your Messiah - the resurrection and the life? You have just witnessed the power of Yahweh and here is proof that those who believe, even though they die, shall live again - behold!' He moved away from the door, shouting, 'Lazarus, come forth!' and to the amazement of all, the lately deceased Lazarus came stumbling over its threshold, still wrapped in the oil and spice soaked linen bindings in which he had been laid to rest four days earlier and blinking in bewilderment at the sunlight. Mary rushed forward and touched his face, sobbing with joy to find it warm and vital. Martha joined her, all terror forgotten in the realisation that her beloved brother was truly restored to her and then everyone began jumping up and down in a great spirit of celebration and delight, hailing Yeshua as the true Messiah.

With all eyes on Lazarus and Yeshua, no-one paid any attention to Balthazar as he slipped inconspicuously out of the crypt, his face strangely pale. He did not join the celebratory party. Instead, making his way quietly through Bethany's modest cemetery to the nearby orange grove where he had tethered his donkey, he lifted his precious burden carefully into one of its wicker panniers, burying it under a homespun blanket and covering the blanket with a layer of oranges taken from the other pannier. Untying the beast, he looped its rope halter over knuckles that still shook slightly and, clicking his tongue in encouragement, led it away, looking like just another grizzled subsistence farmer taking a few goods to market. It was fifteen furlongs to Jerusalem and a comfortable bed at the home of Nicodemus.

Balthazar felt old and drained. He hoped his strength would not fail him.

Jerusalem, Judea, 30 AD

Jerusalem's Second Wall formed the city's north-western and northern boundaries. Outside this wall on the western side, to the north of the Upper City, the ground rose in a small shallow hill; a bare, rocky outcrop that had come to be known as the place of the skull, because it was there that criminals, leading insurgents and others incurring the displeasure of Pilate's judicial system were taken to be crucified. Golgotha was both its name and its nature, for no-one roped and nailed to a wooden cross on its heights had ever returned down that hill alive.

Not thus far.

Balthazar sat under the shadow of the skull, near the entrance to the new cave tomb that Joseph of Arimathea had kindly offered to Yeshua's family - not as a permanent mausoleum, just as somewhere suitable until the Sabbath was past and the Messiah's body could be properly anointed, clothed and borne to the place of its final interment. The old mage buried his face in his hands, his heart grieving. He could not bring himself to attend the crucifixion. How could a father bear to watch his son suffer and die in agony?

For he has become a son to me, he thought. I know I have a son of my own flesh living safe in Damascus, in the house left to me by dear old Melchior, may he rest in peace - and so my duty to the line of Baal is fulfilled - but Yeshua is the son of my spirit. I have been there for him, boy and man; half my life devoted to shaping him for rightful glory, only to come at last to this. When did he become so reckless that he courted mortal danger once too often? Does it all stem from that fateful day when he found his thumb unhallowed by even the smallest drop of Ashar's blood and was obliged, instead, to let me place my own thumb within the hollow? We were both crushed, that instant, by the awful knowledge that the star had played me false - or I had misread its true intent - but, still, I spent my own sole opportunity to use *The Power*, for his sake. How could I not? I love him and I always will.

His mother will blame me; perhaps with good reason. Perhaps the fault, indeed, is mine. Had I the choice to make again, knowing what I know now, would I hold my tongue and let him stay a carpenter's brat? She's up there now, poor Mary, gazing at his thorn-crowned face, willing him to die fast and cheat the Romans of their torturers' fun.

Oh, Yeshua! If only I had stayed my hand in Bethany, when Lazarus took what could have saved you now.

It was approaching the twelfth hour - six o'clock in the evening - when a slow-moving party of four people came into view: Mary Magdalene, with a supporting arm around the bowed shoulders of Yeshua's mother, Mary; these two followed by Joseph of Arimathea and, at the rear, Nicodemus, the two men between them bearing a makeshift funeral litter on which lay Yeshua's body, wound about with a simple linen shroud for decency. Balthazar stood respectfully as they approached the tomb, putting his hands together in silent prayer as they bore the litter into the cave and laid it down.

Thank you, great Surya, for bringing the Messiah back into the bosom of his family and faithful followers, at peace and out of pain at last.

Pausing as she passed, Mary glanced up at him, her face a mask of sorrow and her eyes puffed and red from many hours of weeping. 'You may as well come in,' she said. 'He would have wanted you here.' Her voice cracked with grief.

'Your kindness is more than I deserve,' he answered quietly, lowering his head.

'What was it my son always said? *'The meek shall inherit the earth,'*' she sobbed. 'But I think he was wrong. The powerful won't ever let that happen. Look what they've done to him, a man who never had an unworthy thought and would give his last coin to a beggar...as he frequently did.'

Seeking to comfort and inspire her, he said, 'He was too good for this world. It simply wasn't ready for him. He was the true Messiah, though. You do believe that, don't you?'

'I want to,' she replied, a frown furrowing her brow. 'What is left to me, now, but the belief in what he might have been? But let me ask you this - if the holy spirit of Yahweh was truly in my son and he was sent to be the Messiah, as you always claimed, why does he lie here, dead, at my feet?'

Balthazar shook his head miserably, lost for an answer. 'May I look upon his face?' he asked.

'Mary, we can't stay,' broke in Joseph of Arimathea as he knelt to re-tie a trailing sandal thong. 'Pilate gave over the body at my request, but considering the circumstances, he's likely to send soldiers to guard this tomb and it would be safer if we were gone before that happens. He's already ordered that the three crosses be removed and thrown in some forgotten cistern in an effort to deter insurgents from using the site of execution as a rallying point.'

'How can I leave my child un-anointed?' Mary remonstrated, appalled. 'At least he must be dressed with myrrh and aloe...' On seeing Joseph's expression, she faltered. 'I suppose we could complete the rest of the funerary tasks when we come back after the Sabbath...'

'Joseph is right. You should leave without delay,' urged Balthazar. 'The anointing oils and spices are already laid out and if it will aid your peace of mind, I shall stay and anoint him - even those Roman scum would baulk at disturbing a lowly priest about such sad business.'

'But how will you close the tomb afterwards?' asked young Nicodemus.

The sage considered for a moment. 'If you and Joseph roll the stone the greater way across the entrance, I can finish the job with a hearty shoulder. I'll come to you when all is done.'

And so it was agreed.

Bending to touch the inert, shrouded form, each bid Yeshua a sorrowing farewell and as soon as the stone had been moved they departed, their footsteps quickly fading.

Balthazar stood alone in the cool, deep gloom of the rock sepulchre. Sighing, he began by lighting the oil lamps that stood in nooks hewn in the walls. Banishing the darkest shadows, the flickering light gave the enclosed space a warm cast, gracing the body on the pallet with almost the semblance of life. Padding the stone floor with the cushion he had brought with him that morning, the old sage knelt upon it and delicately drew back the shroud from the Messiah's face. Marred only by the piercings of locust tree thorns, Yeshua's brow was as smooth as pooled wax, his eyes were closed and his wan lips lay slightly parted above his glossy black beard. About to unwind the whole sheet and expose the shattered body for cleansing with a soft, oiled cloth, Balthazar stopped, his eyes fixing on a tiny drop of blood as it oozed from a thorn hole high on Yeshua's forehead.

How can that be? The dead don't bleed.
He's alive!
No, it cannot be...
It must be!

Yet when he bent to the parted lips, he could sense no aura of breath. His urgent fingers found no pulse at the wrist and his ear, when laid against the shroud, failed to detect a heartbeat - but that meant little, his acuity of hearing being much compromised by age.

I must be mad. He can't have survived what he's been through!
I have to be sure, though.
What shall I do?

His eyes kept returning to Yeshua's lips. The answer had to lie in the breath. Without breath there could be no life... and he knew a way to make a certain test for that! Fumbling his thin bronze mirror from a pouch on his belt, he held the cold metal over the Messiah's pale lips, desperate for evidence of the dew of life. Counting to ten, he turned the mirror around, hardly daring to look, but there it was - like the sigh of a mayfly - the most insubstantial and transient of mists, condensed on the surface of the bronze.

Alive! - barely.

His hands visibly shaking, now, he took a precious moment to calm himself before upending his day pack and emptying out all his medicinal pouches in an urgent search for medicaments that might help build on that incredibly delicate wisp of life.

First, following ayurvedic principles, he mixed spikenard, camphor and cinnamon with a little water, a medicine to combat dehydration and help raise low blood pressure. Freeing Yeshua's body of the shroud and supporting his head, he dribbled the concoction between his lips, rubbing his throat vigorously to promote its passage down his gorge. Yeshua's raw, shredded back spoke of much blood loss from his scourging and Balthazar saw that, besides the nail holes in his hands and feet, he had also suffered a shallow spear puncture to his ribs. A thin streak of blood and clear fluid leaked out as Balthazar pressed gently round the wound to assess its severity. His lungs - thank Surya - seemed undamaged. The sage realised, then, why they must have assumed him dead and ordered him taken down from the cross.

The agonising effort, over the hours, of raising and lowering his body on the cross in order to breathe in and out must have compromised his chest tissues and caused an accumulation of fluid in the sac around his lungs. Such fluid often spread to fill the actual lungs of crucifixion victims, leading to death by asphyxiation. After Yeshua lost consciousness from a combination of pain, blood loss and exhaustion, someone had poked him with a spear to test for signs of life and when clear fluid, as well as blood, emerged from the spear wound, they must have thought him dead from drowned lungs. But, by some marvellous chance, the spear had pierced only the pleural sac and, in doing so, had given egress to the fluid that would otherwise have speeded him to his death.

Ironically, that cruel jab had saved his life.

Flushing all the open wounds with salted water, Balthazar liberally applied a beeswax-based herbal ointment softened with flaxseed oil, for the regeneration and closure of the flesh. Stitching together the ragged flaps of the wounds, he finished by covering them with generous smears of honey and bandaged them with clean linen strips torn from one end of the shroud.

Next, he ground together fenugreek; coriander; celery seeds; wormwood, dried chicory and dried parsley, mixing the powder with honey. Honey was a nourishing restorative and the other ingredients supplemented the blood with vital minerals. By the time this medicine was ready, Yeshua's breathing had discernibly improved, but he remained unconscious and his pulse was thready. Patiently, Balthazar wiped his hands on a shred of leftover linen and knelt to pray.

It was several hours before Yeshua's eyelids fluttered and he coughed weakly. Balthazar wiped the thin drizzle of spittle from his lips and propped his head up on the cushion. 'Wake, my son,' he murmured. Yeshua coughed again and raised his eyelids, then groaned as agony filled his world.

'Listen carefully,' said Balthazar. 'You may be the first man to survive a Roman crucifixion, but you are sorely hurt. Swallow the medicine I am about to give you and in my absence, swallow another mouthful each time you wake. I will leave a flask of water and a flask of wine by your side. Sip the water for your thirst and the wine for your pain. When you can, turn to your right side to ease the stripes on your back. Avoid your left side as you took a spear thrust there. Blink twice if you have understood - don't try to talk.'

Yeshua licked his parched lips, meaning to speak, but Balthazar hushed him with a finger and repeated, 'Just blink twice, I said. You are still near death and must not waste what little strength you possess.' Yeshua looked at him and blinked twice, after which he closed his eyes and exhaled a light sigh.

'You are in Joseph's sepulchre,' his mentor told him. 'Do not attempt to leave, even if you regain some strength. You would burst your wounds trying to move the door stone. You will be safe here if you stay quiet. Bite on this cloth to stifle your cries of pain because there will be soldiers just beyond the door.' Saying this, he re-covered Yeshua to his bearded chin with his own death shroud, now dowsed in oil mixed with myrrh and aloe to warm and soothe him.

'I have ministered to your wounds as best I can. Leave the bindings on or your injuries may fester. I must observe the Sabbath and attend those who grieve for your apparent death, but I shall return with help, at dawn the day after tomorrow, to move you to a safe place. Meanwhile, no-one will know you live - for safety's sake. Now, swallow this.' Obediently, Yeshua opened his mouth and Balthazar spooned in some of the herb and honey mixture. 'Sleep and the time will pass more quickly.'

Gathering up his medicinal materials and packing them away, the sage squeezed himself through the small gap between the rock wall and the edge of the stone door. No soldiers were yet apparent. Once outside, he put his shoulder to the stone and heaved with all his strength. Slowly it rolled the last half cubit into place, sealing Yeshua in solitude, with lamps that would gutter out by dawn.

On the first day of the new week, with a peach and lemon sky heralding a fine morning, Balthazar and Nicodemus approached Joseph's sepulchre. To avoid recognition, they were clad in white Zoroastrian robes with hoods obscuring the majority of their faces. Carrying lidded incense pots as if simply wandering through the garden on their way to devotions somewhere nearby, they hoped to deceive the Roman guards into letting them approach sufficiently close to remove the lids and release the fast-acting soporific vapours the pots contained.

They could not believe their good fortune when they found the guards slouched against the scrubby cliff-side next to the tomb, already sleeping peacefully. Setting both pots directly in front of them, Balthazar removed the lids and tiptoed away until the soldiers had succumbed to an even deeper, drug-induced slumber from which, the sage happily assured Nicodemus, they would not wake for hours.

Pushing together, the two men rolled the tomb's door stone aside and the rising sun flooded the sepulchre with golden light.

To Yeshua's slitted eyes, it was as if the silhouettes of two sun-haloed angels had suddenly appeared at the low doorway. Still on his funeral litter, he struggled to his elbows, wincing both from the pain of movement and from the sun's par-blinding effects. 'Hallelujah,' he whispered in awe and gratitude. Once the lamps in their niches had guttered out, he had lain imprisoned in darkness so palpable that his mind had crazed, imagining what might slither up and touch him. The battle to overcome his fear had occupied him so profoundly that it had even dulled his sense of pain. As they came closer, the angels metamorphosed into men and he managed a weak smile for the two who were risking so much to rescue him.

'Good to see you smile, but do you think you can stand and walk, if we help you?' asked the ever practical Balthazar as he whisked away the soiled shroud and cast it aside.

'I can try,' was the uncertain reply.

While Balthazar bound Yeshua's ruined feet in fresh linen, Nicodemus took a simple homespun robe out of his shoulder bag and slipped it gently over the convalescent's head, tying it loosely at his waist with a rope cord. A brown head cloth completed the peasant disguise. Together they lifted him upright and held him until he found some measure of balance. Putting weight on his feet was excruciating, even though they were padded with layers of soft cloth.

'I don't think I can do this,' he panted faintly.

'We only have to get out of sight of the guards. They're dreaming sweetly, but if one manages to resist the effects of my potion and glimpses a dead man walking, it's goodnight all. We have a pallet hidden close by and we'll support you, one on either side. Come on,' Balthazar urged. 'It's just a few steps round the first bend to a bench where you can safely rest.'

Yeshua bit his lip and nodded. He knew he must do this if he wanted to survive.

Much is possible when there is no alternative, but he was pitifully glad when he finally reached the bench and collapsed onto it, grimacing in pain. Leaving him there, his helpers headed for the pallet, disappearing down a side path. They had only been gone for a minute when Yeshua caught sight of Mary Magdalene approaching with a heavy basket over her arms, weeping quietly as she walked.

She's probably bringing the linen bindings meant for my corpse, he thought with a horrified shiver. Dressed as I am, she won't recognise me if I say nothing. But how can I just let her walk on by? He trusted Mary without question, so surely it was unjust to let her grieve for him any longer than necessary? While he vacillated, she walked past with no sign of recognition, only to stop abruptly when she reached the bend, obviously upset and confused by the sight of the open, deserted tomb.

His voice muffled by the cloth wrapped round his face, and with his mind not yet entirely clear on its intended course of action, Yeshua called softly to her, 'Why are you crying, woman? Whom do you seek?'

Mary turned and, assuming him to be the cemetery gardener, gestured in the direction of the tomb and begged to know if he had removed its occupant. 'Will you tell me where you have laid him so I can arrange his removal,' she begged, humbly.

Yeshua could not bear the dreadful grief evident in her voice. His mind was made up. Pulling his face cloth down with one finger, he said, 'Mary!' in a way she was sure to recognise.

'Master?' she cried disbelievingly and ran towards him, meaning to kiss his feet in joy.

'Don't touch me,' he warned her sharply, sure the pain of it would make him scream and bring disaster upon them. She jerked back at his tone, nonplussed. 'There's no need to touch me to see that I have returned - as was prophesied,' he dissembled, not wishing her to know how badly injured he really was.

'What will happen now?' Mary quavered. 'What shall I tell our brethren, Lord?'

Deep inside himself, Yeshua's body told him that he was not long for this world, despite the best attempts of Balthazar. What should he say to Mary? A comforting thought overtook him. As Messiah, surely he was imbued with the holy spirit of Yahweh? He would breathe that spirit upon those who loved him and tell them to go forth and spread the word of the great spiritual redeemer of his people who had given his life to save their souls. Yes, this must be Yahweh's plan - to raise him up as Lord of Heaven, not of Earth. And wasn't the Kingdom of Heaven far greater than any Earthly kingdom?

'My Father calls me and I cannot remain with you for very long,' he told Mary. 'Go quickly; tell our brethren I will prove my resurrection to them before I ascend to Yahweh. Say I will see them in Galilee, at the house of Nathanael in Cana, thirty days from now.'

It gave his aching soul a deep sense of fulfilment to think that when he was gone, he would live on through their belief in his resurrection and ascension to sit at Yahweh's right hand side, ruling both Heaven and Earth in glory!

Cana, Galilee, 30 AD

The only place Balthazar thought truly safe for Yeshua's convalescence was his own home in Damascus. Yeshua argued that it was too far away and that he would rather die amongst his friends and disciples in Galilee, where all who loved him could mourn his passing, at which Balthazar chided him for being so negative - he wasn't going to die. Yeshua wasn't fooled. He'd seen the look in Balthazar's eyes the day he had complained that the wound in his side had begun throbbing ever more painfully under its dressing.

His hands and feet were healing well, no bones having been broken and the nails having been new ones, but the spear must have been soiled, because his pierced side had festered and necrotising gangrene had set in. Balthazar recognised the condition as soon as he unwound the linen bandages and saw the damp, soft, swollen tissue beneath, an unhealthy brown colour, with black around its edges. Soon it would begin to smell putrid. To all intents, Yeshua was a walking dead man and Balthazar's stubborn refusal to accept this fact would not change it.

They had come to Cana, not because it was on their direct route north, but because Yeshua had promised he would see his disciples there; all who could manage it.

He let them touch his hands and feet, to see the healing nail wounds and be reassured that he was living flesh and blood. Even Thomas, the hardest of men to convince, was finally satisfied that the Messiah had truly been resurrected. Nor did Nathanael let him down, welcoming all who arrived and providing enough food for everyone.

Explaining that they would not see him again because he was rising up to join Yahweh, Yeshua told Peter that he now had charge of the flock - conferring on the senior disciple the responsibility of supporting all his faithful followers once he was gone. He made it clear that he also expected them to keep spreading the word that, with love and understanding, eventually the whole of Palestine would be one great and free nation under Yahweh. 'Maybe I'll come back to see that!' he joked. After the simple meal was over, he felt the familiar sick exhaustion creep over him. His eyes taking in their dear faces one last time, yet already feeling strangely distanced from them, his heart bid a silent farewell to his friends and, soon afterwards, he departed unseen, while everyone was busy chattering and helping to clear up. They would simply have to manage without him, now.

Damascus, City State of the Decapolis, 30 AD

Barely conscious by the time they arrived in Damascus, Yeshua survived only days in the comfort of his mentor's home before succumbing to the fever of septicaemia, a frequent complication of gangrene. Balthazar, to his grief, could do nothing save be grateful that Surya had seen fit to bless the Messiah with sleep and a surcease of suffering near the end, rendering his passing a peaceful one. *And so, at last, the dream is over...*

Balthazar and his son, Basem, stood inside a rock-hewn cave tomb half way up a steep ravine on Mount Quasioun, above the city.

Basem, at twenty seven years of age, was an experienced stonemason, a calling of some prestige in Damascus, which always had need of craftsmen able to dress both limestone and the more costly marble used in temples, civic buildings and the homes of the wealthy. Having made Damascus his settled home on inheriting from Melchior, Balthazar had wasted no time in taking a wife and securing his succession. Being, at that time, still of high hope that Yeshua would prove to be *The One*, siring the next generation's Keeper had seemed almost unnecessary, yet without ultimate proof - and whilst still confident of his virility - he had fulfilled his responsibility in that respect; in retrospect, a most wise decision.

'You have crafted a fitting resting place,' Balthazar complimented Basem, his eyes ranging over the carved limestone casket in which they had just placed Yeshua's anointed and linen-bound corpse. He ran his fingers over the beautifully carved sunburst symbol and the eternal promise of *The Power* that decorated the side of the tomb in Latin. Basem had also engraved Yeshua's title and parentage there, as directed by his father.

After saying a number of Vedic prayers, Balthazar took up a woven pouch containing the crucifixion nail he had tenderly withdrawn from one of Yeshua's feet whilst ministering to his wounds. Climbing onto the coffin slab with Basem's help, he laid the pouch in the coffin next to those poor, scarred feet. 'Should any man disturb your peace, let him be pierced with this nail, as you once were,' he intoned, as a curse against tomb robbers, before turning to his son to indicate that it was time to lid the coffin. Even Basem's considerable physical strength was taxed by this task. Balthazar tried to help as much as he was able, but his muscles were now weak with age and it took him some time to recover from the effort. While the old sage rested after his labours, the young stonemason sealed the lid with a fine-ground lime mortar.

'He was not *The One*, but *The One* will be found, my son - not by me and perhaps not by you, but by a Keeper of our line in the fullness of time - and then you, I and Yeshua will all gladly rise, meet and clasp hands again. That is the faith by which we follow the star.' Balthazar bowed long and low in front of the sealed tomb before turning to leave. They ducked out through the chamber's low entrance and Basem walled up the space with ready-prepared mud-bricks. This task complete, they exited the tunnel and Balthazar watched while Basem undertook the huge labour of blocking it entirely with rough chunks of natural sandstone. In a year or two, seeds would take hold and that small section of the gorge would become indistinguishable from the rest, ensuring that Yeshua's remains would enjoy undisturbed peace until the day of *The One*.

In the perpetual, soundless dark of the sepulchre, the two insignificant ossuaries that had already rested there for eons kept silent company with Yeshua. Had anyone turned them round, they would have discovered carved on their hidden sides, in a very early form of Hebrew, the names of their brotherly occupants: Abel and Cain.

Little more than six months later, in bitter sorrow, Basem laid the frail form of his father to rest in a limestone tomb not dissimilar to that of his father's beloved Yeshua. Balthazar had never thrived once Yeshua was gone. Resting one strong, stonemason's hand on the stone seal he had carved on his father's tomb and the other over the matching birthmark on his chest, he vowed he would remain true to the line of Baal as a Keeper of *The Power*.

The casket of the Ancients was safe for another generation and the world rolled on, unknowing.

The Dark Ages

Balthazar's line continued, generation upon generation, the bloodline of Baal mingling with that of the Arabic and Semitic peoples of the near East as wives were taken and sons and daughters delivered of them. But of all the children born, only one in each generation bore the Mark of the Keeper and the casket passed only to the child chosen of the Mark. Those not chosen, however, did not always remain in ignorance of the heritage that had passed them by.

Around two hundred years after Basem's death, a Keeper took a young wife from southern Arabia, descended of the Sabaeans - indigents of the fabled land of Sheba, as it had been known in ancient days. It seemed a fitting match, for the Sabaeans had long worshipped the sun god, whom they called Shams. His wife bore that Keeper six fine sons, the sixth and last, named Adeeb, being chosen of *The Power*. But Adeeb's five older brothers were dismayed, each in his turn, to discover that *The Power* had spurned them - and their combined jealousy of young Adeeb grew ever more bitter and quarrelsome, culminating in a family rift. All five elder brothers left the family home and were never heard from again, passing out of the sphere of knowledge of the line of Keepers.

Once both his parents had passed away, Adeeb journeyed to Jerusalem and became a lay servant in the lately constructed Church of the Holy Sepulchre, built over the supposed site of the crucifixion of Christ at the command of the Roman Emperor Constantine.

Having built a reputation as a learned man, Adeeb was readily believed in his claim that the golden treasure he brought with him was conceived of ancient magic and bore mystic powers. But in truth, he was a bigger fool than the priests and city worthies who paid him heed, for, in consequence of his reckless claim, they wrested the casket from him and placed it under lock and key amongst the crypts and vaults below the Holy Sepulchre. They put their trust in Iesus Christus to mitigate the casket's magic powers and render it a harmless artefact. True to its tendency, however, superstition proved tenacious and the casket remained locked underground for many centuries more.

Consequently, although it remained safe from the acquisitive depredations of Adeeb's brothers, Adeeb's own descendants - the Keepers who continued down through the long years - could only look upon the casket where it lay glittering behind dull iron bars at the back of a narrow, underground kokh tomb, or touch it in the presence of a watchful priest. Dispossessed of their true calling by their forefather's foolishness, any opportunity they might otherwise have had to utilise *The Power* or find *The One* was curtailed and they were obliged to watch and wait out the years, assuming the role of theological scholars, since that calling, at least, kept them physically close to the casket and allowed them to feel they were still its guardians. Nothing of significance changed for the Keepers over the next eight hundred years, save one vital thing - and that was a disaster beyond comprehension.

At some point during those eight centuries - through disuse, misfortune, carelessness or fate - all knowledge of the practical mechanism for activation of *The Power* that resided within the casket of the Ancients was utterly lost to its Keepers.

CHAPTER 8

HOLY ORDERS

Vatican City, Rome, Italy, 18 June, 2016 AD

Immaculately dressed in a pale blue Armani business suit that, oddly enough, served only to accentuate the broadness of his shoulders and the extent of his highly muscular physique, the thirty two year old man strode into the marble-floored, book-lined meeting chamber deep in the heart of the Vatican's archives. Close to the mullioned window at the far end of the small chamber stood seventy-three year old Cardinal Alesandro Mercurio of the Office of the Holy See, a senior member of the Congregation of the Doctrine of the Faith, his red robe and skullcap masking a slight frame and balding grey head.

Mercurio had been taking a moment to appreciate the bold clarity of the white and blue dome of Saint Peter's Basilica, over which a cylinder of white marble columns drew the eye to the final, short spire, topped with an impressive gilded sphere. Brilliant afternoon sunlight engulfed the dome, transfiguring the sphere into the sun's miniature twin, a fiery orb framed against a blue June sky that, for once, lacked the usual heat-haze of Rome's summer months.

Inspiring as the sight was, on hearing the firm footsteps, the Cardinal immediately turned to greet his visitor. Aside from responding to the dictates of courtesy, thought Mercurio, had he kept his back to this particular gentleman, it would have made his shoulder blades prick unpleasantly. Still, one had to make use of the tools the good Lord saw fit to provide and this particular tool had been extremely efficacious on several previous occasions. It was perhaps best not to reflect too deeply on the man's methods, when agents capable of and willing to undertake specialist field work for the Holy See were so few and far between. Such men changed their names along with their underwear. Currently going by the German-sounding name of Raoul Richter and despite his fluency in Italian, German, Arabic and several other languages, the man was, in fact, English.

'Ah, good; you are here - and well, I trust?'

'Yes, Your Eminence.' His agent genuflected, knelt and touched his lips lightly to the ring on Mercurio's out-held hand. The fellow's full head of black hair shone healthily, the Cardinal noted with envy, wistfully recollecting the vitality he, himself, had enjoyed at Richter's age.

'Rise, my son; we have serious matters to discuss that will take some time, so if you would be so good as to pander to an old man's creaky joints, come; let us both be seated comfortably.' The Cardinal indicated two nineteenth century upholstered chairs, placed conveniently close to the antique walnut desk in the centre of the chamber. The desk itself was a Renaissance piece of particular merit. Once he had settled his hips comfortably in his chair, the Cardinal clasped his arthritis-twisted fingers on his lap and said, 'I'm sure it has not escaped your attention that the world's media are making much of the tomb unearthed in Syria.

'I am fully briefed and await your instructions, Your Eminence.'

'A number of reporters are pressing for an audience with His Holiness on the subject, obliging the Prefecture of the Papal Household to prepare a statement to be given at a press conference we understand is imminent. That statement is intended to appease the masses but it will in no way appease our private concerns, which derive from a much greater threat to the Church than that which the discovery of Christ's mortal body is likely to confer.'

The man calling himself Richter shifted in his seat, his suit straining across his shoulders and his knuckles whitening as his large hands gripped its carved walnut arm rests. Although outwardly calm, his smoke-grey eyes and his body language spoke of a barely contained impulse to spring to his feet and commit brutal violence upon whomever or whatever was the cause of the Cardinal's problems.

'Do not concern yourself, Your Eminence: whatever this threat is, I will erase it,' he said in low tones, enunciating his last four words particularly clearly.

Mercurio inclined his head knowingly. 'Your dedication to the faith is unquestionable, my son, but I must warn you that involvement in this matter may hold personal dangers for you. Unscrupulous enemies of the faith are likely to oppose our efforts with all their might - and their might is not inconsiderable.'

'The risk is unimportant. Anything that must be done, I will do. I do not fear death.'

The Cardinal briefly closed his eyes and murmured, 'Saint Mark 8; 35 - *'He who lose his life for my sake and for the gospel's sake will save it'.*' His eyes blinked open again and he smiled.

'Patience: your zeal is laudable and there is a vital task with which I propose to burden you, but first you must listen carefully. We have now received our own photographic evidence of the tomb and its curious inscriptions, obtained by our Emissary who has just this morning returned from Damascus. I want you to look at these photographs.' Mercurio pointed his bony forefinger at a brown folder lying on the adjacent desk. 'Take your time and observe in particular, please, the seal at the centre of the inscriptions.'

The Cardinal's agent opened the folder and examined the sheaf of prints he found inside. When he reached the one that showed the sunburst in close-up detail, he stared at it with keen attention, his pale eyes unfathomable.

Taking his time, Mercurio rose, limped to the far wall and from its bookshelves withdrew a venerable volume, carrying it carefully back to the table. There he placed his gnarled hands on the vellum cover and fixed calculating eyes on the young man before him. 'This contains a copy of a document - an ancient text - that the Congregation has kept from the eyes of men for very good reason,' he said. 'Upon penalty of excommunication, I abjure you to respect and keep secret what I am about to reveal to you.'

'I will die before repeating a word.'

'Certainly, your soul will burn if you *do* repeat a word, for this is the most damningly apocryphal of the so-called lost gospels. Many testaments came to light over time. Not all found their way into the Bible. Some, like this one, were judged inappropriate for inclusion - despite having the provenance and age of similar gospels that were selected and included - and that decision was made during the second century AD, as evidenced by the fact that the Muratorian Fragment, dated to the end of that century, already contained only the four gospels of the New Testament that we see in the Bible today. Many Gnostic and questionable works were also discredited or permanently discarded by Constantine's Council of Nicaea in the fourth century AD. Most were burned. This particular work, for some reason, was not. It is known to us as the Lost Gospel of Basem. The original scroll deteriorated many centuries ago, but has been faithfully hand-copied on robust parchment. It is even embellished with illuminations - most beautifully, I might add.'

Mercurio opened the book carefully to a page he had earlier tagged with a silk ribbon marker. 'A pleasure to behold, is it not?' he asked rhetorically of Richter, who stood and leant over the desk in order to see the double page clearly. 'How good is your Latin?'

The agent shook his head. 'Not good enough, I fear.'

'I thought perhaps not. Mine, however, is excellent and I shall extemporise a translation of the two pertinent passages for you.' From a deep pocket in his robe he pulled out a leather spectacle-purse and shook out a pair of reading glasses, placing them on his nose. His long, thin finger traced a path in the air just above the illuminated text on the page as he reviewed it and condensed its meaning into plain, simple words.

'And the Messiah fell on his knees and prayed to God to help him restore life to the dead body of Lazarus. And he laid his hand upon the corpse of Lazarus but could not bring breath back to his body. So his mage, Balthazar, ever following in his footsteps, brought to him a golden casket and struck it open with his own hand. And God's heavenly white light sprang from the casket, bathing the sepulchre. And Balthazar laid

his hand within the holy light and thence upon the hand of Jesus which still rested on the breast of the dead man. And through the hands of Balthazar and Jesus, Lazarus absorbed God's healing light and, with one mighty convulsion of his chest, expelled the vapours of death and drew living breath once more...'

Seeing that his listener was about to speak, the Cardinal waved a silencing finger at him, turned to a further page tagged with a further silk marker and continued.

'...And when Jesus was taken down from the cross, Joseph of Arimathea received him through the edict of Pontius Pilate, wrapped him in linen and bore him to a tomb in a cave not far distant, where his faithful mage, Balthazar, remained alone to embalm the corpse. But when the mage bent near the mouth of Jesus, he perceived a mist denoting the breath of life. So in urgent haste he anointed the Messiah's wounds with restorative unguents, covered him in a linen shroud and departed the tomb, rolling the stone door over its entrance. And being in fear of the wrath of Pontius Pilate, Balthazar told no-one that the Messiah still lived.

'And when on the third day, Mary Magdalene approached the tomb, she saw that its stone door had been rolled back and it was empty save for a cast-aside shroud. For she did not know that the Messiah was risen and that his mage had returned that morning to remove him to a safe place. And he and his mage were still close by within the garden when Mary came. And when Jesus saw Mary he spoke, saying, 'Weep not, for I am not dead, but risen as prophesied. Tell my disciples I will meet them in Galilee.'

'And when Mary, wondering at this news, had departed, the Messiah and his mage also departed. And the mage warned Jesus that nowhere in Palestine would he be safe from the scourge of the Romans. And he begged him to flee with all haste after meeting with his disciples. And Jesus did flee soon thereafter. Only once did he attend his disciples before departing Galilee and they were amazed, falling down before him and praising him, believing they were in the presence of a holy spirit.

'But Jesus upbraided them for their disbelief that he had risen as a mortal man, causing them to touch his wounds in proof of it. And he told them that he would soon ascend to his Father, the Lord God, in the

Kingdom of Heaven, so it was now their duty to go forth and preach the word of the Lord, for he would not be present to continue this work himself. And thus he departed and from that day forward, no man had sight of him, saving only the mage who went with him.'

Closing the vellum bound book with care, Mercurio said, dryly, 'You may understand, now, why this gospel has been kept in the secret archives of the Vatican.'

Richter bent his head. 'Yes, Your Eminence - because it's a blasphemous corruption of the holy truth!'

Cardinal Alesandro Mercurio's face wrinkled in his effort to phrase his next words carefully. 'The truth is invariably the most difficult thing to extract from the words of men,' he said. 'Let it suffice to say that after much deliberation, the Congregation of the Faith has agreed on the importance of certain key elements of the material I have just divulged to you. It is conceivable that, even though Jesus rose in spirit to heaven, his mortal body may have been removed and buried by someone who would be difficult to trace, such as this Balthazar. Consequently, it follows that the tomb just discovered near Damascus may indeed hold the mortal remains of our Lord.'

His agent's brow furrowed. 'But if the existence of such remains will not shake the Church, what *is* the threat that you perceive?'

'Ah, now we come to the nub of the matter,' said Mercurio. He opened the Lost Gospel of Basem one last time, at the back page. Here, minutely reproduced and decorated in gold leaf, was the same insignia that had lately been photographed on the tomb by the Papal Emissary. 'This, we believe, is the seal of Balthazar,' said the Cardinal, 'and its presence both in this book and on the recently discovered tomb suggests that Balthazar may have played a much more significant role in the life and death of Jesus than we could have imagined. And if we accept that as a possible truth, then we must look more keenly at the first passage I read out to you, concerning the raising of Lazarus.'

'So you think a casket containing the healing light of God might really have existed?' exclaimed Richter, the look on his face suggesting extreme scepticism, if not disbelief.

'It might have - and might still,' was the measured reply. 'Certain distant ancestors of my own - notably, a fifteenth century monk by the name of Brother Dominic Mercurio - certainly thought it did. Consider the Ark of the Covenant, for which men endlessly and assiduously search, despite the lack of evidence for its survival to modern times. If God can house in a little box the means to confer death on those who hate him, then surely, in another little box, he can house the means to confer life upon those who love him.' He felt a gratified surprise that the young man had so adeptly identified the key element of the Lazarus passage after just one hearing. It was pleasing to know that he was employing no dullard. 'Evidence for the existence of this casket is scarce, but we do possess several ancient scrolls bearing the selfsame seal, in wax, as the one carved in stone on the tomb just discovered near Damascus.'

Richter exercised supreme mental control, making his face a picture of innocent, attentive concern. He could not let the extent of his mental intoxication - or his prior knowledge of the existence of the casket - become evident to the old fool lecturing him. Throughout his life, there had been only two desires that fed his passions and filled his dreams - and ownership of this very casket was one of them.

I know it exists and, one day, my hand will be upon it. Day and night I feel its call. It pulses in my blood.

Mercurio could not hope to guess his agenda or the reasons for it, nor did Richter plan to enlighten him. The assassin had already begun working towards the first of his two targets and, now, fate - through Mercurio - was about to offer him the opportunity to take action towards achieving the second.

Unaware of the other man's thoughts, Mercurio continued to press his point home. 'There is further mention of the casket in The Gospel of Basem and, on the tomb just discovered, the lower line of text translates as, *'May the power of the casket protect you until the one comes who will bring light and life to all'*. We have no idea what other inscriptions may await discovery, since the archaeologists will not permit us full access to the coffin until they have completed their in-situ preservation procedures. Only then will the remains be removed to a laboratory, making it possible to see whether anything is written inside the coffin.'

'Are there any clues as to the whereabouts of this casket within any of the texts you hold in the Vatican archives?'

'I have searched exhaustively,' replied the Cardinal. 'One obscure medieval text, written by a Christian priest of the twelfth century, does make mention of a golden casket - but only to say that it is no longer in the Holy City. The writer was attached to the Christian army of the third crusade, who were permitted access to the holy sites within Jerusalem during the three year truce period agreed between Richard the Lionheart and Saladin. This priest, Aloisius, spent time making detailed notes of the scope and condition of the churches he saw - perhaps in expectation that they would soon return into Christian hands. He noted down the name of every chapel, shrine, calvary, room and crypt into which he ventured and amongst those listed for the Church of the Holy Sepulchre was *'The crypt of the casket'*, next to which he added a short annotation, mentioning that a local priest had informed him that this particular tiny crypt had once held a gold casket, housed there from time immemorial and believed by many to have holy powers that would prevent Jerusalem from being sacked, but that the Saracen warlord, Saladin, had claimed it as booty.'

'Not a lot to go on,' said Richter, who already knew very well what had become of the casket in the twelfth century.

'Indeed not. Saladin built fortresses and palaces in a number of cities, to any one of which such a treasure might have been taken. After his death, who can say what its fate might have been? If the casket mentioned was, in fact, Balthazar's, we can, in any case, only speculate as to why it had been hidden for hundreds of years in the crypt Aloisius described.' Mercurio sighed. 'I will keep searching amongst the archives, but do not rely on an answer from that quarter. What I do think likely is that, if it has survived, the casket may still be somewhere in the Middle East.'

'And you wish me to seek it?' There was a restrained yet palpable eagerness evident in Richter's voice as he made this statement.

'Yes. That is your mission if you are willing. This casket may be an object most holy, housing one of God's greatest miracles, or it may not be of God at all. In either case, what has been written of it is suggestive of a power that would be safest held securely within the strong walls of the Vatican.' Mercurio began to hobble up and down in growing agitation. 'Imagine the marvel of being able to use such a power to heal the sick; the dying - perhaps even the dead.' He turned to face the young man. 'Conversely, imagine such a power falling into the hands of the non-believers and evildoers of this world.'

'That must not happen.' Richter was vehement.

Their apparent confluence of aims was most provident, thought the assassin in satisfaction. Not that he believed for a moment that Mercurio would hand over the casket to the Holy See if ever he got his hands on it. The old man's mind was as transparent as the skin stretched over his stricken hands. Did the fool think he could tame the casket's *Power* to such a lowly task as curing his own creaking joints?

I will find it, but it shall never be his.

The Cardinal fumbled in his pocket and drew out a folded document. 'One more thing - here I have a most perturbing request for access to the secret archives. It arrived today, from a British academic who has made similar requests in the past, in line with his antiquarian researches. However, this request is different. It has a local hotel address, which means that Professor Kaye is in Rome already, keen to avail himself and his co-worker of our materials without delay. He specifically asks for access to any works that may make mention of the Magi and their gifts along with any works that offer alternative accounts of the death of Jesus.' Mercurio shook the letter. 'Is this a coincidence? I doubt it.'

'It suggests this professor is dangerously well informed, though it's hard to see how that is possible,' offered Richter thoughtfully. 'He may just be fishing - but I have an idea, if you will permit me, Your Eminence.'

'Go ahead, my son.'

'Tell this man that you are agreeable to granting him access to the archives under confidentiality agreement. Allow me to assist him closely as he pursues his enquiries. I will endeavour to make my services so indispensible that, when he leaves, I will be his first choice of companion if he proposes to conduct a search for the casket.'

The Cardinal stopped pacing. 'That is a good idea. Perhaps, if it does exist, he may even lead you to it. Yes! Go with my blessing and do not cease until you have utterly discredited the Lost Gospel of Basem or else retrieved this object and placed it directly into my hands. Counter any resistance with whatever force is appropriate. I will provide you with the means of diplomatic passage for a sidearm, as usual. Remember, however, that once you leave these grounds, the Vatican will deny any involvement in your activities, should they come under scrutiny or suspicion.'

The assassin's pale eyes gleamed as he placed a hand over his heart. 'Have no fear, Your Eminence. In the name of God, I will humbly obey.'

That evening in his hotel room, Richter stripped to the waist and stood in front of the bathroom mirror, gazing critically at the raised scar on his well-formed chest. Taking his time, he stropped his cut throat razor on a barber's leather, using long, deliberate strokes and, once satisfied with its sharpness, he ran boiling water from the hotel's mini-kettle over the steel to sterilise it. With extreme care, using the mirror as his guide, he made twelve deliberate cuts directly over existing parts of the scar, pausing between successive mutilations to stem the bleeding, disinfect each fresh wound and admire his handiwork.

Soon the skin would heal over, but he would particularly enjoy the period when his body's inflammatory response gave the scar a flaming, roseate hue. If only it would remain that colour permanently, he thought wistfully, it would look truly magnificent.

The new wounds overlaid many older ones, which with time, patience and the effects of tissue fibrosis, had formed the distinctive, raised shape of a star with twelve points - a star just like the one on the seal of Balthazar, just like the one he knew was engraved on the casket and just like the natural *naevus* with which every Keeper was born.

I am the rightful Keeper. The casket belongs to me. For too long, my line has been denied - I have been denied.

I – will – make – it – mine!

Facing the mirror, unblinking, Richter stared at the reflection of his self-made *naevus* and savoured his pain.

Derbyshire, England, October, 1962 AD

'Turn that infernal radio off; I can't concentrate!' grumbled Cyrus Dexter, putting the finishing touches to a rabbit snare he was constructing at the kitchen table. 'Utter rubbish they play nowadays,' he muttered under his breath, twisting the end of a piece of steel wire into a small loop and using pliers to wrap the end of the wire round and round itself to secure the loop.

'It's not rubbish,' contradicted Joanie, his wife, who stood at the sink, washing the dishes. Drying her fingers on her apron, she turned the volume up. 'It's the new Beatles single,' She plunged her hands back into the sudsy water to find the dishcloth and started to sing along to the words: 'Love, love me do... You know I love you...'

Abruptly, Cyrus stood, pushing back the wooden kitchen chair from the formica-topped table. 'I'm going out,' he said, dropping the snare and the pliers into his canvas kitbag and adding his thermos flask, already made up with hot, sweet tea.

'Bring me back a nice brace, then,' called Joanie after him as he shrugged on his hunting jacket and tweed cap.

'Aye, well, we'll see,' was the taciturn reply.

The door slammed and Joanie sighed. She had tried very hard to be a good wife and mother, but she was not sure how much longer she could continue. Something deep inside was eating away at Cyrus and his scheming, haunted look was beginning to scare her. She had stuck by him all through his time in the clink. One stupid mistake and he'd got himself caught. How was it that most thieves could get away with it time after time after time, but Cyrus couldn't even manage to pull off one job before the Bobbies had him banged to rights? And little Seth had only been a year old at the time. Neither he nor his father would ever get those three carefree, toddler years back - and she'd had to carry on alone, bringing up the child and managing the best she knew how.

And now, when he'd done his porridge, instead of spending precious time with his growing son, what devilry was the man up to? Every night it was the same. Come the dusk, he'd wolf down an early supper, make a couple of snares it shouldn't have taken more than an hour to set and then stay out for half the night. God knows where he went, but Joanie suspected it was within the boundary of the nearby Chaumont estate - the very place he had tried and failed to rob four years earlier. What a fool! If he was set on thieving, why not pick ordinary domestic homes in the nearby towns and villages? Why this crazy obsession with Chaumont? Every night she put Seth to sleep with a fairytale, only to lie awake herself, her open eyes staring into the dark, sure that the next knock on the door would be the local bobby to tell her Cyrus had been arrested for wilful trespass, poaching - or something worse.

Cyrus made his way through broom thickets to a remote section of barbed wire fencing at the northern end of Chaumont's grounds. The open fields were dry stone walled, but in the wooded areas, barbed wire fencing was a better protection against the nibbling teeth of roe deer. Throwing his kitbag over the fence first, he dropped down and squirmed through the gap he had previously made at the bottom.

Retrieving his kitbag, he wove through more broom, interspersed with rhododendron, hawthorn and wild privet which, as the land sloped downhill, was replaced by broadleaf woodland. The cover was good and he made quick progress southwards in the deepening dusk.

Reaching open land, he halted, crouching for a moment, his deep-set eyes searching the gloom. From here he could pick out the estate's distant stable blocks, with Chaumont Hall rising beyond them, a few lights shining out from its many windows. No doubt,

His Lordship, Kai Augustus Dexter, the fifteenth Earl of Chaumont, was ensconced in its warm, well-stocked library, while Cyrus Dexter remained an outcast, hunkering beneath the stark branches of an oak in the late October chill, unrecognised as the rightful Earl and owner of the land over which the authorities would claim he was trespassing with intent, should they ever catch him there. It was enough to make a man commit murder, he thought venomously.

His ancestors had all been patient men. Even his own father, when close to death, had told him to bide his time. In any case, it was too late now to think of murder.

Kai had enjoyed his opportunity to gloat, hadn't he?

First, he stuck the knife in by putting me away and then he viciously twisted it when I came out. Why else would that bastard have waited outside the gates of the prison on my release day if not to revel in declaring, as I took my first breath of freedom, that he'd hidden the casket where I would never find it?

Until Cyrus could discover where it was, Kai knew he was safe from physical attack. Only an idiot would kill the only goose that could lay the golden egg.

Cyrus was on a self-assigned mission. No matter how long it took, he would wait and watch - and eventually, he would see something; a trail he could follow or a document he could decipher; a slip of the tongue or an ill-considered and revealing action; something that would give him the tools he needed to begin the long journey home to his rightful inheritance. And if he failed, then Seth would have to continue where he left off. That was all there was to it.

No-one was visible, so Cyrus moved again, hugging the long evening shadows until he came to a tangled grove of yew close to the Dexter family crypt. Accessible down a steep flight of marble steps, the door to the crypt was never locked and the interior made a good place to hole up for a short while on chilly or wet nights. Sometimes he sat cross-legged on the cold, marble floor at the far end of the crypt, leaning back disrespectfully against the base of the first Earl's magnificent, monumental tomb. From there, he could beam his pocket torch onto any of the fourteen marble tombs that marched the length of the crypt in double ranks, to read the proud and lordly epitaphs of his reviled ancestral cousins. Kai's tomb was in place already, last on the left, nearest to the door - empty, but waiting. Its inscription would not be added until his corpse was laid within it. Oh, yes, thought Cyrus, that day will come...

That evening, he had not been inside the crypt long when he heard the unprecedented sound of footsteps descending towards the door. He leapt up and flicked off his torch. God help him if he was caught in here. Clutching his kitbag, torch and thermos, he dived for the nearest cover, the narrow gap between the wall and the third Earl's tomb, holding his breath as the door at the other end of the crypt swung open and a dark figure entered, holding up a storm lantern to illuminate the shadows.

Risking all, Cyrus lifted his head far enough to take a quick look over the top of the tomb, hoping that he was far enough from the flickering lantern to be invisible in the dim recesses of the chamber.

It was Kai...

What in hell's name was he doing here at this time of night?

Setting his lantern down between the armoured feet of the marble effigy of the twelfth Earl, Kai was completely oblivious to the hidden presence of his nemesis at the distant end of the crypt. He stood for a moment, contemplating his own tomb. His effigy already decorated the top of the lid, its head nestled peacefully on its marble pillow; its arms crossed over its chest. One finely sculpted hand gripped a flat-bladed archaeologist's trowel, whilst the other clasped an engineer's drawing in the form of a rolled up scroll.

Kai reached out and pulled off the end-piece of the marble scroll, carved to mask the fact that the scroll itself was hollow. Feeling inside his jacket, he drew out a piece of paper, rolled it tightly and inserted it carefully into the hollow marble cylinder. Replacing the end-plug, he nodded to himself in satisfaction. Who would think of searching for a document within an apparently solid marble statue? Retrieving his lantern, Kai turned and left the crypt, pulling the door closed behind him.

Cyrus smiled in the pitch black.

CHAPTER 9

A CITY OR A CROWN

12 miles West of Jerusalem, The Holy Land, August, 1192 AD

The bedraggled column of men, their armour rusted; their surcoats and mantles faded, struggled through the choking dust up the reverse contour of the low escarpment. Watching them from the height of its broad crest, Richard Coeur de Lion, King of England, Duke of Normandy and Count of Anjou, leader of the third crusade to the Holy Land, knew that the end must come soon. He was weary. It showed in the dull lustre of his eyes. In fact his whole army was weary. They were physically exhausted, fevered and famished. He turned slowly in the saddle, signalling to the mounted knight slightly to his rear.

'This will do.'

'As you command, Sire,' responded Sir John de Erleigh. Wheeling his mount away, the knight began to shout orders to bring the march to a halt. Further orders echoed down the column for commanders to make camp and secure the perimeter. Richard dismounted his black destrier, one of the few they had left. He discarded his helm to take advantage of the light evening breeze, glad to be free of its weight of chain mail. Fresh air cooling his sweat-damp brow, he stared at the sparse scattering of weakly fluttering lance pennants before scanning the landscape with its silhouetted mountains and valleys incised in dark relief against the deepening purple haze of dusk. Dropping to his knees, he silently cursed the arid dryness of the land God gave to Cain.

The wine-dark twilight gave way to the black velvet of a night sky. Aromatic oil lamps mingled their scents with the aroma of burnet tree branches aflame on camp fires, their light flickering off bouche shields bearing red, white and black crosses. Inside the hastily erected, red and white striped royal pavilion, Richard sat on his makeshift High Chair and looked down on a discontented assembly of noblemen and knights.

Bishop Fulk, a thin, scrawny man wearing the black cowl of his order, pointed an accusing finger at the King. 'You promised, Majesty. You promised that we would be in Jerusalem before this month end. Twice have we been within a few miles of the Holy City and been turned back by the Saracen Sultan, Saladin. Now, for a third time, the city is close; a mere twelve miles hence. Have we come this far only to falter - again?'

The accusing tone in the rasp of his voice and the rising murmurs of discontent from knights and noblemen brought Richard to his feet.

'Bishop Fulk, we will enter Jerusalem! But we are fatigued. The men need rest. Some require medical attention and all need food and time to recuperate.'

'And where, Majesty, do you expect to find food in the vast wasteland of this waterless desert? Saladin attacks and cuts off our supply lines at will from all quarters. He has scorched with fire all that lives and moves for a hundred miles in all directions. Pray, in God's name, where do you hope to find sustenance for your army?'

A figure near Richard rose quickly to his feet. 'Bishop Fulk, you are addressing your King; be mindful of your tongue!'

Bishop Fulk turned to confront the broad outline of the man who had admonished him, his voice heavy with sarcasm. 'Ah, Hubert Walter, holy Bishop of Salisbury, what would you know of such earthly matters as an empty belly? Perhaps you can provide manna where all others have failed?'

'Enough!' Stung by the vicious barbs directed at him, Richard strode to the centre of the pavilion, eyes flashing with anger. 'I will not have division within this camp. Bishop Fulk, be silent!'

Bishop Fulk defied the royal command. 'Majesty, you talk of division in the camp! Have you forgotten that it was your temper that led to the defilement of the banner of Leopold of Austria? The anger he roused in you because of his challenge to your leadership obliged him to depart with all his forces. And it was your constant quarrelling with Philip of France that caused him to withdraw from the crusade. In consequence his army is not here to support us in our time of need. With Leopold's and Philip's combined armies we could have been in Jerusalem by now, praying at the Church of the Holy Sepulchre! But, instead, we are alone, without allies. We are severely weakened and demoralised, while Saladin still sits behind the walls of the Holy City - and yet you talk to me of division?'

A steely edge crept into Richard's voice. 'Bishop Fulk, do not imagine that being wrapped in the vestments of the church lends protection from my wrath. Wag your venomous tongue once more and I, myself will cut it out and nail it onto the Golden Gate in Jerusalem!'

Bishop Fulk held Richard's glare for a moment, then tightened the cowl around his shoulders and bowed tersely before quitting the pavilion. Richard strode back to his chair, sprawled in it and stroked his unkempt beard. His outburst at Bishop Fulk had cowed the assembly to an uneasy, heat-stifled silence. Richard drank deeply from a pewter wine goblet, wiped his lips with the back of his hand and looked at the men whose guiding purpose in life was the fulfilment of his promise to restore Jerusalem to Christendom.

For the most part, they were gruff and unshaven; men coarsened by the atrocities of war, their scarred faces bearing testament to their familiarity with the edged weapons of the enemy. Their hair straggled dirtily and the once pristine accoutrements of their trade were showing serious signs of wear. Red crosses had leached to a light rust colour, black crosses were now grey and surcoats were dust-mottled, patched and stitched, no longer giving pretence of any shade approaching the purity of white.

Richard's roving eyes settled on Hubert Walter, Bishop of Salisbury. 'Well, Bishop, do you say more?'

A broad, rheumy-eyed man with a rotund, sweaty face, Hubert stood and said simply, 'No, Sire, I think the Church has had more than its say this night.' He bowed and sat down.

Richard's eyes shifted to settle on someone else. 'What about you, Robert de Sable? As Grand Master of the Knights Templar, you must have a view.' His eyes moved again. 'Or you, Geoffrey de Donjon, Master of the Knights Hospitaller, what say you?'

Both men stood and faced the King. Robert de Sable was the first to speak. 'Sire, under the sign of the red cross I bear witness to the truth of the words of Bishop Fulk. Our victories over Saladin have cost us dear and these past weeks the Saracens have been snapping at our heels, using our own captured knights to lure us into trap or ambush before disappearing into the desert and the mountains. The flower of Christian chivalry is slowly being bled to death.'

Now the balding, grizzled Master of the Hospitallers stepped forward. 'Sire, it would be foolhardy to try and take Jerusalem. We have fewer than fifty knights fit for combat and less than two thousand men under arms, including bowmen. Jerusalem is heavily fortified and even if, by some miracle, it were to fall, we would not be able to keep it rightfully in the Christian domain for long. Many who have fought this crusade at your side at Acre, Jaffa, Ascalon and Arsuf are weary of war and whether we take Jerusalem or not, they want to go back to their homes and their families. Saladin knows this. He is Sultan of all the lands about us, from Syria to Egypt. Another ill-timed, unsupported advance on the city would be disastrous. If we become surrounded, cut off from the sea, under siege…'

Richard held up his hand for silence. Leaning forward he gestured toward Sir John de Erleigh. 'Sir John, does the thought of attacking Jerusalem with a shattered, rag-tag army strengthen your resolve or weaken it?'

The tall, lithe knight, a trusted confidante of the King, pushed back his black shoulder length hair and stood up. 'Majesty, where you lead, my resolve is always strong!'

Richard smiled. 'Well said, Sir John.' He leaned further forward. 'But would you approach Jerusalem or withdraw to the coast?'

'You have sought counsel from wiser and more experienced ...'

'Never mind,' Richard interrupted him, 'It is of no consequence.' Standing, he raised his voice to the assembled knights. 'I will think on what has been said this night. You may retire.'

As the group began to file out of the pavilion with mutterings of dissent, Richard motioned to Bishop Hubert Walter and Sir John de Erleigh to remain. Unbuckling his long handled double-edged sword - the Épeé *Bâtarde*, or Bastard Sword, as they called it - he handed it to a servant. Another helped him out of his surcoat and knee-length, chain mail Hauberk shirt. Pulling on a loose fitting gown, he began to pace up and down.

'What ails you, Sire?' There was a hint of concern in Sir John de Erleigh's voice.

'What ails me, my friend? In the spring, my mother, Eleanor of Aquitaine, sent news that my brother, John, has England under the heel of tyranny. It has become common knowledge among the barons that he is desirous of the throne. You know this and yet you ask what ails me?' In rising agitation, Richard strode over to a long table, grabbed a rolled up parchment and brandished it in the air, his voice thickening in anger. 'And, now, this also ails me!' He slammed the parchment back on the table with a vicious downward swing of his arm. 'It came this very morn, from Archbishop Walter Coutances, with news that my treacherous queynte of a brother is openly plotting with Philip of France to steal my crown and put himself on the throne of England in my stead! Is that ailment enough for you, Sir John?'

Sir John was still struggling to find an answer when Bishop Hubert found one for him. 'Sire, I see you are truly between the horns of a dilemma. Remain here and you lose your crown. Return home and the cause of the crusade, Jerusalem, will be lost. If you were to seek my counsel, then I would say you should send a legation under a white flag of truce to Saladin. Despite rumours of his barbaric nature, he is, I am certain of it, an honourable man. He has great respect for you and will listen if you are willing to come to reasonable terms.'

Richard's rage began to subside and he sank into his chair once more. 'Honourable? How honourable?'

'Remember, Sire, that when your destrier fell under the lance of a Saracen at Arsuf, Saladin sent you two fresh mounts on which to continue the battle. And when, earlier this year, you and your army were near death with thirst and fever, it was Saladin to whom you appealed for aid. He sent fresh fruit and clean snow to melt for water.'

Sir John scratched his dank locks. "Why would an enemy on the verge of victory be merciful?"

'Because his faith, no less than ours, commands him to be merciful to the stricken,' replied Bishop Hubert, still looking at Richard, 'And because the character of the man is such that he would sooner lose an honourable battle than claim a dishonourable victory. He, too, must be weary of Jihad and needless slaughter, Sire.'

Richard hefted his sword in one hand, looking at the leopard of England stamped on the pommel. With his other hand he scooped up the discarded scroll and, employing his two hands as scales, he made the motions of weighing the paper against the steel.

Bishop Hubert seemed to echo Richard's thoughts with his next words. 'Sire, your crown - or Jerusalem. It seems you cannot have both. You must decide.'

2 Miles North of Jerusalem, The Holy Land, 20 August, 1192 AD

The molten midday sun pounded sand into glass on the anvil of the desert. Inside the hastily erected canopy, the lanky Sir John de Erleigh rubbed his hot eyes and looked across the table at the caped figure of Saladin's younger brother, Al-Adil - looked at the thin wisp of his beard, the rich fabric of his turban and the dark, determined face below it. To the right of Al-Adil sat Al-Harawi and Beha ed-Dīn, warriors, agents and advisors to Saladin. To Al-Adil's left was Imad ed-Dīn, secretary, interpreter and scribe. Five paces behind them stood six chain-mailed, iron-helmeted Kurdish men at arms, wearing belts that carried low-slung, curved scimitars. Their lances held rigidly upright, they watched with expressionless faces.

Sweating and puffy-faced in the afternoon heat, Hubert Walter, Bishop of Salisbury, waved his arms across the table littered with maps, drawings and scrolls. Picking up a map of the Eastern Mediterranean, he addressed Al-Adil. 'Richard will never give up the sea ports of Tyre, Acre, or Jaffa, or the towns and castles in the adjoining territories. And despite your argument and resistance, we insist that access and facilities with full protection be granted for Christian pilgrimage to the Holy Sepulchre.'

Al-Adil gave answer through the busily scrawling Imad. 'And if His Highness does not agree?'

Bishop Hubert answered quietly, his voice almost resigned. 'If His Highness is as desirous of a truce as you say, then he must come to terms. Richard cannot take Jerusalem from Saladin and Saladin cannot drive Richard out of the Holy Land. If he does not come to terms, perpetual war, death and misery will blight this land.'

Beha ed-Dīn responded. 'And what would your King say, were he present? Would he be as adamant?'

Sir John de Erleigh answered him quickly. 'We speak on his Majesty King Richard's behalf and we do his bidding. Let it be known and understood by all that, despite pressing matters in England that require his attention, his intent in temporarily departing the Holy Land is not an abandonment of his oath to the crusade of recovering the Holy Sepulchre for Christendom. He simply proposes a truce under treaty, to last three years; three months, three days and three hours from the commencement of the agreement. During this time the Christians will remain within their territory in peace, will make no excursions from it for warlike purposes and will not in any way injure or oppress the inhabitants of the surrounding country. On this, Richard will pledge his sacred word as King and will append his seal! But Saladin must confirm an inviolate peace between Christians and Saracens, guaranteeing all free passage and access to the Holy Sepulchre of the Lord without the exaction of tribute and with freedom to exercise free commerce.'

The tent was a clay oven, its occupants baked as dry as flat bread, but Al-Adil paused for some time in thought before answering. 'We have talked of much this day. We will place your proposals before His Highness. Despite their many differences, he holds your King in high esteem and will give his words weighty consideration. In ten days you will receive an answer…'

'Ten days is too long…'

'Ten days, no more, no less,' Al-Adil re-asserted. 'Many issues have arisen as a consequence of opposing religious beliefs and the resulting bloody conflicts. They are bitter and complex in nature. His Highness will need time to consult with his council and advisors. Ten days!'

Sir John de Erleigh and Bishop Hubert Walter glanced at one another and then both leant forward, arms on the table. 'Very well; ten days.'

CHAPTER 10

A CREEP IN THE CRYPT

Derbyshire, England, 2 June, 2016 AD

Eloi's grandfather, Cyrus, had told him an incredible fairytale when he was a little boy. Cyrus was long gone, now, the victim of a bizarre hunting accident when Eloi was only six - or so Lord Alexander Dexter, the sixteenth Earl of Chaumont, on whose land he was found, had claimed - an accident in which, inexplicably, Cyrus's own neck got caught in the very rabbit snare he had just set. The thin steel loop had sliced his jugular like a cheese wire cuts through ripe Stilton.

Eloi never forgave the Earl and never forgot the fairytale:

Once upon a time, there was a wicked Earl called Simon. He lived in a great manor house surrounded by green fields for as far as the eye could see, all of which he had earned by killing the boy who should have been king - and by killing the child-king's little brother, too. Simon's wicked deeds had made him so powerful and wealthy that, in his vanity, he thought himself more important than anyone else. All that mattered was what he wanted. His pride was even further puffed up by the fact that he was the secret owner of a golden casket of power that only one chosen son could inherit.

This rich and ruthless Earl ruled his household with an iron fist, but despite his wickedness, one day he was lucky enough to become the father of two handsome baby sons - identical twins born only two minutes apart! Yet the first time he saw his twin sons, instead of being delighted, he turned purple with fury.

A Creep in the Crypt

Simon happened to have a little star-shaped birthmark on his chest and had expected his firstborn son, Grimbald, to have one as well. Unfortunately, the elder boy had no such birthmark. It was the younger son, Godwin, who bore it. This didn't suit the Earl at all and he stomped about the manor house in a black mood for weeks, throwing the plates and cutlery on the floor and kicking the scullery maid in displays of petulant temper. He had grown so used to always getting what he wanted that he just couldn't accept that in this most important matter, his desires had been thwarted by fate, a force no man can control.

At last, he calmed down and began to think about the law that meant a man's firstborn son always inherited his title, lands and possessions when he died. He found it easy to decide he would break that law. But it would be hard to succeed without anyone finding out. If he was caught, the king would cut off his head for the scoundrel he was - and the wicked Earl had no desire to lose his head. So he came up with a very clever - and typically evil - plan.

The time came for the birth of his twin sons to be recorded in the kingdom's big birthday book, a way of ensuring that everyone in the land knew exactly who everyone else was and who their parents were and precisely when they had been born, which was particularly important in the case of twins, born only minutes apart. It was now that the Earl put his dastardly plan into action by telling a huge lie. He deliberately wrote his sons' times of birth the wrong way round in the big birthday book, so that it looked as though Godwin had been born first.

And because that lie became the kingdom's official record of his sons' birth, he succeeded in turning his younger son into his sole heir, disinheriting his true heir and denying him the title and lands that were his by right - and all because Grimbald lacked that little birthmark.

When Godwin grew up, Simon explained the truth to him and made him promise he would never tell a soul. This, the young man was only too happy to agree to, for, like his father, he was wicked, proud and greedy and did not wish to lose everything he now possessed. To make sure he would never lose his high and mighty position, he decided to do the most terrible thing. While his twin lived, there was always a chance he would discover the truth - and there was only one way to make sure that never happened. He would kill Grimbald!

Luckily, his murder attempt failed and the wronged Grimbald fled to safety, helped by the scullery maid, who revealed to him the truth about his birth. She had been present at the birth of the twins all those years ago and she knew perfectly well which child had been born first, long keeping that secret out of fear for her own life. A brave and honourable youth, Grimbald went on to enjoy a long, fruitful life and, in turn, passed on to his son the story of the injustice he had suffered. 'Someday,' he told his son, 'We shall win back what was stolen from us, there will be no more wickedness and we'll all live happily ever after'... the end.

Eloi had begged Cyrus for the rest of the story, because, like any five-year old, he knew that all fairytales had to have properly satisfying endings, but his grandfather had gruffly informed him that the rest of the story had yet to be written and that he would only understand the reason why when he was older.

Now, he was thirty two - and he understood perfectly, because his father, Seth, had explained everything to him on his twelfth birthday. Grandfather's fairytale was no fairytale at all. It was the story of his own ancestry and the end of the story would only be written when he took back what was rightfully his - the Earldom of Chaumont and the golden casket of *The Power*. His father had also told him that Grandpa Cyrus, always looking for ways to write the story's happy ending, had discovered a secret map hidden in a hollow stone cylinder on the tomb of Kai Dexter, the fifteenth Earl of Chaumont, a map that he believed must signify a route to the hiding place of the casket.

'Then why didn't he steal it?' the young Eloi had promptly asked.

'Because if the Dexters at Chaumont decide to check on it and find it missing, it might induce them to move the casket to a new hiding place, putting us back to square one. While the map remains in place, they'll assume no-one else has found it or has knowledge of it, so will have no reason to change the location of the casket.'

'But if the map shows where the casket is, why didn't gramps just go and get the casket?'

'Ah, there lies the nub of the problem. The map is a representation of an extremely localised route - tunnels and stairs, somewhere underground, your grandfather thought - but where in the wide world those tunnels and stairs might be, the map doesn't say. For all we know, they could be anywhere from Missus Mop's cellar to the cisterns below the legendary hanging gardens of Babylon. That's why, now and again, we need to make our own check on that map, the presence of which, in its original hiding place, acts as our guarantee that the casket remains wherever the infamous Kai hid it during the period when your poor grandpa was banged up in jail - I'd guess sometime around 1960. But we shouldn't remove the map until we know the general location we're aiming for. At that point, the map will complete the picture and that's when we'll steal it.'

'I'll find out what we need to know,' the boy asserted, methodically pulling the frantically waving legs off a daddy longlegs he had trapped in his fist. 'Leave it to me.'

'I'll have to,' agreed his father, slapping his left leg, which gave off the flat, plastic-and-metal sound of a prosthetic limb - the consequence of a calamitous car crash in his late twenties. Although able to walk, wearing the contraption, his gait was slow and awkward. He had been obliged to accept that his disability rendered him unlikely to be a firebrand when it came to the reclamation of the family birthright.

Instead, he had devoted himself to forging the young Eloi into a physically and intellectually able weapon; a human bullet with a double target - Chaumont and the casket. It was not enough merely to envy, plot and plan. It was time for the disinherited side of the Dexter family to reclaim their own and Seth was confident that his son was going to be the means by which this would be accomplished. All that mattered was the sweet taste of revenge - and after five hundred years of denial, revenge had become an ice cold dish. So he inculcated the boy with an unswerving commitment to the target, bathing him in the furnace of hate and hammering him with tough love and unrelenting training. Throughout that long process, Seth remained blindly convinced that he was working with the purest gold, never conceiving that, in the end, his substrate might prove to be a base metal containing poisonous impurities.

By a sorry quirk of fate, Eloi's inherently unstable mentality was that of a latent sociopath and psychopath and, as a result, his father's efforts served only to prime the fuse of the boy's highly intelligent and calculating form of insanity. In Eloi, resentment blackened to malice; resolution descended into obsession. And far from merely enhancing his personal self defence capabilities, his combat and weapons training reinforced his mindset as an amoral assassin and gave him the technical ability to plan and commit cold blooded murder.

Intellectually sharp, Eloi sought out and soaked up every morsel of knowledge that might help him reach his target, be it religious history; theology; genealogy, cartography or ciphers. In the process, he found that spiritual faith appealed to him on many levels, not least because of the mystic nature of *The Power*. Secretly, he began talking to God about his holy quest and in the fullness of time he heard a voice inside his head whispering back in answer, giving him advice, instruction and praise.

He was rapturously elated. The Lord God of old was with him! The whispers told him to seek employment for his killer's hands, doing the work of the Lord.

It was not long afterwards that he carried out his first contract for the Vatican.

Over time, backed by what those omnipotent whispers urged him to believe, Eloi conceived the certainty that, as well as his anticipated elevation to the seventeenth Earldom of Chaumont and ownership of the golden casket, he was being primed for an even higher destiny.

'You are of the blood of the Ancients,' the whispers reminded him. *'Don't let the lack of a birthmark stop you from believing you can be a true Keeper.'* From that point, it was only a short step to his final conviction - and God's whisper confirmed it.

'You shall have Chaumont, the casket and The Power. And you shall be The One with the ultimate choice - to gift life or withhold it!'

His exultation was complete.

Mine shall be the second coming of the Messiah!

God warned that if he embarked on this journey to personal divinity, he could trust no-one. *'Let any who oppose you feel my wrath through you,'* God whispered, *'For I am a jealous God!'*

Eloi thought about this. Aside from the current Earl of Chaumont and his daughter, who obviously needed to be removed, who else of the blood might be plotting to take his place? He could only think of one person. At first unwilling to believe that his own father would ever betray him, he nevertheless began to look for any telltale signs of incipient betrayal in his father's words. Seth's niggling disapproval of the way Eloi was leading his adult life began to achieve a new and damning significance.

I wonder, he thought; did you batter all that training into me, father dear, only so that I would obediently play patsy - under your constantly critical eye - while right from the start you planned to step in at the climax and steal the prize?

In time, his paranoia matured. His mind had long been consumed with burning suspicions and today, at last, he was going to test them out. Seth had commanded that it was time to check up on the map. On previous checks, Eloi had followed his father's precise instructions, never touching the rolled map inside the marble scroll but, instead, merely removing the scroll's lid and confirming the map's continued presence within. Now, it occurred to him that this was a useless practice. Without drawing it out and examining it, how could he be sure that it was Kai's genuine map and not a deception left there to make a fool of him? The answer was obvious, so this time he planned to defy his father. This time, Eloi would do what *he* thought was best - and, when he announced what he had done, Seth's reaction would reveal *his* true intent.

Eloi did not wait for dusk to cover his trespass - early morning was the best time for a brisk walk. No rabbit snare was going to choke him in the dark, thanks very much. Knowing the terrain as well as he knew his hymn book, he had no trouble picking a daylight route that he was content would never put him in the direct line of sight of any of Chaumont's staring windows. Anyway, he thought, it's a Sunday. The vile progeny of Godwin are probably still tucked up in their goose feather duvets, snoring off their Saturday night indulgences. Sleep on, he thought, rounding the reed-strangled rim of the lake and relishing the fact that one day soon he would find a way to extend that sleep eternally.

Having deliberately selected the north-western approach to the Dexter family crypt that avoided sight of the Hall, Eloi did not see the Earl exit from Chaumont via the conservatory door and make his way round one side of the formal garden, past the stables and on towards the rise that lay to his north, where a large copse of trees masked the crypt's pergola from view. Notwithstanding the temperance of the June morning, he was wearing a black coat out of respect for the dead, because his destination was the crypt. Although a Greek revival marble pergola had been added, above ground, in mid-Victorian times, the large burial vault commissioned by the first Earl early in the sixteenth century lay underground, with its door at the bottom of a steep row of steps. The site had probably been chosen because the topography of the land guaranteed good drainage down to the lake on the north-western side of the rise. From the pergola, there was a wonderful panoramic view of the lake and the woods rising beyond it.

Approaching from the south, Lord Alex Dexter climbed up the narrow woodland path through the beech trees towards the summit of the rise at the same time as Eloi Dexter ascended the same rise from the northern side, where he paused for a moment amongst a stand of ancient yew near the summit to admire the spectacular vista that he was certain would, one day soon, belong solely to him.

Circuiting the pergola to its northern side, the Earl reached the top of the steps that led down to the crypt and rested, slightly winded from his climb up the hill. It was his habit to recover his breath before entering the crypt to pay his respects to his wife. Charlotte's remains already occupied their joint stone tomb, a monument designed to accommodate both man and wife, so that, when his own time came, they would be together, always. Closing his eyes, he put his hands together and began to pray, sad that his daughter, Sam, lacked the strength of faith in spiritual redemption from which he took comfort. Perhaps she would come to it in time.

Eloi finished his climb through the yew and came in sight of both the marble pergola and the Earl, who stood facing the steps with his head bent in prayer and his back towards Eloi. Eloi's calculating mind raced. There couldn't be a better opportunity - a secluded spot with no witnesses - the easy contrivance of an unfortunate 'accident' using those marble steps as the weapon - why wait? He took a deep, silent breath, darted up the few yards of grassy slope that separated him from his intended victim and, both hands connecting with the middle of his victim's back, shoved the unwary Earl forwards, hard. The force of the impact expelled the air from the Earl's lungs and he gave a low *whooph* as he shot forward and down.

His assailant watched him topple, missing the first nine or ten steps entirely before touching ground, his momentum then carrying him head first down the last few steps to crack his temple on the marble flags at the bottom. His body crumpled limply and blood slowly began to pool around his head. After waiting for a few moments, Eloi followed more sedately down the steps. Straddling the still form, he bent to feel for a pulse at the neck. Pleased to find none, he judged that the angle and force of impact had caused instantaneous death, with the cervical vertebrae slamming through the base of the Earl's skull into his brain. It was a most satisfactory outcome.

'That's payback for gramps,' he told the dead man.

Taking a handkerchief from his pocket, he wiped Alex's neck where he had touched it, then tucked the rag away again and returned up the steps for reassurance on the matter of witnesses. He need not have worried. The only source of movement in the vicinity was the dew-fresh morning sunlight dancing a jig on the rippling water of the lake below. Eloi's mouth twitched in gratification and he descended again, stepping lightly over the late Earl to enter the crypt. Closing the door behind him and pulling out his torch, he flicked it on and went directly to the marble scroll.

Depositing the torch on the cold marble belly of the Earl's incomplete effigy, he unplugged the scroll and slid two fingers inside its hollow tube to withdraw the contents. Illuminating the unrolled map in the beam of the torch, he saw that the description passed down from his grandfather had been entirely correct. The drawing did look like a complicated set of underground passages, although he supposed it could represent alleyways - or rabbit runs, even, for that matter - and it also had a number of intriguing scribbled annotations. It was the real deal; that was the main thing. Just as he was re-rolling it to return it to its hiding place, God, in His wisdom, whispered to him.

'You have scattered your enemies with your mighty arm! Now receive my blessing and the great gift I give unto you. Use it well, my son.'

'Thank you, great Lord of Hosts; oh, thank you,' he murmured breathlessly, briefly throwing back his dark-haired head and raising his eyes until their grey irises almost disappeared from view, leaving the blank, white sclera prominent. Now that he was dead, the Earl would no longer be checking up on this map - so there was no need to leave it here. This was God's gift to him!

What about the Earl's daughter? She was an enemy he had yet to confront. Did she know about the map? Even if she did, she was going to be too distraught over her father's demise to worry about it. The map was probably only a secondary backup, in any case. For a moment or two he contemplated the practicality of abducting Samantha Dexter. He knew, in great detail, the methods that the Inquisition had once employed to extract confessions from heretics.

If she knew the casket's location, those same methods would easily wring that truth from her lips. And afterwards, he could fashion an ingeniously original end for her - something so exquisitely agonising that the bitch would beg to die...

Think about that pleasure later. Right now, concentrate on clearing up and getting out of here.

Folding rather than rolling the map, he tucked it into the zip pocket of his lightweight camouflage jacket, re-topped the hollow marble scroll, shook out his handkerchief again and wiped the marble wherever he might have touched it. Confident that no evidence of his presence remained, he retrieved his torch and left the crypt, flicking off the beam as he exited and stepping casually over the Earl's corpse to climb the steps and make his way quickly and cautiously north towards the estate's boundary.

Seth was purple with anger. 'You did *what*?' Eloi had just told him of the morning's events and of bringing Kai's map away with him.

'You hate it when I use my initiative, don't you, father?'

'You kill a man on the spur of the moment and call it initiative?'

'It had to be done sooner or later.'

Groaning, Seth wiped his open hand down his face in an agony of indecision. 'Maybe it did. I just don't think now was the right time - and you did it without getting any information about where the casket is!'

'I'll get that from the girl - all in good time.'

'But the map - that was an error of gargantuan proportions! Unless you've made discoveries you haven't told me about, we still have no idea what location that map relates to - so all you've done is make it close to certain that Samantha Dexter *will* find it gone and *will* move the casket. After all I've told you - I can't believe your stupidity. I've raised a bloody moron!'

'No. You've raised a man who knows what he's doing and isn't afraid to do it, unlike you. You just want me to be a pawn under your control, don't you? But you don't have the guts for the dirty work it'll take to get our inheritance back! And even when I've bathed in the blood of our enemies to reach the target, you still won't be satisfied, will you? Don't think you've got me fooled any longer. You haven't!' Eloi screamed in his father's face, his own face white with fury and his eyes sulphurous.

Seth took a shying step back, shocked by his son's vehemence. 'You're out of control, Eloi,' he blustered.

'Ah, yes! Control! That's the keyword, isn't it? You manipulating bastard! Think I'm your bloody puppet - and at the end of the show you can just snip my strings? Snip-snap!' Eloi made snipping scissors out of two fingers of his left hand and waved them wildly in Seth's face. 'Think I'm going to let you see me off so you can be Lord Muck and play God with *The Power*? Think I don't know your game? Fuck you! *I'm* going to be the God, not you!' and with those words, Eloi flicked the thump lever to release the blade lock on the Falcon Stiletto pocket knife he had been hiding in his closed right fist.

Closing in on his father with one swift step, he viciously slid the five inch blade between Seth's ribs at just the right angle to pierce his heart. Seth's eyes opened wide in shock and disbelief as he fell to the floor. He was dead within moments.

After his violent act of patricide, Eloi sat down on a kitchen chair and forced himself to perform breathing exercises until his temper cooled. God began whispering to him again, telling him not to worry.

'Your father betrayed you. He deserved to die. Remember My words in the Old Testament: I will render vengeance unto Mine enemies! Unlike your earthly father, I will never betray you, for I love those who love Me.

'Your conquests are righteous, My son - and see, you have vanquished two of your three key threats in just one day! What you must do now is to cleanse this dwelling place with healing flames - just one more tragic accident.

'For the Lord loves justice and does not forsake His godly ones; they are preserved forever; but the descendants of the wicked will be cut off!

'Everything is going to be alright - perfectly alright.'

CHAPTER 11

DOUBLE-EDGED GIFTS

Church of the Holy Sepulchre, Jerusalem, The Holy Land, 2 September, 1192 AD

Saladin watched from his slightly raised dais as a white and yellow robed messenger ran into the courtyard of the Church of The Holy Sepulchre to throw himself upon the ground, arms outstretched. The Sultan inclined his head, giving the man permission to speak. The messenger came to his knees, head bowed and said quietly, 'Your Highness, the Franks draw near. They are at *Bab el Amud* - the Damascus gate on the north wall.'

Under the clear blue sky of early morning, Saladin's face remained impassive beneath his conical, mailed qipehaq helm. It was the face of a man weary of the futility of war; tired of fighting a valiant, stubborn, but beaten enemy, whose refusal to accept defeat had wounded his army deeply and drained him of resources. Small and frail, with a short, neat beard, he was seated on a simply carved Lebanese pine chair. Behind him, as if protecting the steps leading into the Holy Sepulchre itself, his double-ranked personal guard of armoured Mamluks stood motionless but alert. To either side of him stood his council of Isfahirs and Ustadhs, army leaders and senior commanders. Further away, on both sides, small clusters of Amir Jandars, the governors of important citadels, sat cross-legged on richly patterned Persian rugs. Each pattern bore one deliberate error in its weave, for only Allah was perfect.

Hearing the hostile roar of distant crowds, he turned to his younger brother, Al-Adil, who tried to look appropriately apologetic.

'My Lord, thousands line the streets of the city all the way up from the Via Dolorosa crossroads. They voice the animosity and anger which they have long harboured against these invaders. Many are eager to avenge the wrongs they have suffered, particularly those who are friends and relatives of the hostages who were massacred at Acre by the infidel Richard. Do you wish them silenced?'

'No!' Saladin's response was sharp. 'Let them bay. Anger is no longer anger when it is spent. Perhaps, when they come to know the Franks a little better, their mood will change.'

Imad ed-Dīn, Saladin's secretary, bowed as he uttered softly, 'My Lord, they are here.' The brassy, clarion call of trumpets and the heavy, rhythmic beat of kettledrums announced the entry of the Franks, as the huge courtyard gates with iron studs were pulled open. Their small procession, escorted by Kurdish lancers, entered slowly, keeping wary eyes on the Mamluk guards lining the base of the courtyard walls. Drawing close to Saladin, Sir John Erleigh, Bishop Hubert Walter and the accompanying knights knelt with due respect.

The Sultan stood, extended his arms and spoke, using Imad as his interpreter. *'Assalaam alaikum* - in the name of Allah the most beneficent and compassionate, I bid you welcome. Knights of the cross, you kneel before me as foes. Rise as friends.' Imad clapped his hands and waved for seating to be brought. Saladin continued. 'What news of your King, Richard Coeur de Lion?'

Sir John Erleigh rose to answer. 'Your Highness, most powerful amongst the most powerful, I beg to inform you that although His Majesty is still bedridden with fever, his condition is improving. He commands me to convey to you and this assembly his greetings, felicitations and most humble apologies, for his absence on such a momentous occasion grieves him sorely.'

Saladin smiled a touch thinly.

'Highness, His Majesty also commands that in his name I make fair and rightful exchange of sealed documents for the agreed declaration of truce.' Sir John Erleigh presented the document of truce to Imad, who read it aloud and bowed before passing it on to his Sultan. Saladin's equivalent was flourished and it too was read aloud, ending with the rejoinder that the truce, thus agreed upon, was to continue in force for three years, three months, three weeks, three days and three hours and that, at the end of that period, both parties would be considered released from all obligations arising under the Peace of Ramla and that either was then at liberty to resume the war.

Sir John Erleigh beckoned to one of his knights, who came forward bearing a long slim package wrapped in white Damask silk. Sir John Erleigh slowly un-wrapped it and bowed to Saladin. 'King Richard has commanded me to gift you this, his battle sword, not as a token of surrender, but as an act of faith in your word that he has no further cause to use it.'

Saladin's dark eyes glistened as he viewed the jewels set into the quillion of the long-handled sword. Drawing it part way out of its scabbard, he traced with his fingertip the fuller - the blood gutter - of the Épée *Bâtarde* that had dispatched so many of his warriors to Paradise.

As Sir John Erleigh slowly withdrew, Imad said quietly to Saladin, 'My Lord, Richard has gifted you his oath and honour, bound up in his sword. It would be customary to return a gift equally valuable, equally precious.'

Saladin glared at his secretary. 'Give me the solution, not the problem,' he muttered.

Thinking rapidly on his feet, Imad murmured, 'Highness, I am led to understand there is a small but richly worked gold chest or casket...'

'A gold casket...Where?'

'Locked in a crypt beneath this church, I am told.'

'Have it brought to me. I will judge its worth.'

In celebration of the truce, the feast in the citadel was well under way. Imad entered the banquet hall at the head of a small procession. He bowed before Saladin, who sat cross-legged on tasselled silken cushions behind a low table laden with grain-stuffed roasted pigeons, herbed goats' cheese and ripe black dates.

'Highness: the casket.'

He ushered forward a slightly built, middle-aged, grey-templed man of scholarly demeanour, wearing white cotton robes and carrying a package swathed in linen. The man bowed nervously before placing the object on the table and unwrapping its swaddling to reveal the dull lustre of old gold. Saladin stopped eating, wiped his hands fastidiously and scrutinised the casket before carefully picking it up, as though by testing its weight he could put a monetary value on it. Replacing it on the table, he enquired, 'And to whom did this belong?'

Imad answered, 'It is a treasure of *el kuds esh sherif* - of Jerusalem, the Holy City itself, My Lord.'

Saladin straightened, his thin lips parting in a smile. 'If it belonged to the city - then it is now mine. How did Jerusalem come by such a treasure?'

Imad beckoned to the scholarly man who hovered behind him. 'With respect, my Lord, this theologian, Abdul Hamid, lay-servant of the Praised One, is perhaps best placed to answer such questions.'

The scholarly man took two paces forward and knelt before the Sultan. 'My Lord, no-one knows its origin. It has been in Jerusalem longer than living memory.'

Saladin looked at the casket more closely, drawing a thin bladed knife from his belt to point at the centre crest. 'This sun emblem with its strange markings - what does it represent? It's not Arab, Jew, or Frank.'

Hamid stared hard at the floor. 'No, my Lord. It is ancient; believed to be Indo-Persian, but there is no certainty.'

Saladin's eyes glinted dangerously. 'How do you know this, scholar? And tell me, why is such a treasure kept in darkness, away from the eyes of men?'

Hesitating, Abdul Hamid struggled to find suitable words. 'It is said that it possesses... mystical properties. Both the priests and the imams bow to custom and legend, so the casket remains hidden underground, where it has been for hundreds of years, barred with an iron gate in a kokh crypt beneath the Church.'

'Has anyone ever encountered the so called *mystical* properties of this box?'

'No, my Lord.'

'Seen them; felt them?'

'No, my Lord.'

'Heard them; smelled them?'

'No.'

'Then what is there to fear?'

'Beyond the fear, there is a legend, my Lord, which says that so long as the casket is safe in *el kuds esh sherîf*, the city can never fall.'

Saladin snorted in laughter, his mirth echoed by his courtiers until he held up one hand for silence. 'Jerusalem fell when the armies of Allah forced the Frankish Kafir, Balian of Ibelin, Lord of Nablus, to abandon the Holy Citadel… perhaps the legend fled with him into the desert to wither and die.' There was more laughter.

Imad bit his lip. If the casket was not acceptable he would be obliged to miss the feast to locate an alternative gift for the Christian King. Thinking quickly, he said persuasively, 'Highness, if the city can fall whilst under the safeguard of this casket, then it can fall again, perhaps next time back into the hands of the crusading Franks. Better it were gone!'

Uncertainly, Saladin turned back to the casket. 'I want no rumours of further danger spreading about the city. The people are restless enough as it is.' His face lightened. 'This object is not revered of Islam or Christianity, so if I gift it together with its supposed mystic protective powers to Richard Coeur de Lion, as a material token of my respect, then in truth I am gifting only a pagan protection that is proven to have failed already. This is perfect!'

On hearing these words, Abdul Hamid prostrated himself before Saladin, his voice pleading. 'Highness, I beg of you; do not send the casket out of the Holy City. Or, if you choose to gift the casket to the infidel King, please gift me with it!'

Taken by surprise, Saladin leaned back. 'Why would you ask this of me?'

'My Lord, I am the designated guardian of the casket and for years have made deep study of its strange symbols and markings. To be parted from it would deprive me of my life's work and cause me much distress.'

'Are you learned in such things?'

'My Lord, I speak Hebrew, Arabic, Latin and Greek. I have an understanding of the language of the Franks. I am versed in many sciences and...'

'Enough.' Saladin cut him off. 'You are a free man, are you not?'

'Yes, my Lord.'

'If I were to gift you to Richard, you would become no more than a chattel chained to this gold box and the vexatious ways of the Kufaar for the rest of your days. Is that your wish?'

'My Lord, I have always been a slave to my work, so it matters nothing to me where I go or under whose aegis my humble and worthless efforts continue.'

'Pray, what of your family? If I gift you, they must go with you!'

The sorry fellow came to his knees, 'Highness, my wife died during the siege of Jerusalem. I have just one son, Haleem, who is a good boy and devout of his duty. He will do his father's bidding.'

'My Lord,' interjected Imad, impatient to join the revellers who were fast emptying the bread baskets and meat platters, 'Why not send both casket and scholar to Richard and advise him, with diffidence, to keep them ever near him, so that he may be the first to benefit should the scholar complete his understanding of the mystic powers of the casket. It will not have escaped you that this Abdul Hamid will then be in an ideal position to keep us well informed about our erstwhile enemy's future intentions.'

Saladin's eyes twinkled. He raised a goblet of freshly iced water and drank deeply. Dabbing his lips with a delicate white cotton cloth, he nodded decisively. 'Let it be so. Give the golden casket - and this man and his son - to the Knights Templar to take to King Richard.' He pointed a thin forefinger at Abdul Hamid and said, 'Do not fail me. It is the will of Allah!'

Double-Edged Gifts

The Ionian Sea, One Day's Sail East of Acre, 9 October, 1192AD

The last pink streak of dawn was sweeping the decks of the caravel-built hull of the buscia magna *Frankenenef* as she yawed and pitched on the growing swell of the sea. Richard Coeur de Lion steadied himself, gripping the hand rail up on the forward castle deck and fighting a surge of nausea as he tried to catch a last glimpse of the smudged white sails disappearing over the horizon to the west.

Baldwin de Bethune, Count of Aumale, the only other man on the deck, clutched his heavy cape tightly to his body. A tall, lean, angular man with thick brown hair and hawk-like features, he growled pensively, 'There goes what remains of your army, Sire. God speed them on their way to England; would that we could be with them.'

Richard nodded. 'They will need all the help God can spare, with corsairs swarming along the North African coast and Philip of France's war ships prowling on the approaches to the Straits of Gibraltar. I hear Philip also has ships deployed throughout the Bay of Biscay -with some sightings even as far north as the English Channel. That is why I ordered our vessel to part from the fleet. I cannot risk capture, nor do I intend to fall into the hands of Philips's allies. Tomorrow, God willing, we shall make landfall at Corfu, where we shall alight in favour of a smaller vessel and sail for Aquileia in the Adriatic. From that port we hope to make safe passage overland as pilgrims to Saxony - and thence home.'

Baldwin's eyes narrowed. 'The Adriatic is controlled by Henry, Emperor of Byzantium, who bears us no friendship. Germanic soil will also be hostile and our company is small - I fear it will prove a hazardous journey, Sire. We could do with the likes of Sir John de Erleigh and Hubert Walter among our numbers.'

Richard eased the bulk of his robust frame away from the ship's rail. 'They will land on English soil ahead of us. I have entrusted them with the task of forestalling John's treacherous alliance with Philip to depose me and steal my crown.'

Baldwin de Bethune lurched with the rolling of the ship. 'Bishop Walter seemed quite taken with Abdi... Abu...'

'Abdul is the man's name.' Richard gave a one-sided smile. 'Abdul Hamid and his son, Haleem - indeed, they make an interesting pair. They seemed strangely content with Saladin's decision to attach them to his gift. The Bishop thinks the learned Hamid can teach us much about the ways of the infidel. Personally, I'm convinced that the Saracen schemers had some ulterior motive for gifting them to us along with that golden casket.'

'Perhaps, Majesty: nevertheless, the casket was a magnificent gift, with or without Hamid and his son. I'm inquisitive - what is your plan for them if, as we fervently pray, the fleet comes safe to the shores of England?'

The creak of the rigging and the flapping of the fore and aft lateen sails momentarily distracted Richard as he grasped the hand rail again. 'I am told it is Saladin's personal wish that they remain always close to the casket, ostensibly that the scholar may continue his esoteric researches concerning its supposed mystic powers of protection. Consequently, I have issued Bishop Walter with an edict that the scholar and his son be housed in the Tower...'

Baldwin expressed little surprise. '...As prisoners, Sire?'

'Not as such. Hamid is an oddity from a distant land with no means of self support, which makes him and his son my - responsibility - shall we say? My edict is for his protection. In the Tower he will be afforded quarters and a small stipend and will be allowed to continue with his scholarly studies. The casket will be placed in the treasury, but it will not be counted as being *of* the treasury - and I have instructed the Bishop to keep an ever watchful eye on all the elements of our new gift. Being a man of true Christian faith I have little time for mysticism, but Saladin has shown himself to be an honourable man, so respecting his wish is the least we can do. No doubt, given time, both men will become part of the established order and be forgotten - swallowed whole into the administrative belly of the crown.'

The Captain of the *Frankenenef*, a Greek of sullen countenance who wore long flowing robes, a red turban and a black cummerbund with a long curved knife thrust into it, climbed the wooden stair that led up to the castle bridge and bowed before Richard. 'Lords,' he said gruffly, pointing towards the south-west, 'Rough weather soon come - you go below where safe, please?'

Richard looked at the Captain, then at Baldwin de Bethune. There was rancour in his voice as he queried rhetorically, 'After the storm of the Saracens, what ill can these waters do?'

As the *Frankenenef* continued to yaw and pitch its way toward the rocky island of Corfu, banks of ominous storm clouds began to darken the face of the Ionian Sea. The rising winds soon had them scudding towards the Adriatic, where the storm would exact a heavy toll.

CHAPTER 12

HOW BIG IS A NUCLEAR BOMB?

Rome, Italy, 19 June, 2016 AD

'So far, so good,' whispered Kaye to Sam as they left the office of Monsignor Rafaello de Luca, Prefect of the Secret Archives of the Vatican. 'Mercurio excelled himself this time - getting us through the red tape this fast. Jury's out on the chaperone - but if he can speed things up a bit for us...' He trailed off as their new companion came within earshot.

Having confirmed the academic nature of their request and described what sort of material they were seeking, Kaye and Sam had signed confidentiality agreements covering all documents housed under the Vatican Museum's Cortile della Pigna, in the underground, custom-built, two-storey archive generally known as the Bunker. The Vatican Archives were located in several different sites within the Apostolic Palace, but the Bunker was reserved for parchments requiring controlled humidity: works of great age or value and documents of a particularly sensitive or provocative nature. They had been careful to omit any mention of a gold casket and gave, as their reason for seeking archival access, the pursuit of an academic project 'tracing the supplementation of early Christian writings with non-doctrinal material of questionable origin, whether fanciful or derived from earlier pagan myths'.

Rather unusually, the Prefect had assigned another lay researcher to facilitate their search for useful material, introducing him as Doctor Raoul Richter, a theological historian. 'You will find this gentleman well versed in the physical locations of texts relevant to your inquiry,' de Luca explained. 'He has already been here for several months, conducting research on topics not dissimilar to those in which you accord an interest. I wish you *buona caccia* - good hunting - and trust this arrangement will prove mutually beneficial.'

Richter shook hands with them and smiled. Looking into his evenly tanned face as she took his hand, Sam's first impression was antipathetic, for no good reason save that Richter's smile was restricted solely to his lips; it never touched his unusually pale grey eyes, which retained a dissociated yet intense look that Sam found disconcerting.

'I'm so pleased to meet you, Doctor,' he said to Kaye. 'I've come across some of your work in the Journal of Codicology and Paleography. I believe we have a mutual friend in Professor Fred Heyes at the University of London.'

'Fred Heyes?' echoed Kaye, caught off-balance. 'Jolly good.' He could not place Richter within the circle of academic palaeographers he knew, nor recollect coming across any papers published in the field by anyone of that name. 'Fred's very strong on middle English and medieval genealogies. I've a lot of time for him,' he commented, making a mental note to phone Heyes and ask about Richter. It was embarrassing to be caught at a professional disadvantage. 'How do you happen to know him?'

'He was most helpful to me in some projects I've been working on,' answered Richter. 'Medieval inheritance laws; ancient family trees; some documents in middle English I had trouble with; that kind of thing.'

'But that's not your current interest?'

'No: here in Rome I've been working on a long term project looking at the reasons why some gospels and epistles were assimilated whilst others were rejected for inclusion in the main theme doctrines of the early Church. This has led me to a study of several documents I think you will find particularly challenging. I'd like to start by showing you the Lost Gospel of Basem, since, amongst other surprises, it offers a very unusual rendition of the crucifixion and ascension of Christ. It's believed to date from around 50 AD but was almost certainly not written by a Christian. Shall we..?' and with that, he opened the Prefect's office door and ushered them out ahead of himself.

Richter's arctic eyes bored into the small of Sam's back as she strolled on ahead, innocently admiring the stately, historic buildings of Vatican City, their terracotta and white beauty set against the lush viridian of the manicured gardens they were traversing en route to the museum under which the Bunker lay. It had been hard to hide his flicker of recognition when de Luca had introduced them, minutes ago. He could barely believe his good fortune.

Just because she has a little star on her breast, she thinks the destiny of mankind is in her hands. But she is ignorant of how she figures in my plans and her blind hubris will be her downfall.

The Lord God hath delivered unto me mine enemies in confirmation that my righteous accession is His omnipotent and indisputable will!

The Power of The One shall usher in the Day of Judgement - and this woman shall be judged according to her wrongs!

Sam and Kaye sat in a secluded reading room deep inside the Bunker, to which Richter had brought the Lost Gospel of Basem and a script written by a certain Father Aloisius of Veronia in the late twelfth century. Kaye's translations confirmed, in both his and Sam's view, that the casket mentioned in the texts was undoubtedly Balthazar's - the one they sought. Nor did it escape their attention that the emblem on the back page of Basem's gospel was a match to the one figuring as the centrepiece to their mystery. They glanced at one another when Kaye turned the last page and found it there, but his slight frown was sufficient to prevent Sam from passing comment.

'This part bothers me,' he muttered, pointing to the section Basem had written about the raising of Lazarus. 'Look how it makes a mockery of one of the holy miracles of Jesus!'

'Oliver,' said Sam, 'You've probably never questioned your faith. You accept what the Bible teaches, so I realise how difficult it must be for you to swallow what's written here.' She bit her lip, not sure how much to tell him. 'Trust me, there's more to this than meets the eye - I have a personal letter you don't know about that will shed some light - I'll show it to you later. I think you should keep an open mind.'

Registering Sam's reference to a letter whose existence she had not previously divulged, Kaye blinked, filing the fact away without comment. 'You don't understand,' he countered. 'This Basem claims it was Balthazar's intervention that raised Lazarus. Even allowing for leeway in translation, his script suggests that God's healing power came from the casket, via Balthazar, to Jesus. I can't accept that. It's hard enough to believe that Balthazar actually remained in Galilee with Jesus, though I concede that's possible - and I'll even allow that the casket may have been proffered as a gift supposedly conferring power to the Messiah - but to imbue it with the healing power of God? No, that's ridiculous.'

Yet even as he was speaking, his mind flashed back to the ninth Earl's impassioned note concerning the death of his son, Jasper and it occurred to him that on the basis of Basem's assertions, a very different interpretation of that note was now possible - one where George spent all night trying to open the casket because there *was* some power inside it that would enable him to save their son's life. Kaye found himself suffering the beginnings of a crisis of faith - and did not like it one bit.

'If that part gets your goat, you must be absolutely livid about the later section covering the crucifixion,' said Sam. 'I mean, if Jesus didn't die on the cross, how can he have been resurrected? And if he wasn't, doesn't that run contrary to the very core of your faith?'

'Yes,' replied Kaye, trying not to sound acerbic. 'Unfortunately, it also makes a horrible kind of sense - if Christ's body really is inside that tomb in Syria. One might conjecture that Balthazar took him north to Damascus, well away from Roman Judea and its attendant dangers and that, ultimately, he died there. But I'm finding all this very difficult to come to terms with, Sam. I'll need time to think about it.'

'Who was Basem, do you think?' interposed Richter, softly. He had been sitting so quietly at the end of the glass-topped table where they had laid out the precious manuscripts that they had almost forgotten he was there.

Kaye shook his head to clear it. 'This gospel has been dated to around 50 AD, you say? That's twenty years after the crucifixion. So,

Basem had to be someone who either knew Jesus or had the story related to him by someone who had known Jesus.'

'That makes sense,' agreed Sam. 'But no-one named Basem appears in the Bible, so I doubt if Basem knew Jesus well enough to be a first-hand witness. Just a minute...' She quickly scanned the Lazarus section of the translation again. 'According to this, the only person inside Lazarus's tomb with Jesus was Balthazar, so only they could have known the details of what happened in there. Surely it's more likely that if Balthazar was with Jesus to the end, as this gospel suggests he may have been, it would have been Balthazar who passed on the story to Basem. Perhaps Basem was a close friend of Balthazar...' She paused; '...Or his son.'

His son...

Sam's mind revolved. Her father had predicted she would reach the point where she wanted to take on the Keeper's mantle - was this the beginning of that epiphany? If Balthazar was a Keeper and Basem was his son, Basem was probably a Keeper too. And if the Keeping of the casket always passed down the same family line, across all the centuries to her father and finally, to her, as evinced by the star on her chest, then she was looking at something written almost two thousand years ago by one of her own direct ancestors. What an incredible thought! And Basem was perfectly clear about what the casket held - the power to redeem death. Not only that, but it was obvious that Balthazar knew exactly how to access that power and had done so successfully; so if she could discover the casket and the trick of opening it... could she use that power too?

'Well, Doctor Richter...' began Kaye, his voice bringing Sam back from her reverie.

'Do call me Raoul.'

'Thanks, Raoul. Sam's suggestion may have merit, but whoever Basem was, it comes as no surprise that this gospel never made it past the Council of Nicaea, does it?'

'No indeed. In fact, I think it was rejected far earlier. But I have to say that, as a consequence of coming across it, I was quite intrigued by the casket it mentions and this other, much later, document appears to offer a possible hint as to the fate of that object.' Richter indicated Aloisius's scroll. 'The casket seems to have acquired the cachet of a sort of latter-day Ark of the Covenant in some respects. Could God have used it as a tool to help his only Son? What do you think?'

Kaye was stumped. The question was phrased innocently enough, but was it the product of a hidden agenda? Why had Richter picked up on the matter of the casket so quickly? Then again, anyone reading this would be bound to wonder about the object of Godly power that the writer claimed had taken centre stage in a miracle of Jesus. Finally, he answered, 'I don't think we have any corroborating evidence that might help with that question at present. Let me read Aloisius's text again.'

Kaye tapped a finger on the annotation Aloisius had made concerning the Crypt of the Casket, located somewhere unspecified in the labyrinthine vaults of the Church of the Holy Sepulchre. 'It looks as if some casket - perhaps the same one; perhaps not - was taken as war booty by Saladin.' He paused, remembering that one of Sam's scrolls was a letter from Saladin's brother to one Abdul Hamid, who had accompanied Saladin's gift to Richard the Lionheart. Was the Saladin connection a coincidence? Or, considering the fact that at some point the casket must have come to England in order to end up belonging to Sam's family in Derbyshire, could Saladin's gift, in fact, have been Balthazar's casket? He concluded that it was entirely possible, but did not want to voice the thought in front of Richter.

'Have you come across anything else you think might interest us?' he enquired. Turning to the last page of the vellum-bound book that held Basem's gospel, he revealed the sunburst seal and said, 'For example, I wonder whether, during your research here, you happen to have noticed any other documents that include this emblem? I think it may be associated with a sect of non-conformist zealots who evinced an alternative version of the holy truth, much as Basem perpetrates in his gospel.'

Sam smiled at Kaye's fabrication, but did not contradict him. He was just being sensibly cautious.

Richter rubbed a chin that was developing a haze of stubble as the day wore on. Cardinal Mercurio had mentioned that the Vatican he␣d a few other documents sealed with the Mark of *The Power*, but he would need time to ask where they could be found. 'I might have come across something similar, somewhere,' he lied. 'Let me have a think and another look in some of the cupboards I've explored over the last few weeks. Perhaps by tomorrow I'll be able to help you out with that enquiry.'

'Much appreciated,' said Kaye politely.

'Shall we call it a day for today, then?' suggested Sam.

'Good idea,' agreed Kaye, stretching. 'I could do with some fresh air.' It was claustrophobic in the underground reading room, hemmed in on three sides by heavily carved wooden cupboards that covered the walls from floor to ceiling. 'Can we meet in here tomorrow morning at ten, if it's not keeping you from your own research, Raoul?'

Richter inclined his head. 'Not at all; I'm delighted to be of help.'

Sam said little as they walked back to their hotel in the late afternoon sunshine, dodging the milling crowds in the vast expanse of Saint Peter's Square. She remained pensive, thinking about what the day had revealed and wondering how much she, in turn, should reveal to Kaye. He was equally un-talkative and Sam judged that he was having trouble dealing with the successive faith issues that the discovery of Christ's tomb and the content of Basem's gospel had raised. Here I am, she thought, beginning to accept - in part at least - a faith concept that could shake the world, while Oliver's world is being shaken by a struggle to reconcile his faith with what he is learning. How ironic.

As they reached the hotel, Kaye said, abruptly, 'You mentioned a letter earlier. Are you willing to share it with me now?' His handsome face was unreadable but his tone carried a trace of resentment.

'Of course,' answered Sam, wishing she had come clean sooner. She hoped his chagrin was not going to ruin their working partnership, which she felt had been developing well, up to this point.

'Why didn't you show me this before?' Kaye paced the length of the well-appointed sitting room of Sam's suite, halting when he reached the brocade drapes that adorned the tall window and turning to face her, her father's letter in his hand. 'How can I help you solve your mystery if you're only going to feed me bits of information as and when it suits? What else don't I know about?'

'Nothing!' Sam swept her auburn hair back angrily. 'It should be obvious why I kept that letter to myself until now! Aside from it being personal, I originally thought it was nonsense and, anyway,' she admitted, dropping her eyes, 'I was embarrassed. I thought Daddy might have had a screw loose.'

'Ah. I hadn't considered that,' said Kaye sheepishly, his irritation dissipating. Returning to the centre of the room, he sprawled on one of the armchairs ranged around a large coffee table to re-read the letter, more slowly this time.

Sam felt the need to expand on her reticence and subsequent change of mind. 'The letter said it was a family secret, so I couldn't very well share it with a complete stranger, could I? But with all the evidence that's building up and with what we found out today, it's become clear that, even if it is peculiar, it does make some kind of sense. It isn't necessarily the sort of sense either of us feels comfortable with, but we have to face the possibility that at least some of it may be true - and may be important.' She stopped, satisfied she had made her point, then, whimsically changing subject, added, 'You do know you have a pencil stub sticking out from behind your ear?'

'Damn,' said Kaye. 'You noticed.' He looked up from the letter and gave a quirky half smile. 'Habit of mine, I'm afraid. I was going over some of your documents again while I waited the half hour. I said hello to Ghulam as well - he told me he'd been in heaven all afternoon, otherwise known as a Ferrari showroom.' Kaye removed the pencil and tucked it into his shirt breast pocket. 'Listen; can I ask you some questions in relation to this letter?'

Sam sat down again and nodded. 'I thought you might want to.'

Reclining into the cushioned backrest of his chair, Kaye made a cathedral of his fingers and said, 'First, I assume you have the birthmark the letter refers to - in which case, would it give offence if I asked to see it - if it wouldn't compromise your decency, that is?'

A slight blush freshened Sam's cheeks. 'Not at all,' she murmured and unbuttoned her silk blouse just far enough to pull back one edge and reveal the raised, pink mark over her heart.

Kaye peered at the mark and exclaimed, 'It *is* the star on the emblem; even to the twelve rays...'

Self-consciously re-buttoning her blouse, Sam said, 'It could just be a coincidence, of course.'

'Did your father have the same birthmark?'

She shrugged. 'Believe it or not, I never saw his chest. He was a very private man in that respect. I have to assume he did, though. Why would he lie?'

'And he never told you *anything* - the content of this letter came as a complete surprise after his death?'

'Correct.'

'So, you discovered all the other documents subsequently, by following the letter's instructions?'

'Yes, Oliver. There really aren't any other secrets. You know as much as I do, now. I just hope you will respect my father's wish and keep this to yourself.'

Kaye gave a wry smile. 'I can't see any of my usual journals continuing to respect my professional reputation if I send them a submission that relies on the scandalous evidence presented by a lady's bosom. I think you're safe on that score.'

Sam smiled, but then her face clouded. 'So far, the mystery only seems to have deepened,' she said. 'I wouldn't blame you if you wanted to duck out at this point. I'm not sure I can see there being much profit either professionally or financially for you in all this.'

Kaye looked at her lovely, strained face; at her mournful green eyes. 'Money and fame - generally overrated,' he said softly. 'Let's go and save Ghulam from ruining his eyes reading car engine stats and see if he'd like to join us for dinner. I always think better on a full stomach and we have a lot to consider if we're ever going to find that casket of yours.'

Just before retiring that night, Sam decided to put the folder containing their onward flight tickets into the hotel room safe already housing the Chaumont documents, her passport and other valuables. Crossing to the vanity table to pick it up, she paused, frowning. Her memory told her she had left it in the middle of the table with its back edge resting up against the bottom of the mirror. Now, the folder was not quite touching the mirror and lay at a slight angle on the desk, off-centre. Typical, she thought. You pay for six-star service and the maids can't even dust neatly. Yawning, she picked it up and locked it away safely, then went directly to bed. Her dreams were haunted by fleeting glimpses of Kaye's startling blue eyes, but every time she tried to look squarely into them, they blinked - and when they opened again, they had changed to a pale, smoky grey.

Rome, Italy, 20 June 2016 AD

Promptly, at ten in the morning, Richter appeared at the sliding glass door of the reading room in the Bunker, deep below the Vatican Museum. He was holding a single scroll and laid it gently on the table in front of Kaye and Sam, who had been reviewing a second century Gnostic text they had found that gave a very different slant on Judas Iscariot's betrayal of Jesus, as recently translated by a foremost authority in Coptic script. Whilst interesting, however, it had not shed any further light on their mystery.

'Good morning,' he said brightly as he entered the room. 'I trust you both spent a pleasant evening in the eternal city. Regarding your request, I've come across this. I'd passed it over in my own research because it's a medieval document, rather too late to be relevant to me, but, as you can see, it is wax-sealed with what I think is the same seal represented in the Gospel of Basem - and I take my hat off to you for honing in on that seal. I would never have thought anything of it, myself. I have no idea, however, what its link is with this medieval script, since I didn't bother to translate this when I first came across it.'

'How kind of you, Raoul,' said Sam. 'Thanks.'

'I'll pop back in a while to see whether you found it of use.'

'Fine,' replied Kaye, already reaching for the scroll.

Richter left quietly, not wishing to appear too overtly interested in what they were doing. The fish must be played very gently, now.

'He seems a decent chap,' commented Sam to Kaye.

Kaye gave a slight nod. 'I think he's genuine. I phoned Fred Heyes in London last night and he confirmed he'd done some work for Raoul. By all accounts, he's a private researcher, not connected to any university or theological institution, but a frequent visitor to the Vatican and the author of a couple of papers in theological journals. Fred said Raoul had been trying to fill some gaps in his personal genealogical history, which apparently has late medieval aristocratic connections.'

Sam was relieved to hear that Richter had checked out. 'I wasn't sure about him to begin with,' she admitted, 'But he has been awfully helpful.'

'Let's see what this document tells us' said Kaye, drawing on his white cotton gloves and looking critically at the wax seal with a magnifying glass. The imprinted seal certainly resembled Balthazar's. He unrolled the scroll and set weights on its corners. It was written in medieval Arabic that, once translated, proved to be a short account making mention of an unusual occurrence - the unwilling baptism into Christ of a Moslem called Haleem. 'The script begins with a date,' said Kaye: 'Month of Ramadan, 604 AH. I'll have to work out what that would be in the Christian calendar.'

Sam was puzzled. 'Aren't they both the same?' she asked.

Kaye explained. 'The Islamic calendar is completely different from the Gregorian one. Its year zero is our 622 AD - because that's when the prophet Muhammad moved from Mecca to Medina. Making things even more complicated, the Islamic calendar is made up of twelve lunar months, totalling 354 or 355 days, not 365 days like ours.' He dug a credit card sized calculator out of his wallet and did some rapid sums. 'There have been 1395 years since 621 AD and that equates to 1434 Islamic years.' He made another calculation and said, 'So the Islamic year 604 AH is 1192 AD, by my reckoning. That seems a reasonable date, looking at this script. Now, let's see what the text says...'

'Hang on,' interjected Sam. '1192, you said? Why does 1192 ring a bell? I'm sure you mentioned that year when you were explaining something about one of the documents you translated for me back at home.'

Kaye frowned; then his face cleared. 'By George, you're right - well, almost. What I think I said was that 1193 was when Saladin died. So, if I remember my crusades history correctly, 1192 was the year Richard the Lionheart made a truce with Saladin because he couldn't take Jerusalem by force.'

'Saladin again? He does keep cropping up, doesn't he?'

'Let's keep that in mind as we see what Haleem has to say for himself.'

'My beloved Shamsa, it is so hard to say goodbye to you. Just as the white stork flies north, so must I, in a great ship with white sails that will bear me away to live in a cold, far away land, but unlike the stork, I shall not return, for I am cast into bondage and will be a vassal of the Frankish king until the day I die. You may ask why I accept such a destiny. It is because my father has offered himself to meet the needs of the great lord Sālah al-Dīn and where my father goes, I must follow. To leave the golden city of Jerusalem is a bitter draught to swallow, but more bitter yet is parting from you, my beautiful Golden Moon.

'Do not mourn me, for I will be gone from you not only in fact but also in faith. My father tells me that within the hour we are to be baptised in the name of Iesus - Isa, as we have always called him. To survive amongst the Christians, we must adopt their ways, my father says. So today I will become one with the infidels and after that, your father will banish me from his threshold, so this letter will be the last from your loving Haleem. Try to forget me - let your father find you a worthy husband of the true faith and, please, for my sake, be happy. For my part, I will never forget you, sweet Shamsa, for the

moon in the sky will remind me of your beauty every night of my life. Farewell forever, my love.

'Under the seal of my father and in the name of Allah, Haleem Hamid.'

'It's a love letter!' exclaimed Sam. 'Oh; how sad. He sounds very young and terribly lovesick - poor Haleem.'

'They tended to wed around age fourteen or fifteen - and still do in some places, like the Yemen - so yes, I expect he was just a kid,' said Kaye. "Shamsa' translates as 'Golden Moon', by the way - a pretty name for a sweetheart. That's irrelevant, anyway.' Kaye cleared his throat. 'What *is* important is the boy's family name and his father's seal - and the fact that they were both off to England under the orders of Saladin.'

Sam blinked. '...His name? Of course - Hamid, like Abdul Hamid! Do you think this is the son of the man named in that Arabic letter I found in Chaumont?'

'The date is right; the name is right and the seal is the clincher. I would say it's a certainty.'

So, here's another of my distant ancestors, thought Sam. He must have found an English girl in the end - and probably forgot all about poor little Golden Moon.

'Which suggests,' added Kaye meaningfully, 'That the gift Saladin gave to the Lionheart *was* your casket and was sent by ship to England with the Hamids to guard it...'

'...And then it eventually ended up in my family, somehow,' Sam finished for him.

Kaye looked at her sharply. 'Or, rather, it never left your family,' he corrected. 'Remember - you've got the star on your chest and I'd lay odds that it's a birthmark linked to a very dominant genetic marker. I dare say all the Keepers of this casket have had the same birthmark - and you can probably count Haleem, Abdul, Basem and even old Balthazar the mage as your direct ancestors. I bet Simon Dexter had the mark too - and all the subsequent Earls of Chaumont.

To sum it up, your ancestors have been keeping a continuous and extremely watchful eye on that casket for at least two thousand years, which, at the very least, is an extraordinary story of devotion to a perceived duty - making it even harder to understand how such an oh-so-carefully guarded casket can have disappeared without a trace!'

'Yes,' said Sam meekly, impressed with his razor-keen analysis. 'I agree with almost everything you say.'

'What don't you agree with?'

'The two thousand years bit - I think that's too conservative an estimate. Surely that seal was engraved on the casket when the casket was originally made and I'm inclined to believe the casket has been around for as long as that Sanskrit legend - at least four thousand years and possibly a lot longer.'

'Evidentially slim, but possible,' conceded Kaye, nodding as he embraced the idea.

Sam was on a roll. 'And, if my father was serious - and right - about my being the latest in a long family line of Keepers, he must have been equally serious about *The Power* I was supposed to be guarding - in fact, I'm starting to believe that the casket is what holds that *Power*.'

'You're telling me you think there's a little gold box out there somewhere that contains the ability to bring the dead back to life?'

'Yes.'

Kaye snorted derisively. 'Now, that I *do* find hard to swallow.'

'But I thought you were the one with spiritual faith?'

'That's exactly why I think you're nuts to believe that a man-made object could contain that kind of power! Despite being a Catholic, I don't take everything I read in the Bible - and most especially in the material that never even made it into the Bible - as the literal gospel truth. The truth has been squeezed, remoulded, enhanced, edited, misinterpreted and mistranslated by generation upon generation of readers, writers and believers. Why do you think Constantine held the Council of Nicaea? It was exactly because there were so many varying accounts of the so-called truth floating about that he decided it was time to make a decision about which bits the Church should adopt as its one and only creed from then on. Heavens, it was only at that Council, in 325 AD, almost three hundred years after he'd died, that hundreds of Bishops of the era formally voted in favour of Jesus being part of a single, Trinitarian Godhead rather than merely a sub-deity, distinct and separate from God the Father. Please, Sam, be sensible and take what you've read with a big pinch of salt - otherwise I think you're going to be dreadfully disappointed later on.'

'How big is a nuclear bomb?' asked Sam abruptly.

'Beg pardon?'

'A nuclear bomb - what size? Say, the one that demolished Hiroshima, for example.'

'Oh, I don't know - missile-sized - several tons in weight, I should think. Why?' He wondered where she was going with this tangential query.

'Well, think about it. The atomic bomb was man-made and just look at the power *it* contained! And haven't they kept refining nuclear technology ever since? I hear you can vaporise half the planet now with something you can hide in a suitcase!'

Kaye gaped at her. 'But that's modern technology.'

'I know. And it demonstrates that mankind has the ability to invent small boxes holding enough power to cause Armageddon, so why couldn't someone, way back before recorded history began, have invented something that would fit in a small box and have the power to restore life, rather than take it?'

Outclassed by a complete amateur in an academic debate for the first time in his life, Professor Oliver Kaye could not think of a single appropriate thing to say.

Richter chose that moment to breeze into the reading room. 'Saved by the bell,' breathed Kaye.

'How are you getting on?' enquired their new buddy, all smiles. 'If you've finished with that scroll, I'd be happy to return it to its designated place in the Archives. Was it of interest?'

'Not directly pertinent,' answered Kaye. 'Thank you anyway.' He carefully rolled up Haleem's love letter and returned it to Richter.

'Unfortunately, we'll have to cut our research here short for the present. We have to fly out of Rome this afternoon on other business.'

Richter displayed mild surprise, followed by relief. 'Actually, that lets me off the hook rather handily,' he said. 'As it happens, I was about to let you know that I shan't be able to assist you for much longer, since I'm leaving Rome, myself, later today. I've been incredibly lucky. The Cardinal mentoring my theological studies has arranged for me to visit the contentious tomb just discovered in Syria - I'm sure I heard you mention it yesterday at some point, so you've obviously seen the news this week. It seems the archaeologists are so protective of the site that virtually no-one is being permitted inside the tomb. Only the Papal Emissary has been in so far and I'm to be given access on the basis that my research is Vatican-approved. Anyway, it's been a pleasure meeting you both - and I wish you good luck with your project.'

Sam looked askance at Kaye. Leaving aside the phenomenal coincidence of both destination and timing, what Richter had just indicated about the difficulty in obtaining access to Christ's tomb might mean that without some type of official sanction, they themselves would be barred from entry. Neither of them had given any thought to that possibility. But nor had they told Richter their forward plans, so there was no way he could have known that they were also heading to Damascus. The latter thought was reassuring.

'Raoul,' she said quickly, 'Do you believe in serendipity? Because by some spooky quirk of fate, our destination happens to be Damascus, too, and although our primary goal is unrelated, we had hoped to visit the newly discovered tomb whilst in the area. Unfortunately, we hadn't considered the fact that access might be a problem. I don't suppose we could be awful nuisances and impose on you to incorporate us under your official umbrella, as it were, so that we can get inside to have a proper look at it?'

'Good heavens,' he exclaimed, raising his eyebrows. 'Don't tell me you're on the four forty flight as well?'

'Going via Amman.'

'Are you sure you're not following me?' asked Richter, winking.

'Perhaps we should be,' laughed Sam. 'You seem to have your trip far better planned than we have.'

'The archaeologists are only expecting one researcher,' said Richter, rubbing his chin. 'Let me see....' He brightened. 'I expect I could phone them before arriving and ask if you can accompany me. I'll spin them a line.'

'We're putting you to a lot of trouble,' commented Kaye. 'I can't thank you enough.'

Richter smiled. 'No problem - anything to help fellow researchers seeking the truth. I'll see you on the plane, then.' He waved the scroll at them, turned and left the reading room.

I don't care what anyone says about the man, thought Sam. His eyes still send shivers down my spine. They're dead-pools.

CHAPTER 13

TWO PRINCES TOO MANY

The Tower of London, England, 23 June, 1483 AD

The inner ward echoed to the playful sound of childish laughter as Edward and Richard Plantagenet amused each other in the Constable's garden. Observing them through the mist of a light morning drizzle, Simon Dexter tightened the belt around his brown leather jerkin and adjusted the sheath of the rondel dagger at his waist. At close to six feet high in his knee-length calfskin boots, he was of swarthy complexion with a thick mane of black hair. The curved nose and slightly Levantine features of his face gave him the cast of a wayward brigand as he glanced up at the sentinels pacing the battlements - their long-tailed, German-made sallet helmets and shouldered halberds a grim reminder that the Tower was not only a fortress and a royal palace, but also a prison.

'Two hundred and ninety years?' Even disguised by a heavy Italian accent, the surprise in the questioning tone was obvious.

Dexter returned his attention to the speaker. 'Truly, Brother Dominic: my ancestors, Abdul Hamid and his son, Haleem, were gifted to Richard Coeur de Lion by Saladin - exchanged for Richard's Épée *Bâtarde*, the famous bastard sword. They were brought here on Richard's orders, under the protection of one Hubert Walter, the then Bishop of Salisbury.'

'I see. Forgive me, but one cannot help noticing that Abdul Hamid is not an English-sounding name. So, tell me, how did the family name of Dexter arise...?

'Hamid was a scholar; a seeker of truth. The Bishop was much impressed with his studies, engaged him in a wide variety of tasks and came to consider him invaluable. It was he who termed Abdul 'better than a second right hand' and dubbed him with the name Dexter. Haleem formally adopted Dexter as his family name - perhaps he believed it would help him blend with the culture in which he found himself obliged to remain, having no hope of returning to his native home in Jerusalem.'

'Ah! That makes sense.' Dominic Mercurio hesitated, fingering the almoner that depended from his frayed cord belt. He made his next comment appear casual. 'I can understand how he might have pined for the wonders of the Holy City. I, myself, was there several years ago. Come to think of it, whilst wandering through its bazaars, I heard tell from a Genoese trader that Saladin also gifted Richard with some trifle stolen from its holy role in the Christian Church - a fabulous, hand-crafted, golden box of inestimable value. Have you heard aught to confirm such a tale?'

Dexter dismissed the idea, his expression a study in innocence. 'I know of no such box, golden or otherwise. If such a treasure existed, which I find exceeding doubtful, it must long since have been lost; sold... or, more likely, proffered as a royal bribe - ha!'

The Augustinian monk shrugged disarmingly. 'No doubt you are right.' He changed tack. 'I was thinking... the binding of your ancestor to the crown happened centuries ago - has no Dexter ever sued for the renunciation of that outmoded bondage? Do you, yourself, remain here from choice?'

Dexter's lips narrowed. Mercurio's straggly tonsure and worn black habit belied the shrewdness of the man. 'The gift was in perpetuity,' he responded tersely. 'Petitions have been made more than once to dismiss the pledge of responsibility and, though succeeding monarchs scarce knew of my ancestors' existence, all petitions were refused. We have been and continue to be vassals, bound to this place, yet not prisoner to it, servants without a master, free to come and go, yet not leave for good. You might say that we have become lost in the thread of the fabric of the Tower and, so, remain here, generation upon generation, in the absence of leave to venture forth and seek our own destinies.'

The monk wrestled with the issue of Dexter's strange situation, trying to think of some suitable philosophical reply, but finally gave up and merely shook his head in bewilderment and sympathy. Changing the subject, he waved an arm in the direction of the two princes and said, haltingly, 'They seem carefree and full of summer joy this morn, but their physician told me he visited them yesterday and found them in a state of abject melancholy. What can we hope for them?'

Dexter pursed his lips. 'I do not concern myself with matters of state. Those that offer unsought opinion should know that they speak at peril of their lives…'

Undeterred, the monk continued. 'I fear that their uncle harbours a ruthless streak that is malevolent in nature. He has taken it upon himself to postpone the coronation of King Edward and even now seeks to have Parliament declare the heir to the throne a bastard, thus invalidating the boy's claim to the crown. Is there no confining the evil of the man and his yearning for power?'

Dexter said quietly, 'Brother Dominic, as I have already made clear, I would advise you of the poor wisdom of making such thoughts known freely. These are treacherous times. Being here at the behest of His Eminence Angelo Cato, the Archbishop of Vienne and the court of King Louis the Eleventh of France, to report on the state of affairs of this nation, you may think, erroneously, that your patrons' influence will save you from the English scaffold, should you utter treasonous words. Think again! Whilst Richard's guest, I urge you to let caution be your mentor. Come; let us out of this rain before we are drenched.'

Crossing the grounds to the gothic mass of the White Tower, they climbed the wide stairs that spiralled up to the second floor, passing westwards through the main banqueting room to enter the cool of the King's private chapel of Saint John the Evangelist. Mercurio gazed down its fifty five foot length. Four massive round stone columns on either side supported the barrel-vaulted ceiling. The Apse held four more columns of equal girth in a semi-circle that raised the chapel to the height of three floors. Above the slab of the marble altar, stained glass windows portraying the Virgin and Child; Saint John the Evangelist; Edward the Confessor and a figure of Christ, together diffused the light into pastel hues that pushed back the harsh shadows of the Apse.

Mercurio felt the texture of the Caen stone columns, caressing them with ink stained fingers. 'Is it true that William the Conqueror imported all the stone for the Tower from France?'

'Yes,' answered Dexter, 'Along with the masons to carve it. He didn't trust Anglo-Saxon craftsmen to do the work.'

The monk fell silent for a while, contemplating the enormity of the chapel. When he spoke again there was a deliberate tone to his voice. 'Surely a fortress such as this must have many dark and secret places. Would you not say so?'

Dexter, suspicious of what might dangle from the bottom of this thread, answered evasively, 'Possibly; who knows?'

Mercurio ploughed on. 'If there are, one might suppose that, over the generations, such knowledge would become known to a line linked as closely to the Tower as yours has been.'

Dexter recalled how his father had revealed to him the many secrets of the Tower before his death. No other family line had habitually inhabited the Tower for as long as the Dexters. True, the Plantagenets could trace their ownership rights further back in time, but for the most part they had chosen to live in stately castles like Baynard's to the west of the city and in homes scattered around the country. Monarchs and their administrators came and went, but the Dexters - and the casket - remained. Dexters had been present when most of the towers were built - the Garden Tower, the Beaufort Tower, and all the others. They had seen the castle expanded and reinforced and each generation had become familiar, in turn, with every stone and timber.

The monk was astute. The accumulated knowledge of the Tower's secrets had indeed been passed down from father to son, reinforced and supplemented by personal experience. As a boy, Dexter had exhaustively explored the corkscrew twist and dusty turns of every building and tower. No-one now alive, save he, knew all their concealed panels, spring traps, cubby holes and hiding places. Blank walls sprang open to his touch and he could insinuate himself behind any of the Tower's many spy holes to oversee and overhear the conversations of others. Some of his best kept secrets were those hidden doors that accessed subterranean tunnels beneath the moat - leading to the town and a transient freedom.

'Would you not agree?' Mercurio pressed, snapping Dexter out of his reverie.

'Yes, I would, Brother Dominic, if it were the case. Alas, the opposite is the truth. If the Tower holds any dark secrets then they are well kept from me.'

Dexter's stone walls, like those of the Tower, were impenetrable and the confounded monk acceded defeat, asking no more questions and, instead, taking his time to assimilate the atmosphere of the chapel before eventually kneeling in prayer at the altar. As Dexter stared hard at the back of the bowed head of the penitent, the last words of his father flooded into his mind.

'Never acknowledge its existence or reveal its place of concealment, for the casket belongs to The One, not to you. As its Keeper you are merely its guardian. Beware any who speak of it; let them not into your mind and never trust in the shallow friendship of men!'

As he went down on one knee to join Brother Dominic in prayer, he swore a silent oath. When opportunity presented, he would petition the King to sever the unjust shackle of his vassal pledge. Whatever it took to achieve it, he *would* have his freedom.

The Tower of London, 25 June, 1483 AD

On the upper floor of the White Tower, the late afternoon sun filtered through leaded windows set into the council chamber's thick, white-washed, stone walls. Its light illuminated Richard Plantagenet of the house of York; Duke of Gloucester; Lord Protector, Regent and uncle to the twelve year old Edward the Fifth of England, as he paced impatiently up and down. The tread of his boots on its worn oak floorboards echoed back from the chamber's massive ceiling, which was supported by ponderous, criss-crossed beams of timber. Thirty-one years of age, of medium height, with a pale, even featured face, an aquiline nose and shoulder-length, loosely bobbed brown hair, his thin lips gave him a fierce expression about the mouth.

Apparelled in fine hose below a fur-edged, purple doublet worked with gold thread - and padded heavily on the left shoulder to disguise the deformity of his raised right shoulder - he obsessively twisted the signet ring on the third finger of his right hand as he halted, turned on his heel and addressed the three men who had just entered from the staircase at the other end of the chamber. 'Is it done?' His voice was sharp, the question even sharper.

Henry Stafford, Duke of Buckingham, a tall, florid man, replied in a sombre voice, 'It is done, Your Grace. The petition was put to the Lords and commoners of the realm assembled at Westminster and they have declared invalid the marriage between your brother, Edward, and Elizabeth Woodville. That union, made without the consent of the Lords, was conducted privately and clandestinely without the edition of banns and was thus bigamous, since Edward had pre-signed a contract with another woman.'

Richard crossed the expanse of the chamber to close in on Buckingham, whose face was now almost as red as the loose fitting gown he wore. 'Was evidence laid before them?'

Buckingham nodded. 'Yes indeed, Your Grace. Robert Stillington, the Bishop of Bath and Wells and erstwhile Lord Chancellor of England, swore on oath, as promised, that King Edward the Fourth had contracted a secret marriage to one Lady Eleanor Talbot in 1461; that he, as Bishop, had conducted the ceremony and that the Lady Eleanor was still alive when Edward IV married Elizabeth Woodville in 1464. That act of bigamy renders any issue from Edward's marriage to Elizabeth Woodville illegitimate.'

Richard turned and began pacing again, adopting a moderate tone as he endlessly twisted the ring on his finger. 'So by decree of Parliament, my nephew, Edward, the supposed King of England and his brother, Richard, Duke of York are both bastards - and neither may take the throne?'

Sir Robert Brackenbury, a beefy man clothed in a black gown over a heavily pleated skirt, added his voice. 'The Lords spiritual, temporal and the commons have all declared that you, Your Gra - Your Majesty, are the rightful heir and true King of England.' Upon these words, the three men knelt in homage to the newly acclaimed King Richard III.

Richard's voice fell slightly as he emphasised each word he spoke. 'I want more than a declaration from Parliament. I want my brother's bigamy and the bastardisation of his offspring entered into the scrolls - a *Titulus Regius*.'

Buckingham replied without lifting his head. 'It shall be done, Your Majesty.'

The beginnings of a smile tugged at the corners of Richard's thin lips as he bade the three men rise. Addressing the third man, who had yet to speak, he said, 'Catesby, you are appointed Chancellor of the Exchequer, Chancellor of the Earldom of March and Knight of the Body.'

William Catesby bowed low: 'As Your Majesty commands.'

Richard turned to Brackenbury and said, 'Sir Robert, you have served loyally. You will take the office of Constable of the Tower.'

Brackenbury seemed slightly ill at ease. 'If it pleases Your Majesty, I have affairs to attend to in the north...'

Richard cut him off. 'See to them quickly, Sir Robert. The nobility is not to be trusted. There is treachery in the air and I need true men of mettle at my back.' Striding over to a high backed wooden chair, made comfortable through the simple addition of a deep blue throw rug embellished in embroidered fleurs-de-lis, he sat for a moment to ease his oft-aching back and scrutinised the three men with an authoritative air. After a moment, Buckingham posed the obvious question.

'What's to become of the two boys, Your Majesty?'

Richard pointed a long finger at him. 'I place them in your charge, Buckingham. Where are my dear nephews housed at present?'

'In the Garden Tower, Your Majesty, in the care of Sir James Tyrell.'

'And how are they kept?' The question was direct; unexpected. Buckingham hesitated slightly before answering.

'They are kept well, Sire, served by only one man. He supervises their daily fresh air and exercise in the Constable's garden, oversees their meals and attends their general needs.'

'Who so serves them?'

'One Simon Dexter: he is most able, Sire.'

'I know of this man. He is an oddity of the palace, as was his father, and his father before him, and their fathers before them. Watch him well, Buckingham. What of other matters?' Seeking easement, Richard leaned against the high back of his chair. Due to his scoliosis, the muscles supporting his misshapen spine were under constant strain and frequently bound themselves into hard knots, causing severe discomfort.

'Majesty, we must expect that Elizabeth Woodville will now bear you great enmity and that she will be intent upon the return of both her sons. How is this to be resolved?'

Richard frowned but did not answer.

Buckingham continued. 'Sire, there are rumours that Henry Tudor, Earl of Richmond, is in Brittany and has become desirous of the crown not yet placed upon your head. If he allies himself with the Welsh Tudors and with the Woodvilles, who have very strong ties with the nobility of the north…'

Richard came abruptly to his feet. Grasping the ivory hilt of the boar's head dagger that depended on a gold chain from the leather belt at his waist, he spat venomously, 'Earl Rivers, Lord Grey *and* Sir Thomas Vaughan had their necks bared on the block for the headsman's axe at Pontefract Castle this day - on my warrant. That will be my threat to Henry Tudor and the Woodvilles and their kin, or any who commit to treason against the Crown!' Twisting his ring again, his eyes narrowed as he paused to deliberate. 'This evening I retire to the Lanthorn Tower where I will spend the night. Early on the morrow I return to Baynard's castle. You, Buckingham, will come to me there, after noon, with the Lords. You will lead them to acclaim me as King and petition my reluctance to take the throne. Effect this well, Buckingham, being mindful that a flawless performance will go in your favour.'

Buckingham bowed. 'If it pleases you, Sire, I'll take my leave to go about the King's business.'

Richard nodded his approval and, as Buckingham withdrew, transferred his attention to Brackenbury. 'Sir Robert, I desire that the two boys not be objects of the public gaze. Have suitable quarters prepared for them in the Tower proper. Now leave: I wish to be alone.'

Brackenbury and Catesby bowed, backing toward the spiral staircase at the north end of the chamber.

Alone and re-seated in the roomy chair, Richard quaffed Burgundy wine from a pewter goblet. Dark, lugubrious thoughts ran through his mind. While the princes drew breath he would never feel secure. Giving his ring a particularly vicious twist, he called out loudly, summoning the captain of his guard. 'Recall the Duke of Buckingham immediately,' he ordered. 'I have urgent matters to discuss with him.'

The Tower of London, 9 July, 1483 AD

Above Traitors' Gate, the late evening shadows obscured Simon Dexter's face as he leant against the wall of the chamber that housed the windlass for raising the Tower's portcullis. He had chosen the location for this meeting carefully, to ensure no prying eyes or ears would compromise its secrecy. It remained to be seen whether such care was truly necessary, but the man he had come to meet had been adamant that no-one should be privy to their conversation. Dexter had lived all his life in the midst of the intrigue of the English Court, where most walls had ears - usually his own - so had not been overly surprised at the request for a clandestine venue.

Facing him at the foot of the narrow spiral staircase that led up to the Wakefield Tower, Henry Stafford, Duke of Buckingham, garbed in a fur-edged, grey velvet gown, a long summer cloak and a black rolled cap with a jagged ribbon liripipe, looked ill at ease. 'I am obliged to inform you,' he said slowly, 'That His Majesty's present disposition does not look kindly upon the granting of your petition.'

Dexter launched away from the wall, hands outstretched. 'How can Richard, the royal crown barely three days upon his head, not grant a petition to end the grossly unjust requirement that demands my service and the service of my family in perpetuity? Why does he refuse me the freedoms that other men take for granted?'

Buckingham looked into Dexter's dark, flashing eyes. Despite several hundred years of intermarriage with English women and a change in surname to deflect prejudice, when he was angry, those eyes still spoke of their fiery Middle Eastern heritage.

'I did not say that the King will *not* grant your petition. I said only that he is not, at present, disposed to look kindly upon it - although, perhaps, the performance of one service may deserve another...' Buckingham's words trailed off suggestively.

Dexter held Buckingham's gaze. 'Speak plainly, Your Grace. I do not care to riddle at so late an hour.'

Buckingham's gaze shifted away from those unsettling eyes. 'In blunt, then, the crown does not rest easily upon the King's head. He is assailed by inconveniences and rumours which dog his wellbeing by day and haunt his sleep by night. Consequently, he will not entertain supplications and petitions, unless by granting them, some measure of progress is achieved in the matters that weigh so heavily upon his brow.'

'He's a-feared of Henry Tudor, Duke of Richmond, that much I know. What else?'

'Indeed,' Buckingham agreed. 'It is common knowledge that Tudor has designs on the throne and is raising an army even as we speak. I fear there is little that you may contribute to alter that fact, but of equal import to the King is a resolution to the unfortunate matter of the young princes who languish not far from where we stand. It cannot be expected that his Majesty raise his own hand against them - but all good advice dictates that it were best they be done away with.'

Dexter seized on the desire evident in Buckingham's tone. 'Best for whom, I wonder: Richard - or you?'

Buckingham flung back his cloak with a snarl, grasping the hilt of his sword, drawing it and feinting at Dexter in one fluid movement. Dexter instinctively parried Buckingham's vicious downward slash with his long bladed rondel dagger. The ring of Damascus steel against Toledo blade filled the chamber as Buckingham spat through clenched teeth, 'You dare talk in such a manner to me? I am the King's mouthpiece in this matter.'

Unperturbed, Dexter balanced lightly on the balls of his feet and kept his dagger at the ready. 'It is also widely observed that you are a man of ambition, Your Grace. If Tudor were successful in disposing of Richard, then, with the two princes removed, your claim to the crown through your mother's lineage would be strengthened. Only Tudor would then stand between you and the throne.'

Buckingham stepped back and straightened up, the blade of his sword rasping as he slid it back into its scabbard. 'I concede you are no-one's fool, Dexter. Nevertheless, I am Richard's man while he holds the throne. So, do we continue our conversation? If you can watch your tongue, we may yet find agreement.'

Warily sheathing his weapon, Dexter answered, 'Speak on.'

'The boys must cease to be a thorn in the side of the King - and soon. Attend to this matter for the Crown and you will find the Crown grateful.'

Dexter drew breath through his teeth and whispered, 'You advocate high treason. If so accused, I would die a traitor's death!'

'Treason,' answered Buckingham calmly, 'is an act against the Crown or the realm. These lads have nought to do with either. They are just, regretably, in the way. As their attendant, you have ready access to their quarters and I have confidence that you are more than capable of devising a way to accomplish the desired outcome.'

Dexter bowed slightly at the inverse compliment. 'Nevertheless, such a distasteful task will command a high price.'

'The Crown's gratitude will encompass any reasonable price. Name yours.'

Dexter paced, thinking. If the princes were to go - at any cost - then why should another profit from the deed? Why not he? Had not his ancestors wiped the backsides of the English monarchs and cleared up their sorry little messes for generations, all in hopes that one day, an opportunity of this calibre would finally arise - a chance to attain independent position and wealth as security against an ever-changing and hostile world? Murder - particularly of royal children - was a heinous price to pay for such security, but Dexter remained ever mindful that his ultimate allegiance lay with *The Power*. His own security and that of his descendants would best assure the safety of the Keeper's secret. The most serendipitous benefit in this affair had to be the fact that the casket he had long kept hidden could at last be removed entirely from the royal court and housed far away, wherever he made his home as a free man. He made his decision.

'I think you already know what I most desire, my Lord: it is my freedom. I want the shackles of my bloodline's serfdom struck off and I want this grant of perpetual freedom in writing, sealed by the King's own hand.'

Buckingham interrupted him to accede. 'Perform this service and I guarantee you shall have that wish.'

'Not so fast, my Lord. There is yet more. I also want position and lands to provide a fair living.

Buckingham hesitated slightly. 'I imagine that an Earldom would confer the level of position you had in mind; yes? As for your future provision, let me see.' He thought for a moment. 'I am aware of several adjacent holdings in the Shire of Derby which, if combined, would generate an income of between three and five hundred pounds a year. I don't believe that would be too difficult to arrange. Just one proviso, in your own interests; to avoid idle gossip or pointed fingers of suspicion, I would propose that title and lands be formally bestowed only after the *Titulus Regius* has been approved and confirmed by parliament.'

Dexter's eyes darkened with mistrust. Had agreement to his demands come too readily? Perhaps the Duke had no intention of honouring his words. How could he make betrayal an unpalatable proposition? 'There's more,' he said quickly.

Buckingham pursed his lips and sniffed loudly.

Dexter's voice was firm and even. 'The King has a dagger with a white boar's head hilt and his motto, *'Loyaulte me lie'*, engraved on the blade. I want that dagger.'

Buckingham frowned. 'That is a most strange request.'

'If my hand is fated to do this deed for the King, it is only fitting that it should wield the King's dagger.'

Sighing, Buckingham gave in. 'It will be difficult, but I will see that the weapon comes to you. Have I your hand on the matter now?'

'Patience, Your Grace: there is yet one more item I require. Richard wears a signet ring bearing his crest and it, too, bears his motto inscribed on the inner …'

'How are you privy to what so few men know?' Buckingham burst out, his voice betraying his surprise.

'If all my store of such knowledge was free to you, my lord, you may trust that, in knowing it, your mane would stand on end!'

'But the King's own signet ring! Have you taken leave of your wits? He would never agree to relinquish it to me, let alone you. And what, in the name of heaven, would you do with it? Just having it about your person would incur the penalty of death!'

'The King's ring will be his covenant to me; his word that what I do is done with impunity - and trust me when I say that it will never be found about my person.'

'You would doubt the word of Richard?'

Dexter gave a short, dry bark. 'I would doubt the word of *any* king in such a matter - especially this one!'

Buckingham remained silent for a moment. 'And in return for his signet ring, what proof will His Majesty receive of the completion of your task?'

'Richard shall have the rings of Edward and his brother - that his crown may sit more comfortably on his head and that he may sleep easier at night.'

Buckingham sucked on his lower lip, looking troubled. 'I am unsure. Persuading Richard won't be easy - he can be very difficult,' he began.

Dexter shrugged. 'You have the crux of it. I will not negotiate. Take it or leave it, as you will. Of course, if the King would prefer to effect the deed by his own hand or find some other servant willing...'

'No,' Buckingham interrupted quickly. 'You have my hand on it. I will attend upon Richard and you shall have your price. He is at Greenwich Palace this day but shortly he will move to the castle at Windsor. How long before..?'

'Soon - and as confirmation, I will present to you a sprig of broom concealing the two rings. Thereafter, no further word must be uttered on this matter.'

Buckingham nodded, but looked puzzled. '...Broom?'

'*Planta genesta* - the origin of the name 'Plantagenet' - I think it most apt.'

'Ah. And the...' Buckingham hesitated to mouth the word, '...Remains? What will become of them?'

Dexter knew he was now in control. 'That need not concern you, for therein lies my further protection. Should I find I am betrayed, rest assured that the childish fingers of the dead shall point most clearly in the direction of the cause of their sudden and premature demise.'

Gathering his cloak about him, ready to depart, there was a threatening tone to the Duke's final words. 'Do not fail me, Dexter, or your head will be upon the block!'

Dexter returned his threat with a half smile. 'If I fail you, Your Grace, then surely both our heads will be upon the block.'

CHAPTER 14

HALF A CLUE

Damascus, Syria, 20 June, 2016 AD

Ghulam had booked their party into the Beit Khan, a restored palace that had been turned into a small but luxurious hotel in the historic Old City of Damascus. They expressed surprise that Richter had made no advance accommodation arrangements, but he shrugged, saying, 'I'm a last minute kind of guy - it makes life more of an adventure.' He shared their taxi from the airport and, since the hotel had vacancies, booked in when they arrived. 'Handy to be in the same hotel, since we're visiting the tomb together,' he pointed out as they crossed the exquisitely tiled central courtyard, stopping briefly to admire its old stone fountain.

'We might as well hire a car, Ghulam, if you're willing to drive,' suggested Sam.

'Yes, Miss'm, I'll make arrangements as soon as I've unpacked for you.'

Over the years, Ghulam had shortened 'Miss Samantha' to 'Miss'm', a designation they both rather liked and which she had no intention of asking him to change for a more formal title following her father's death. Following Sam to her suite, he unpacked her case while she, having showered, changed and worked out how to use the room safe, went out onto the terrace that overlooked the courtyard and sat down to read a document she had never really taken the time to look at properly before - the account her grandfather, Kai Dexter, had written of his trip to the Holy Land in 1959.

A large, beautifully marked moth lay on the patterned tiles in Sam's suite, its soft wings splayed like a fallen Icarus. It was unmoving, but, noticing it, Ghulam gently picked it up and held it in his closed fist for a few moments, using the other hand to open one of the windows. Leaning out, he opened his fist and blew on the moth to give its wings some lift before launching the tiny creature into the air. Like a sycamore seed, it began to spiral down, but soon it stabilised and, beating the air more purposefully with every stroke, it fluttered away over the red tiled roofs of the old city souks. Ghulam nodded in satisfaction. It's just a matter of understanding how things work, he thought. Closing the window, he completed his work and made a call to reception to arrange for a suitable hire car to be delivered as soon as possible. Locking the suite, he found Sam on the terrace and returned her key to her.

'Thank you, Ghulam. Did you sort the hire car?'

'A Mercedes GL class SUV, Miss'm - it will be here in an hour or so. It should be suitable for rougher terrain outside the city limits.'

'Good thinking.' Sam looked at her watch. 'It's too late to do much today, especially after the long overnight haul. Can you get a city map and work out the best route to the Umayyad Mosque? We want to visit the tomb of Saladin - Oliver thinks it's next to the mosque, which should be easy to find because it's the biggest one in the city centre. We'll be heading out of town tomorrow, but Doctor Richter should be able to give you directions to the tomb site.' Ghulam's unremarkable Asian face remained impassive, a habitual demeanour giving people the impression that his mind was as devoid of complex thought as his blank face suggested. They were mistaken.

'Yes Miss'm. I'll go and unpack my things before the car arrives.' And with that he left her to her sheaf of papers, his lithe form gliding silently away.

Sam returned to her grandfather's discourse on the new Israel. Of course, she thought, it *was* a very new country when he went there, having only been created after the Second World War – in the late forties, wasn't it? She had assumed his trip was for pleasure, but as she worked into his text, it transpired that he had headed a small group of archaeologists invited to assist during the start-phase of a major renovation of one of the greatest Christian sites of pilgrimage, the Church of the Holy Sepulchre, which got underway in 1959 after five centuries of damage, desecration and neglect. That was interesting, thought Sam. The casket had been kept in that church for goodness knows how long before Saladin snaffled it and gave it to the Lionheart. Was that just a coincidence or had her grandfather held a special interest in the site because of what he must have known about its link to the history of the casket?

She read on.

> *'The Rotunda needed much work,'* wrote Kai. *'We instructed local masons to trim stone in the style of the 11th century to repair damaged areas in keeping with the original, whilst in other parts of the Church, stonemasonry in 12th century style was required. I spent some time at the western end of the Church, where a narrow, cave-like entranceway leads off the dilapidated Syrian Orthodox Chapel of Saint Joseph of Arimathea and Saint Nicodemus.*
>
> *'On the other side of this unlikely doorway, carved into the blackened limestone bedrock, is a maze of first century Jewish cave tombs - kokhim, as the locals call them. Whether or not this church was built on the site of the crucifixion and burial of Christ, it was certainly built on the site of a burial ground of Christ's era. The tombs were blocked with a mixture of building detritus and stored items. Having had this material moved, I found that the first tomb on the right side bore, at its rear, the long-rusted remains of a few iron bars in the form of a grille - I wonder what could have lain behind that grille in times long past?'*

I think I know the answer to that as well as he did, mused Sam and turned the page.

> *'Off that particular tomb lay more discoveries, hidden from immediate view by a square door-stone, which I removed with*

great difficulty, even though it was quite small. Taking a lantern, I crawled through the low, sloping passage now revealed, which quickly widened and became a small chamber, high enough for me to stand clear of the curved, tomb-like ceiling. But this was not a tomb, for there were no stone benches at its sides and at the far end, a flight of worn steps led downwards.

'I knew that a limestone quarry had been worked here, before and during the time of Christ, and wondered if perhaps the kokh tombs had been an access point to underground workings connected with the quarry. However, whatever the origin of the steps, they led me into an underground maze I had never thought to discover, stunning in its extent and complexity and with numerous hazards to negotiate in transit, such as cistern pits, cramped dead-end passages, vertical shafts and the like. Clearly this was unsafe territory for the incautious feet of pilgrims to the Church, so, on my final exit, I arranged for a strong cedar door to be constructed to block access to the crypt that formed the entry point to the maze below.

'I locked the door myself and instructed the Latin, Greek and Armenian communities to leave it untouched for safety's sake - they are quite used to leaving things untouched, since nothing falling under communal ownership of the sects has been moved since the 'Status Quo' agreement of 1757. If even one door is left open that ought to be closed, there is unseemly brawling amongst the clerics as a consequence of perceived offence.

I had two keys made, one of which I retained - but annoyingly lost whilst journeying home. I hid the other where none, I trust, will ever find it. If that door should, one day, need to be opened, it must either be hacked down with a mighty axe or opened by one who has read this document - if they are clever enough to work out where the surviving key is located. Only those of my descendants who bear the mark will ever read this document, so I may go to my eternal rest content that the maze will remain a hidden mystery for as long as needs be.

'Dear descendant, whomsoever you may be, note that the key, should you require same, can be found by following the instructions given below, followed by secondary details to be found on the back of the stone altar in the chapel named for the discoverer of the true cross:

> *'A keeper of old laid the Mark of The Power*
> *In full sight of all, who, unknowing, walk o'er.*
> *Where one of its rays lights the way to the dawn...*

'One thing I am sure of is that the damnable Cyrus Dexter will never know anything of this trip, for having failed in his attempt to thieve that which is most precious to my family, I have had him locked up by the Magistrates for several years. And good riddance, say I - my long dead cousin Grimbald certainly has a lot to answer for. Until I apprehended his villainous descendant and better understood his misconceived motivations, I would never have guessed that any of the severed line of Grimbald had survived to this day and age - and every one of them, it would seem, a rogue or an assassin!'

This was getting very interesting. A hidden key... a failed thief... and someone amongst her ancestors called Grimbald. That name was familiar. Where had she read it recently? Sam sat back, her face screwed in concentration as she tried to remember. After a moment the answer came to her - it was sneering Simon's younger son. He must have been thoroughly disenchanted to learn that he had missed out on the Earldom - and it sounded as if his side of the family had split away and gone on to produce a string of questionable descendants, culminating in this Cyrus whom her grandfather had caught, denounced and had jailed for attempted theft of... *that which is most precious*? It had to be the casket.

Why, though, was granddad glad to have made the trip to the Holy Land without Cyrus knowing? Before Sam had time to think about that, Kaye appeared and took a chair opposite her, looking refreshed in clean, lightweight slacks and a short-sleeved shirt. It was the slight droop of his azure eyes that gave away his underlying tiredness - that and the yawn escaping him, which he politely covered with a hand.

'Poor old thing,' she joked. 'It's all too much for you, this jet-setting, isn't it?'

'Less of the old, if you don't mind. I'm only thirty three - youngest professor in the faculty, I'll have you know.'

'Don't worry, I won't tell them you can't hack it outside the ivory towers.'

'Ha! That comment only serves to demonstrate your ignorance concerning the vicious day-to-day cut and thrust that goes on in academia. You've got bags under your eyes too, by the way, fair lady.'

Sam grinned. 'But they'll be gone in the morning, unlike yours.'

'I'll be the judge of that when tomorrow comes,' he retorted amiably. 'So, now we've finished insulting each other, what's the plan of action?'

Sam shuffled the pages of her grandfather's trip notes together and said, 'A long cold drink, I think, while we wait for the hire car to turn up. Ghulam's dealing with that. Then I thought we might visit Saladin's tomb.'

'Good - nothing but a tourist interlude, I expect, but you never know.' Kaye yawned again. 'Where's Raoul?'

'I haven't seen him since we arrived. The visit to Mount Quasioun is tomorrow, so I'll leave a message to say we'll meet him at eight for breakfast.' Sam spotted a waiter and beckoned for service.

Shortly after they had finished their drinks, Ghulam returned, wearing black slacks, a white, long-sleeved shirt and a tie with the Dexter family crest on it. He looked cool and smart. 'The car is ready, Miss'm. Do you wish to leave for the Umayyad Mosque now?'

'Yes, let's do that, please,' replied Sam, picking up her sheaf of papers. Reading the remainder could wait until later.

A bored guard sat on a hard wooden chair in the tiny porch of Saladin's mausoleum, which stood next to the north western corner of the massive Umayyad Mosque. They had not entered the mosque itself, but did venture into its courtyard to glance at the central ablution fountain, said to mark the half way point between Istanbul and Mecca. Now, nodding politely to the guard, they picked up a small leaflet in Arabic from his rickety table and entered the mausoleum.

'Oliver, are you able to translate that leaflet on the hoof, by any chance?' asked Sam. 'It would be nice to know what I'm looking at.'

'It's not hugely informative,' replied Kaye. 'It says that Saladin died in 1193 of a fever and was initially buried in the Citadel fortress, but was moved here two years later - presumably it took two years to build this place. There are two sarcophagi, as we can see... it says the ornate marble one was presented by the German Kaiser, Wilhelm II, in 1898. He intended it to replace the old wooden sarcophagus, but no-one wanted to disturb Saladin's rest, so they simply plonked the new sarcophagus next to the old one and left it there.'

'So the body of Saladin is in the wooden one?'

'Not exactly: Muslim practice is to bury the dead and place the sarcophagus over the top of the grave, so the sarcophagus is just a shell protecting the confines of the grave.'

Worn carpet runners covered the speckled tile floor around and between the two sarcophagi, both of which were substantial oblong boxes with tent-shaped lids rising to human head height. Whilst the marble gift of the Kaiser was fully visible, Saladin's wooden sarcophagus was loose-covered with a heavy, peacock-green, satin drape, highly embroidered in cream silk thread with Arabic text on all four sides as well as on the lid, each panel embellished with borders of stylised fuchsias. Around the upper edge of the body of the sarcophagus, the drape was trimmed with heavy silk braid from which dangled large cream silk tassels.

'How beautiful,' murmured Sam, reaching out to run one of the tassels through her fingers. 'They must still revere Saladin to decorate his tomb like this. What a shame we can't see the actual wooden structure - although at almost a thousand years old I expect it's rather fragile.'

'The Arabic on the cover says: *'Oh Allah! Be satisfied with this soul and open to him the gates of Paradise, that being the last conquest for which he hoped'*,' translated Kaye, looking round from a close inspection of the text. Sam was there and nodded, but Ghulam was nowhere to be seen. A moment later he popped out from the far side of the sarcophagus and beckoned urgently.

'Professor, Sir, could you come and help me please,' he said very quietly. 'I seem to have dropped my contact lens.' Then he put a finger to his lips. Puzzled, Kaye walked round to the back of the tomb and crouched down next to the chauffer, who proceeded to lift up the bottom edge of the satin drape, revealing something written on a small panel of the geometrically fretted wood beneath. 'Do you see my lens anywhere?' continued Ghulam, for the benefit of the guard's ears.

'I'm feeling around on the carpet for it,' answered Kaye, understanding the ruse now. He peered quickly at the ancient Arabic text on the panel. It translated as:

'Here, too soon, must I lie at rest, his Bastard Sword upon my breast,
Yet, even ancient mystic gold will not stop Richard growing cold.
Only Allah has our measure, freeing us from earthly treasure:
He that heeds men's suffering cries earns greater gifts in Paradise.'

Pulling down the drape again, Kaye stood, saying, 'I've found your lens. Let's go before you lose it again.' He winked at Sam and headed for the exit, saying nothing of what he had seen until they were cooling off in the Mercedes' air conditioning while Ghulam drove them back to the Beit Khan.

Repeating his translation of the hidden verses to Sam, Kaye said, 'I know the Lionheart's battle sword was named the Épée Bâtarde - which means the Bastard Sword. I surmise that Richard gave the sword to Saladin and, in return, received a gift of ancient *mystic* gold - it's got to have been the casket, so these verses are confirmation of what we had begun to suspect.' Ever the historian, he could not help adding, 'I'd say those two enemies actually bore a great respect for one another, from the value and significance of their gifts - I wonder if the Bastard Sword is still on Saladin's breast? That would be some treasure in its own right!'

'We'll go back and steal it later,' laughed Sam.

After they had gone, Richter, having observed their visit from a safe distance, entered the mausoleum himself and spent some time inside, looking for anything that might account for the big grin apparent on Kaye's face as he had strolled out of its doors. Unsuccessful, sweating and jetlagged, he kicked at the marble base of the Kaiser's sarcophagus in frustration and stormed out past the open-mouthed guard, hailing a cab back to the hotel. There he showered, then spent some time admiring his inflamed scar in the bathroom mirror while he thought about how pleasurable it would feel to put a gun into Samantha Dexter's proud, aristocratic mouth and watch her terrified, pleading eyes as he slowly squeezed the trigger.

CHAPTER 15

A DILEMMA AND A DEED

The Tower of London, England, 11 July, 1483 AD

Two days had passed since his meeting with Buckingham. Simon Dexter trod quietly up the secret staircase between the Garden Tower and the Wakefield Tower. Half way up, he stopped, raising his lantern to illuminate the inner wall in quest of the stone that bore a carved leopard's head with oddly empty eye sockets. Locating it, he inserted a bronze key into the beast's right eye and pushed it home, hard. Turning the key one hundred and eighty degrees to the right, he was satisfied to hear the muted clunk as a section of the wall eased forward, then to one side, revealing a windowless recess secreted in the thickness of the wall, its only feature a small oak bench upon which rested an object covered in black velvet.

Stepping inside the cubby hole, Dexter placed his lantern on the bench and carefully peeled back the velvet wrap to expose the golden casket with its sunburst relief. Running his fingers over the arcane signs and symbols engraved on its domed lid and around its sides, he pondered on their lost meaning. Their very mysteriousness served only to heighten his inexplicable affinity for the ancient object of power. Its gleaming precious metal caught and reflected the lantern light, magnifying and softening it to push back the crypt-like darkness of the chamber.

Pulling a cylindrical, copper scroll holder from his belt, Dexter removed the protective cap from one end and slid out the contents, holding the vellum documents close to the lantern to illuminate them. They were warrants and Letters Patent from the King. The first stated a renunciation of the perpetual servitude of his bloodline and granted him and his heirs the status of free men. The second conferred upon him elevation to the Lords - a peerage in the form of an Earldom together with the lands, income, properties and estates, holdings and all else of five recently vacated Manors to be joined under his new title, in the Shire of Derby. The scrolls were signed and dated July tenth of that year and bore the Sovereign's great Seal of State.

The corners of Dexter's lips formed the ghost of a smile. It widened as he up-ended the copper tube to spill a small black leather purse into the palm of his hand. Opening its drawstring, he removed the royal signet ring that signified the oath of King Richard and held it up to the lantern light to read the inscription - *'Loyaulte me lie'* - engraved on the inner rim. Content, he replaced the ring in the purse and laid it on the bench. At its side he placed the boar's head dagger which bore the same inscription.

The Duke of Buckingham had, so far, kept to his word. Dexter wondered what Stafford's own price had been for mediating this matter. It had also been through Buckingham's help that Richard had waylaid and captured the young King Edward the Fifth at Stony Stratford and the Duke had consequently been rewarded handsomely with titles and honours. What more could the man desire, Dexter wondered, that drove him to wager all he already possessed - even to his very life - on this dangerous undertaking? The reward must be extraordinary to justify the risk. But it was not his business to conjecture. It would suffice that he should receive his own due rewards - and a long life in which to enjoy them.

His mind shifted to the job in hand as he eyed the meagre chamber. Only three men had seen its interior in more than a hundred years - his grandfather, his father and himself. He was critical of its dimensions but satisfied that it would serve the purpose he had in mind. Thoughts of the task ahead began to gnaw at his conscience. For as long as he could remember, he had despised the way the monarchy and its supporting mesh of nobility brutalised and enslaved those beneath them in order to maintain their own rank and privilege. Now, by his own actions, he was about to make it his destiny to become one of those he held in contempt and to complicate matters yet further, doubts as to whether he was capable of double murder in cold blood had begun to weigh on him. Carefully removing a round leather phial with a pewter lining from the hip pocket of his jerkin, he placed that, too, on the bench and looked at it, considering its contents.

Earlier that day he had paid a clandestine visit to the Captain of a Maltese ship he knew to be currently docked on the Thames. Unobserved, he had lifted a flagstone in the cellar floor of the Byward Tower. The narrow steps leading down were treacherously slippery and, making his way through the tunnel beneath the Tower moat, he had shivered as water drips from the roof dampened the hood of his featureless, brown wool cloak. Trying to avoid brushing against the wet, mould-slimed walls, he could not stop himself from wondering how much longer the tunnel could withstand the enormous pressure from above before it collapsed in on itself. He did not favour the idea of being engulfed in a lethal torrent of water, mud and stone.

Captain Rafiq was a rough, stubble-chinned trader, half-Egyptian, half-Syrian; a Muslim Arab apothecary who imported and dealt in rare unguents and - if no questions were asked and the price was right - poisons. Dexter had asked no questions, paid Rafiq in gold, and departed with a potion containing ground mandrake and henbane, their bitterness masked by exotic, aromatic spices that would delay, for a very short time, the effects of those two deadly compounds.

Now, alone in the dim, lantern-lit recess, as he contemplated the insidious murder weapon housed in the innocent-looking phial, Dexter's conscience troubled him, the moral conflict within his own mind beginning to shred his earlier resolve. He raised one hand, inserting it inside the breast-slit of his doublet to feel the star-shaped *naevus* on his chest. It seemed to pulsate in rhythm with his speeding heart as his doubts fired his nerves. Placing his other hand on the warm, living gold of the casket, he waited, attempting to compose himself; at last the pulsing slowed and then ceased. Reason returned; resolve again took command.

A Dilemma and A Deed

His destiny having been inculcated into him by his father, his life's purpose centred round the casket. All that mattered was its preservation until *The One* was found - and its safekeeping in the hands of the Dexter bloodline was a sworn and sacred duty which stretched back far beyond even the time of Abdul Hamid. It was his beginning, middle, and end. Nothing else mattered. As his father had told him, *'...in taking action to preserve the casket and keep it safe there can be no right or wrong; only what has to be; only what must be done'*.

Dexter breathed in deeply. He was ready. Gathering the items on the table to his person, he re-wrapped the casket and picked it up. He would now hide it in his own quarters, safe from dangerously inquisitive eyes, until he departed the Tower for good. Slipping out of the chamber, he sealed the entrance. Later, he would risk the moat tunnel once more, this time to pay another visit to Segmar, the crabbed old hag with a stooped gait who was a fount of knowledge concerning wild shrubs and herbs. She had already advised him that she knew where *planta genesta* grew and, for a silver half-groat, would provide him with a freshly cut sprig close to the full yellow of its blooming. 'A pretty blossom for a heart's keepsake,' she had cackled knowingly - and he had not disabused her.

An hour later, quitting the grounds of the Tower once more, he distracted his mind by considering how to style his new Earldom. He was at liberty to pick any one of the five Manors' names. He spoke them aloud to see how each sounded: Hoddington; Blackleigh; Elmsdale, Stone End and Chaumont. Four were blunt, northern names that sounded uncultured to his ears. Only one rolled off his tongue with a courtly, aristocratic lilt. Chaumont, he thought, warming to the sound of it: yes, he would become the Earl of Chaumont.

The princes were agitated. Identically dressed in pleated, scarlet tunics with gold lace across the chest, tapering to the waist, they also both had straight, fair hair cut to the nape of their necks. Edward, tall for his twelve years and handsome in appearance, peered longingly through a leaded window set into the thick stone wall of the Garden Tower and begged, 'Why will you not let us go out to the garden?'

Simon Dexter half bowed and slowly shook his head. 'I regret, Your Majesty, that his Grace the Duke of Buckingham instructs that you should, for a measure, remain here in the Garden Tower for safety's sake.'

Richard, aged ten, had been standing by the huge fireplace that was laid into one wall, with deep recesses on either side. Leaving the fire's warmth, he moved across the room towards Dexter and made his complaint in the sweet, piping tone of one whose voice has yet to break. 'We are not sleeping or eating well. We have felt sickly of late and the doctor says we need the light and warmth of the sun and more exercise if we hope to improve our humours. Surely even Buckingham cannot deny us these rights?'

Looking around the chamber - at the floor tiled in green and yellow with patterns that included flowers and fleurs-de-lis; at the grandly carved four poster bed with velvet damask drapes and at the tapestries depicting hunting scenes that hung around the walls - Dexter shrugged and said, 'But your quarters are richly furnished and comfortable, are they not? And as to whether Buckingham can deny you the use of the garden, I would respectfully remind you that he acts only under orders from Richard, your uncle.'

When Edward answered, there was pleading in his voice. 'Then we *must* see our uncle and ask why he commands our confinement.'

'He will not come to you at present. He resides at Greenwich but soon proceeds to the castle at Windsor and may not return for some time. Have patience. Fortitude and forbearance are both princely qualities.' The princes looked at one another and Edward gave a small, unhappy shrug of submission. There was a moment's silence and then Dexter, pretending a yawn, said apologetically, 'Forgive me; tiredness creeps up on all men.'

Richard seemed surprised. 'Tired? How so? It is only late noon!'

Dexter seized the opening he had engineered. 'Like you, Sire, I have been suffering great difficulty in sleeping of late. I prevailed upon the kind nature of Brother Mercurio, who was good enough to prepare a potion for the problem. Alas, when I sip of it too early I must to my bed long in advance of my usual hour.'

Edward was intrigued. 'And you have partaken of this potion how long since?'

'About one half hour ago.'

Edward pressed his case. 'Do you think he would ... I mean, for us?'

Dexter shook his head as he ran fingers through his thick black hair. 'No, not this day, I fear. He is attending a meeting of clerics at Westminster Abbey before attending Midnight Mass.'

The brothers' disappointment was clear. Richard asked, 'Do you, by chance, have any of your potion to spare? We would gladly pay for it.'

Playing out the ruse, Dexter shook his head again as he patted the bulge in the hip pocket of his jerkin. By the pounding of his heart, the shortness of his breath and the uncomfortable rush of blood through his veins, he recognised that this was the moment of truth. He swallowed, repulsed by the thought of what was to follow.

In God's name, they're just children! How can I force my hand to this atrocity?

His father's words echoed again in his unwilling mind: *'...there is no right or wrong; only what has to be; only what must be done'.*

'You are most generous, Sire, but I do not want your money,' he assured Richard. 'I will gladly oblige you both for the sake of your fatigue.' Pulling the leather-covered phial out, he placed it next to a full water jug on a side table and fetched two small, engraved silver goblets from a wall shelf near the fireplace. He poured a little water into each goblet, chasing it with carefully gauged doses of his 'sleeping draught'. Rafiq's words reminded him, *'...just a thimbleful will do the job'.*

Swilling the noxious fluid in the goblets to mix it well, he handed one to each of the princes. 'It is not the most pleasant drink to quaff, I fear - I recommend you down it in one gulp while it remains at the height of its efficacy. You might feel its effect very quickly, so it would be wise to recline without delay. I know it is yet early to be abed, but you will feel the better for it on the morrow.'

The two boys smiled at him in thanks, threw back their heads and swallowed their draughts to the dregs, exclaiming and making faces at the bitter taste. Setting down their goblets, they jumped onto the bed and lay down as he had bid them. By virtue of its novelty, the whole affair seemed almost a game to them.

Dexter spent a few minutes looking thoughtfully through the window at the garden below - a haven of dappled sunlight, droning bees and the nodding heads of scented summer flowers - a haven these boys would never stroll and play in again. Donning his cloak to leave, he gave the two drowsy boys one final glance. They lay peacefully sprawled on the embroidered coverlet, their blond locks mingled and their guileless arms around one other in what would be their last brotherly embrace.

His gorge beginning to rise at the thought of how those innocent young faces would soon contort in pain and how their small bodies would writhe and arch in agonised convulsions as the toxins wracked ruin on their delicate internal organs, he departed swiftly, quietly locking the great, steel-strapped door behind him.

Concentrating on emptying his mind of guilt, Dexter skirted Tower green in the approaching dusk and made his way towards the Gothic structure that was Beauchamp Tower, built during the reign of King Edward I. Conceived with defence in mind, it was now used to lodge prisoners of rank who needed to be well guarded. Toward that line of work, Rulf, the man Dexter sought, was well suited. Rulf stood in the shadow of the tower, dressed for duty in a sallet helmet and a brigandine, a leather jacket lined inside with strips of metal riveted together for sturdy protection. Built more like a siege trebuchet than a man, he took in his stride the weight of his Italian falchion, a single-edged heavy battle sword easily capable of shearing mail and crushing light armour.

Dexter made no acknowledgement of Rulf's presence. He continued round the green at an even pace and made his way to the chamber directly above Traitors' Gate, knowing that, having seen him, the guard would follow.

As soon as they were together inside the plain stone chamber, the guard's gruff voice was equally plain. 'You have it?'

A Dilemma and A Deed

Dexter gave a brief nod. Throwing Rulf a purse of gold, he studied a face scarred from battles fought at Edgecote Moor, Losecote Field, Barnet and Tewkesbury. Rulf caught and weighed the purse in his hand. He unfastened its drawstrings with big, clumsy fingers, checked the contents and looked up, scowling.

'You said there would be more.'

'Yes, there will be - much more, once the job is done - enough to purchase ten casks of ale and buy the services of enough whores to keep even a bull like you satisfied for a year!' Dexter smiled to himself. Of all the human traits he had encountered there was one above all others that he knew he could invariably rely on - greed.

A section of tiled wall at the side of the fireplace in the Garden Tower made a low grating sound as it swung open. Two figures moved silently and quickly to the four poster bed where the princes lay, their small, blanched faces lifeless and their lips drawn back from their teeth in rictus grins. Judging by the way the spasms had contorted their bodies, their deaths must have been excruciating. Dexter pointed at Richard's body and ordered, quietly, 'This one first.' He forced the acid of rising bile back down his throat.

Rulf lifted the limp form so that Dexter could spread a thick blanket beneath it. As Rulf lowered the child's body and straightened his limbs for wrapping, Dexter said, 'One moment.'

He lifted the boy's right hand and drew the ring off its third finger, slipping it into his belt pouch. Unsheathing the double edged dagger Buckingham had provided, he placed the point above the boy's heart, pausing only for an instant before thrusting it deeply into his chest, once only. Removing and wiping the dagger on the prince's scarlet sleeve, he beckoned to Rulf and said softly, 'Now, wrap and bind him well.' Rulf busied himself with the unpleasant task.

Dexter moved around the bed and took the signet ring from the third finger of Edward's right hand, housing it safe with his brother's. In its stead, he slid onto the boy's pale finger the signet ring procured through his own foresight; that of the King. To prevent the man-sized ring from slipping off the slender digit, he passed a piece of twine between ring and finger, looping it up to the wrist and tying it off. If the bodies were to be discovered within the King's lifetime, the identity of the orchestrator of their murder would be clear to all.

Plunging the dagger through the heart of the late heir apparent to the throne of England, he looked across at Rulf. 'I'm finished. You can deal with this one now - and hurry.' Obediently, the guard wrapped the second body in a thick blanket and bound it with cord.

As Dexter led the way with a lantern, Rulf manhandled both the corded bundles through the narrow door at the side of the fireplace, out of the room and up the narrow stone stairs to Dexter's secret cubby hole. There, Dexter opened the doorway with his key and motioned for Rulf to take the bodies in. Flushed from his efforts, Rulf unstrapped and doffed his helmet, laying it down on a step as he wiped the gathered sweat from his brow, then he dragged each of the bodies inside, in turn, unceremoniously dumping one on top of the other.

'No,' commanded Dexter, 'Place them apart.'

Rulf grunted. 'Why bother; they're dead, aren't they?'

'Because I say so,' Dexter replied sharply. 'That's why. In any case, they were royal princes. Show some respect!'

Rulf grunted again as he turned and knelt to separate the blanket-wrapped bundles. This act presented his back to Dexter, who moved up behind him with rapid stealth. Before Rulf could utter a cry, Dexter clamped one hand firmly under the man's chin and pressed the other to the back of his grizzled head, while planting a knee firmly into the centre of his spine. Giving the head a sharp, savage wrench to the left, he felt and heard the snap as the cervical vertebrae dislocated, severing the spinal cord. After one further wrench to be certain, he let the guard's body slump to one side.

Avoiding Rulf's blankly accusing eyes, Dexter fumbled in the dead man's pocket to retrieve the purse of gold bestowed earlier, muttering, 'My need is greater than yours.' He felt little remorse for ending the life of the mindless brute but, nevertheless, his hands were shaking as he stepped beyond the threshold of the recess and secured the door. His nature tended more to that of a courtier than a killer

A Dilemma and A Deed

and he prayed that circumstance would never again call upon him to commit such acts of physical violence. He also prayed that no breath of air would disturb the mortal dust in that stone-sealed chamber until the very Tower itself crumbled to rubble. *'In pace requiem,'* he whispered as he descended the stairs for the final time.

Returning to the princes' quarters in the Garden Tower, he straightened the bed linen, alert for any telltale signs of blood, but, knowing that a dead heart pumped no blood, he was unsurprised to find no stains. Picking up some loose pieces of cord that Rulf had dropped, he was also mindful to wash and dry the two silver goblets he had used to deliver death. He opened the window and flung the swill water down onto the garden below. After taking one last look round at the tidy room, notable now only for its emptiness, he departed by the main entrance, leaving the door unlocked.

The Duke of Buckingham stared hard at Dexter. The intense tone of his voice betrayed his calm exterior. 'And so, shall his Majesty sleep better this night?' The words echoed slightly round the vaulted chamber above Traitors' Gate.

Dexter nodded. 'I'll warrant his dreams will be the sweeter for the knowledge that you have received this token.' He opened his left fist to reveal a near-flowering sprig of broom, in which nestled the signet rings of the two princes. 'I have fulfilled my promise - I expect Richard to do likewise.' He dropped the costly sprig into Buckingham's outstretched palm.

The Duke wasted no time in picking out the rings and pocketing them. 'You have nought to fear. It is manifest that to renege would go against Richard's own best interests. Does anyone else know what was accomplished this night?' The question was asked in an innocuous manner, but Dexter knew what prompted it.

'You have no cause for concern, Your Grace. All you need know is that I have put in place a guarantee that, in the case of my betrayal, will most assuredly be the undoing of you both. On that you have my solemn word.'

Buckingham gave a hollow, nervous laugh. 'We are all pledged, each to the other; let all be forgotten and all will be well.' He regarded the yellow-budded broom still in his hand and frowned, saying, 'I know it signifies the task completed, but tell me, Dexter, when I present this twig to him, what, pray, do you expect the King do with it?'

For the first time in all the years the Duke had known him, Dexter actually smiled.

'He can shove it up his golden crown for all I care!'

Nottingham Castle, England, 12 August, 1485 AD

Simon Dexter, Earl of Chaumont, chafed by the burnished breast plate he wore strapped over his mail shirt, leaned out over the battlements high on castle rock. A light meadow fragrance of scythed grass infused the air as the sun burned off the last of the early morning mist. In the middle distance, beyond the meadows and marshes to the south of Nottingham, the silver ribbon of the Trent glistened as it curved in the flow of its journey to the sea. Straightening up, he pulled on one studded leather gauntlet and eased his battle sword in its scabbard before turning to his manservant, Lovell Caeg, of whom he enquired, 'Where's Richard?'

'In the oratory of the Black Tower chapel, my Lord, holding a council of war with the Bishop of York and those Lords and Noblemen loyal to his cause.'

'Loyal to his purse, more like,' Simon snorted, winking at Lovell. Less than thirty years of age, the broad-shouldered manservant stood taller than six feet and sported a head of thick, cornstalk hair. Simon had discovered him, gaunt with hunger, a craftsman without work and in desperate straits, living with a young wife and three ragged children in a daub and wattle lean-to on the outskirts of Hoddington village on Chaumont land. The Earl had put food in their bellies and had clothed them. At that time, Simon had already decided which of the five empty manor houses on his lands would be his seat - a sprawling pile of timbers and thatch nestling in the wooded folds and agricultural land of South Derbyshire. Some of the heavy beams of the hall were Saxon-hewn and others had been added later, but all

A Dilemma and A Deed

were in need of renovation. He had put Lovell and his skills to good use plundering materials from the lesser manor houses to repair and expand his new home. Now, almost two years later, Lovell was at his side as his personal squire, more friend than serf.

'The King seems low in humour,' Lovell commented.

Dexter scowled. 'Aye, that may be, but if I'd lost my only son and heir last year, followed by my wife this year, I would be in low humour too. Now he's planning to engage in the toils of war to prevent Henry Tudor from attempting to pull the crown of England off his head - again.'

'Again, my Lord?'

Dexter slowly pulled on his other studded gauntlet as he made reply. 'In October of the year before last, the crown not yet three months on Richard's brow, the Duke of Buckingham, disenchanted by the King's failure to keep his promises, conspired with Tudor, inviting him to return from exile and marry Elizabeth of York. For his part, Buckingham agreed to raise an army from his estates in Wales and join Tudor against Richard. With ten thousand crowns from Francis of Brittany and five thousand mercenaries, Henry's fleet set out from Brittany to invade England, but a storm drove his ships back to port. Buckingham's army, beset by the same storm, deserted when Richard's forces came against them. Buckingham was publicly proclaimed traitor and tried to escape in disguise, but was turned in for the bounty Richard had put on his head. He was convicted of treason and felt the kiss of the axe-man's blade in Salisbury on the second day of November that year.'

'Forsooth, why did the Duke risk all?'

''Twas power lust that ruled him, Lovell, plain and simple.' Gesturing at the King's war standard fluttering atop the new tower, Dexter added, 'If you're in want of any symbol that embodies that kind of greed, look no further!'

Discordant trumpet fanfares rent the air as King Richard III and his entourage of Lords and advisors left the Black Tower. Mounting his white Surrey, Richard scarcely glanced in Dexter's direction as he made his way down the slope to the barbican and the main gate.

Behind him, to the dull thud of a drumbeat and flying pennants, two dozen fully armoured knights led a disciplined column of half-armoured men-at-arms in kettle hats, bearing a lethal selection of halberds, glaives and other pole-arms, their metal tips glinting in the sun. As the column snaked its way down through the heavily guarded gate, Lovell asked, 'Where does he go, my Lord?'

Dexter shook his head. 'Probably down Castle Gate into the market to whip up the gander of his troops. Men from Repton and Newark are expected to arrive today to rally to his banner. Perhaps he goes to greet them.' Leaning forward to look out over the battlements again, he peered down. A hundred and fifty feet below, the thin slash of the River Leen lapped its way past the base of the rock before sluicing past the French and English boroughs of the town to join the river Trent further downstream. Men swarmed around boats moored to temporary jetties, as cargos were off-loaded and hauled up to the castle or manhandled into the storage caves carved within the rock itself. In the meadows to the fore, archers were at practice, loosing goose-feathered shafts at the butts. All this activity, Dexter thought, and for what? For an over-decorated, hollow metal circlet and for power, honour and glory, never mind the rights or wrongs of it.

Lovell disturbed his reverie. 'My Lord, someone approaches.'

The Earl turned and spied a stocky man with a bushy beard, dressed in mercer's garb, making haste up the escarpment to the battlements. Reaching them, slightly out of breath, the fellow bowed to Dexter. 'My Lord, Sir Cedric of Farndon sends you his greetings and awaits you with his companions at The Trip to Jerusalem Inn.'

'What companions?'

'I know not who they are, My Lord, only that there are three; four if you count Sir Cedric, who await your pleasure.'

Dexter paused before answering. These were perilous times and vigilance was paramount. Before he made his next move he had to be certain, beyond doubt. 'You have something for me from Sir Cedric?'

The messenger removed a small square of parchment from his belt pouch, unfolded it and presented it to the Earl. One corner was torn off, leaving a jagged edge. The parchment bore no written word, merely a red wax seal with the impression of a dragon. Dexter took a shred of paper from his purse and matched it to the torn corner, scrutinising the fit closely to confirm that the messenger had truly been instructed by Sir Cedric of Farndon, a secret envoy of Henry Tudor. 'Tell Sir Cedric that I will be pleased to meet with him and his companions very shortly,' confirmed Dexter, looking up again. The messenger nodded briefly, turned on his heel and was gone.

'Will you require me, my Lord?' Lovell asked.

'Yes. Stay close, but not too close. I need you to watch my back while I'm engaged at the inn.'

The Trip was crowded and filled with the noise of big, rough men attired in stinking leather brigandines, who argued and shouted over their pots of ale as Dexter elbowed his way through their mass to a patched leather drape covering the entrance to one of the ground floor caverns at the rear. He left Lovell there with instructions to let no-one pass. The sandstone cavern, its strong odour of sweat and ale mingling with the haze of smoke from oil lamps, was large enough to accommodate a rough plank table, around which four hooded men sat on uneven benches.

Dexter seated himself at one end, poured ale into a spare clay pot and acknowledged Sir Cedric of Farndon with a nod before placing an irregular shaped piece of wood on the table. He slid it towards the nearest of the other three men, who in turn produced a similar piece of wood, slotting it into the first piece. The others followed suit and when all four pieces were together they formed a six inch diameter plaque with the outline of a red dragon in the middle. Dexter examined the disc closely before breaking it up and handing the pieces back. As the men removed their hoods, Dexter said quietly, 'To business, Sirs...'

Sir Cedric cut him off. 'My Lord, I did advise that we meet in secret, not in some hole at the back of a clamorous tavern ...and, pray, who are these others you have called to our tryst?'

Dexter's eyes narrowed. 'When there is reason to be secretive, guile is better enacted in the face of all men so they may recognise not what they see. As for these strangers, know that they are knight emissaries who carry the pledged word of the allies Henry Tudor seeks to help him defeat Richard. I have spent many months earning their trust and bringing them together - and so to business. What news of Tudor?'

Sir Cedric cast a glance over his right shoulder. Satisfied that no-one was in earshot, he unrolled a hastily drawn map of England and the Welsh borders. 'Henry left Harfleur on the first day of August, landing near Milford Haven six days later with two thousand French mercenaries and a handful of Lancastrian and Yorkist lords and knights. Though he enjoys a strong following in Wales and the Marches, at Shrewsbury he had only five thousand men under his banner.'

One of the three knights, a grizzled veteran, spoke up. 'Where is he now?'

'After the long march through Wales, his men were weary, so he is temporarily encamped at Lichfield. He wishes to march south to meet Richard, but with only five thousand men against Richard's estimated fifteen and a half thousand, he is hesitant. Without the support I trust shall be pledged by your masters, he must flee back to Brittany. If he stands alone he will be badly mauled.'

The grizzled man spoke again. 'My master, Thomas, Lord Stanley, is married to Tudor's mother. He commands, alongside his brother, six thousand and more of Richard's army and is most reluctant to take up arms against his son-in-law. Besides, Richard has taken one of Lord Stanley's sons, Lord Strange, as hostage against his future good conduct. Stanley will not pay fealty or homage to any man, King or commoner, who would act thus, especially a scullion dog like Richard!'

On the other side of the leather drape in the main room of the inn, men were bellowing ribald songs.

One of the other knights joined the conversation. 'Aye, well said. I speak for the brother, Sir William Stanley. If Tudor gives his word, on oath, that he will make good the promises broken by Richard, then Sir William pledges his support.'

Sir Cedric looked at the third knight. 'So you must speak for Henry Percy, Earl of Northumberland?'

'Aye, I do. He commands three thousand men and will stand on the field of battle beside Richard but will not participate in the fighting unless it goes badly for Henry - then he will be Henry's man. Tudor knows the terms of the alliance. Does he agree to accept?'

'Yes,' Sir Cedric answered quickly. 'I am authorised to agree on his behalf to all his allies' terms. Where will our forces combine?'

Dexter answered, 'On the field of battle, Sir Cedric, wherever that may be. If my counting is not amiss, Tudor's army will be swelled to about fourteen thousand and Richard's reduced to roughly six thousand. The Earl of Northumberland and the Stanleys must march with Richard when he moves south to Leicester in a few days. His resources are stretched to the limit and support for him is already crumbling. One whiff of treachery on the part of his Lieutenants and it will be he who retreats, possibly to Warwick Castle, or Kenilworth, or even back here. Thus, the field of battle will be the moment of truth.'

'Very well,' Sir Cedric conceded, 'And your terms, my Lord? What do you desire of Henry Tudor?'

Dexter spoke in low, earnest tones. 'Tudor knows well my desires. If he is victorious over Richard, then for the part he knows I played in that victory I want his pledge that my position, title and lands are guaranteed for me and my heirs and their successors for all time.' He handed Sir Cedric his irregular shaped section of the dragon disc. 'In return, this is my pledge of fealty to him and his heirs and successors.'

Sir Cedric looked at the other three men. Each in turn handed him their piece of the disc. Then all stood and raised their pots of ale in a common toast. *'Le Roi est mort; vive le Roi!'*

Silently, one by one at short intervals, they left the inn. Dexter was the last to go, pushing his way out through the drunkenly boisterous mob, Lovell following unobtrusively.

Dexter had already determined that, come the day Richard marched south, his own men would not form part of the column. He had fulfilled his obligation of fealty to Richard by answering his call to arms, providing fifty-five able bodied, fully armed men. But they were not Richard's men - they belonged to the land; they belonged to Chaumont. He wiped rivulets of sweat from his brow. Richard would have his men butchered in the slaughter of some battlefield for a cause they neither understood nor cared about. Would Richard find him another blacksmith, another stone mason or men to reap the harvest or scythe the long summer grass? No! So when Richard's army moved, he would instruct his men to slip away quietly before battle was joined. They would find their own routes back to Chaumont. The work to be done there bettered anything Richard could offer them.

Lovell exclaimed, 'My Lord, if I am not mistaken, the Steward of your household seeks you out!'

Surprised, Dexter looked where Lovell was pointing. Thomas, an elderly, sinewy man, was dismounting from a windblown, dapple grey mare. As he approached Dexter he bowed slightly. 'My Lord, I have come in haste and am relieved to discover you in such timely fashion, for I bear important news.'

'Then speak it, good Steward.'

'My Lord, in the early hours of yesterday morning your wife gave birth. You are a father!'

'Is it a son?'

'No, My Lord...'

'Dexter's eager smile faded slightly. "Tis a girl child.'

Thomas's creased face smiled broadly. '...No, my Lord, *two* sons! Your wife is delivered of twins - two boys with just minutes between their births. Upon my soul, my Lord, you have my heartfelt congratulations.'

Dexter's mind was racing. Two sons! He grasped Thomas by the arm. 'Are they well - do they have...is everything...I mean...?'

'Yes, My Lord, they are healthy and strong. The second-born has a slight blemish on his chest, but the doctor says it is of no matter.'

Dexter breathed a sigh of pride and relief and released Thomas's arm. 'And my wife, the Lady Isobel, how does she fare?'

'She fares well, My Lord, and wishes you Godspeed home.'

Dexter pressed coins into the Steward's hand. 'Thank you Thomas. Thank you! This is good news indeed! Go, slake your thirst and hunger and when you and your mount are rested, return to Chaumont and inform the Lady Isobel that I will soon attend her.' As Thomas led his mount away towards the inn, Dexter grinned and said to Lovell, 'Back into the crush, man. Fetch out a large flagon of ale and two pots, quickly!'

Lovell returned from the inn with his load to find Dexter leaning on a crumbling sandstone wall at the side of the road, watching infantrymen file past, followed by a dozen newly forged cannons resting on stout carriages boasting iron-bound wheels that screeched on the uneven cobblestones. Filling two pots from the flagon of warm, pungent ale, the serf passed a pot to his Lord, who raised it in a toast: 'To the newborn!' His eyes softened as he looked at the weather-beaten face and rough, callused hands of his serf. 'Only once in a man's life does fate touch him with a firstborn and when it does, he should mark that time well. What say you?'

Lovell fidgeted uncertainly, unsure what answer was required of him. He said simply, 'Aye, my Lord.'

Dexter's face was grave for a moment, echoing the gravity of the words he was about to utter. 'When you return to Chaumont it will be as a free man.'

'But...My Lord...I have little money! I cannot afford to pay for my freedom...'

'No payment is required, Lovell. I am granting you - no, returning to you and your heirs - that which I have no right to withhold; your freedom. You will be welcome to stay on Chaumont land and work for me as a free man, or you can seek your fortune further afield; the choice is yours.' Before Lovell could respond, Dexter stood up and beckoned. 'Come, we must return to the castle. I have duties to perform and the King's commander will not take it kindly if I am found wanting.'

In the humidity and rising dust of the late morning, Dexter and Lovell trudged up the hill to the barbican. Below, in Nottingham market, Richard was rallying men to his white boar banner and making ready for war.

The Field of Redemore, Bosworth, Leicestershire, England, 22 August, 1485 AD

After two hours of unmitigated slaughter, the battle was done. Weary of looking through the slit of his pivotal visor, Henry Tudor removed his helm to reveal sweat-slicked, dark brown hair; similarly coloured eyes, thin eyebrows and a wide, slim-lipped mouth. He let his armoured courser pick its own way amongst the mud and blood-smeared slain.

It had been a brutal and near ruinous engagement. At its climax, Richard had seen Tudor's red dragon banner crossing the field with obvious intent to spur Northumberland into committing his force. Believing Henry had left himself isolated, Richard led a charge of a thousand knights, thinking to kill him and end the battle in one fell stroke. Henry's standard-bearer, William Brandon, was the first to fall to Richard's vicious attack. Discarding his broken lance and grasping his battle hammer, Richard and his knights began to hack their way through to Henry, who sat astride his courser surrounded by a defensive schiltron of pike-men.

Unfortunately for Richard, William Stanley chose that moment to advance his four thousand red-coated retainers to attack Richard's right flank. Unable to withstand that onslaught, Richard's army, both knights and infantry, broke and fled. Richard was now the one isolated - encircled by Lancastrians. Caught in a dense, struggling mass of men and horses, his helmet was knocked from his head, a misfortune that proved his undoing when he was dragged from his horse by a Welsh halberdier-man and the press of men closed in on him, hacking and stabbing. The killing blow was a savage slash from a broadsword that sliced his skull open to the brain. Dead, his armour and clothes were torn from him and his naked, bloody corpse was further mutilated before being unceremoniously slung over the back of his white Surrey and roped like a sack of oatmeal.

As Henry steadied his mount, Lord Stanley rode up, Richard's crown in his fist, a golden diadem that had once graced the late monarch's helmet.

'Lord Stanley, how came you by such a trinket?' Henry's question was half jest, half surprise.

Stanley gestured wildly as he answered, 'I found it hanging from a thorn bush yonder, Sire, but I warrant there's a more fitting place for its settling!'

'Well thought and even better said, Stanley,' Henry answered with a grin.

Stanley raised the glinting diadem so that all who stood nearby could see it. 'Sire, all here acknowledge the royal person of our Sovereign Lord, King Henry VII and the heirs of his body!' Kicking his steed closer, he reached across and placed the crown on Henry's head, then, standing in his stirrups with his sword held high, he loudly proclaimed, *'Le Roi est mort; vive le Roi!'* The cry spread and 'Long live the King!' began to roll out of men's mouths all across the battlefield.

Richard was the more experienced and competent commander, but the double-edged swords of treachery and betrayal have won the day for Henry, thought the blood-streaked Simon Dexter as he looked down on the scene from a nearby hillock, his expression wry and his sword arm aching. He had little stomach for the butchery he had just witnessed and even less desire to join the tumultuous mob below, drunk with victory and thrusting their gory weapons high in the air to cheer their new monarch. Besides, he had got what he'd come for. Safely tucked away in the pocket of the tunic beneath his cuirass was his own piece of the Tudor dragon disc. Henry Tudor had returned it to him in acknowledgement of his debt when they had met at Atherstone before the battle, affirming his pledge that if he was victorious, Dexter would remain a Lord and that his Earldom and estates would be guaranteed for all time.

Remounting his courser, Dexter turned his back on the carnage and spurred the animal forward, his thoughts turning inwards. The long years he had spent prowling the Tower's secret passages and dark corners seemed little more than a dream now. He would let those memories slide away. Across his brain there flashed a rapid sequence of unbidden images - a leather phial - fine, blond hair tangled on a flowered coverlet - small clenched fingers... He shook his head violently to banish those lingering nightmares for the last time. No-one would ever know what had befallen the vanished Princes: with both Buckingham and Richard dead, that dark secret was safe.

And his much greater secret, that of the casket of the Ancients, would now be safe as well, protected by its Keepers, unhindered, generation upon generation.

He was, in truth, at last a free man, never to walk again in the shadow of another. Digging his heels into the flanks of his courser once again, the Earl urged the heavy bay into a ponderous canter and with the faithful Lovell following, headed north to Chaumont.

CHAPTER 16

PRAYERS FOR SUCCESS

Mount Quasioun, Damascus, Syria, 21 June, 2016 AD

'Four days in this hellhole,' complained Umarah, 'And I always get the midnight to four shift.' A drop of sweat fell from the end of his nose as he shifted his elbows on the unforgiving rock. 'What's the use? We're never going to get near that place...'

'Will you shut up?' hissed Bashir, training his binoculars on a Mercedes SUV coming up the gorge road. 'That's no press car,' he muttered, turning the dial slightly to bring the vehicle's occupants more clearly into focus. 'Four people inside: the driver is dark-skinned; probably Asian; the rest are Europeans, I'd say.' He watched as the vehicle drew up and stopped near the archaeologists' camp, his dark eyes calculating.

The new arrivals got out, one an under-dressed woman who immediately exclaimed at the arid heat and then pointed up at the hole in the craggy cliff. The blond man answered her just as the big archaeologist with the lush beard came out of his tent and waved at them all. But it was the dark haired, muscular-looking man who first walked forward to greet the archaeologist, shading his pale eyes with one hand.

'Couldn't be press - no cameras,' commented Alim, leaning on his elbows to crane over the edge of the gorge.

'They're climbing up to the tomb,' said Bashir. 'I think they're going in.'

'They must be important,' asserted Alim. 'No visitor has been inside since that Catholic came. Why are they letting a woman in? That's what I'd like to know.'

'That's easy to answer,' said Umarah. 'Christian men have no control over their women. They let them choose their own husbands; have control over their own money; wear clothes like whores... I mean, look at the brazen hussy with her bare shoulders and her jeans clinging to her legs so you can see the shape of them; shameful.'

'Women were created by the devil; our Khassahs teach us so,' confirmed Bashir, licking his lips and reluctantly handing his binoculars to Alim once he had enjoyed a close examination of the exposed parts of the woman's rather fine body. 'But as you say, Alim, these foreigners must be important, so I want to know who they are and why they're here.' He made a quick decision. 'I'll follow them when they leave. If they're staying in the city, I'll find out where and, when I return, I'll bring fresh supplies and cold drinks. Keep a man on watch. I'll be looking for a full report when I get back.' He wriggled backwards until he was sure he could stand without being seen from below, shook red sand from the folds of his didashah and hurried away to negotiate the rocky slope down to their camp and onwards to the Sham parked a mile down the dirt road. He decided he would drive to the first junction and wait for the Mercedes to pass - then simply follow it.

Sam expressed surprise at seeing the cave tomb entrance protected by two armed militia men, so Laurent explained about Rousseau's murder. As he spoke, it was clear from his harrowed expression that he had taken the loss badly.

Kaye said, 'We are very sorry to hear of this appalling incident. I'm sure the police are doing all they can to bring the culprit to justice. Unfortunately, this bears out what I predicted on hearing of the discovery of this tomb, which was that it could cause a lot of trouble because of its faith implications. I understand why you would assume tomb robbery, but have you considered the possibility that your colleague was killed for spiritual rather than material reasons?'

Laurent pulled at his beard. 'Unless the police catch whoever committed the crime, we'll probably never know.' He drew a deep breath and lightened his tone, smiling at all four of them. *'Alors -* enough talk of poor Alain. I don't want to cast a cloud over your visit and you will be amazed by what you are going to see; that I can guarantee.' He led the way up to the tomb, indicating the best footholds on the steepest section and cautioning them all to make use of the rope that had been set as a guideline and handhold. 'Mind your heads going in,' he warned. 'I'll go first so I can help you through the gap into the sepulchre, which is about three metres along the tunnel. It's rather cramped inside, as Jean is still working on the in-situ preservation of the remains. We sent a sample away for carbon dating and, before you ask, we do expect an accurate result.'

'How long does such a test take?' asked Richter as they reached the tunnel entrance and gathered on the narrow ledge there.

'I don't want to bore you with science,' smiled Laurent, 'But it's worth explaining why we have to wait a while for the results. Carbon dating relies on measurement of the concentration of carbon-14 in the sample. All living things continuously take up carbon atoms as they breathe and eat, but this stops when they die. The proportion of radioactive carbon-14 to normal carbon-12 is naturally around one to one billion and it decays with a half life of around five and a half thousand years.'

'Sorry, what is 'half life', exactly?' enquired Sam.

'That's the time it takes for half the total amount of carbon-14 in a sample to decay to its stable isotope, carbon-12. Because of the low concentration and long half life, it's difficult to measure the carbon-14 concentration in any given archaeological sample of a few grams, so the test is done by a very sensitive spectrometer that, in simple terms, counts the amount of carbon-14 present - but this takes several days to do. By comparing that result with the normal concentration we know would have been present when the plant, animal or human died, we can determine the age of the sample.'

'Clever stuff,' said Kaye.

'The technique is very reliable, except where more recent organic contamination may affect the result. In this case, however, we can be confident that the corpse has remained uncontaminated since it was laid to rest.'

'There have been many issues over the dating of the Turin Shroud,' commented Richter.

'True, although personally I support the scientific findings,' answered Laurent. 'But it's only to be expected that those with faith in the shroud's authenticity will find it hard to accept evidence that refutes their beliefs. Shall we go in?'

One by one they bent their heads and entered the tunnel, noticing an immediate drop in temperature that became even more marked once they had squeezed into the sepulchre itself. The chamber was well lit with rechargeable solar-powered lighting and Desselle stopped work to welcome them. On a field bench set up at the back of the chamber they could see treated samples of tissue, teeth and hair taken from the mummified corpse, some in tubes containing chemical solutions, some embedded in epoxy resin, awaiting transport to a laboratory for ultra-structural observation using an electron microscope and for tests to see whether DNA could be recovered. Samples of the shroud had also been conserved for analysis. It was clear that modern archaeology was not all about trowelling dirt.

'My work on the primary remains is almost complete,' Desselle told the visitors. 'Tomorrow we propose to lift the mummy carefully into an inert polymer body-bag from which we will pump out the air, leaving a semi-vacuum to conserve the remains as well as possible during transport to the laboratory in Paris.'

'Assuming we can overcome the Syrian red tape and get permission to relocate the remains,' added Laurent. 'We're working on that.'

Richter nodded his understanding, his gaze fixing on the side of the limestone coffin. The lighting made it easy to see the Latin inscriptions and the sunburst carved in the centre of the text.

The Mark of The Power!

He exulted silently at the sight of the symbol, his first direct contact with new physical evidence of that which he sought; that which consumed him, day and night.

Sam and Kaye, too, were drawn to the sunburst, though they were careful not to let their faces show the extent of their interest. It's larger than I'd realised it would be, thought Sam, and all the details are so clear on it. It's as if someone carved it only yesterday.

Richter already knew what the inscriptions said, having been told by Cardinal Mercurio. Kaye, however, was mentally translating the bottom inscription as he listened to what the French archaeologists were saying.

'May the casket's power protect you until the one comes who will bring light and life to all.'

His stomach muscles knotted and his heart thumped in his chest. Could he be mistaken? Could 'casket' just mean 'coffin'? Why would a coffin be seen as having power, other than as a protective stone shield, which fact would surely not have deserved mention? The one who brings light and life to everyone could mean God, I suppose, he thought, but, in that case, why not just say Yahweh? Try as he might, he could only conclude that the sentence literally meant what it said - fitting perfectly with what he and Sam had already learned about Balthazar's golden casket.

'What do you make of the inscriptions?' he asked Laurent, indicating the coffin.

'My eyes are like hawk's balls from staring at those Latin words for hours,' groused Laurent, making his visitors smile at his literal translation of the French idiomatic phrase that, in English idiom, would be expressed as having bags under the eyes. 'The Latin is simple enough and the upper text is unambiguous. It plainly states that Jesus, son of Joseph and Mary, crucified Messiah, was interred here. Since the tomb still had its brick seal intact when Alain found it, we can be pretty sure that the remains in the coffin are the remains placed there originally. There can have been no substitute. We'll send samples of the mud-brick for analysis and carbon dating, to see if the age of the seal and the age of the remains concur - and whether that dates them to the first century AD. I think it highly likely, considering the design of the coffin and all that we have established so far - though it's likely that the chamber itself is even older. We are confident that the individual buried here was, indeed, crucified. The mummified hands and feet show signs of having been pierced, probably with iron nails. We can test for ferrous content at the lab.'

'And the text underneath the sun carving?' prompted Sam, who, unable to read more than a few words of Latin despite two years of school lessons in the language, was still in the dark about the meaning of the lower inscription.

'A bit of a puzzle, really,' answered Laurent. He translated it out loud for Sam, who was stunned. It took all her self control to keep her face fixed in an expression of polite academic interest. 'It's not something I've ever seen on any tomb before, although admittedly our team has specialised in medieval tombs, not tombs of the first century. It may be an obscure blessing of the era, but I'd welcome your opinions,' he added.

'I'm sure you're right,' said Sam quickly and continued with another question. 'Have you come across any other inscriptions on or inside the coffin? I can't see anything from where we're standing.'

'No, nothing,' confirmed Desselle. 'Something may be chiselled into the base of the interior, but we can't check that until the remains have been lifted out. I have come across one oddity, though. There's an indent in the shroud, near the feet. It's quite pronounced and something I would normally expect to result from some small, heavy object left on top of the grave clothes.' He shook his head. 'Here, though, there was no object, although I did find a few shreds of fibre in the base of the indent - strands of a coarse, woven fabric quite different from the linen of the shroud itself. I can only conclude that there *was* something lying there that is now gone.' He shrugged. 'Perhaps Alain or one of his temporary local helpers removed it, whatever it was.'

'What's in the two small clay boxes behind us?' Richter wanted to know.

'No idea,' said Laurent. 'We've only worked the main find so far. They're probably ossuaries that were already here before the larger coffin was added. Multiple-burial sepulchres were quite common. How they got this big limestone coffin up this mountain I don't know, but it may have been brought in pieces - we haven't examined its construction yet.'

Throughout their time inside the tomb, Ghulam had remained silent, asking no questions but allowing his eyes to range over everything in the chamber. Had anyone noticed, they might have been surprised to observe that he spent some time focused on the shadowed, uneven rock ceiling about two feet above his head. The centre of attention for the rest of the party was the tomb of Christ and they never looked upwards, or, indeed, spared a glance for the unobtrusive chauffer, so it was only Ghulam who noticed and memorised the text lightly scratched on the roughly tooled sandstone roof.

Now, at last, he spoke. 'I'm sorry to say I'm experiencing an insignificant but growing sense of claustrophobia. I think I'll return outside, if nobody minds.'

'Oh dear,' said Sam. 'Of course, you must go out.' Laurent solicitously accompanied Ghulam to assist him down the cliff to the dirt road.

The group's mood of intense enquiry dissipated with the interruption and Kaye's mind was jolted into a different train of thought. 'Doctor Desselle, he said, 'I imagine, as a scientist, that you see this primarily as a site for scientific study. My own academic specialty is as an historical linguist, but, as a Christian, I can't help being spiritually awed, standing here, where it seems almost certain that I am in the presence of the mortal body of our Lord. Would you mind if I took a moment to pray before I go?'

Sam looked at her feet, always discomfited by overt displays of religious belief. While she respected people's right to follow their faith, she could not respect the actual beliefs, being genuinely incredulous that even the most intelligent people could be blind believers. I'm not a bigot, she thought, but how can people swallow the two thousand year conglomeration of inaccurate, superstition-driven, dogma-ridden misrepresentations of the facts concerning the life of a man who simply taught love and peace in the context of his time and location? In fact, why have people, all through history, needed to invent and worship gods? Does it all stem from the simple fact that we can't explain our existence? Is our species' ego so huge that we feel we're bound to be the centre of attention of some universal creator, or are we just so terrified that death brings oblivion that we have to believe in an afterlife of everlasting bliss? Why can't we simply accept that we're mortal creatures and get on with making this world the best it can be for everyone, while we're here?

Desselle had not expected Kaye's request, now seconded by Richter, but he could understand their urge to express their faith. 'Certainly,' he said. 'I'll step outside and give you privacy, but, please don't touch or remove anything from the sepulchre. No mementos, gentlemen!'

'I'll come out with you,' Sam told him.

Leaving the two men alone with their God, Sam and Desselle bent low through the dark tunnel and emerged, blinking, into the relentless sunlight. Standing with her back to the rock face and closing her eyes, Sam momentarily revelled in the sensation of heat on her face and arms, while Desselle gazed out over the gorge, reflecting on the irony of the fact that the Papal Emissary who had visited days earlier had never once requested an opportunity to pray.

Inside the ancient chamber, Kaye and Richter knelt before the coffin and bowed their heads in an attitude of prayer.

With the fire of a zealot built into his psyche, Richter had toyed with Catholicism over the years, finding temporary solace for his unrealised spiritual ambitions in its uplifting rituals, his ego feeding from its aura of ancient and ultimate power. In truth, however, his unshakeable belief was purely in the Old Testament God of wrath and vengeance - *that* was the God a man really needed on his side in this unjust world.

He knelt, but did not pray to Jesus. It had suited him to be seen as a professed Catholic to further his career as a mercenary agent supporting the Vatican's cloaked activities, but his faith in the wishy-washy Jewish love-monger was as much a false construct as Mercurio's avowed reason for employing him to search for the casket. That was a sham he had seen through immediately. The glamour of *The Power* had poisoned the Cardinal and Richter was certain that if the casket were ever to pass into Mercurio's hands, the Vatican would never learn of the fact. Once Richter had found the casket, he would enjoy killing the scheming Cardinal. Perhaps even before that. When it rose unbidden in his mind, he instantly repressed the unpalatable idea that his faith in his destiny as *The One* was, similarly, a false construct, as was the Keeper's *naevus* on his chest.

When Kaye raised his head and opened his eyes to see Richter's fixed on the sunburst, it occurred to him that it could not have escaped the man's attention that this emblem was identical to the one in Basem's gospel. Back at the Bunker, Richter had already seemed interested in the casket and, having now seen the tomb inscription, must have put two and two together, though it was impossible to know whether he thought the casket still existed. Should we bring him into our confidence, Kaye wondered, rather than risk him veering off on a parallel course leading to later conflict?

As if echoing Kaye's train of thought, Richter turned to him, smiled and said, 'I bet you're thinking the same as I am - that Balthazar was here; perhaps Basem, too. We're all going to have to realign our spiritual understanding to accommodate the new evidence that's building up.'

Kaye nodded thoughtfully. 'It's hard to refute, now that I'm actually here,' he admitted, 'But I find that, somehow, I'm okay with it. What if this *is* the mortal body of Jesus? Is that going to destroy my faith? I don't think so. When I die, I'll be leaving my own mortal body behind, but my soul will live on in God's heavenly kingdom - that's my belief through the teachings of Jesus. He still died for my sins, as far as I'm concerned.'

What Richter said next was even more direct. 'That's a first class answer on matters spiritual and intangible. Now, let's consider earthly things. The casket Basem wrote about was a tangible, physical object - and not just any old object - it belonged to Balthazar and might even have been used to bring Lazarus back to life. What if it's as real as this tomb and still exists? I don't mean to pry, but I think *you* think it still exists and I think you and Samantha are looking for it. Am I right? Because, if I am, I'd love to look for it with you - and co-publish our findings, if, against all the odds, we come up trumps. What do you say?'

There seemed little point in denying the truth. The highly perspicacious Richter had worked it out, despite their caution. 'The casket would be an extraordinary archaeological find,' Kaye replied carefully, 'But you're speaking to the wrong person. It's Sam that's calling the shots - I'm just the hired help. I think we'd better all sit down together for a chat back at the hotel and you can ask her the same question you just asked me. I'll go along with whatever she decides. I can't say fairer than that.' He stood up.

Richter also rose, brushing a few grains of fine sand from the knees of his lightweight slacks. 'You're an honourable man,' he said. 'I hope Sam knows how fortunate she is to have engaged your services. I thought, perhaps, that you were romantic partners, but a business arrangement actually makes everything easier, doesn't it? I'll look forward to that chat at the Beit Khan.'

Sam's romantic partner...? Chance would be a fine thing, Kaye thought.

Taking a last, lingering look at the tomb, they ducked out through the mud-brick hole and made their way back along the low tunnel to join Sam and Desselle in the furnace of the desert noon. The two militia men currently on duty sat to the left of the tunnel entrance, their feet dangling over the edge of the drop, under an overhang that provided a narrow strip of shade. They looked hot and bored.

Climbing back down the cliff, Desselle took the lead, calling foothold directions to Kaye, just behind him. Letting them get well started, Richter followed and Sam came last. The first twenty feet were particularly sheer and Sam, game, but not at ease with heights, was relying on Richter to guide her descent.

'It's a bit of a stretch but there's a good place for your left foot two feet down and a foot to your left', he said from below.

She extended her leg blindly for it, unable to look down in case her vertigo made her wobbly, but at full reach, she could not feel any ledge or indent in the sandstone cliff. 'Am I anywhere close?' she asked through gritted teeth, feeling the strain building in her arms as her sweaty right hand began slipping down the guide rope, giving her a friction burn.

'Another four inches down, directly below you,' Richter's call advised.

Your legs must be longer than mine, she thought. I'll have to let go of the guide rope to do this. She committed herself to the action, releasing her hold on the rope and letting her body drop - but her foot never found the promised hold. She completely lost her balance and her right arm flailed wildly.

His heart missing a beat, Kaye yelled, 'Watch out, above!' cursing the fact that he was too far below Sam to be of any practical help.

Sam dropped away from the cliff with a short, sharp scream - and would have plummeted thirty feet had it not been for Richter, whose strong right arm whipped out and caught her bodily as she passed him. Her ribcage slammed painfully against the rock, winding her, but he continued to hold her securely until her scrabbling feet found purchase and her trembling hands re-established a firm grip on the guide rope. Her Dolce and Gabanna sunglasses were less fortunate, spiralling down to splinter on the rocks below.

'Butterfingers,' said Richter lightly. 'Are you alright?'

'Oh my,' breathed Sam, panting. 'My legs are jelly. If you hadn't stopped my fall...' Her pulse was still racing in shock.

'...The whole of you might have been jelly; I know. But you're safe now. Just take it slow and steady the rest of the way.'

'You saved my life.'

'Not at all - I just happened to be in the right place at the right time - you fell straight into my arms,' demurred Richter modestly. He had almost made a mistake, he thought, relieved that, in her panic, she had failed to notice that the foot hold to which he had been directing her did not exist. It would have delighted him to see her broken body sprawled at the foot of the cliff, but just as she lost her balance, he had changed his mind. The time wasn't right yet - and there was so much he wanted her to know before he finally quenched the light in those aristocratic eyes. Meanwhile, he could put this little episode to good use. After all, how could any woman refuse a request from the man who had just saved her life? Lady Samantha Dexter didn't know it yet, but she was about to add a fourth member to her treasure hunt team.

Damascus, 21 June, 2016 AD

'Zikar? Ali be with you. Listen, I'm parked round the corner from the Beit Khan hotel in the old city. I am about the *Dhu Samawi's* business. Can you join me? I need some backup.' Bashir spoke quietly, holding his cheap mobile phone close to his ear to keep out the sound of the city traffic.

'Give me half an hour.' The reply came from the third most senior member of the Brotherhood of the Sabaeans. 'Do you need me to bring anything?'

'Money - and a change of clothes for me; we both need businessmen's clothes that will go unremarked in a top class hotel. And a lock pick. Have you a pistol to hand?'

'Yes, an army issue Makarov some Sunni freedom fighter unfortunately misplaced - unfortunate for him, that is; lucky for me.'

'Bring it.'

It had been easy to follow the big, shiny Mercedes back from Mount Quasioun into the city, where Bashir's dented Sham was undistinguished amidst the urban traffic. He stayed about four cars behind his quarry and when it turned into a dead end lane in the old city and parked outside one of the best hotels in Damascus, he simply drove past the end of the lane and took the nearest parking space he could find. Whoever these people were, they had plenty of money, he thought, his eyes hot with envy. While waiting for Zikar, he scouted the vicinity of the Beit Khan, checking for escape routes other than its main entrance and enjoying the sense of importance it gave him to be doing something active rather than merely lying on a lump of rock, straining his eyes through a pair of binoculars. He clenched and unclenched his fists as he walked, in the manner of a man itching to release his pent up frustration through an act of physical violence.

Having noted the service entrance near the kitchens at the back of the hotel, along with the presence of a steel fire escape that passed several windows on its climb to an access door on the third floor, Bashir bought mint lemonade from a street vendor and returned to his car to quench his raging thirst. Unconsciously, his fingers sought out and fiddled with the ancient crucifixion nail he still had stuck through his belt. It was his talisman in the hunt for the casket and the pain he felt as he repetitively drove the tip of his middle finger against its rusted point helped him to focus and kept the red mist of his anger from descending to block all rational thought.

A blue Ford Transit van pulled up and Zikar climbed out, a burly man in his prime, with pocked cheeks, a hawk-like nose and a luxuriant moustache, dressed in a traditional, formal evening kaftan and white gutrah. He had brought similar for Bashir, along with a beard trimmer.

Inside the van. Bashir exchanged his dirty didashah for the clean kaftan. 'What about shoes?' he asked. Wordlessly, Zikar passed him a pair of brown brogues with cream socks stuffed inside them. Bashir looked at them disparagingly. 'I hate brogues,' he muttered, but put them on anyway. 'At least they fit.' He slipped his knife inside one deep pocket, tucked the wrapped crucifixion nail into the other and looked Zikar up and down quizzically. 'Where's the pistol?'

'Strapped to my right calf; I have plenty of cash and some other bits and pieces in my pockets as well. Now, are you going to explain what this is all about?'

Richter changed for dinner before making an international phone call.

'*Pronto?*'

'Your Eminence? It's Richter. Can you hear me?' The line was full of hissing static.

'With difficulty,' came the quavering sound of Mercurio's voice. 'I'm about to go into a meeting. What's the problem?'

'No problem,' answered Richter. 'But you need to cancel your appointments for the next couple of days and come to Damascus on the first available flight. I have information I can't give you over the phone. You should also visit the tomb here, because they're about to move the body and you'll be able to see what's in the base of the coffin. They won't let me in for a second look. Phone me on my mobile number to let me know your arrival time tomorrow. I'll pick you up.'

'Is it that urgent?' queried the Cardinal. 'Can't it wait... days?' The line was disintegrating.'

'Can't hear you - it's a really bad line. See you tomorrow,' said Richter loudly and broke the connection.

He had decided not to defer the gratification of putting an end to any threat the Cardinal might pose.

No-one gave the two traditionally attired Syrian businessmen a second glance as they crossed the hotel's open courtyard, entered the lobby and turned to climb the curved staircase leading to the upper, open air terrace. The key to success was to blend in to your environment perfectly - to behave as if you belonged and knew exactly where you were going. It was early evening and the restaurant section was scantily occupied, making it easy for Bashir to identify the foreigners, who sat at a table overlooking the courtyard, chatting as they picked at a variety of small dishes of local appetizers.

Bashir and Zikar strolled casually round the terrace, settling at the table nearest to Sam's group, a perfect spot from which to evesdrop. Bashir only spoke Arabic and English, so was relieved to hear the latter language as he sat down. Zikar ordered tea and meze from the attentive waiter and then the Brothers of the Sabaeans sat back, murmuring occasionally to one another in Arabic, but concentrating very carefully on what was being discussed at the next table. Their arrival caused no abatement in the foreigners' flow of conversation, which either meant that they had nothing to hide, thought Bashir, or that they naively assumed that no-one was interested in what they were saying. He hoped the latter reason applied.

'I was impressed by the meticulous work they were doing to conserve samples for analysis,' said Sam.

'Yes, it's a difficult site to work, up that ravine in the middle of nowhere. Talking of which, can you imagine how hard it must have been to carve that sepulchre out of the solid rock?' commented Kaye between olives.

'They thought it was probably an existing cave,' reminded Richter, reaching for a dolma.

'Well I'd rather they hadn't picked such a dangerous, inaccessible place,' said Sam ruefully. 'If not for Raoul, I'd be on a marble slab tonight, next to that poor archaeologist who got murdered!'

Zikar raised one eyebrow at Bashir, who nodded imperceptibly, taking credit for the kill.

'All the more meze for me, if that had happened,' quipped Kaye, loading his plate with second helpings of flatbread, hummus and olives.

'You're a heartless beast,' responded Sam, glaring at him.

'Not at all,' he replied, grinning; 'Just a hungry one. By the way, while I'm eating your share, you might want to consider a proposal that your knight in shining armour put to me earlier, after you left the tomb. I told him it would be your decision.'

'...A proposal?' Sam had picked up the menu but put it to one side again and looked questioningly at Richter.

He took the cue smoothly. 'Yes, Samantha. I took the liberty of mentioning to Oliver that it's become clear we have shared interests. Independently, we've reached the conclusion that the casket mentioned in the literature we've researched - and on the tomb we saw today - may still exist. Oliver didn't deny that you and he are trying to locate it and I'd certainly like the opportunity to examine and publish on - well, co-publish on - such an amazing and theologically significant artefact, if it can be found - so I wondered if you'd let me join your quest on the basis that combining our intellectual resources might add benefit? I promise I'll make myself useful on the team.'

Hearing this, a rush of blood suffused Bashir's face and set his cheeks on fire. His English vocabulary was limited, but good enough to understand that these English pigs knew about the casket. In fact, they were actively looking for it! How could they possibly know about it? And what *did* they know, exactly? He *had* to find out. He'd had a feeling about them from the moment he saw them - and his instincts had been right on the nail. *On the nail - ha!*

Zikar observed Bashir's barely contained agitation and, in fear of a rash outburst from the younger man, put a cautioning finger to his lips, covering the brief action with an innocuous comment about the food in front of them. It was vital to remain calm and anonymous.

Sam felt a rush of emotions, one after the other. Her initial dismay that the cat was out of the bag was replaced by surprise that Richter had caught on to the quest, but, when she thought about it, there was more than enough material in the Vatican and on the tomb to put any thinking person on the trail. Next came a wave of mistrust - how could she be sure he wasn't up to no good? That unkind thought made her blush inwardly with guilt because she really had no reason to mistrust the man. He had helped them willingly in the Vatican archives and without his assistance they might never have gained access to the tomb - not so fast, at any rate. And he saved my life today, she reminded herself. That has to count for a lot. It would be a relief not have to worry constantly about what to say and what not to say in front of him. Searching Kaye's face, she tried to gauge his attitude to Richter's request.

'It's your call,' Kaye said evenly in response to the unasked question evident in her eyes. He had no wish to influence her and felt it was not his place to try, despite his reservations. In her heady flush of gratitude to Richter, he worried that Sam was forgetting both what her father's letter had warned her about trusting strangers and what he, himself, had said, before they left Chaumont. He couldn't bear the thought of her getting hurt in any way and with that thought - and remembering how he had felt a couple of hours earlier when he thought she was falling off the cliff - Kaye realised that Sam's welfare was more important to him than any golden casket, however valuable and mystical it might turn out to be.

Sam turned to Richter. She thought she knew what she was going to do but she needed a bit more time to reflect - and to tell Kaye, in private, about what her grandfather had written. 'If you don't mind, Raoul, I'd like to think about your proposal overnight.

I'll give you my answer in the morning. It's not a decision I want to make too lightly. I hope you understand.'

'Take all the time you need,' replied Richter. 'By the way,' he added, indicating the menu by her elbow, 'May I recommend you try the kibbeh with quince sauce as a main dish?'

'Kibbeh?'

'The local spiced lamb sausages. I hear they're to die for.'

CHAPTER 17

A LIFE SAVED TWICE; A MAP LOST ONCE

Damascus, Syria, 21 June, 2016 AD

The dull roar of night-time traffic, the wailing calls to prayer from the tops of minarets, the cries of tired children and the sirens of distant police cars, along with the subtle, mingled scents of smoke, spices and kebab meat... all these intrusions on peace were banished when Ghulam closed the window shutters in Sam's suite. He put his hands together in traditional obeisance and bade his mistress goodnight before exiting through the connecting door to his own room. Shortly afterwards, there was a knock on Sam's main suite door and she opened it to admit Kaye.

'Thanks for coming,' she said gratefully. 'I've been reading my grandfather's notes and they're a lot more useful than I'd realised from the one page I'd glanced at back home - though a bit puzzling in places. I need your help.'

Kaye pulled up a chair at the hexagonal mother-of-pearl-inlaid walnut table on which Sam had laid her sheaf of notes. 'Fine - let's have a look.'

Sam leafed through the papers. Having explained something of her grandfather's trip, she went on to share the most intriguing sections of his notes.

'One day I'd certainly like to find out more about the villainous Cyrus Dexter, my erstwhile distant relative. I wonder what happened to him after his years in prison,' she said, turning a page. 'Ah! Here's what I really wanted you to look at.' She passed the page to Kaye, who read it, only speaking aloud the three lines of the clue to the location of the key Kai had hidden.

> *'A keeper of old laid the Mark of The Power*
> *In full sight of all, who, unknowing, walk o'er.*
> *Where one of its rays lights the way to the dawn...*

Working out its meaning as he spoke, he said, 'So, a long time ago, someone put a representation of the casket's emblem somewhere visible, where people pass over it as they walk. The mark was *laid* - I wonder if that means *laid* as in inlaid - like this table,' and he tapped the mother-of-pearl as he spoke.

'Or like an inlaid design on a floor?' contributed Sam.

'Could be - it would fit the bill and people certainly walk over decorative stone floors in lots of public places. The last line might mean that one of the sunburst's rays points at something to do with the dawn - a window, maybe...'

'The dawn is associated with the east,' pointed out Sam.

'True. Unfortunately, we don't have the rest of the clue to hand so we shouldn't speculate. Where does he say the rest of his clue is?' Kaye's query was rhetorical, since he was already re-reading the relevant paragraph. 'Here we are.' He read the important phrase aloud: '*...On the back of the stone altar in the chapel named for the discoverer of the true Cross*'.

'I don't know who discovered the true Cross,' admitted Sam. 'In fact, I had no idea it had been discovered, though I do know there are supposed to be bits of it in Catholic churches all over the place. But I always reckoned those were all fakes, contrived to bolster belief and encourage people to keep on attending mass and putting their coppers on the collection plate.'

Kaye said, 'Damn it, woman. You're such a cynic.'

She shrugged. 'I just say it as I see it.'

'You could look it up on the internet,' he said. 'But, as it happens, I already know who found the true Cross. The Emperor Constantine - who convened the Council of Nicaea, which I mentioned the other day - had a mother named Helena who was a fervent Christian. So much so, in fact, that she trotted off to Jerusalem, looking for the site where Jesus had been crucified, but received no co-operation from the Christians there, who mistrusted her motives. Undeterred, she bagged a local who revealed, under torture, that the temple of Aphrodite - Venus, to the Romans – built some time after the death of Christ, stood directly over Golgotha and the tomb of Jesus. It seemed a likely place to dig for two good reasons. Firstly, the emperor who had commissioned the temple was anti-Christian and might have deliberately built his temple intending to obliterate the Christians' holy place and, secondly, the physical location was right - just outside the walls of the old city, which is where the Bible says crucifixions always took place.'

'But how could she dig up a whole temple?' asked Sam.

'If you're the mother of the Emperor I guess you can do just about anything you want,' replied Kaye. 'Anyway, that's exactly what she did. She had the temple totally demolished, which was a huge act of courage and faith, bearing in mind that there were a lot of pagans around who still worshipped there at that time.'

'What did she find?'

'Several tombs, I think; one with a round stone door at one side of its open entrance, along with, so accounts of the matter say, three wooden crosses near a small rise, next to what used to be a limestone quarry at the time of Jesus. Apparently, a miracle took place when the true Cross was lifted out of the disused cistern into which someone had thrown it. It's said that Helena also unearthed the *titulus crucis*.'

'And that would be...?'

'...The piece of wood that Roman soldiers habitually nailed at the top of a cross with the reason for the execution written upon it. I'm sure you know what was written on the *titulus crucis* of Jesus.'

'INRI,' said Sam.

'Yes - INRI - King of the Jews.'

'I've never quite understood that. I thought he was arrested and condemned for claiming to be the Son of God. Why didn't they put *that* on his *titulis crucis*, I wonder? Anyway, thank you for the history lesson,' said Sam, 'But to get back to the point - I suppose we need to look for a stone altar in a place called the Chapel of Helena, then?'

'Probably *Saint* Helena - the Church raised the lady to sainthood for her efforts, although her canonisation may also have been influenced by the fact that her emperor son commissioned a church to be built on the site to preserve it for all time as an icon of Christianity. And that church, of course, is...'

'...The Church of the Holy Sepulchre,' Sam finished for him, nodding. 'By the way, when were the accounts about the finding of the true Cross written?'

'Oh, at various times after the event, by historians,' said Kaye.

'Well, there you are, then,' said Sam triumphantly.

'Sorry?'

'I mean, they're not first-hand accounts. They could be lies, or at least embellishments of the truth. The bits of wood Helena found, if she did actually find any, could have been any old bits of wood really - just like I always thought.' She sat back and crossed her arms smugly.

Kaye sighed and smiled wryly. 'There's no convincing a heathen, is there?'

Sam ignored his comment. 'Where *is* this Chapel of Saint Helena, that's the question?'

Kaye considered for a moment. 'I'll look it up, but my guess is that it's exactly where your grandfather was when he hid his key - in the Church of the Holy Sepulchre itself. I've never been there, but I know it's a rambling place that has dozens of chapels - think of the length of the list that twelfth century fellow, Aloisius, made, for a start.'

Uncrossing her arms and sitting forward again, Sam voiced an exciting thought that had just occurred to her. 'And maybe the Mark of *The Power* is on the floor of the same Church!'

'Don't jump to conclusions. Is it likely that such an arcane symbol would be in plain view somewhere at the very centre of all that is most holy to Christianity?'

Sam shrugged. 'I don't see why not. Maybe it's so small that it's hardly noticeable - although, in that case, it'd be hard for us to find it.'

She frowned at that thought. 'Anyway, there are tons of pagan symbols decorating churches all over the world, including some that have been adopted as Christian symbols. For example, did you know that the Pope's gesture of benediction - the one with his forefinger and middle finger raised - was originally a fertility symbol of the pagan god, Ba'al?'

'You're kidding?'

'I'm not - and it gets worse. Ba'al became corrupted to Beelzebub - so, when the Pope raises his hand in benediction, what he's really saying is, 'The Devil wants your ass."

'I'm utterly shocked at you,' exclaimed Kaye, laughing and shaking his head.

Sam looked smug again. 'There's no convincing the faithful, is there?'

'Touché.'

'In any case, there must have been generations of Keepers linked to the Church of the Holy Sepulchre while the casket was there, up until Saladin gave it away. Perhaps one of them commissioned a new floor and had the emblem built into it. After all, people in general would see it purely as a decorative design.'

'I'm impressed with your argument,' said Kaye, 'But before we go rushing off to Jerusalem - how is finding your grandfather's key going to help us? We're looking for a casket, not a key.'

Sam was stubborn. 'Keys unlock doors. And who knows what's hidden in the tunnels behind the locked door granddad installed? He might have left clues there that will lead us to the casket. The casket itself might even be hidden there!'

'Hmmm.' Kaye was not convinced. 'Lara Croft, here we come. It sounds like a wild goose chase to me, but hell, that's what academic sabbaticals are all about, usually.' He poured himself a locally brewed Barada beer from the mini-bar. 'Cheers!'

'There are several pages I haven't read, yet,' Sam reminded him. 'Perhaps we should look at them now?'

Kaye relaxed onto a sofa with his beer. 'You go ahead. Tell me if you find out where the casket is.' He sank back into a pile of tasselled cushions and closed his eyes.

'Thanks for nothing,' muttered Sam under her breath. She began reading. The final pages appeared to have been written some time after the earlier ones.

'...Several years after my return from Jerusalem, Cyrus was released. On that day, to save him from successive, fruitless attempted burglaries, I informed him that during his sojourn at the pleasure of Her Majesty, the object of his desire had been hidden in a new location that I alone knew and which he would never find. I offered him my hand and enough money to set him up in a decent trade, but he refused both, at which I was not entirely surprised. The whole business with Cyrus made me conscious of the fact that Alexander, my only son, is not yet of an age to be taught his future responsibilities - and, mindful of the venom in the last look Cyrus gave me before he spat in my face and turned away, I felt it imperative to secure details of the location of my son's inheritance where they could be found in the event of my untimely death.

'To that end, I have made a map to act as a physical guide and have sealed it with the Mark. But the map is nothing without the knowledge of how to pass through its domains, for I have guarded the prize with more than mere walls. If he is half the man I expect him to be, in time, my son will know enough and be both brave and cautious enough to overcome the obstacles I have set in place. The means to enable him - or, indeed, any future Keeper - to come safely into the presence of The Power are either indicated on the map or will become apparent during the journey itself, with the appropriate level of mental perspicacity. Anyone making the attempt would be wise to draw on the courage of the beast supporting our family Coat of Arms. I have also made a false version of the map, with misleading annotations to trip up the unwary - or any future thief of Cyrus Dexter's stock - though I pray that no misbegotten heir of his seed exists!'

That crook really scared granddad, thought Sam. Reading between the lines, she gauged that Cyrus's gall went far beyond the natural sullen resentment of being jailed for theft. Could such intense bitterness and hatred have been nurtured down through the centuries all the way from the time of Grimbald? Of course, she didn't know how Grimbald became estranged from her side of the family. Even though I can't imagine sneering Simon making a great father, he would surely have given his younger son a privileged lifestyle and a permanent home at Chaumont, she thought. Perhaps the rift wasn't his fault. Perhaps it was a nasty case of sibling rivalry. She gave a little sigh. Her own family was gone and she couldn't help feeling that even dysfunctional relatives were preferable to the endless empty corridors and silent rooms awaiting her when this trip was over. She had begun this quest for her father's sake, but had it turned into a self-indulgent excuse to delay dealing with the realities of life without him?

Dropping that uncomfortable train of thought, she decided that her most immediate concern was the matter of the map. There had been an annotated map of sorts amongst the documents she had brought with them. It was sitting in the room safe. She had never looked at it, but now she must, because the question uppermost in her mind needed a definitive answer. Was hers the true map - or the false one?

Kaye had nodded off on the sofa. Tired, herself, after the long, hot day, Sam rose and crossed the room to the safe, transferring his half-finished glass of beer from his tilting grip to a side table as she passed by. She couldn't help noticing that he looked even more boyish with his face at rest, his blue eyes closed and a shock of corn-blond hair drifting to soften his lofty temples. He was good looking; intelligent; interesting, reliable - so why, she found herself wondering, was he still single at thirty three? Pressing the four digit combination, she opened the small hotel room safe that was housed in a cupboard against one wall and withdrew all her documents, rifling through them until she found the single-page map. Putting everything else away and locking the safe again, she relaxed on an easy chair facing the sofa and the shuttered windows behind its sleeping occupant, to examine the peculiar drawing in comfort.

A Life Saved Twice; A Map Lost Once

It was impossible to decide which way up to hold the map. Its annotations had been scribbled in a higgledy-piggledy fashion; some sideways, others, upside-down. Turning the sheet over, she looked on the back for broken wax, an ink-imprinted seal or anything to suggest that any kind of insignia had ever been present. There was nothing. A lead weight settled in the pit of her stomach. If this was her grandfather's deliberately falsified version, how much of it, if any, would be of any value to them? Turning the sheet over again to try and make sense of the complicated, squiggly lines on it, she began to find it hard to concentrate, her blinks becoming ever slower. One final blink and her eyelids remained closed, her head gently drooping to her chin, the map still in her hands.

Bashir left it to the dignified looking Zikar to stroll casually after the English group when they left the terrace. The pale-eyed man, whose name sounded like the plaintive call of a lion - Rowwl - split off and headed downstairs towards the hotel's reception area, while the other three made their way through the hotel's third floor lobby and took the left-hand corridor, along which the hotel's two best suites were located. Zikar continued past without looking at them as they unlocked their respective doors, the small Asian man and the woman entering one suite, while the fair-haired man went into the other. Continuing round the quadrant as if heading for his own room, the Syrian doubled back after a few minutes and was at the corner of their corridor again when the fair-haired man opened his door and walked out. Jerking back to remain unseen, Zikar heard him knock on the door of the other suite, where he was quickly admitted. On hearing that door close again, Zikar quickly made his way back to the terrace, where Bashir looked at him questioningly.

'Come,' whispered Zikar. 'One of their rooms is temporarily unoccupied. Let's check it out.'

It was fortunate for them that the historic style of the hotel did not suit modern electronic card entry. The imposing suite doors had ornate brass fitments that were key-operated. In under a minute, the lock pick had been put to good purpose and the two men slipped inside Kaye's empty suite. Having spent several years in the army,

Zikar took a natural lead and, moving furtively, indicated that he would handle the bedroom, leaving the living area to Bashir. They searched systematically, turning out cupboards and drawers, throwing cushions and pillows out of their way and scattering Kaye's personal effects as they felt inside pockets, flinging aside each item as it proved useless. Bashir ripped up the living room's elegant soft furnishings with his Khangar dagger, half looking for anything that might relate to the casket, half out of sheer pique that these people could afford to live in such opulent luxury. He found the room safe but could not open it, which made him even angrier.

Appearing at the bedroom doorway, Zikar shook his head. He had been almost as unsuccessful as Bashir, his only find some travel paperwork that bore the names Samantha Dexter, Oliver Kaye and Ghulam Gupta. Furious at their failure, Bashir kicked the sofa he had been demolishing. Then a sly, determined look replaced the rage on his face. He walked over to the window and leant out to check the location of the fire escape he knew to be on this side of the building. Seeing that it descended between this and the next suite, with access from both, he turned and whispered urgently, 'We may not get another chance. Whatever they have, it must be in the other suite. They won't be armed, so that pistol of yours will guarantee their compliance - and we can get out using the fire escape before they have time to raise an alarm.'

In his ground floor room, Richter washed his hands in the bathroom, then sat on the edge of the bed and unbuttoned his shirt to rub some antiseptic on his throbbing scar, wondering why he felt restless and uneasy. He was confident that Samantha would welcome him into their group tomorrow morning, so why the sense that something was wrong, somehow?

There had been something odd about those Syrians on the adjacent table...

Re-buttoning his shirt, he went and opened his room safe, reaching in for the side holster containing his compact Beretta 85FS Cheetah. He had carried it with him from Rome in the Vatican Diplomatic Envoy's satchel provided by Mercurio, backed by appropriate Vatican paperwork for customs purposes. This comprehensive diplomatic umbrella shielded him from luggage and body searches and he was waved on without having to participate in the security screening process all normal travellers were obliged to endure. The fact that the Vatican was an independent city state in its own right had proved a godsend to him on more than one occasion in respect of the carriage of clandestine arms.

Closing the safe, he strapped on his shoulder harness. With the holstered pistol snug below his left armpit, he concealed it beneath a lightweight casual jacket and left the room again, his behaviour that of a tourist taking an innocent evening stroll around the hotel. Fluent in Arabic and always professionally alert to his surroundings, he had understood every word the Syrians had spoken. Sparse and innocuous to the point of vacuity, their conversation had been atypical of the locality and there had been something about their body language that made him scent danger. In all likelihood, their presence at the adjacent table was coincidental and, whatever they had in mind, it was unlikely to have anything to do with the casket - but better safe than sorry, he thought grimly, deciding that his first check would be Sam's corridor, just to make sure all was quiet in that quarter.

Ascending to the terrace, he found it deserted. The older Syrian had risen to follow Sam's party into the upper lobby, he was certain. Of course, both might have returned to separate rooms if they were staying in the hotel, but he doubted that they were resident. Few locals could afford the tariff at this hotel. It was also possible that they had left the hotel during the short time he had been in his room, but, again, his sixth sense told him otherwise.

Zikar was not even obliged to pick the lock on Sam's suite door, because she had not thought to re-lock it when she let Kaye in. Depressing the handle gently, Zikar felt the door give. Quickly, he bent, lifted the hem of his kaftan and drew the Makarov out of his calf holster before nodding to Bashir. Flinging the door wide, they burst in, halting in surprise when they saw both the woman and the fair-haired man sleeping peacefully in separate chairs and utterly oblivious to the violation of their privacy.

Richter strolled to the third floor lobby door, pulled it open and went inside. He bore left down the corridor off the lobby and, at the next corner, sneaked a look down the length of the suites-only corridor. No-one was visible, but he caught a glimpse of Sam's door closing. Rounding the corner and continuing past Sam's suite at a half run, he approached Kaye's door. It was slightly ajar and he pushed it fully open with the fingers of his left hand, his right hand reaching under his jacket for the Beretta.

The sitting room had been comprehensively trashed. Richter wondered if he would find Kaye's bloody corpse sprawled in the bedroom, but it, too, proved devoid of life and had also been rifled, albeit without the senseless destruction apparent in the other room. Kaye's clothes lay scattered and the contents of his bedside drawer had been tipped out onto the duvet cover. Taking in the scene at a glance, Richter turned on his heel and raced out of the suite.

Bashir saw a hand-drawn diagram drooping loosely in the woman's hands and lunged forward boldly, whisking it from between her fingers. Seeing more papers scattered on the table nearby, he swept them up with one hand, roughly folding the wad and stuffing it into the deep pocket of his kaftan. His actions roused Sam from her light doze. Alert in an instant at the sight of the intruder, she sprang to her feet, shouting, 'What the hell..!'

Her loud yell startled Kaye awake, but before he could react, Zikar, whom Sam had not even realised was present, seized her slender body from behind, throwing his left arm forcefully across her chest and grabbing her right elbow in a vice-like grip, pinioning her arms to her sides and immobilising her. Holding her close against his body, he brought his right arm up and round, brutally jabbing the muzzle of his gun into the soft flesh under her chin. Sam abruptly stopped struggling when she felt the bite of the cold steel. One bullet and she knew she would be dead. Loose strands of her long auburn hair trailing across her face from the brief struggle, her eyes sought Kaye's in desperate appeal.

'No!' cried Kaye vehemently, springing from the sofa in horror.

Bashir turned on his fellow Sabaean. 'What's the idea? Are you mad? Use the damn gun to make them co-operate, I said, not take fucking hostages!'

'Easier this way,' returned Zikar, his eyes hard.

Muttering under his breath and drawing out his dagger, Bashir carved the air threateningly in front of Kaye. 'You - sit down,' he ordered authoritatively, speaking in heavily accented English. 'Be quiet and no-one gets hurt.'

Kaye's eyes darted from the blade to the gun and back again.

'Sit or die!' screamed Bashir, pointing his Khangar at Kaye's heart. '...Now!'

Richter reached Sam's door in a few quick steps. From inside came a sharp feminine outburst, followed almost immediately by a shocked negative in Kaye's unmistakeably English voice. This was followed by a staccato of Arabic, full of colloquial invective and very revealing as to what was going on inside the room. Not good, thought Richter and burst into the room. Diving, he rolled behind the nearest armchair, rose to a crouch and drew his pistol all in one swift, fluid movement, yelling in Arabic, 'Drop your weapons and get on your knees, scum!'

Ghulam had been reading in bed and although the raised voices of Sam and Kaye reached his ears, he assumed they were merely having a heated discussion. It wasn't until he heard a strange voice yelling in Arabic that he realised there must be a problem. Wearing only his pyjamas, he slithered out of bed and padded barefoot to his bedroom door, where he very slowly depressed the brass handle, opening a crack just wide enough to see what was happening, whilst hoping not to be seen himself. It took only a few seconds for him to assess the situation.

Holding his breath and sucking his cheeks in with concentration, he silently re-closed the door. Fetching a bedroom chair, he wedged it under the door handle before flinging himself across the bed to reach for the telephone. Dialling zero, he mouthed a calming mantra under his breath, praying that he could get through to the reception desk and make someone understand him before the worst happened.

Seeing pale, unblinking eyes and the barrel of a Beretta targeting him, Bashir reacted by launching himself at great speed past the shocked Kaye, using the sofa as his springboard and dropping behind it, next to the shuttered window. Zikar spun rapidly to face Richter, hauling Sam round with him to form a human shield. He answered Richter's demand defiantly. 'I have a better idea. You throw your gun over here, or I will kill the woman.' To demonstrate his willingness to carry out his threat, he repositioned his own pistol with the barrel to the side of Sam's forehead, compressing her cruelly against his body with his left arm. She gave an almost inaudible gasp.

'Do it,' Kaye begged Richter through clenched teeth. 'Throw your gun down. Don't risk Sam's life, for God's sake!'

'She'll be fine. These guys are pussies,' retorted Richter calmly. 'I'm going to count to three,' he said loudly. 'Don't test me.'

'Brother - let's go!' Bashir still had his head down behind the sofa. The dynamics weren't entirely in their favour now, but that wasn't why he wanted out. What had made his neck hairs prickle was written in their antagonist's ice-cold eyes - and it spelled one word – *death*.

'One,' counted Richter, conversationally.

Zikar spoke. 'We're leaving. Nobody move or the whore dies.' He repeated himself in English and began backing towards the window, taking Sam with him, his pistol still pressed to her head.

Counting on Zikar to cover him, Bashir leapt up and threw open the shutters, then the window. Moving fast, he launched his body over the low sill and out onto the small square steel grille that marked a turn in the zigzag fire-escape. As he leapt, his kaftan billowed, its pocket gaped and a solitary sheet of paper fell from it and fluttered to the floor.

'Two,' counted Richter; loudly.

Reversing until his heel hit the wall, Zikar cautiously stepped backwards over the sill, releasing his grip on Sam at the last instant and giving her a hard shove in the small of her back that sent her staggering forwards to sprawl full length on the mosaic floor. Bashir was already bounding down the fire escape and Zikar followed him at high speed. Their shoulder blades unpleasantly pricking in anticipation of well-aimed bullets, neither man dared to look back.

By the time Richter reached the window, the Syrians had already hit the ground, split up and were running fast, keeping to the alley shadows. He would have needed his Enfield 303 sniper rifle to be sure of hitting them. Richter impassively holstered his pistol and closed the window, bolting the shutters firmly. Then he closed and locked the suite door.

'Wow,' said Kaye, giving him a hard stare. 'That was a most impressive performance, Doctor Richter.' He would have said more but was already busy helping the winded Sam up, half expecting her to burst into a flood of tears.

Instead, despite the fact that she could not help shaking from shock, she angrily pushed her glorious mass of hair back from her face with both hands and glared at him with her lips compressed in a *don't you dare contradict what I'm about to say* kind of way. 'I wasn't gasping from fright, you know,' she blurted out. 'That son of a bitch was squeezing my ribs so tightly I could hardly breathe.' Then her self-anger vented. 'Oh: God! How could I have been so stupid; so complacent? Why did I let myself fall asleep? And why in hell's name didn't I lock the door? Those bastards have got away with granddad's notes - and the map!'

Kaye raised his eyebrows. 'Heavens, Sam, you're not to blame. I was the one who nodded off first - I should have stayed alert. It's my fault and, in any case, the most important thing is that you're not hurt.' He paused, looking worried. You aren't hurt, are you? Perhaps you should sit down. Should I get you a brandy or something?'

'No,' she said, crossly. 'I'm absolutely fine. Nothing's damaged except my pride.' Truth be known, she was more dismayed by the fact that it had been Richter rather than Kaye who had leapt to her rescue than she was by anything else. Noticing the piece of paper on the floor, near the window, she stomped over and retrieved it. It was the final page of Kai's notes, which she had not even finished reading. At least the thieving swine don't know they might have a false map, she thought with aggrieved satisfaction, folding the sheet into her own pocket.

At that instant there came an unexpected and loud rapping on the suite door, startling everyone. A voice from the other side of the door shouted, 'Are you alright in there, Miss'm? The hotel manager will be here in two shakes. I wish I could speak Arabic. It was quite difficult to make them understand me.'

Unlocking the door to admit her chauffer, Sam shook her head, smiling, while Kaye and Richter simply gaped at him.

'I really must look up the Arabic phrase for '*Please come quickly; there's an armed robbery in progress*',' continued Ghulam as he entered the suite, still barefoot and wearing only his Paisley patterned pyjamas.

'How on earth did you get out of your bedroom?' Sam wanted to know.

'Through the window,' confessed Ghulam. 'My Tae Kwon Do is a little rusty and unlike the heroic Doctor,' - here he put his hands together and gave Richter a small bow - 'I don't possess a weapon, so I thought it best to phone Reception for help. Having accomplished that, I went to my window and found it was easy to jump from there onto the fire escape steps. I did so on the basis that the terrorists might use the same route to make good their escape and that my humble presence, crouched behind the hotel bins at the end of the alley, might enable me to see where they went. Consequently, I can tell you that they each left in a separate vehicle - an old grey Sham saloon and a cobalt blue Transit van - both of which were parked round the corner from the hotel.'

'See,' said Sam sagely to Kaye. 'I told you he was indispensible. Thank you, Ghulam.'

'That was very courageous of you,' added Kaye.

'Not at all, Sir; I was just doing my job. Have you a slip of paper, Miss'm? I must write down the vehicle registration numbers before I forget them. Then, if nobody needs me, I shall go and wash my feet. The area around the bins was less than wholesome, I'm sorry to say.' He lifted one black-soled foot to demonstrate.

'And let's not forget you, Raoul,' exclaimed Sam, turning towards him. 'You're indispensible too. Ghulam is right - you *are* a

A Life Saved Twice; A Map Lost Once

hero. That's *twice* in one day you've saved my life. I just don't know what to say.' She paused. 'Actually, I do - and I'm not even going to wait till morning to say it - my answer to your proposal has got to be yes. Join us, Raoul and let's work together as a team on this casket business. I think it's safe to say you've proved your worth.'

Kaye clenched his jaw, then opened his mouth as if to say something, but closed it again without speaking.

Richter smiled broadly. 'Delighted to,' he confirmed, but had no opportunity to elaborate because at that moment the Beit Khan's plump, sweating manager arrived, with a beetle-browed hotel security officer, to learn what had transpired. His attempts to placate and reassure his honoured guests were little short of comical, punctuated as they were with much bobbing and bowing and the repetitious mopping of his face with a red handkerchief. Armed robbers? How horrifying! No outrage of this sort had ever happened in this esteemed establishment before. Was anybody hurt? Had any valuables been stolen? Did they want the police called? They must rest assured that their safety was paramount in his concerns...

The room became a buzzing hive of people talking and gesticulating. Only Richter remained quiet, other than to interject occasionally to overcome language barrier issues. Sam felt she had no choice, really, but to reassure the manager that everyone was fine and that nothing had been stolen. Just imagine the poor fellow's conniptions if I told him the thieves had stolen my secret treasure map, she thought with a wry smile, sitting down, at last, exhausted.

Ghulam gave the hand-wringing manager the intruders' vehicle registration numbers to be passed on to the police, but Kaye quickly made it clear that they had no wish to get involved in a police investigation. 'By all means follow this up from the perspective of hotel security. However, we will be leaving Damascus in the morning and we don't want any trouble. I'm sure we'll all be fine, now. We'll lock our doors and I hardly think lightning is likely to strike twice in one night, eh?'

The manager bobbed his head like a nodding donkey. He would smooth their path and there would of course be a substantial discount on their bills to compensate them for this unfortunate experience. Kaye was finally able to usher the barrel-belly and his minion out, closing the door behind them and leaning back against it with a huge sigh of relief.

Richter, who had been perching on a sofa arm, stood, saying, 'You must be very weary. I know I am. I'll leave you to it, shall I?'

Sam gave a mighty yawn. 'I can't remember the last time I felt this tired. See you in the morning.'

'I'm heading for bed too,' said Kaye. The die was cast and he would just have to deal with any consequences as they went along. He felt galled at the apparent ease with which Richter seemed able to command Sam's admiration and trust. Why did women always do that - fall for the fake hero instead of the chap who really had their best interests at heart? 'Goodnight, Sam. We can sort out our plans when we've all had a decent rest. You *will* lock this door when we've gone, won't you? Never mind what hour it is; just call if you need me.'

She held up her room key and waggled it at him, nodding.

He opened the door for Richter and followed him into the corridor, closing the door firmly behind himself. Bidding him goodnight, Richter made to walk away but Kaye stopped him with a hand on his forearm.

'Just one question, Raoul, if you don't mind: not that we weren't damn glad of it, but what's a theological historian doing packing a gun?'

Richter gave Kaye a surprised look. 'I brought it for personal protection. I can't speak for you, but I wouldn't feel comfortable in Damascus unless I was armed. After all, it's a civil war zone, isn't it? It beggars belief what these people are doing to each other. Did you see the latest news? An eleven year old kid helping wounded patients at a local hospital just got killed by a mortar bomb. The Russians may have persuaded these madmen to stop gassing each other with sarin, but there are other dangers - as we've just experienced. The Vatican actually insisted I carry a weapon for self defence; in fact, they provided it, along with the diplomatic pass that got it through the airports. And, as you say, we've all had reason to be glad of that, tonight.' He gave a small, nervous laugh. 'I just wish I knew how to shoot the blasted thing. Fooled the bad guys though, didn't I?'

Kaye clapped him on the back. 'You can fool them like that any time, as far as I'm concerned. All credit to you, Raoul - or maybe I should call you Bond; James Bond!' He winked to complete the jest and turned towards his own suite.

'Austin Powers or Johnny English, more like,' Richter called after him and, maintaining his charade of bonhomie, headed down the corridor whistling jauntily until he rounded the corner.

Kaye stopped and turned to watch the receding figure, his smile fading. You might have fooled the thieves and you've certainly fooled Sam, he thought, but I don't think you've quite fooled me. Your room is on the ground floor, so what were you doing up on the third floor outside Sam's suite at just the right moment to play hero? I may be wrong, but my nose is catching a faint whiff of the distinctive and foetid smell of *rattus rattus*.

He reached his suite to find the door inexplicably ajar. Hesitantly pushing it wide open, he surveyed the vista of destruction in front of him and let rip with a stream of invective far worse than Sam had mouthed a little while earlier. Picking his way through the god-awful mess, he hauled the room phone out from beneath a heap of disembowelled cushions, dialled Reception and demanded the manager. It was going to be a long night.

CHAPER 18

A MERCURIAL MASSACRE

Damascus, Syria, 21 June, 2016 AD

Deep in the Alawite enclave of Wurud, Bashir finally stopped the Sham and got out. Zikar's Ford Transit had kept up with him as they manoeuvred through the narrow streets of the old city to make sure of their getaway, turning often and always using the less travelled byways and alleys. Now both vehicles drew up in the dust of an unpaved parking lot close to the home of the *Dhu Samawi*. Zikar discontentedly slammed the van door, only to turn and see Bashir, in a buzz of elation, thrust his fist high in the air in a triumphal salute.

Zikar dismissed the gesture sourly. 'Your premature victory celebration is like an under-ripe olive: it looks good but tastes bitter.' He opened the back of the van and tossed Bashir's dirty clothes to him. 'We may know some of their names but we know nothing else except their intent.'

Resentfully, Bashir said, 'I stole their papers. Soon we'll know much more.'

'Peace! Whatever you have to say, keep it behind your tongue until we are off the streets. And don't expect to get any rest tonight. First, we must give those papers to the *Dhu Samawi* - he reads English better than you or I. And you do realise that our enemies won't hang around in Damascus now they know they have competition? We'll have to follow them - and that means you'll have to collect Alim and Umarah from Quasioun. And we'll need fresh clothes - and transport that no-one can trace back to us. Come on. There's no time to waste. Time enough for crowing when the job's done.'

Deflated, Bashir trailed behind as Zikar strode to the Lord of Heaven's house.

Inside the Khassah's spacious prayer room, surrounded by icons of Christian saints, framed texts highlighting the proclaimed godheads of Ali, Muhammad and Salman and a wall niche containing a small altar with candles, kept lit for the sake of the Ma'na - the incarnate essence of the Alawi Trinitarian Godhead - the Brethren gave their report to the *Dhu Samawi* and Bashir fished the stolen papers out of his kaftan pocket, spreading them out on a low table for their leader to peruse.

The Khassah's wife, unveiled in the way of Alawi women, had learned to mitigate her husband's natural disrespect for her sex by anticipating his needs and supplying them in an unobtrusive and deferential manner, so had quietly entered after a few minutes to pour wine for the three men.

'Ah, good,' beamed the Khassah. '...The Servant of Light! A few drops will restore us for the night's labours. Leave the bottle with us, Catherine. I'll call if we need anything else.' It was quite common for Alawis to bear names of Christian origin because of the Christian elements of their complex religion. But, being unclean and without souls, women were never taught anything of this most secretive of faiths. Even men were only initiated into its holy mysteries over a period of years, although *taqiya* - the vital art of religious dissimulation - was impressed upon them from the age of sixteen, when initiation began. Chameleons of faith, Alawis were adept at claiming to practice the faiths of others with whom they mingled, whilst never actually revealing their own beliefs, knowing that to unveil their holy secrets would invoke the swift retribution of death, followed by the humiliation of reincarnation as a lowly animal, a lot normally reserved only for unbelievers.

When Catherine had gone, the Khassah put down his wine glass and reached for the papers Bashir had brought. They were numbered and the third page ended half way through a sentence, which, as he pointed out, must mean that one or more additional pages were absent.

Bashir was annoyed with himself. 'I'm sure I picked up four pages as well as the map,' he said. 'One must have dropped out of my pocket.'

'Then we must make do with what we have,' was the philosophical reply. The Khassah went on to read the document while the others waited impatiently. He summarised the main points of interest for them and said, 'Clearly, the casket of the Ancients has, at some point, fallen into the hands of English Christians. From this document I see that in the middle of the last century the casket was hidden by one such - and despite the failure of the writer to be direct about the location, I believe we will find it in Jerusalem, most likely within spitting distance of where our miserable ancestor, Adeeb, was obliged to leave it - within the confines of the Church of the Holy Sepulchre. There is apparently a key to a particular door in that church; a key that is also hidden. This is where the English will be going, I guarantee it. We don't need to follow them - rather, we should attempt to precede them.'

'We must go quickly, then. My guess is that they will be leaving Damascus in the morning,' cautioned Zikar. 'As foreign Jewish sympathisers, they'll be able to enter Israel by the official route. But as Syrian nationals, how are you planning to get us through the Quneitra Crossing?'

'I'm not,' replied the Khassah. 'Aside from the occasional Druze bride or pilgrim, they don't let civilians through at Quneitra any more. I doubt that's the route the English will take and if they don't go that way, or if they fail in the attempt, they'll have to catch a ferry to somewhere like Cyprus and fly from there. We'll go the quickest way - overland - but not by any official crossing. Have you forgotten my uncle?

'...Ishmail? Oh, yes - I remember him. Before the Six Day War they let him in to study at the university in Tel Aviv, didn't they? He ended up staying in Israel permanently.'

'Correct to a fault, my dear Zikar. But you left out the most important fact.' The *Dhu Samawi* smiled. 'Ishmail's son, Moses, grew up to join the Israeli army and is a senior officer now. Father and son both changed faith to become Jewish - practicing *taqiya* at its most sublime, I might say - but I know I only need to make one call and a message will reach Moses, who will act upon it for the sake of his true faith. Rest assured there will be no Israeli patrols in our vicinity tonight and transport will await us once we have crossed the border at the place I have in mind. But it must be done at night, so we shall make preparations over the next three hours and leave no later than one in the morning.

'Bashir, phone Alim and explain that he and Umarah must make their own way back to the city or wait to be collected. Perhaps Matthew will oblige? We'll take my car and leave it near the border. Be back here at midnight and bring Hafiz with you - like you, he has the heart of a warrior. Choose functional black clothes, wear walking boots and pack small rucksacks only - we must travel light. Is everything clear?'

The others nodded. 'What about the map?' Bashir asked.

The Khassah sighed. 'I will need to study that further. It represents the final mystery that I believe will lead us to the casket itself. My initial thoughts are that it depicts tunnels and rooms - perhaps crypts or vaults of the church. It may show the layout of what we will find beyond the door we must unlock. The notes in specific places on the map may be important. We will refer to them when the time comes.'

He glanced at the ever-burning candle in the wall niche, then at the ever-ticking second-hand on his wristwatch. 'The time for thought is over. May the light of Ali ibn-Talib guide us all in our endeavour. Now - let's get moving.'

Mount Quasioun, Damascus, Syria, 21-22 June, 2016 AD

Bored beyond endurance, Alim and Umarah had given up watching the routine activity around the tomb. Once it grew dark and quiet, instead of setting a night watch, both of them retired to camp to eat the last of their stale flatbread with the contents of the last few containers of preserved food - olives, dolmas, artichokes in olive oil and some tinned lamb stew that would have been passable if heated up, but had to be eaten cold because they were not allowed to light a camp fire. Removing his mobile phone from his pocket and placing it beside him, Alim cocooned himself in his wool blanket against the night chill of the desert and fell into a deep sleep. Umarah rolled himself up next to his Brother, neither man stirring even when the phone, nestled in a fold of Alim's blanket, vibrated repeatedly during the darkest hours.

Waking in the clear light of dawn, Umarah, youthfully refreshed in spirits, brushed his teeth in a splash of water from his canteen, rewrapped his gutrah against the coming sun and relieved himself amongst the rocks near the camp tent. He shook Alim awake and said, 'Bashir will be back this morning.'

'He'd damn well better be,' growled Alim, rubbing his eyes. 'He knows we need supplies and, without him, we've got no way of getting home other than by walking down this mountain.'

'It's not that far,' said Umarah, shading his eyes to look down the steep mountainside towards the city, a grey mass with a smudge of dawn pink on its distant rooftops.

'Not for a mountain goat like you, perhaps. When he does turn up, he'd better find us where we ought to be - on duty on the cliff top, ready to report that nothing of any interest happened overnight.'

'We could always make something interesting happen,' offered Umarah with a grin, bending to pat the stock of his rifle.

Damascus, Syria, 22 June, 2016 AD

Cardinal Alesandro Mercurio's pique at being urgently summoned to Damascus was balanced by his desire to discover what could be so important that Richter had taken such an unprecedented step. Had his agent obtained proof of the existence of the casket? Lord above, might he even know where it was? Barely able to contain his acquisitive curiosity, the Cardinal had cancelled his impending appointments and booked an overnight flight to Damascus, via Istanbul. It was pricier but faster than the Jordan route, arriving in Damascus at eight thirty the next morning.

By eight in the morning, Sam's group had been regaled with the tale of Kaye's ruined suite, had breakfasted and had taken the decision to leave Damascus and drive directly to Jerusalem. Sam no longer felt safe in Syria. Ghulam made use of Kaye's 3D tablet to reserve suitable hotel accommodation in Jerusalem and by eight fifteen they were packed and ready to leave.

At first, Richter declined the offer of a seat in the hired Mercedes, saying he would sort out his own transport and meet them on arrival, but Sam argued that, although not normally in favour of guns other than for shooting pheasants and rabbits, on this occasion, all things considered, she would feel a great deal more secure if he - and his pistol - accompanied them in the same car. Unless they travelled to Cyprus and from there to Tel Aviv, the only way to get into Israel was the direct route south, through rebel-occupied territories bordering the Golan Heights. It was unlikely to be a trouble-free journey.

The bitch's insistence was annoying, thought Richter, since it would oblige him to rethink his plans regarding Mercurio, but he could hardly refuse her on that basis.

Excusing himself for a moment and finding a quiet corner, he dialled the Vatican from his mobile, but was informed by an assistant secretary that the Cardinal was en route to Syria for an unofficial visit to the tomb recently found there. He tried Mercurio's private mobile number, but it went to answer phone. Realising that Mercurio must still be airborne, Richter left a brief message.

'Apologies, Your Eminence, but I'm unable to meet you on your arrival in Damascus due to my obligation to accompany the professor's party, set to depart for Jerusalem as I speak. I recommend you take a cab from the airport to visit Christ's tomb - an experience you would be sorry to miss - and follow on to Jerusalem thereafter. I'll phone again once I've arrived there.'

Rejoining the group waiting in the hotel lobby, he graciously acceded to Sam's pleas and called for a porter to take his baggage out to the car. Settling their accounts, they left the Beit Khan and were already on the ring road out of Damascus by the time the Cardinal's flight landed.

Mount Quasioun, Damascus, Syria, 22 June, 2016 AD

Alim finally checked his phone, to find four increasingly irascible messages from Bashir.

The first message said, 'Why aren't you picking up? If Umarah's on night watch he should have the phone and be able to pick up while you're asleep. Get back to me. I've got important news.'

The next spat, 'Damn it, Alim, pick up! Where are you? If you're both asleep I'll have your hides when I see you.'

The third was in similar vein, but it was the fourth, recorded at close to one that morning, that revealed Bashir had utterly given up on them. 'Sleep on, fools. But when you do finally hear this, you're not going to like it. The *Dhu Samawi*, Zikar, Hafiz and I are leaving for Jerusalem right now. Our raid on the foreigners has borne rich fruit and we're going for the prize without delay. You two are a complete waste of time and you can either start walking down the mountain or wait for Brother Matthew to phone about collecting you. Personally, I'd just as soon leave you up there, you worthless drizzles of shit. You're a disgrace to the Brotherhood!'

The message ended abruptly, but not before Alim's ears had begun to burn with a mixture of shame and fury. They had been summarily abandoned by their Brethren - excluded from their right to be part of the main event - demoted to the ignominy of tramping home alone or waiting for a lift, like little kids after school. His hand shook as he passed the phone to Umarah. Let him play the messages for himself. There was no need to guess what his response would be.

Umarah put the phone to his ear, his face darkening as he listened. His subsequent outburst was predictable. 'He could have collected us before they left for Jerusalem! But no, that was too much trouble. They don't care about us - not even the *Dhu Samawi*! It's a deliberate plot to deny us our share of the glory! ...Brethren? Huh! What a bunch of bastards!' Beside himself at the calumny perpetrated against them, he stamped his foot on the bare, red rock and clenched his fists tightly, his dark eyes flashing at Alim. 'I'll show them who's worthless. They'll eat their words by the time I'm through, trust me!'

'But what can we do?' Frustrated, Alim plucked up a loose chunk of stone and cast it with vicious force at a large boulder.

Umarah grabbed up his rifle and feverishly ran his hand over the magazine, checking it was securely in place before lifting the weapon high and brandishing it in front of Alim. Born of a long line of Alawites who, for hundreds of years, had entrenched themselves in the inaccessible Jabal al-Nusayriyah mountain ranges of north-west Syria to escape religious persecution, his ethnic pride rose up and filled him with fierce determination.

'I don't know what you intend to do,' he cried, 'But I'm not spending the day tossing pebbles or hanging around so Matthew can fetch me down the mountain in his arms, like a lame goat. I'm heading uphill - and today I mean business!'

He turned and commenced a nimble ascent of the precipitous side of the ravine, his boiling rage lending him an unprecedented burst of energy. Unwilling to be cast as a coward, Alim armed himself and hurried after Umarah.

Switching on his mobile inside the terminal at Damascus International Airport, Mercurio collected Richter's message. It was intensely aggravating - he would have to contain his desires for longer than he had hoped. But the professor's move to Jerusalem seemed full of informed promise. Matters were proceeding at a much faster pace than Mercurio had expected. Good! And his agent was right, thought the Cardinal; he should avail himself of the opportunity to visit the intriguing tomb before leaving. Why not, indeed? Pocketing his phone and rolling his wheelie bag behind him, he crossed the thronged concourse in the direction of the taxi rank. Climbing into a yellow cab, he said, in passable Arabic, 'Please take me to Quasioun.' It was his first opportunity to use a language he had taken the trouble to learn, using audio-tape lessons, in case he was ever called upon to officiate as Papal Nuncio in any of the Arabic-speaking countries.

The cab driver shrugged. 'It's a big mountain,' he replied in Arabic. 'What road?'

The Cardinal pulled a newspaper out of his carry-on and unfolded it to show the cabbie a photo of the tomb. 'I want to see the tomb of Jesus Christ,' he tried.

The cab driver rolled his eyes, having already taken in the Cardinal's collar. 'May Allah preserve us,' he muttered, putting the car in gear and moving off. 'That'll be the dirt road, then.' Assuming that his passenger could speak Arabic fluently, he began prattling in that language as he drove along the main route north towards the city bypass. His liver-spotted hands loosely clasped on his lap, Mercurio nodded at intervals and smiled encouragingly, imagining that the driver was suggesting things to see and do while in Damascus, but, in reality, discovering that he did not know as much Arabic as he had thought.

Bypassing the city and leaving the main road, the cab wound through the scrubby groves and scattered dwellings of the Quasioun foothills and eventually bore left onto a steep, switchback track that led up the mountain proper. The air temperature was rising quickly in the fierce sunlight, but the Cardinal was obliged to let his perspiration gather, unable to interrupt the driver's flow of Arabic to ask for air-conditioning. As they rose higher above the city, the track was dwarfed by the uncompromising stone steeples of a narrow gorge; a chasm cleaving the eroding sandstone that made up the backbone of the mountain. Arid and inhospitable, it made Mercurio wonder why tombs had been constructed in such places - unless their very isolation was the appeal. Here, at least, he mused, gazing up at the towering cliffs, there was respite from the agony of human suffering going on below in the world's oldest, still-inhabited city. A man could free his soul in a place like this.

At last the yellow cab rounded a double curve and pulled up sharply, its wheels crunching on layered flakes of sandstone at the edge of the dirt road. A cloud of red dust rose and an unexpected breeze carried it forward up the noose of the gorge, blocking Mercurio's view of the heights.

'Please wait,' he said and got out of the cab. As the air cleared, he caught his first glimpse of the tunnel entrance, along with the two armed militia men sitting under an overhang next to it, their legs dangling casually over the edge of the ravine. And was that another guard up on the summit? There appeared to be a rifle in his hands, but why was he dressed in traditional garb rather than in uniform?

It was almost two hundred metres to the cliff top and the Cardinal began to raise his hand, meaning to shade his eyes so that he could better see the fellow who had accomplished that climb. As he did so, the man in question stepped up to the very edge of the precipice, his didishah billowing slightly in the desert breeze. Abruptly, he raised his rifle, took aim and fired. The high velocity bullet sped towards its target so fast that the sound of its discharge reverberated from the surrounding cliffs only at the same instant as the missile itself hit the centre of the Cardinal's forehead. Mercurio toppled backwards, dead before his body hit the compacted dirt.

Echoes from the shot continued to resound in the narrow gorge as the startled militia men clambered to their feet and looked around wildly. The unmistakeable crack of the rifle shot even penetrated the short tunnel to the sepulchre and brought Laurent and Desselle scrambling out in concern. Leaning over the precipice, they looked down in shock at the body lying on the dirt road below.

'Get back!' yelled the militia man closest to them, waving his arm urgently; the wisdom of that advice borne out as a second shot rang out, zinging off the rock only a foot away from the guard who had just cautioned them. He flattened himself against the cliff and the archaeologists hurriedly scuttled back inside the tunnel entrance.

'These militia guys were meant to be a visible deterrent, not target practice for terrorists!' Desselle was both indignant and alarmed.

'I know. And if that sniper takes out our guards, what do we do then?' Laurent exclaimed. 'We're effectively trapped! Thank God we sent young Yves and Philippe back to Paris yesterday with all the samples. I can't imagine what I'd have said to their parents if anything had happened to them.'

As he spoke, one of the militia men ducked into the tunnel and pressed a button to activate the two-way radio clipped to his combat jacket. He began a rapid conversation with whoever was receiving his call - Laurent hoped he was requesting urgent backup. Gingerly, Desselle poked his head out of the tunnel and spotted the other guard, his rifle raised, crouching behind a protective boulder with his head craned up to scan the heights above. Acquiring a target, he took aim and fired off a burst of shots. Whoever was attacking them must be up on the brow of the ravine.

Desselle drew back and cursed. 'Why did I leave my pistol in the blasted tent - today of all days?'

'Mine's on a ledge in the tomb,' Laurent remembered, brightening. 'I'll fetch it. Thank goodness the local police saw fit to issue us with side-arms.'

Crouched at their feet, the other militia man finished his radio call and un-holstered his own Makarov pistol, passing it to Desselle. 'Take,' he said. 'You may need.' He pointed upwards. 'I go - how you say? ...Like fish? No... Like crab: over rocks; up to top. Get behind gunman - then is easy go *takka-takka-takka*.' The gesture he made with his automatic rifle at this point was very expressive. He nodded briefly at the speechless pair and edged round the right hand side of the tunnel entrance, keeping his body close to the cliff as he began to look for a quick and quiet way to gain height.

Outside, two more shots rang out and there was instant answering fire from the pinned down militia man. Seeing Desselle's face paling as he gripped the Makarov thrust into his hand, Laurent turned and scrambled along the tunnel to retrieve his own pistol.

Repeatedly ducking away from the spray of bullets coming from below and then darting forwards and firing back at his enemy, Umarah was elated to hear the militia pig emit a pained cry as a bullet winged the soft flesh of his left arm.

A few metres away, Alim, yet to engage, knew that there would be no stopping Umarah now. Having worked himself up into a state of furious desperation, nothing would suffice but the satisfaction of a complete bloodbath.

Umarah called to his Brother in glee, 'See, Alim, they're sitting ducks! Ul-ha! Ul-ha! Ul-ha!' His battle cry rang out over the gorge.

As Laurent returned along the tunnel, his gun primed, he heard both the shots and the militia man's cry of pain. Scrambling past Desselle and out of the tunnel, he dived for cover behind a heap of rock-spoil, scanning the skyline. Hearing the triumphant ululation ring out from above and glimpsing a white-robed figure, the big Frenchman screwed up his eyes in concentration and fired.

Umarah's jubilant cry ended in a choked gasp as Laurent's bullet took him in the chest. Dropping from suddenly nerveless fingers, his rifle clattered onto the rocks as he toppled from the clifftop, his didishah billowing into angel's wings. Cartwheeling off an outcrop part way down, he continued plummeting to the road below, where the final, thudding impact left his lifeless arms outstretched towards the adjacent Cardinal, as if in supplication for redemption. Losing its graceful angel wings, his didishah deflated and settled over the broken corpse like a shroud.

'No!' screamed Alim, frantically scrambling to the edge of the chasm to look down in horror at the small, still form far below him. Beyond rational thought and torn by unbearable guilt at his failure to save his fellow Samaean from martyrdom, Alim sprang erect, uncaring of the risks. 'I will avenge you, Umarah,' he sobbed and took aim at Laurent, his index finger closing on the trigger.

Intent on his role as a harbinger of vengeance, Alim was unaware of the militia man who had successfully ascended the cliff further up the gorge and worked his way across the crags to get a clear shot at the surviving sniper. As Alim's trigger finger moved, the militia man loosed fire squarely from behind, spraying him with a merciless barrage of bullets that ripped ragged holes through the back of his didashah and stung shards from the rocks around him. As blood bubbled from his lips and darkness rushed in to claim him, Alim raised his own martyred eyes to the blue sky, then his body made its long swan dive to join Umarah's.

For a short space of time in the aftermath of the slaughter, silence reigned in the Quasioun gorge. Then the militia man on the summit called out to his partner to confirm that the brow of the gorge was clear of targets. Desselle rushed out of the tunnel with a first aid kit and knelt to assist the wounded officer who sat slumped against the boulder behind which he had been hiding. And Laurent sat down suddenly, weak at the knees. He had never killed anyone before.

At the onset of the gunfight, the cab driver had ducked down into his front seat well, where he had remained, with his eyes tight shut. Now he emerged, gripping his fare's hand luggage, only to drop it when he saw the three bloody corpses scattered around his cab. But he had seen death up close many times during the course of the civil war, so, after thanking Allah for sparing him, he began scouring his cab for bullet holes and bewailing the fact that he would not get his fare, now.

Reinforcements arrived forty minutes after the incident was over. A dozen men jumped out of two armoured trucks and, having established that the gorge was clear of gunmen, set several guards, while the rest began loading the bodies that littered the dirt road. Meanwhile, the team from the accompanying military ambulance conducted an efficient rescue of their wounded colleague, who was strapped into a field stretcher and rope-lowered down the cliff.

Laurent and Desselle were shocked when the frail, elderly body of their murdered visitor was identified from his passport and personal effects as a Catholic Cardinal. They had received no forewarning of his arrival and were at a loss to understand how anyone else could have known about it in order to plan his assassination. It was hard to believe that the Cardinal had simply turned up at the wrong moment.

Feeling emotionally drained - as well as afraid for their own personal safety - the archaeologists agreed that the remains in the tomb should be removed to the morgue at Damascus police headquarters until the official sanction to ship them to Paris came through. Perhaps, if the tomb was left boarded up and it was clear that work here was finished, it would stop attracting both visitors and trouble. The press could scarcely fail to get hold of this story and the murder of a Cardinal at the site of the tomb was bound to cause an international furore.

An hour later, the two thousand year old mummy, cocooned in the stretcher lately used for the militia man's rescue, began its journey down the mountain under military escort. Desselle went with it in the military ambulance, while Laurent stayed to clear up the tomb and strike camp before following on. A few militia men remained long enough to board up the tunnel entrance and paint a simple warning in Arabic on the rough wooden panels: *'Danger! Do not enter! By order of the Directorate General of Antiquities and Museums and the Damascus Province Police'*.

Desselle rattled around inside the ambulance, one hand steadying the stretcher that was no more than a simple pallet. Looking at the shrunken, shroud-wrapped mummy it cradled, he could not help wondering how many millions around the world would consider the action of removing Christ from his tomb as sacrilege. Would he and his co-workers be praised for their scientific rigour, or vilified for disturbing the Son of God's eternal rest? It seemed an ironic twist of fate that the physical return of the Messiah to the world of men was a 'second coming' that no-one could have envisaged, following, as it did, on the heels of a trinity of bloody deaths. Desselle concluded that this inauspicious fact, along with Christ's current corporeal state, hardly rendered this a resurrection likely to reflect the heartfelt hopes of true believers.

CHAPTER 19

REACHING THE PROMISED LAND

The Syrian-Israeli Border, 22 June, 2016 AD

Masked Syrian rebels had recently abducted a dozen United Nations peacekeepers on patrol in the demilitarised zone between the Israeli-occupied Golan Heights and Syria. Ironically, this was a boon to the Sabaeans because, in response, the UN forces had temporarily curbed their patrols in the area, which reduced the risk of being seen. The Sabaeans had, in any event, less to fear from the UN forces, there merely to observe, than from stray groups of dangerously unpredictable rebels.

From Damascus they drove to Izraa before turning west to Nawa and Al Rafeed, then cut off to the south, down a small country road through the barren hills, turning west again on another, even smaller road that petered out into a dirt track. Where the paved road ended there was a small, disused quarry and it was here that they left the Kassah's car.

Donning black gutrahs and darkening their faces with charcoal-grease, they shrugged on small rucksacks and began to trek uphill, walking in silence, with the *Dhu Samawi* leading the way. The waning moon gave enough light to prevent stumbles as they followed the goat tracks that ran erratically through the scrub-dotted rock outcrops. Traversing two kilometres without incident, they approached the top of a rise and halted. The *Dhu Samawi* beckoned to Hafiz and whispered an instruction. Hafiz nodded and continued to ascend, alone.

At the summit, he crouched amid the thorny scrub to minimise his outline against the skyline and, from there, made out a regular man-made structure extending across the hillside some thirty metres down the farther slope. In the darkness no detail was visible, but it had to be the border fence. Hafiz knew that beyond the fence ran a road along which UN jeeps or tanks often drove - but no vehicle lights were visible tonight and the only sounds he could hear were the distant, throaty chatters of a pair of argumentative rock hyraxes. To let the others know it was safe to proceed, he performed his own speciality animal call - the gekkering of red foxes at play. The apparently deserted hills were, in fact, full of wildlife. Hares, gazelles and even packs of wolves and golden jackals were known to roam this disputed stretch of wilderness. Any listeners would remain unconcerned, for the natural night noises of wild animals were commonplace here.

He barely heard his Brethren approach, they practiced such stealth. Looking round, he nodded and set off, remaining bent low as he angled downhill to the fence. Reaching it, a light tap on his shoulder indicated he should move aside and let the *Dhu Samawi* walk ahead of him on the dirt track that ran alongside the structure. Their leader sought a red ribbon tied to the barrier - the promised sign to confirm that the alarm system on this section of the fence had been temporarily deactivated to allow their safe passage. When Syrian rebels began infiltrating the demilitarised zone, the Israelis had rushed to install a new mechanism to foil any attempt to breach the border fence; this they accomplished by incorporating into the mesh of the fence a sensory fibre, sensitive to the slightest touch. Only if the sensor alarms housed on the Israeli side were switched off would it be safe for the Brethren to cut a gap in the mesh.

Just as he began to think Moses had failed them, the *Dhu Samawi* saw something flutter weakly against the far side of the fence at head height. It was a ribbon, although he could not distinguish its colour in the darkness. They would have to risk it, anyway - it was unsafe to loiter here much longer. Beckoning to Zikar, the Khassah made cutting movements with his fingers and pointed at the fence. Slipping his rucksack off, Zikar freed a set of heavy duty diagonal pliers and tentatively snipped one wire, then paused.

No alarms went off. Ali be praised; Moses had come through for them!

Zikar snipped furiously, slashing the mesh from ground level up for a metre or so, then peeling the loose corner back to create a crawl gap. In turn, each man dropped to the ground and passed into Israel on his knees, like a penitent pilgrim. Rucksacks were handed through separately.

The last man through was Zikar himself, who untied and pocketed the telltale ribbon before they moved on down the hill, keeping their descent as direct as possible on the basis that their transport was supposed to be parked directly below the safe section of fencing - and there it was - an Israeli army Saymar Musketeer, a light armoured vehicle resembling a camouflage-painted Range Rover. Parked with keys in the ignition, its back seat was piled with four Israeli army uniforms into which they quickly changed, bundling their black clothes into their rucksacks and hiding them out of sight, before wiping each other's faces clean with rags.

With Hafiz at the wheel, they drove sedately along the UN access road, headlamps on to create the impression that they were on legitimate army business. Passes and order papers had been left in the breast pockets of their uniforms to assist the illusion. At the crossover point between the UNDOF Alpha Line and the Israeli-occupied Golan Heights there was a small checkpoint, with two UN personnel on duty.

The only Hebrew speaker amongst the Brethren, Hafiz was responsible for talking them through this checkpoint. Drawing up at its barrier pole, he greeted the UN soldiers in Hebrew, explaining that they had come from Mount Hermon in the north east on a UN-liaison and fact-finding mission and were now in transit to their unit in Western Galilee. He flashed their passes and papers and they were waved on without further question, the red and white pole dropping back down behind them.

'By Ali, that was almost too easy,' he muttered as they joined Route 98 and headed south.

'Thanks to your prowess in Hebrew, Hafiz. But let us also remember what we owe to Moses,' commented their leader. 'Without his help, we'd have been flying to Istanbul and who knows how long it would have taken to contact the right people there to get Kurdish papers suitable for entry into Israel?' He suddenly smiled as an amusing thought struck him. 'One could say that my cousin has veritably lived up to his name, for indeed, Moses has led us to the Promised Land!'

Adopting a more sober demeanour, he added, 'But we have yet to reach Zion. This vehicle and our uniforms will only take us as far as Tiberias on the west side of the Sea of Galilee. We must hope that my cousin fulfils his last duty by meeting us there and providing civilian transport. I will rest now. Wake me when we reach the town.' The *Dhu Samawi* settled back in his seat and closed his tired eyes. The worst dangers of their journey were past and he could afford to relax for a little while.

The Quneitra Crossing, The Syrian-Israeli Border, 22 June, 2016 AD

The army guards on the Syrian side of the Quneitra Crossing were heavily armed. Afraid of the international political consequences of trying to take the Crossing, the Rebel forces had let it be and President Assad's army still controlled both the Crossing and the through-route to it from the town of Khan Arnabeh on Route 7, the main road south west from Damascus. The Druze apple trade from Israel into Syria continued on a daily basis, with UN trucks carrying crated apples over the border and returning empty, the fruit being reloaded onto Syrian trucks for transport north to Damascus. Despite the semblance of normality evinced by this regular trade, the stability of the area was highly precarious and no-one was taking any chances.

Ghulam approached the Syrian checkpoint slowly and brought the Mercedes to a halt the moment an army officer put up his hand, a hundred metres away from the barrier. 'I'm going to let down all our windows,' he said, nervously, 'So they can see we mean no harm.

And I suggest everyone keeps their hands visible - these gentlemen don't look too friendly.'

Four soldiers approached, pointing their rifles at the car. 'It's very dangerous in this area,' the senior officer amongst them barked, speaking in Arabic. 'You shouldn't be here. Where have you come from? Out of the car and give me your papers - immediately!'

'What's he saying?' whispered Sam.

'Just do as I do,' replied Kaye. He opened his door, got out, proffered his passport and spoke in Arabic. 'We are all British Nationals and this man is a Vatican Emissary with diplomatic immunity.' He indicated Richter, who had also climbed out. Ghulam and Sam followed and all of them handed over their passports, visas and, in addition, in Richter's case, his Vatican papers.

'We are a delegation en route to Jerusalem in connection with the archaeological discovery of the possible tomb of Jesus Christ near Damascus. That is where we have just come from,' said Richter, also in Arabic. 'Professor Kaye and I are theological historians. We are due to meet a Cardinal from Rome in Jerusalem later today and this is the only route that can get us there in time. We ask for your kind co-operation in providing exit stamps and facilitating our transfer to the Israeli checkpoint.'

They endured a string of questions and there was some suspicious muttering amongst the soldiers while the officer took their papers into the checkpoint building, but after a ten minute wait they saw him reappear and as he drew close, he nodded, saying, 'Your papers check out. They are stamped and you may proceed. I hope you have informed your hire car company that you will not be returning your car within Syria, as this is a one-way crossing. No return - understand?' He handed back their documents.

Kaye nodded. 'No problem.' He switched smoothly to English to say to his companions, 'Get in the car, everyone.'

The officer had to have the last word. 'We have helped you today because we are a progressive and peace-loving nation, eager to promote international cultural and religious co-operation - but there are no guarantees that the Israelis will see fit to accord you the same consideration. They may arrest and deport you - I cannot say.'

He waved them forward and a soldier pressed the button that electronically opened the high gates. Keeping his speed low, Ghulam took the Mercedes through and the gates swung shut behind them.

'All this aggressive security and these high fences - it's awfully intimidating, don't you think?' commented Sam in a small voice as they traversed the breadth of the no-man's-land separating the Syrian and Israeli checkpoints.

'It's meant to be. Israel and Syria are technically still at war,' said Richter shortly. 'Israel has had control of the Golan Heights since the Six Day War, but the Syrians consider it rightfully theirs and the international community has never affirmed it as Israeli territory. And with the Syrian civil war escalating, Israel is getting jittery about what might happen if the rebels decide to lob more than the odd, stray Scud across the border.'

'They've been launching missiles?'

'Now and then: better hope they don't choose today to start doing it again. That Syrian soldier wasn't joking when he said this was a dangerous area.'

'Will the Israelis let us in?'

'God willing,' murmured Richter, cocking his head slightly to better hear what the Lord was whispering to him.

'Follow Me into the Promised Land and I shall restore your birthright. Your enemies shall be as chaff in the wind and, like King David of old, you shall rule, but, this time, my covenant with you shall be forever.'

Ahead of them, the Israeli gates opened and a UN jeep drove through to meet them some distance inside the no-man's-land area. Ghulam stopped the car and everyone got out again, Sam felt very vulnerable under the scorching sun of mid-morning. She clutched her passport and smiled hesitantly at the two UN officers who got out of their jeep and approached on foot. They, too, were carrying weapons, but at least they weren't pointing them at anyone in particular.

'Surely it's obvious we're non-Syrian civilians, just from our clothes,' she murmured to Kaye.

'I expect they're trained to assume nothing - and since I don't speak much Hebrew,' he replied, 'I can only hope they understand English.'

Sam looked surprised. 'I thought you spoke everything.'

He glanced sideways at her and saw she was being entirely serious. 'I'm overwhelmed by your high opinion of my linguistic capabilities,' he said dryly, 'But no-one speaks every language fluently - and I specialise in dead languages, don't forget. I've translated quite a few old Hebrew texts, but I've never had to speak modern Hebrew aloud.'

'Papers,' demanded the first UN officer in a clipped, efficient tone. It was hard to identify his accent but he looked northern European. He took all their documents and leafed through them, comparing the passport pictures with the faces in front of him, one by one. Finally he looked up and spoke in English. 'You are all British civilians?'

'Correct,' affirmed Kaye. His companions concurred.

'As you are here, I suppose you must be in some kind of trouble. Are you claiming refugee status?'

'Good heavens, no!' said Sam, tartly. 'Do refugees usually arrive in a Mercedes?' She drew breath to continue, but Kaye tapped her arm urgently in warning and she took his hint.

'We're a research expedition team,' he extemporised. 'We had no idea that the overland route from Damascus to Jerusalem was as fraught with difficulty as we have discovered it to be. We're academics working in collaboration with a Vatican representative, who is here with us.' He indicated Richter. 'As you can see, we all have the correct entry and exit stamps for Syria, having been to Damascus, briefly, to see an ancient tomb there. Now we're heading for Jerusalem to visit some more tombs.'

'Aside from a few Druze, by special arrangement, no civilians have been permitted through this crossing in over three years,' replied the UN officer, shaking his head. 'I can't imagine what you were thinking to attempt this route, sir.'

'I apologise on behalf of us all,' Kaye said, humbly. 'We're happy to co-operate with any checks you need to carry out. Our colleague's Vatican papers confer diplomatic immunity, if that helps...'

'Ah - diplomatic - I see. That makes a difference. Diplomats don't count as civilians. Which one is the diplomat?'

'That would be me,' said Richter, handing over his Vatican papers. 'Doctor Raoul Richter...'

'Richter?' broke in the UN officer, staring at him with fresh interest. 'That's a German name, not an English one - but your passport is English.'

'My grandfather was German,' lied Richter, smoothly. 'But I'm a born and bred Englishman. By the way, if you can't read Italian, I have an English version of my papers in my diplomatic bag. No German version, though, I'm afraid.'

'Interesting coincidence, your name,' said the UN officer. 'I'm German, myself - and my name also happens to be Richter.'

Sam smiled nervously. 'Perhaps you're related,' she suggested.

The UN officer shrugged, his features remaining deadpan. '*Wer weiss?* Who knows? It's not an uncommon name. Now, listen carefully, please. I am going to let you come forward to the gate. You will wait in your vehicle while I have your identities checked electronically.' He held up their documentation. 'I will need these, but they will be returned to you if they are in order. You are incredibly fortunate to be in possession of a diplomatic pass. If legitimate, it will facilitate your entry into Israel - and we may be able to waive a full body search.'

The wait was longer this time. After thirty five minutes, everyone was roasting inside the Mercedes, which provided no air conditioning with its engine off. At last the gate opened in front of them and two UN soldiers waved them through, directing them to pull in to the right, by a low building with a sign that read: 'UN Checkpoint - Al Quneitra'. Ghulam surrendered his car keys to one UN soldier and a second one escorted their party into the building. Their car was searched and their luggage brought inside while they stood in line waiting to pass through a scanner. Richter was conducted to one side, together with his small suitcase and diplomatic bag, avoiding these procedures.

Sam glanced across the room enviously. 'I do hope this doesn't mean the rest of us will have to submit to full body searches,' she lamented.

'If you arrived in Israel by plane, they would probably do a full body search at the airport,' the UN officer checking their luggage told her. 'However, this crossing is UN-controlled and we are able to use our discretion. In this case it will be sufficient for you to walk through the scanner. Please ensure you have no metal items in your pockets.'

Once through the scanner and reunited with their luggage and with Richter, they approached a counter where the German named Richter stood waiting for them, their passports and papers on the counter in front of him. He stamped each one in turn and handed it back to its owner. 'I am issuing emergency visas, which you must pay for here,' he advised them. 'These will remain valid for one week only, so if you intend to remain in Israel longer than that, you must approach your embassy for extended visas. Please do not attempt to cross either way at Al Quneitra again. We have made an exception for you this one time only.'

Waving away their thanks, he issued their visas and Sam, the only one with the foresight to have brought with her some Israeli New Shekels, paid in cash for them all. 'Yours is my treat,' she told Richter, re-zipping her Burberry tote-bag. 'Without your diplomatic pass we'd have been caught between a rock and a hard place'.

It was with immense relief that they meekly trailed after the German, who led them outside and back to their searched vehicle. 'Do you have a road map of Israel?' the UN officer asked Ghulam, handing back the car keys.

Ghulam shook his head.

'In that case, I advise you to turn right at the end of this road and, afterwards, left onto Route 91 towards the Sea of Galilee. Follow signs to Tiberias and there you will find shops, maps and touristic services. Have a safe stay in Israel.'

The black Mercedes pulled away and the German shook his head as he stared after it, his lip curling in bemused disbelief. Only the English would attempt a stunt like that. Were they caught in a time-warp of imperialistic self-delusion, or were they just a nation of blind optimists? Either way, they seemed to believe themselves invulnerable to harm wherever they went in the world. Crazy, every one of them... *total* übergeschnappt*!*

Jerusalem, Israel, 22 June, 2016 AD

The Sabaeans exchanged their military disguises for nondescript western clothing and a rental car in Tiberias, courtesy of Moses, who assumed they had fled the troubled Syrian capital in fear of their lives and offered to help them find accommodation and jobs. The *Dhu Samawi* expressed sincere gratitude for all that he had done and explained that they were not, in fact, planning to be in Israel for long. They had come on urgent, private business and would be returning to Syria via normal commercial routes in due course. No, of course they weren't involved in any type of intelligence operation or terrorist activity! Moses need not worry. By helping them, he had not in any way compromised the safety of his adopted homeland; not at all. This was a personal matter only. May he and his loved ones be thrice blessed by Ali ibn-Talib!

By seven in the morning, they were on the outskirts of Jerusalem, arguing over the city map with which Moses had provided them, in the typical manner of tourists who could not decide whether car parking; accommodation; breakfast or the proximity of key attractions was their most important priority. In due course they found all, including a modest guesthouse above a spice bazaar in the north-western Muslim Sector of the Old City, an easy walk away from the Church of the Holy Sepulchre. Believing that they were, at the very least, a day or more ahead of their rivals, they broke their fast heartily with big bowls of shakshuka - a simmered egg and tomato stew - some cucumber and tomato salad and a dish of cheese-stuffed, fried-dough parcels called bourekas, before retiring to catch up on their missed hours of sleep.

CHAPER 20

AN INSPIRATIONAL SALUTATION

Jerusalem, Israel, 22 June, 2016 AD

By noon, Ghulam had successfully negotiated Jerusalem's teeming city streets and brought his charges safely to the door of their hotel, the Royal David, located in the Mamilla District at the south-western corner of the Christian Quarter of Jerusalem's Old City. Its suites overlooked the ancient Jaffa Gate and the imposing, crenellated bastion that was the Tower of David. Entering the Old City on foot through the Jaffa Gate and bearing left at the end of the street would put them on Hanotzrim Street, the hotel concierge told them; from there, it was only a five minute stroll through the dense warren of alleyways - jam-packed with colourful market stalls - to their desired destination.

While they were grabbing a snack and quenching their parched throats with chilled tamarind juice in the hotel's mezzanine bar, Kaye pointed out that they would need to do some practical shopping before they could contemplate a visit to the Chapel of Saint Helena. He smiled at Sam. 'I don't think the Greeks, Armenians, Copts or any other sect would appreciate us pinching their votive candles to provide the light we'll undoubtedly need if we do find the key to the door your grandfather spoke of - we'll need to buy good, big torches.'

'And a water bottle for each of us, Miss'm?' suggested Ghulam with feeling. They had all suffered from the heat that morning.

Sam turned and studied him critically. 'Considering the claustrophobia you suffered when we were in that rock sepulchre yesterday, I believe you ought to think twice before going into any more small enclosed spaces, Ghulam. I would certainly be the last one to ask it of you.'

Her chauffer shook his head. 'You don't need to worry yourself about that, Miss'm. Could I be a good car mechanic if I was claustrophobic? I've spent half my life tinkering with oil filter wrenches in confined spaces. No - I just needed an excuse to remove myself to a quiet place where I could concentrate on memorising some letters I saw in the tomb but had no means to copy onto paper at the time.'

Sam patted Ghulam's arm as if to console him in advance for her next words. 'I appreciate your thoroughness, but there was no need for you to do that,' she said gently. 'Oliver is our 'letters' man. And, never fear, he remembers exactly what was written on Christ's coffin, don't you Oliver?'

Kaye nodded. 'You're a good chap, Ghulam, but I've got that one covered.'

'I'm very glad to hear that, Sir.' ...*But I don't think you have, quite.* The short verse he had seen scratched into the rock ceiling in the tomb was still puzzling Ghulam. He had memorised it, translated it and knew exactly what it said, but had no idea of its significance, if any - and he wasn't about to disclose what he knew in front of Richter, despite the fact that the good Doctor was part of their team, now. Ghulam simply didn't trust the man: he had emotionless eyes.

'Aside from getting torches and so forth,' said Sam, 'I've still got the last page of my grandfather's notes to read before we start adventuring. But there's no huge hurry to get going, is there? I mean, those Syrian terrorists can't have followed us - they'd never get through at the Quneitra Crossing, would they?' Deceived into a false sense of personal safety by the distance they had just put between themselves and Damascus and lulled by the comfortable familiarity conferred by the cosmopolitan environment of her new hotel, Sam felt a surge of reckless confidence.

Her logic being superficially sound, Kaye readily agreed that there was time to gather their thoughts - and review the paperwork - before heading to the shops and then the Church of the Holy

Sepulchre. Richter made no comment, appearing to be happy to go with the flow, but the group plan of action having been settled, he did have one suggestion to make.

'Listen, while you're all gathering clues, or whatever, why don't I scout about and get the bits and pieces we need?' He gave a conspiratorial wink. 'I know I can trust you not to go running off treasure hunting without me.' He judged this offer might get him some brownie points and it would also, more importantly, provide him with an excuse to spend some time alone. Keen to tie up loose ends, he had already phoned Mercurio once since reaching the hotel, but the Cardinal had failed to pick up and remained an elusive threat in his mind.

His more immediate concern, however, was the palpable threat posed by the Syrians. Who the hell were those bastards, anyway? In all his years of clandestine fact-finding, he had never come across a link between the casket and any radical Muslim group. Knowing your enemy was the first step to defeating him - and he had been guilty of the fundamental error of believing that the identity of all his enemies was known to him. He'd thought he was in full control of the game, but these Syrians were the lethal wildcards that proved the Lord God was still testing his resolve. That naive pretender, the Dexter bitch, might dismiss the potential dangers, but Richter had recognised in the Syrians' eyes the same single-minded obsession that lay in his own. He only wished he knew how many would come, for come they would - and soon.

'That's very kind of you, Raoul,' smiled Sam, thankfully.

As adept as an Alawi at keeping his true thoughts and beliefs hidden, Richter smiled back pleasantly for her benefit, plucked his room key-card from beside his empty glass and strolled away towards the elevators.

Like honey from a fractured comb, golden afternoon sunlight poured through the windows of Sam's elegant penthouse suite. Indoors, the sense of peace accorded by strategically placed iris, rose and cyclamen arrangements was challenged only by the susurration of an efficient air conditioning system.

An Inspirational Salutation

Outdoors, one might be forgiven for concluding that someone must have wrongly awarded Rome its cachet as the Eternal City, since that particular epithet was more pertinent in every way to the Old City of Jerusalem. If eternal meant endless, or incessant, then the Old City aptly met those criteria. The constant honking of frustrated cabbies; the interminable *phut-phut-phut* of mopeds winding precariously between orange-laden trucks and dusty local buses; the sonorously clanging church bells; even the whispered prayers and supplications of Christians, Moslems and Orthodox Jews, each had its place in the interminable cacophony that overlay the worn and secretive stone buttresses, crumbling arches and meandering alleyways of a metropolis whose origins lay much further back in time than those of Rome.

The pulsing stream of humanity also seemed perpetual, its varied composition reflecting the volatile diversity of spiritual and secular passions in this unique location. Through her windows, Sam watched tourists; guides; Coptic priests; awed pilgrims of all nationalities; veiled Moslem herb-sellers; shoppers and traders flowing through the Jaffa Gate in both directions. Considered its main entrance, the Jaffa Gate sliced through the encircling, medieval stone walls guarding the Old City and gave access to the ancient maze of streets that led to some of the holiest shrines of Christendom, Islam and Judaism.

On the eastern side of the Old City stood the separately walled area of Temple Mount, dominated by the oldest Islamic building in the world, the seventh century Dome of the Rock - housing the rock from which Muhammad was said to have ascended to Heaven. Its great golden dome was easily visible to Sam even from this far away. She also made out, in a more central location, the smaller, plainer dome of the fourth century Church of the Holy Sepulchre - housing the rock upon which Jesus Christ was said to have been crucified. She marvelled at the series of discoveries and revelations that had brought her to this extraordinary place. And then she contemplated, in more sombre vein, the destiny awaiting her beneath that distant dome, in Saint Helena's chapel and beyond.

Kaye had also been absorbing the view for a few moments. Turning away from the window, now, he watched Sam as she unfolded the rescued final page of her grandfather's notes, noticing how the glancing sun infused her glossy, auburn hair with a halo of amber light. You're one hell of a beautiful woman, he thought - but so much more as well. You shake off experiences that would send the majority of people scuttling back home to the safety of their armchairs - falling off sheer cliffs and being held hostage at gunpoint by terrorists, to name but two - and whatever the setbacks, your confident determination just bounces back. You openly appreciate the good things in life, but your sense of duty always prevails over self-indulgence. And you never give up...

'I give up,' said Sam, startling Kaye out of his reverie. 'What can he possibly mean by that?' She stabbed her finger at something on the page she had been reading.

'Read the problem bit out aloud and I'll see if I can help,' suggested Kaye.

'I might as well read out the whole passage; it's not very long.'

Kaye sat down at a nearby table to listen, leaning on his elbows and making a cathedral of his fingers.

'...Before I close, let me add one item of vital information that, for prudence' sake, is not written on the map or apparent on the route. If you, Keeper, intend to trace my steps, note this well and solve its conundrum or reap no reward.

'At the end, this letter alone will offer you one small element of hope when the walls close in around you, and all seems lost. To reverse your unfortunate situation, you must know, to the very letter, the potent meaning of the spiral inscription that is written in the tongue of the Ancients on the Mark of The Power. Pray upon that element of hope and your prayers shall be answered.

'Good luck and may your steps ever be guided by your duty to The Power and your hope for The One.'

'That's all there is,' said Sam, disconsolately. 'I can't make head or tail of what he's talking about, other than the bit about needing to know the meaning of the inscription on the seal. It looks as if we have

An Inspirational Salutation

to decipher that and use it to solve the rest of his cryptic conundrum, or else...' She broke off abruptly.

'Or else something quite nasty will happen to us, I imagine,' finished Kaye for her, looking troubled. Wasting no time, he fished his trusty notebook out of a deep jacket pocket and flipped through it until he found the scribbled symbols he had copied from the emblem on the *Sanskrit* legend on the day he first met Sam. Casting a professional eye over them again, he sucked his lip indecisively before offering an opinion. 'I do think these symbols are letters and I'm rather coming round to the idea that they represent a kind of *proto*-Sanskrit.'

'*Proto..?*'

'Yes; a root language that pre-dates true Sanskrit - the forerunner to it, if you like.'

'So, in other words, they're in a totally unknown language. But that means we can't possibly decipher them!' Sam was aghast at the thought of coming this far, only to be thwarted by a few prehistoric squiggles.

'Hold your horses, ma'am,' scolded Kaye mildly. 'I didn't say they couldn't be translated. You haven't got some two-bit charlatan sitting here, you know.' His fingers went automatically to his ear, but found no pencil stub. 'Oh, rot,' he muttered. 'Anyone got a pencil?'

'Will this do, Sir?' Ghulam, who had been using their en-suite wi-fi to read an online article about the Israeli car market, padded across the lounge with a hotel courtesy pen.

Taking the pen and nodding his thanks, Kaye looked sympathetically at Sam's quiet, unobtrusive factotum and said, 'How will you occupy yourself, Ghulam, now that we don't need to drive anywhere for a while? It'll be a bit of a bore for you, won't it?'

Ghulam put his hands together deferentially to indicate that he meant no offence by what he was about to say. 'You underestimate me, Sir. A Hindu is never without the means to occupy his mind and body. Let me give you an example, if I may. Whenever I can, at sunrise, I address my spiritual and physical well-being by performing the *Sūrya Namaskāra* - the Sun Salutation.'

Kaye was fascinated. 'What does that involve?'

'I am honoured by your interest,' replied Ghulam. 'The Sun Salutation makes for an auspicious start to the day. It consists of ten yogic postures, these being assumed in successive flowing movements to complete one namaskar. I utter twelve sacred mantras in a specific order and, for each mantra, I perform one complete namaskar.'

'I feel ashamed to admit it,' said Kaye, 'But I wasn't even aware that Hinduism involved sun-worship.'

'Oh, yes,' said Ghulam, smiling. 'We have the oldest religion on Earth, you know. The ancient sacred texts - especially the Rig Veda - still guide our path and are a source of many of our favourite prayers. In fact, my favourite mantra when performing a namaskar comes from the Rig Veda.'

'I'd like to hear it,' commented Kaye. 'Do you say it in English or in Sanskrit?'

Ghulam chose to answer Kaye's question by speaking the mantra aloud, in English:

'Throughout the dusky firmament advancing, laying to rest the immortal and the mortal; borne in his golden chariot he cometh, Savitar, God who looks on every creature.'

Good grief, thought Sam, in whom Ghulam had never confided on matters of faith - sun-worship: how anachronistic. Intellectually, she could understand why ancient cultures had deified the sun. Giving light and warmth and making plants grow and animals thrive, the sun was fundamental to the survival of mankind. No wonder primitive, ignorant people had seen it as a god. But for anyone in the twenty-first century still to be worshipping the sun - well, that just seemed bizarre.

Then a humbling and unwelcome thought struck her. What was her father's creed if not an unconventional form of sun-worship? Hadn't the Sanskrit legend claimed that the sun's life-force had been captured and locked up in the casket - and hadn't *The Power* even fought to escape that fate before Baal bent it to his will? If factual, that cast the sun as some unimaginable kind of living being; if not a god, then certainly godlike in its powers.

An Inspirational Salutation

And after all, whom but a god could bring the dead back to life? And wasn't a god supposed to be 'unimaginable'?

The distinction between *The Power* as a force born of technology and *The Power* as the living spirit of a god-like being began to blur in Sam's mind in a distinctly jarring epiphany.

'So, I speak it aloud in English - but I can also write it in Sanskrit,' said Ghulam, proudly. 'Look.' He took back the pen he had lately proffered to Kaye and carefully wrote out the mantra in its original tongue:

आ कृष्णेन् रजसा वर्तमानो निवेशयन्न अमृतं मर्त्यं च ।
हिरण्ययेन सविता रथेना देवो याति भुवनानि पश्यन ॥

'So you know it's written from right to left,' Kaye noted. 'Excellent! Have you a grasp of the alphabet and how it translates, or do you just understand its meaning through having learned the mantra by rote?' He turned to the spiritually-challenged Sam and said, by way of an aside, 'The Rig Veda is a sacred Indian text over three thousand years old. It relates the mythology of the Hindu gods in the form of a thousand hymns - all written in Sanskrit, of course.'

'I had no idea you knew Sanskrit, Ghulam,' said Sam weakly, unable to improvise a more intelligent response because her mind was still trying to make sense of - well - everything.

'No, Miss'm; why should you?' replied Ghulam, beaming a white smile against dark skin. 'And nor would you know that we consider Savitar, the solar deity mentioned in my mantra, to be a vivifier - a life-bringer.' He paused, then added, diffidently, 'I've been thinking, you know, that perhaps it might be the soul of Savitar inside the casket, Miss'm. Who knows?'

Sam's jaw dropped. So did Kaye's. Ghulam had never appeared to be remotely interested in matters connected with the casket. His unexpected observation, however, suggested otherwise.

Ghulam's gave a small, quirky smile at their obvious shock. 'I may not say much, Miss'm, but your welfare is most important to me - so I tend to listen rather carefully to the conversations going on around me when they appertain to you or any matters important to you.' He turned and looked at Kaye. 'If you don't mind sharing with me the text you wish to understand, I'd like to try and help, if I can.'

Kaye pursed his lips in pretended consideration and then grinned, patting the empty seat next to himself. 'The more, the merrier! Sit yourself down, Ghulam, old boy.' He passed his open notebook to his new work-buddy. 'That's my best effort to copy what was inscribed on the seal... the one you've no doubt overheard us discussing.' Ghulam blinked at the symbols on the page.

प्र क्र (gap) ई स्व र

'Only those five symbols appear in the spiral; the same five repeated multiple times,' Kaye told him. 'I wrote them down in the same order that they appear, spiralling inwards to the seal's centre and I wrote 'gap' to indicate where there was an obvious gap suggesting the end of one word and the start of another. But although they look very like Vedic Sanskrit, they don't match any words I know in that language - and now I'm beginning to wonder whether they only look so much like Sanskrit because I added the typical Sanskrit upper bars to them myself. What do you think?'

'Let's see how it might sound to say them aloud as if they were Sanskrit, but in the Latin alphabet,' suggested Ghulam. He gave it a try. "*Pra - kr - is - v - ar*.' Hmm. The '*is - v - ar*' syllables sound vaguely like a shortened version of the Sanskrit word Ishvara, the 'I' of which we would capitalise, of course, because Ishvara means 'the personification of Vishnu'.'

Kaye picked up the hotel pen and wrote down 'personification of Vishnu'. 'Remind me about Vishnu,' he said, diplomatically.

'He is God, of course,' replied Ghulam, shrugging. 'But Ishvara does not mean Vishnu, exactly.' He cast about for the right words to explain. 'Vishnu is the Creator. And what he created was the universe, right? Now, we believe that because God exerts total control over his own creation, he is, in a way, one with that creation - God and the universe rolled up in one, if you like. So we would say that Vishnu is the supreme cosmic spirit, indefinable, whilst Ishvara, which literally translates as 'one with and different from his creation',

An Inspirational Salutation

is used to identify the aspect of God that is a tangible force, having material impact upon our world. These are subtle definitions - not easy concepts for a non-Hindu to comprehend.'

'I'm totally lost,' admitted Kaye.

'Sorry. Just think of Ishvara as 'the supreme cosmic force', if you like.' Ghulam peered at the symbols in the notebook again, borrowed the pen back and wrote down his shortened definition of Ishvara. Then he said, 'That leaves us with *'pra - kr'* - or *'prakr'*. I'm trying to think of any words I know in Sanskrit that contain *'prakr'* within them.'

'There's the word *'prakrti'*, of course,' murmured Kaye, almost dreamily. 'Doesn't that mean energy, or something?'

'Yes! Yes, of course!' Ghulam grew quite animated. '*Prakrti* is the energy or potency used by Ishvara to effect the material impacts he desires on the universe, our world and ourselves.'

Grabbing the pen out of Ghulam's hand with a sudden *prakrti* of his own, Kaye wrote *'Prakr Isvar - Prakrti Ishvara'* and looked hard at it. Judging that the latter phrase was almost certainly derived from the former, he scrawled down the English translation and with a huge whoop, launched the redundant pen across the room like a paper dart.

"*The Potency of the Supreme Cosmic Force*' - that's what it means!' he cried, pounding the table in elation before jumping up and pumping the hand of an overwhelmed and grinning Ghulam.

Sam, who had been a mere onlooker in this play, clapped her hands at the men's quick success. 'You're absolutely extraordinary, both of you...' She launched into a litany of praise, but never finished, because, in one impulsive stride, Kaye filled her vision, grabbed her hands, pulled her to her feet and began swinging her round in a heady whirl, his eyes a pair of flashing sapphires.

'Gracious! What's got into *you*?' she gasped happily, her surprised eyes upturned to his. The poignant, misty sadness that so often occluded them was absent, Kaye saw. Now they were dancing eyes, full of green fire.

'If you're labouring under the delusion that I'm a boring boffin, it's only because you've never attended one of my faculty grant award parties,' he quipped breathlessly and with that, although he could easily have whirled on and on in the heat of that green fire, he brought the lady gently to a halt and delivered a brief, celebratory peck to her left cheek. She did not shy away from the gesture; nor did she return it. Instead, she simply bestowed upon him one of her rare, glowing smiles and squeezed his hands before letting go of them.

'You're not boring,' she promised him. 'Not in the slightest.'

As Sam received her fleeting kiss in the Royal David Hotel, four men dressed in nondescript, baggy clothing entered the vast, stern emblem of Christianity that was the Church of the Holy Sepulchre, just another statistic amidst the surging crowds of pilgrims and tourists, each of whose shuffling feet was contributing, infinitesimally, to the wearing away of the time-smoothed paving upon which so many thousands had walked for so many long centuries.

But unlike the rest of the multitudes, these four had not come to marvel at its hallowed chapels; or to rub their scarves, reverently, on the Stone of Unction, where it was said Jesus' body had been prepared for burial, or even to dip their heads in prayer before any of its many ornate altars. Nor had they come to stand in line with the Christian pilgrims waiting to enter the Holy Sepulchre itself, that most sacred place where Christ was believed to have lain for three days, before rising, resurrected, in promise of eternal life for all those who chose to follow his teachings. That intangible promise seemed more real and gave more comfort to the mortal masses when they could touch some seemingly tangible evidence of its origin, so they queued for that precious moment of hope.

The four men entering the Church did not seek comfort or hope.

They had no need of promises.

They had come with one purpose only: to find a clue, a key and a casket - a fifteen-thousand-year-old receptacle which they believed held the real power to demonstrate the consummate, undeniable, tangible proof of resurrection that mankind had sought and yearned for since time immemorial, a proof that, after two thousand years, Christianity, like all the other religions of the world, had failed to deliver with certitude.

An Inspirational Salutation

No wonder they pushed impatiently through the milling crowds in the Anastasis, bypassing the crusader-built Catholicon containing the main altar of the Church, in their haste to reach the Chapel of Saint Helena as quickly as possible. The divine miracle of life from death - and the ultimate power to control that miracle - was almost within their grasp.

CHAPTER 21

PLAYING 'FOLLOW MY LEADER'

Jerusalem, Israel, 22 June, 2016 AD

Kaye and Sam had jotted onto one sheet of paper all the mysterious clues they had discovered that might help them in the practical aspects of locating the casket. And Richter had returned, bearing powerful torches, filled water bottles and belt loops through which to hang the items. He seemed to be in excellent spirits, desite the heat. Only he knew that the reason for the spring to his step was the news he had just managed to extract, over the phone, from a shocked personal secretary at the Vatican.

Cardinal Mercurio had been taken care of without him having to lift a finger. The Lord God was truly working in mysterious ways to benefit his chosen second Messiah.

The party donned clothes suitable for clambering about in tunnels and tombs, although Ghulam insisted on keeping to the dark trousers, white shirt and tie he considered to be his work uniform. 'In case of accidental mishap,' he explained, 'I would want my mother to know I went properly attired. She has always been very particular about observing the proprieties.'

Sam smiled. 'When you were a kid, I bet she told you to wear clean underwear every day in case you got knocked down by a car on the way to school.'

'Naturally,' replied Ghulam. 'Indeed, she has never stopped telling me.'

With their water bottles and torches on their belts, sturdy non-slip shoes on their feet and the clue-page in Sam's zip pocket, they were ready to go.

At the eastern end of the Church of the Holy Sepulchre was the Ambulatory, with three chapels beyond it. Between two of the chapel entrances lay a set of steps which led down to the underground Chapel of Saint Helena, a twelfth century Armenian Church and a place less visited than most, being modestly adorned in memory of Helena's pious simplicity. The Chapel was shadowed, its low-strength lighting giving it an aura of sanctity and mystery. No-one else was present when the four Sabaeans arrived.

Stepping over the low chain that spanned two huge stone pillars near the Chapel entrance and crossing the intricate mosaic floor the chain had been placed to protect, the *Dhu Samawi* approached the altar at the far end of the room, his three companions hanging back to keep a watchful eye on the entrance in case a priest or other visitors should appear. Climbing with sacrilegious disregard over the waist-high, ornamental cast iron railings that barred access to the altar itself, he slipped through the narrow gap to the left of the high stone edifice, into what was little more than a crawl-space at its rear, where, wedged like a pebble between the unforgiving stone of the altar and the equally solid rear wall, he knelt in the semi-dark, his eyes ranging intently over the smooth, grey blocks of limestone that formed the back of the altar.

There was something...

Peering closely at one particular stone block about three feet above the floor, the *Dhu Samawi* manoeuvred his torch out of his pocket and illuminated the inscription scratched into its surface. His chest heaving in a mixture of mental excitement and physical discomfort, he read the words that completed the partial clue written in the notes Bashir had stolen.

'A keeper of old laid the Mark of the Power
In full sight of all who, unknowing, walk o'er.
Where one of its rays lights the way to the dawn

Was now supplemented by:

It points to where Christ wore a crown made of thorn.
There, penitent, kneel, but abstain from the rock:
Beneath and behind lies the key to the lock.'

Memorising the new lines, he rose and carefully backed out of the narrow space. Just as their leader reached the railings again, Zikar stepped into the Chapel entrance, momentarily blocking the activity within the Chapel from the view of the group of tourists descending the stairway. Quickly, the Lord of Heaven vaulted the railings, strode back across the thousand-year-old mosaics and stepped over the guard chain, instantly taking up the pose of an innocent spectator of the holy monuments around him. Zikar stepped aside to let an incoming swarm of tourists shoulder past him.

'Got it,' the *Dhu Samawi* whispered to his Brothers, as he turned and moved sedately towards the stairs, threading apologetically through the softly chattering group who were now gathering to admire the mosaic floor. The three Sabaeans fell in behind their leader and soon they were back up in the Ambulatory, looking for a place to sit down while they considered the meaning of the stanza. There were plenty of empty rows of pews in the Catholicon and no-one disturbed them as they unobtrusively occupied one, their heads bowed in apparent prayer.

'The Mark of *The Power* has twelve rays,' muttered the *Dhu Samawi* quietly, having repeated the full stanza for everyone's edification. 'Assuming it is represented somewhere within this building, I'd say one of its rays points eastwards - perhaps towards a specific icon or painting of Christ being crucified... did anyone bring a compass?' He raised bushy, grey brows at his Brethren, who shook their heads.

'Then we must become tourists and leave no chapel, crypt or forgotten corner of this shrine unvisited.' The Lord of Heaven sighed. 'With the help of Ali, one of us will notice what we seek. Let your eyes cleave to the floor beneath your feet, for I am strongly of the view that the Mark will be found set in stone in a location where people frequently walk.'

Hafiz grunted in chagrin. 'They walk everywhere. In fact, half the time, you can't even see the damn floor for the crowds.'

'We passed the Calvary earlier. Isn't that the place of crucifixion?' hissed Bashir in sudden agitation. 'And, literally speaking, where Christ wore his crown of thorns?

'Yes! Of course...' The *Dhu Samawi* pulled hard on his beard as if berating himself for not having made that connection himself. 'Quickly - let us go and pay homage at the rock of Golgotha, Brothers.'

The four men filed out of the pew. Bearing left just before the Catholicon's exit, they climbed a broad flight of steps that passed through a stone archway, beyond which further, narrower steps gave access to that area of the Church built over and around the small, rocky outcrop that Saint Helena had identified as the true site of the crucifixion of Christ. Just as the Syrians disappeared from view beyond the archway, Sam's group entered the Church almost directly below, unaware that they were already lagging behind in the race to find the casket.

At the top of the stone steps lay the Catholic Chapel of the Nailing of the Cross, bearing on its vaulted ceiling a twelfth century mosaic depicting that cruel act for which the Chapel was named. Adjacent to this was the lavishly decorated Greek Orthodox Calvary - a sanctified Aladdin's cave infused with the candlelit glitter of gold - where pilgrims flocked to see the rock of Golgotha, protected under glass and visible on both sides of the altar. That altar - a simple, stone table topped with a brown marble slab, over which hung an aerial forest of golden-hued sanctuary lamps - attracted an endless queue of believers waiting for their turn to kneel, alone, within its confines and, through a small, silver-rimmed hole at the back, reach down to touch the bedrock itself at the very spot where their Lord had died to redeem them.

Unknowingly tracing the footsteps of the Sabaeans - and about twenty minutes behind them - Sam and her party, having found the inscription in the Chapel of Helena and reached the same conclusion about the most likely place to find the Mark of *The Power*, entered the Greek Chapel of Calvary, the Twelfth Station of the Cross on the Via Dolorosa.

They had anticipated a need to quarter the Chapel in search of a symbol that might be hard to find but, in the event, there was no need. That which they sought was right before them in plain sight. Sam stopped in her tracks, astonished.

The foot-polished stone floor occupying the body of the room directly in front of the altar bore not only the patina of a thousand years but also, as the decorative element forming its centrepiece, the unmistakable twelve-pointed, wavy-rayed orb that was the seal of Balthazar, set in pure white marble on an obsidian background. At least five feet in diameter, its black rim was bounded by a broad hoop of white, accentuating the impact of the design and isolating it from the remainder of the floor, which was comprised mainly of tan and cream marble flagstones.

Over this blatant symbol of *The Power* tramped the myriads, as they had tramped for an eon, oblivious to its significance. Their eyes and minds were fixed immutably on the rock of Golgotha and the elusive promise of eternal life.

How incredibly bold one of her long-dead ancestors had been, thought Sam, to place the sunburst here at the ultimate heart of Christianity. And how that stonemason must have laughed to himself as he lovingly carved and shaped that enduring emblem, knowing that out of all the people in the world, only one Keeper in each generation would ever be able to recognise it for what it was. She stood before the handiwork of her nameless forebear and shook her head in wonder.

Finally she turned to Kaye and chided him, with gentle humour. 'Oliver, I told you Christian churches were full of pagan symbols. Now do you believe me?'

'No choice, really, have I,' he answered, wrinkling his nose at her. 'More to the point, if you'll pardon my pun, the guidebook says that the altar in here faces west, which means that the ray directly facing it must be pointing east.'

'*Where one of its rays lights the way to the dawn, it points to where Christ wore a crown made of thorn,*' murmured Sam, watching a pilgrim drop to his knees at the altar in front of her. 'I know where the key is, Oliver.' She let the direction of her gaze demonstrate the answer. 'But I'll let you do the kneeling. I never was much of a one for penitence.'

Richter listened in fascination to their soft exchange. They may have included him in their party, but had not seen fit to explain all the details of the cryptic clues to be solved and the steps required to reach the place where Kai's map would come into play. He had that map tucked securely in his pocket against necessity, but had, in any case, memorised all its annotations. They had hidden their top cards from him, so it was only fair that he should keep his own aces close to his chest until the time was right. Then the arrogant bitch would learn the meaning of penitence!

Kaye waited in line and, after ten minutes, was rewarded with his own personal opportunity to kneel down, under the altar slab, on the cool stone floor.

Abstain from the rock, he thought. *Beneath and behind lies the key.* Well, I won't abstain from touching the rock of Golgotha, now that I'm actually here. I may never have the chance again. But, assuming that the key isn't beneath or behind the rock itself, the clue can only mean that once my arm is through the hole, I need to feel around underneath and behind it. This is - literally - a blind act of faith... and with that thought, he bent forwards and plunged his right arm through the hole at the back of the altar, his splayed fingers questing for the solid surface of the sacred rock below him.

Having satisfied his desire in that respect and having prayed, briefly, with his eyes closed and his fingertips on the bedrock, he began to withdraw his arm slowly, bending it at the elbow so that his hand could explore the space just behind the hole. Abruptly, one of his knuckles scraped on wood and he carefully felt his way into what his fingers told him was a slim, open-fronted, box-like enclosure. Mapping its extent by touch, he panned from side to side before straining right to the back in case the elusive key happened to be wedged against the rear wall of the tiny compartment. His extended fingers examined every last cubic inch of Kai's clever hiding place, but to no avail. The ledge was empty.

Bitterly disappointed, he rotated his elbow and drew his arm out from the hole, backing out from beneath the altar before climbing to his feet and moving away to allow the next pilgrim to take his place. Rejoining the others, they could see from the expression on his face that his venture had been unsuccessful. 'Nothing,' he confirmed grimly, then elaborated on his terse statement. 'Well, Kai's cubby hole was there, alright, but either the key must have fallen out of it, which I consider unlikely, or else some filthy thief got here before we did.'

Sam looked utterly crestfallen. She had been so confident that all would be as her grandfather had written. 'That's it then,' she said sadly. 'It's a dead end.'

'If I might ask,' ventured Richter, 'What was this missing key supposed to unlock?'

'A particular door, here in the Church,' replied Sam disconsolately.

'Haven't you ever heard of a lock-pick?' enquired Richter dryly. He had a finely crafted set of them in one of his pockets.

Sam frowned at him. 'Yes, of course I have - but I don't happen to have one and wouldn't know how to use it if I did.'

'Oh, it's quite easy, Miss'm,' broke in Ghulam, joining the muted conversation unexpectedly.

Sam looked at him askance.

'I always carry a bit of thin wire around with me in case I lock myself out of the car,' admitted her factotum sheepishly. 'I can get into some makes in less than thirty seconds. I think I'd have a fair chance with your door, though it might take longer than thirty seconds.'

'This chap never ceases to surprise me,' commented Kaye to Sam.

Sam's face lightened. 'Superman personified; didn't I tell you so?'

'Shall we pop along and have a look at the door in question, then?' suggested Richter, winking at Ghulam. 'Seems a waste not to, while we're here...'

Behind the Holy Sepulchre, at the west end of the Rotunda, between two of the many massive pillars that supported its great dome, lay the entrance to the neglected Syrian Orthodox Chapel of Saint Joseph of Arimathea and Saint Nicodemus, a lacklustre, dilapidated chamber without so much as an altar. A low, uneven, cave-like opening at its rear gave access, via a short passage, to a small complex of empty, first century, Jewish rock tombs known as kokhim tombs, their roughly hewn and dirty limestone interiors not worth more than a cursory glance from the few who bothered to venture that far, their eyes by then having become accustomed to expect the opulent, if occasionally tarnished, magnificence apparent in the main chapels of the Church.

Following the leads given in Kai Dexter's informative notes, the *Dhu Samawi* led his Brethren to this forgotten corner, the pilfered key clutched tightly in his right hand. It had been demeaning to have to act out that stupid kneeling ritual in the Calvary, but the reward justified the blasphemy. He was in high spirits at his skill in analysing the latter part of the poetic clue, an accomplishment that had delivered the key into his eager hand. His temples might be greying but his brain was still a fine tool. His heart swelled with longing and desire, almost to the point of physical pain, at the thought that before the day was over, he might discover the casket and take possession of his rightful place both as The Lord of Heaven and, more importantly, of Earth.

The blessèd scrolls cannot lie - they say that the Dhu Samawi who finds the casket will be The One. It is my right and privilege. So I must be The One. I AM THE ONE!

Striding through the deserted Chapel of Saint Joseph and Saint Nicodemus, he lowered his head slightly to enter the rock-hewn tunnel leading to the kokhim tombs, the others following on his heels. From there it took only moments to reach an old but sturdy wooden door, painted black, set into the solid rock wall on the right hand side of the passage at the point where it opened out into the tomb complex proper.

Just as the Englishman's notes had described! The *Dhu Samawi* was doubly elated.

Only here, in this one iconic Church, could a door have been left locked and untouched for over sixty years. The entrenched, centuries-old disputes between the six Christian sects holding custodial responsibility for specific portions of the building precluded any modifications to its designated communal areas, since gaining the unanimous agreement required to implement such change was a sheer impossibility. The well-known 'immoveable ladder' was testament to this extraordinary state of affairs. At some point in the early nineteenth century, someone had placed the ladder on a communal exterior windowsill. No-one knew to which sect that person had belonged and, consequently, no sect dared move the ladder in case it disturbed the fragile status quo, provoking the wrath of other sects. The ladder had remained in the same position ever since, a bizarre symbol of the divisions that continued to dog the Christian world.

Inserting the precious key into the ordinary-looking keyhole beneath the door's brass handle, the *Dhu Samawi* held his breath and turned the shank slowly. For an interminable moment the key stuck, part way through its turn; then the internal lock mechanism clicked and the key completed its rotation freely. His lungs released their pent up air in a sigh of relief and, taking a firm grip on the handle, he pulled open the heavy door, its dry hinges creaking in protest after their protracted period of disuse.

The small, enclosed space on which they now gazed looked like a typical, two thousand year old kokh tomb, with its unevenly stippled limestone walls and shallowly rounded roof. There was even the usual indented channel running the length of the tomb, intended to carry away water - and other fluids. Unlike a typical tomb, however, at the back of this one lay an ancient, rusted grille, behind which a small raised stone platform was apparent. Bashir, looking over the *Dhu Samawi's* shoulder, said, wonderingly, 'This is the very crypt where the Christian priests locked away the casket after our cursed ancestor, Adeeb, told them of its powers - I am sure of it!'

'Yes,' whispered the Lord of Heaven. 'You are right. The casket *was* here for many hundreds of years. Even now, its aura lingers in the air of this place.' His gaze moved to the left of the grille, to the old wooden boards nailed tightly together over the low entrance to a further passage. 'And my bones are telling me that its current resting place is not far distant from where we stand. Come. Let us open the way!'

Because it had taken the Sabaeans several minutes to pry apart the boards blocking the entrance to Kai's maze, Sam's group reached the black door only ten minutes after the opposition had, in the manner of Alice's white rabbit, vanished down the hole they had uncovered. It was an unpleasant shock to find the door slightly ajar, since, aside from Ghulam's disappointment that he was not required to demonstrate his lock-picking skills, it was only then that full understanding hit home - someone had preceded them.

'It has to be those Syrian thugs,' said Sam, biting her lip. 'They're the only ones who could possibly know about the key and this door apart from us. How in hell's name did they manage to get here before us?'

'Men like that... who knows what resources they can call on? Terrorists seem to be able to cross borders only too easily, don't they?' Kaye frowned, thinking rapidly. 'They can't be very far ahead of us, surely? We haven't exactly dawdled since the Syrian incident.'

'I half expected this,' commented Richter. 'And in case you were wondering, I did bring my pistol along. I had a feeling it might be needed.'

'God, I hope not,' muttered Sam, bundling her thick auburn hair into a pony tail and securing it with a scrunchie. 'Anyway, while we're debating, the bad guys are getting even further ahead of us. Come on, everyone. There's no time to lose!' And with that, stepping into the crypt, she pulled the torch from her belt, flicked it on and knelt down to crawl into the dark tunnel at the far end. The only good thing, she thought as she shuffled along its narrow length on all fours, was that the Syrians almost certainly had the false map. She was not ashamed to hope that they would follow its misleading clues and get completely lost in the maze. Then again, she reminded herself sourly, they might have the wrong map, but *she* didn't have the right one.

Which means we might end up getting lost down here ourselves, she reflected uneasily, ducking her head even lower to miss a lumpy outcrop of rock that jutted down from the roof of the passage.

We could get lost, yes. Or topple into some god-awful hole in the dark. Or even fall foul of one of granddad's anti-Cyrus traps. In fact, we could quite easily end up dying in here...

CHAPTER 22

LOST IN THE LABYRINTH

Beneath the Church of the Holy Sepulchre, Jerusalem, Israel, 22 June, 2016 AD

After a few metres, the low tunnel ended in a cramped chamber with the saving grace of a roof high enough to permit the four men to stand erect and from which spiralling stone steps descended, plunging through the bedrock. Hafiz shone his torch downwards, but the curved blackness sucked up his feeble beam and bounced it back at him, refusing to yield its secrets. He shrugged fatalistically. 'Let me go first, Lord of Heaven, so I can catch you if you trip.'

'May Ali bless you, Brother,' replied the *Dhu Samawi*. 'Lead on.'

The steps were narrow but the tunnel roof arched sufficiently to give adequate headroom for a comfortable descent. Hafiz counted off the steps as he went down. 'Twenty four... and a sloping tunnel ahead,' he called from the bottom, flashing his torch over the pitted and blackened limestone passageway falling away in front of him. Passing down the steps and along the tunnel in single file, the men emerged into a natural limestone cave formed by water erosion in prehistoric times when the land above enjoyed a more temperate climate. Short, knobbly stalactites clustered over their heads along fault lines through which water must once have seeped. Since there were three tunnels radiating from this diminutive cave, they paused to allow the *Dhu Samawi* to consult the sketched map in their possession. He was now certain that it depicted the very labyrinth in which they found themselves.

Realising that one end of the meandering drawing closely resembled what he had seen of the kokhim complex and taking that as his starting point, he was able to trace the path they had taken to their current location. 'Yes, now I see where we are. Good; good!' he exclaimed, relieved beyond words to discover that the previously incomprehensible diagram was, after all, going to prove an invaluable guide. 'We should take the right hand tunnel from here. The others fade to dotted lines with a bar drawn across them - they must be dead ends.'

'And after that?' demanded Bashir, frustrated by the slow, deliberate demeanour of his leader and eager to race on to their goal, his mind already envisaging the rich golden glint of the casket in his torch beam and how it would feel to lift the weight of the fabulous prize in his own two hands.

An uncharacteristically intolerant frown deepened the furrows lining the *Dhu Samawi's* brow. Leadership was an overwhelming responsibility. The unthinkable consequences of failure loomed huge in a mind already challenged by the onset of severe taphophobia - that unspeakable terror of being buried alive. He swallowed drily, battling to blank out the horrid image of being trapped down here, unable to move while the millions of tons of solid rock above him descended implacably, inch by agonising inch, compressing his lungs to jelly and crushing his bones to powder.

'...One step at a time, fool!' He shook the map for emphasis. 'The man who fashioned this also wrote of hazards to be overcome on the route. In speed lies disregard and in disregard, danger. Mark me well and curb your insolent impatience.'

Cowed by this unexpectedly severe rebuke, Bashir subsided into thin-lipped silence.

'Lord of Heaven - can we be sure the casket is truly down here?' asked Zikar, seeking reassurance.

'My bones tell me it is. So let us reach it safely.'

They proceeded with caution, the constant twists, turns, slopes and steps of the maze making it impossible to retain any spatial awareness of their position relative to the Church way above them. One thing only was certain. Slowly but surely, they were descending ever deeper into the ancient limestone roots of the hill of Golgotha.

She could have cut the pitch black air with a knife. Sam had always considered fear of the dark to be a childish trait. But now, with only the fitful wavering of a few torches to help them negotiate the unknown, she began to make her own personal acquaintance with mankind's primordial terror. At the same time, perhaps in response to her extremely limited vision, she found her other senses intensifying. As the four members of the group walked in single file, the dull tread of their combined footfalls sounded abnormally loud to her. Using the left hand wall of the tunnel as a positional benchmark, Sam had taken to running her fingertips along it continuously as she moved forwards and so sensitive had her sense of touch become that the sulcate stipple of the chiselled rock felt like Braille, couched in some arcane tongue.

The gently sloping tunnel opened into a small natural cave with three possible exits. It was the first time they had been required to make a choice. Longing for her grandfather's map, Sam felt a new fear grip her. What if they went the wrong way? They might miss Kai's traps, but getting lost could be even more dangerous. She played her torch aimlessly across the exit tunnels, thinking, *eeny-meeny-miny-moe*.

As the ranging beam arced across it, a small area above the arch of the right-hand tunnel revealed itself to be much whiter than the surrounding rock. Curious, Sam brought the beam back to the spot - and gasped.

'Hey! Look at this.'

The three men crowded closer to peer at what she had found.

'It's a pig,' declared Kaye, bemused. 'Someone's chipped away the dirty surface of the limestone to form the animal shape in the clean white rock underneath: clever.'

'It's not a pig,' corrected Sam, 'It's a boar.'

Kaye looked dubious. 'If you say so - same difference, either way.'

'Actually, I think the difference is significant. I'm pretty sure granddad's notes said something about remembering to draw on the courage of the beast supporting the family crest. Now I think I know why.' She suddenly shifted her torch beam, pointing it directly at

Ghulam's chest to highlight the Dexter family crest embroidered on his tie. 'Look at the animals supporting the shield - on the left, a unicorn representing purity and, on the right, a boar representing *courage*. I think he carved that boar there as a sign to take that tunnel!' Sam made a mental note to herself not to dismiss as a throw-away line anything that Kai had written.

'You know, I think you might be right,' conceded Kaye, impressed with her powers of deduction. 'Is everyone in accord?'

Ghulam and Richter acquiesced, the latter already knowing that Sam's choice was correct. He could have pulled out the map to show them, but it was still too early to let the cat out of the bag. *Let the bitch sweat it.*

The *Dhu Samawi* let Hafiz take the lead. The tunnel was high and broad and there were no annotations on the relevant section of the map to suggest a special need for care. Its limestone rock floor was gritty with loose rock dust, but level and even, so Hafiz strode ahead confidently, his torch aimed at the ground just in front of him. Consequently, because its frayed end was about four feet above the floor and his torch beam glanced on it only at the last moment, he almost walked into the rope dangling from an iron ring bolted to the tunnel roof.

His automatic reaction was simply to push the unexpected obstruction away from his face without breaking stride, while raising his torch to better illuminate the passage in front of him, by which time he had already taken another couple of steps. What came into view in his raised light beam was a line of similar dangling ropes spaced along the centre of the tunnel for the next six or seven yards, but by the time his mind had processed what he was seeing, it was already too late.

The crunch of his boots on limestone dust remained the same, but with his final step, he only had time to note that the underlying echo of his footfall had taken on a vaguely hollow attribute before the apparently solid rock floor dropped from under his feet. Camouflaged by a thick layer of coarsely ground limestone, a centrally pivoting steel plate had been secured across the top of an oblong vertical shaft spanning the entire width of the tunnel. The weight of a man stepping onto one half was more than sufficient to cause the whole plate to pivot on its axis.

Hafiz threw his arms up wildly in an attempt to grab a rope end as he lost his footing, but the steel plate swung down so fast that he simply slid off the end of it and vanished, amidst a great shower of grit. One continuous, high-pitched scream tracked his fall in the ears of his horrified companions. The scream ended abruptly when he reached the bottom of the shaft, which, whilst not tremendously deep, had a particularly well-sharpened set of wooden stakes set in an upright position at its base.

Even before the meaty thud of Hafiz's impalement, the steel plate had righted itself to lie grit-free and exposed before them, its polished metallic surface gleaming innocently in the torchlight.

Still a few yards back from the death-dealing trap, the *Dhu Samawi* clenched his fists and threw back his head, emitting a roar of fury and anguish. Restraining the urge to rush forwards to try and help, or indeed to run in the opposite direction, he spread his arms as a barrier. 'Don't move,' he hissed to the two men behind him. 'There's nothing we can do to help Hafiz now. He is lost to us - a martyr in the name of *The Power*!' He bowed his chin to his chest and intoned, 'May Ali have mercy upon his soul and bear him straight to Paradise.' Then he turned to his fellows and stated, grimly, 'We need no more martyrs, so set your grief aside and concentrate. Somehow we have to get past this abominable contraption.'

'How did he not see the solution in time?' lamented Zikar. 'It's so obvious. All we have to do is keep our weight off the metal by swinging arm-over-arm along the ropes! Look, I'll show you. Shine your torches ahead to light my way - I'll need both hands free.' He shoved his own torch into a deep pocket, ran forwards and grabbed the first rope, high up, reaching for the next in line as his momentum swung him forwards. Keeping up a rhythm in that manner, his feet only inches above the floor, he crossed the pit and pivot safely, dropping to the ground only when he reached the last rope.

Bashir followed with monkey agility and the less physically able Lord of Heaven went last, experiencing much greater difficulty. Three quarters of the way across, he lost momentum and became stranded, dangling one-armed over the steel plate, his nerveless fingers beginning to slip down the rope. He was saved from the same fate as Hafiz only through the intervention of his Brethren, who instantly leant forward to circle his waist with strong arms and wrench him bodily to safety. The *Dhu Samawi* relinquished his failing grip and allowed himself to be propelled forwards, sprawling gratefully onto the reliable limestone floor, where he remained for some moments to regain his breath.

At last he recovered his dropped torch and stood. 'Right: let's move on - very carefully,' he said. 'Courage, Brothers; we don't have far to go, if I've read the map right.'

What he did not know was that from there on, their map would lead them falsely.

Moving as speedily as they dared through the twisting midnight passages, Sam's team heard a dreadful, extended screech followed by an unearthly, hollow cry, reverberating from somewhere ahead and below.

'Well, that proves we've got company,' said Kaye, nervously. 'It must be the Syrians - and not too far away, if I'm any judge.'

'It would seem they've encountered a problem,' commented Richter, straining his ears in hopes of further audible feedback.

Sam gave a shiver, the hairs on the back of her neck prickling. 'Whatever it was, it sounded bad.'

'But it suggests they haven't looted the casket yet,' pointed out Richter, his pale eyes as lambent and unblinking as those of a latter-day Gollum.

Only minutes later they, themselves, came to the steel plate and the line of ropes.

Kaye put out a cautionary arm to stop Sam. 'Something tells me this was the cause of those unholy cries we heard, so stay still and let me investigate,' he said firmly. Sam nodded mutely, staring at the strange set-up. With extreme care Kaye knelt and exerted light pressure on the smooth steel with one hand. The sensitive pivoting mechanism responded immediately and the plate depressed beneath his touch. 'Ah!' he said. 'I see what we have here.' Curiously, he shone his torch into the gap and the beam glanced off the walls of the hidden vertical shaft, affording him an unpleasant glimpse of a contorted human body some twenty feet below, the pointed ends of half a dozen sharp stakes thrusting up through the limp corpse. *One down, then. Sam had better not see this, though.*

'It's a mousetrap for people,' he said as he rose. 'Step on the steel and you'll plunge into the deep shaft that's right underneath it.' He looked at Sam. 'I hate to say it, but I'm pretty sure Kai must have installed this to catch out the unwary. He certainly wasn't messing about, was he?'

'Did it work?' asked Sam, bluntly.

'Is that all you can say, Genghis Khan? I didn't know you were so merciless! Yes, it worked - but don't you dare look.'

'I won't - and I'm not merciless. Rather them than us, though. If they hadn't got here first, it could have been one of us down there, instead.'

'I can't argue with that.' Kaye looked at the ropes. 'We don't have a plank handy so are you up for a monkey-swing? There doesn't seem to be any other choice.'

'Let's do it.'

One by one, the three Syrians squeezed through a tight cleft that delineated the end of the rugged passage down which the map had directed them. There had been an alternative tunnel but, on the map, an annotation written next to the relevant junction read, '*Take a sinister turn*' and the *Dhu Samawi* interpreted 'sinister' to mean left just as 'dexter' meant right, in Latin. They had taken the left hand passage.

The cleft opened into a cavern far larger than the grotto they had come across earlier. Stalactites and stalagmites adorned it in abundance and it was clear that serious scrambling and clambering would be necessary to navigate the obstacle course over which their torches danced. Zikar scouted the route ahead, leaving Bashir to assist their leader. 'Follow me at your own pace,' he said. Because the cavern was so obviously a natural geological formation, he felt confident in dismissing any worries concerning man-made traps.

Lowering himself down between two gargoyle-like stalagmites, he began to pick his way through the extraordinary wonderland, shining his torch on the extravagant flowstone and travertine sculptures above and around him. Multi-tiered wedding cakes vied with crystalline fountains for his attention and, as he angled his torch beam upwards towards the central dome of the cavern, he could make out several clusters of long, icicle-like stalactites.

Behind him, as he rounded a frilled crinoline-petticoat of a buttress, he could hear Bashir talking the Lord of Heaven through a challenging array of conical stalagmites. Then his eyes caught sight of what lay ahead across the more even sweep of rock favouring the centre of the cavern. Dominating his vision, the domed cavern roof boasted a spectacular stalactite chandelier composed of several dozen slender icicles, immediately beneath which, within a circular pool of water only a few feet in diameter, stood a large, mushroom-shaped stalagmite resembling an inverted baptismal font - and, resting on top of that mushroom, an object that glimmered with a rich, alluring lustre under the effulgence of his torchlight.

Here, then, lay the culmination of their deepest desires; the fulfilment of their dearest dreams.

At last... The golden casket of the Ancients!

'Ali be praised! I've found it!' he cried out in rapture and raced towards the mushroom, splashing into the pool in his haste to reach the casket. The water was shallow, but the smooth calcium carbonate coating that formed its saucer-like base was extremely slippery. His feet went out from under him at the first step.

Landing on his back with a gargantuan splash, he was fortunate to suffer no more than a winding, a couple of banged elbows and a slightly twisted ankle. He even managed to retain a grip on his all-important torch. One unnoticed consequence of his minor misadventure was the displacement of an appreciable volume of water. The abrupt introduction of his bulk generated a wave that radiated outwards, lapping over the pool's calcified rim to fill the unobtrusive gutter measuring its circumference. From there, the liquid flowed away rapidly along an unremarkable channel carved in the sloping rock floor, only to vanish down a small plug-hole at the edge of the cavern.

Emerging in another limestone cavity directly below, that same stream of water poured down into a conveniently placed container that formed one end of a metallic, fulcrum-weighted kingpin. The weight of the water tilted the kingpin on its axis, raising its far end sufficiently to touch and release the metal clip that had been holding a sharp axe in place. The released axe swung in a pre-determined arc, slicing through the highly tensioned, vertical rope that rose into a natural rock fissure above.

That vertical fissure connected, higher up, with a similar, horizontal fissure that extended, within the strata of the limestone, all the way to the heart of the cavern roof - directly above the pool where Zikar had just taken his tumble. Through this hidden airspace ran the rope, at last leaving the fissure to pass down through a deliberately bored hole accessing the underside of the roof of the cavern, a few short inches below. There the rope ended in a knot securing it to a tempered steel ring, which in turn was screwed into the back of a disk of Bakelite about eight feet in diameter, built to integrate with the natural formations surrounding it. Attached to the underside of the disk, the slender stalactites that Zikar had assumed to be natural were, in reality, Bakelite spears, supported internally by steel rods that tapered to needle-sharp tips.

The sliced end of the rope snaked upwards at great speed in response to the downward pull of the weighty Bakelite chandelier at its other end, a construct no longer prevented from dropping once the rope restraining it had been cut.

Down in the pool, Zikar had barely raised himself onto his complaining elbows when his torch beam caught the huge stalactite cluster above his head dropping towards him. His mouth opened in disbelief but he had no time to cry out before the chandelier slammed down on top of him, its battalion of lances piercing his unprotected flesh.

The weight of the array caused the majority of the imitation stalactites to splinter on impact, such that the disk came to a final rest at an angle, blanketing Zikar, the mushroom stalagmite - and the golden casket.

The crashing boom that signified this event ran round and round the cavern in a dull, thunderous rumble. Both Bashir and the *Dhu Samawi* ducked automatically, thinking that the cavern roof might be collapsing, but as the deep, grumbling echoes died away to silence, they paled and glanced at one another, now sharing a different fear.

'Zikar!' shouted Bashir, 'Answer me!' There was no reply. Scrambling as fast as they could over the inhospitable terrain, the two men rounded the crinoline buttress and took in their first view of the disaster site, over which a coronal haze of rock dust scintillated in the flashing beams of their torches. Approaching closer, their boots crunching on shattered shards of Bakelite, they saw the steel ring with the long rope attached, its coils now looped in loose, untidy piles on the ground - and they saw Zikar's waterlogged boots protruding from beneath the rounded edge of the formidable disk.

'Quick! Help me,' cried the *Dhu Samawi*, setting down his torch to light the scene and setting his shoulder to one side of the rim of the eight foot disk. Bashir ran to its other side and between them, with a mighty shove, they heaved the dread weapon away from its victim, letting it fall outwards to land with its broken lances thrusting upwards in a fittingly vicious salute to their purpose. Sadly, shifting the disk proved to be of no avail. Zikar's dead eyes, round with shock, stared up at his Brethren through the shallow water that covered his face.

Beside himself with grief and horror, the *Dhu Samawi* raised shaking hands to his temples, grabbing fistfuls of his greying hair and tugging at them. 'Oh, Zikar!' he moaned. 'Why did you run on ahead? What drove you to this evil fate?'

'I heard him shout something like 'I've found it',' whispered Bashir slowly. 'What did he find?' Playing his torch beam over the ruined area, his heart momentarily jumped when the light glinted off something gold - but sank into his boots when it proceeded to glint off several more things that were also gold. Collecting the four broken chunks and squatting, he reconstructed the three dimensional jigsaw and revealed what the stalactite chandelier had broken asunder. He held it up for his leader to see.

It was the golden casket.

And yet it was not...

What the burning eyes of the *Dhu Samawi* beheld was a facsimile; nothing more than a detailed plaster imitation adorned in gold leaf, but convincing enough, in an encroaching darkness relieved only by one wavering lamp, to have lured the worthy Zikar to his terrible fate.

Her group halting at a mystifying Y-junction, Sam was stumped. There had been no further evidence of their enemies since the scream and roar several minutes ago - and since they were not present at this junction, it had to be assumed that the Syrians had either made an arbitrary choice of direction or had been guided by the map they had stolen.

The sharp-eyed Ghulam pointed out that over each of the two tunnels they faced, mathematical addition sums were scratched into the rock. Over the left hand tunnel the sum read '37 + 4', whilst over the right hand tunnel, the sum read '38 + 3'. Both added up to the same figure, 41, but that meant nothing to any of them. There was momentary silence while Sam, Kaye and Ghulam racked their brains over the mystery.

'*It is time, chosen One,*' whispered the Lord God in the mind of his worthy acolyte.

Yes! Richter thought - and a passionate, epiphanous joy gripped him. Backing away from the others, he drew his pistol out of the holster concealed under his jacket and released the safety catch. The click was so faint as to be indiscernible under normal circumstances, but in the primaeval dark and silence of the maze, with their ears more acutely tuned to sound, the click echoed audibly. Everyone turned their heads at the unexpected metallic sound.

'How gratifying to have gained your attention so quickly,' said Richter, pleasantly, pointing the pistol at them with his right hand and shining his torch into their shocked faces with his left. 'Now, don't move unexpectedly, or this weapon might go off - even if I miss, a ricochet is bound to cause injury. But trust me when I tell you this: I never miss.'

'What do you want?' rasped Kaye, staring bleakly at the man he had never really trusted. All at once it was horribly clear that Richter's 'charming and helpful' act had been a consummate deception and Kaye belatedly realised that his own unvoiced suspicions had been all too accurate. At what cost had he failed to tell Sam his fears? He slated himself bitterly.

'I want to help you, actually,' Richter answered in a matter-of-fact tone. 'I happen to have in my possession a map of this maze and I believe it could prove quite useful at this juncture - if you want to be sure of selecting the right route.'

Sam blinked. 'You've got my grandfather's authentic map - how *could* you have?'

'Never mind how. But I assure you I'm telling the truth. Kai's annotation concerning this junction says, "*Without arms, what would be left of Old Glory?*" Richter wagged the pistol at them. 'There. I've done my bit. Now it's up to you to work out what dear grandpapa meant by it.'

Richter's hostages looked at one another blankly.

'No-one wants to be stuck down here any longer than necessary, so I suggest you get on with it,' prompted Richter, his tone terse. 'Remember; I don't actually need all three of you to help me complete this journey - and the clock is ticking.'

Incensed at the perfidy of the man to whom she had accorded utter trust, Sam blamed herself for the predicament into which she had put her companions. Funny how the possible imminence of death crystallised one's mind about what was truly important. The casket was irrelevant, now, she thought. All that mattered were the two people she cared about. Ghulam wasn't just a family retainer; he was a faithful friend who had always had her best interests at heart and Oliver... Oliver was so many things, but most of all - and she could no longer avoid acknowledging it - he was the man with whom she was falling in love. There; it was out in the open at last - well, mentally speaking.

She couldn't bear to lose either of them, which meant she needed to think fast.

Kaye watched as a plethora of wrenching emotions chased one another across Sam's face and his heart went out to her. 'We'll work it out; don't worry. Let's start with Old Glory,' he said gently. 'He must mean the American flag; agreed?'

Sam nodded tensely, biting her lip.

'Also known as the Stars and Stripes...' Kaye mused, his throw-away comment beginning a convoluted train of lateral thought in Sam's mind.

Kaye continued. 'The word 'arms' has several connotations. Arms as in weapons...' He glared at Richter's Beretta at this point. 'Arms as in human limbs...'

'...And arms as in heraldic crests,' blurted out Sam. 'Like a flag represents a nation, a coat of arms represents a family. And it's not only Old Glory that has stars and stripes - the Dexter Coat of Arms has them too. Look!' She stabbed a finger at the fine example displayed on Ghulam's tie.

Kaye made the tie an object of close scrutiny.

Upholding the arms were the boar and unicorn Sam had mentioned earlier. Over the escutcheon, a crowned helmet was embellished with sprigs of broom. The escutcheon itself was quartered, with the upper left quadrant bearing white stars on a sable field; the upper right - a sable scimitar on white; the lower left - a sable keep on white and the lower right - white, wavy lines on sable.

'That has to be significant,' he concurred, looking up again. 'But what can we extrapolate from it?'

Ghulam straightened his tie self-consciously. 'If the right answer to the riddle is one of the two mathematical sums,' he speculated, 'Do you think we might need to count something?'

'Like what?' Sam felt as if her brain had atrophied.

'Like the numbers of stars and stripes, perhaps. There are twelve stars and ten stripes on the Dexter crest. What about Old Glory?'

'Fifty stars for the fifty States,' said Kaye, perking up. 'I don't know how many stripes, though.'

'I do. I had to memorise all that stuff for a school project on the US, once.' The words tumbled out of Sam's mouth. 'It's thirteen - and now I know the answer to the riddle! *Without arms, what would be left of Old Glory'...* What do you get if you subtract the Dexter stars and stripes from the ones on the US flag?'

'Thirty eight stars and three stripes,' replied Kaye almost instantly.

'So it's the right hand tunnel!'

Richter gave them no time to celebrate. 'Let's move,' he ordered. 'Single file - the lackey first; then you, professor: Samantha will accompany me at the rear.'

Ghulam shot him a look of pure hatred but obediently turned to enter the tunnel. Kaye hung back for a moment, facing the shadowed silhouette behind the glaring torch beam. 'Don't hurt her,' he said. 'Or I'll kill you. Understand?' He entered the tunnel without waiting for a reply.

Richter closed on Sam. 'You can ignore the hired help's charming display of empty valour - because he doesn't have one of these,' he said and prodded her spine brutally with the muzzle of his pistol to push her forwards.

'Rot in hell,' spat Sam between clenched teeth as she stumbled ahead of him through the tunnel archway.

With two of their group horrifically dead, the unspoken fears of the survivors were reaching a new peak.

Bowed by the guilt of having failed his Brethren and fearful of what might await them ahead, their latest loss prompted the *Dhu*

Samawi to form a new resolve. In all conscience, how could he drag the youthful Bashir into further life-threatening danger? The destiny of destinies was his alone and he must rise above his fear and shoulder the burden. These thoughts occupied his mind as the two men picked their way across the cavern to its far reaches, seeking the exit.

Conversely, rising fear served only to fan to incandescence the rage that constantly smouldered behind Bashir's dark, desiring eyes. His pent up fantasy of bloody revenge on the infidel who had conceived the diabolic deaths of his comrades had no outlet, since the fiend responsible was almost certainly long dead and beyond his reach. Right from the start, everything had gone wrong; every possible obstacle had been placed in his way; every evil had beset him and everyone had worked against him. It added up to nothing less than a conspiracy to keep him from his goal! Feeling for the crucifixion nail he still carried in his pocket, he ground his thumb hard against its pitted tip, the pain re-purifying his mind to its single purpose.

Another cleft gave rise to a tall but narrow passage beyond the cavern. Here the *Dhu Samawi* stopped and turned to face his young companion, his features echoing his emotional struggle. 'From this point, the map shows only this passage, bending to lead to one final room,' he told Bashir. 'We know what must lie in that room - but our journey has already exacted so terrible a price that it gives me good cause to fear further mortal risks for any seeking to claim the casket. I cannot let you share those risks. I am *The One*. It is *my* fate; *my* destiny... and I must face it alone.'

'You expect me to stay here?' growled Bashir, his face darkening to thunder, 'And let you simply stroll up and pocket what so many have died for? Now I see the truth! Leaving Alim and Umarah behind was deliberate, wasn't it? And the displays of grief you've shown for Hafiz and Zikar - all a sham!'

The *Dhu Samawi* blanched and extended a shaking hand towards Bashir. 'No!' he exclaimed, mortified. 'You're wrong, Bashir; completely wrong. My motives are pure and my intent honourable. Can you not see? I'm simply trying to protect you!'

'I don't need protecting!' yelled Bashir. 'And what makes you so sure *you're The One*? A few disintegrating scraps of parchment in the cupboard under the candle of Ma'na? We're all supposed to believe those blessèd scrolls, but they're nothing more than myths and legends that are slowly crumbling to dust - you don't *know* what the truth is!'

'*On behalf of all the Brothers of the past, the present and the future, whomever shall hold the venerated position of Dhu Samawi when he receives the casket into his hands shall not be found wanting, for he shall prove to be the true redeemer. He shall be The One...*' In a shocked whisper, the Lord of Heaven recited the passage from the ancient scrolls on which the Brotherhood of the Sabaeans had long relied, regarding the role which he fervently believed was destined to be his. '*And he who follows a path other than that which the blessèd scrolls teach shall be re-named for the despised Adeeb, and shall be deemed outcast from the Brotherhood, to be slain on sight, that he may arise as a lowly beast in the next reincarnation.*' The *Dhu Samawi* gazed disbelievingly at Bashir. 'To be an outcast, Bashir - is that what you want?'

A murderous glint appeared in Bashir's eyes. 'You say only the *Dhu Samawi* can be *The One* - only the oldest amongst the Brethren. If you had died at the first trap, Hafiz would have taken on your role, and after him, Zikar. But they're already dead, aren't they? So if you die now, who will become the next *Dhu Samawi*..?'

The *Dhu Samawi's* eyes widened in unbelieving dread as he saw Bashir slowly draw his Khangar dagger from its sheath.

'I will!' Bashir answered his own question, his eyes blazing intensely as he advanced on his leader with the dagger raised to strike. '*I will*...and then *your* destiny becomes *mine*!'

CHAPTER 23

LET THERE BE LIGHT

Beneath the Church of the Holy Sepulchre, Jerusalem, Israel, 22 June, 2016 AD

At the head of the strung-out group, Ghulam was making steady progress when his torch bulb began to flicker. Then it pinged and the light went out, leaving him groping in the dark. His fingertips losing contact with the wall, he stopped and shouted, 'My torch has blown!' His words echoed and re-echoed with imposing hollowness - suggesting he had just entered some kind of huge space. 'But I think I've hit a big cavern. Be careful as you reach the end of the tunnel.'

Drawing close, Kaye's torch illuminated the tunnel's exit arch. 'Let me past,' he suggested to Ghulam, practically. 'Then you can follow my beam.' Ghulam stepped aside, Kaye exited the tunnel and Sam followed, her head held defiantly high, with Richter's gun hovering close behind her. The group congregated within the overlapping cones of light produced by the three working torches. Beyond their immediate area, a limitless black void pressed in. Under their shoes, telltale chisel marks denoted that the rock had been painstakingly levelled and, immediately in front of them, the solid ground dropped away in an apparently sheer chasm of unknown depth. Ghulam's cheeks turned two shades paler. One step more and he would have fallen over the edge.

'There must be steps somewhere,' growled Richter. 'Find them, professor, before I lose patience and send sweet little Samantha down this cliff the quick way.'

Moving to the lip of the ledge, Kaye peered down, swivelling his torch to illuminate the cliff face below and to each side. Relieved to see the beginning of a narrow flight of steps descending in switchback fashion a few feet away to his right, he also noticed an additional man-made feature, the purpose of which was much less obvious. Hugging the uneven, steeply sloping walls several feet below him, on both sides of the steps, were deep gullies carved out of the craggy limestone in horizontal lines that stretched away in both directions beyond the limits of his beam. Backing away from the chasm, he turned right and began walking slowly along the ledge. Reaching the top of the steps, his arcing torch glanced off a large steel lever with a knob at the top in the shape of a boar's head, rising from an oblong hole in a steel plate set in the rock floor of the ledge, just a yard further on. It looked like some kind of ratchet mechanism. Kaye quickly examined it for instructions of the 'pull me' kind, but the steely eyes of the boar regarded him blankly, giving no clues away beyond the fact of its presence.

Richter was becoming impatient. 'What have you found? Are there steps?'

'Yes,' said Kaye. 'Here; where I'm standing. Come ahead, all of you. There's a lever here, too - I'm going to pull it but I have no idea what will happen as a result, so keep close to the wall, just in case.' Ghulam was quick to join him and stood with his back to the rock, peering curiously at the lever.

'Why pull it if you don't know what it will do?' asked Sam nervously, edging up to Ghulam. Richter was right behind her.

'Because it has a boar's head on it,' answered Kaye. 'When we last saw a boar, it meant '*this is the right path to take*', so I'm assuming this means the same.'

Without waiting for their captor to command otherwise, he grasped the knob and pulled the lever back in its oblong socket, just as Ghulam spoke up, saying, 'I believe you might have found a God machine.'

'What do you mean?' whispered Sam, close to the tears she had been promising herself she would not shed.

Ghulam spread his arms wide and spoke.

No....!'

Twisting his body away from certain death, the *Dhu Samawi* fled along the narrow tunnel, his torch flashing wildly from wall to wall. Sixty feet above his head, Christian pilgrims shuffled their feet, patiently waiting to enter the Holy Sepulchre, a more forgiving tomb than the long coffin of darkness that offered no escape route to the *Dhu Samawi's* desperate eyes. Through his panic-stricken gasps he could hear Bashir's pounding boots behind him; feel Bashir's burning eyes on his vulnerable back. He was so fraught with terror that he did not even sense the rock beneath one foot depress slightly as his racing heel hit it. The weight of that heel activated a hidden hair trigger mechanism that, in turn, caused a slim, steel blade to spring out from a horizontal niche in one wall of the tunnel, directly across his path, at neck height.

The *Dhu Samawi* ran full tilt into the finely honed edge of the blade and self-decapitated instantly, his headless body tottering gruesomely for a couple of faltering steps before collapsing to the ground, its limbs jerking aimlessly for a few moments before falling limp. His head's forward momentum carried it through the air, over his dead body, landing beyond and rolling for several yards before coming to rest. Pumping from the severed neck, blood spread in a black pool, filling the hollows in the rough limestone floor.

Skidding to a halt in momentary stupefaction, Bashir lowered his dagger and then, his blood lust transmuting into an appeased grin, he laughed in paranoid delight. After all the earlier horrors, the trap-setting fiend had finally worked his evil to a useful purpose. Sheathing his own blade, Bashir ducked carefully under the much longer blade that had caught out the *Dhu Samawi*, stepped over his erstwhile leader's mutilated corpse and continued along the tunnel, his eyes aglow with anticipation.

In expectation of a well appointed chamber ahead, filled with the mysterious effulgence of the waiting casket, he rounded the corner - in his mind, indeed, he was already lifting it from its stone pedestal, feeling its deeply graven embellishments beneath his touch; hefting the solid, immutable weight of it in his hands - only to drop his torch in shock when its beam bounced off a blank stone barrier directly in front of him. His heart missing several beats, he bent rapidly to retrieve the vital tool and then ran up to the solid face of the rock, frantically panning both the torchlight and his free hand over every square inch of its hewn surface. Eventually, emitting a low moan, he slumped to his knees in front of it, beating his fist repeatedly on its unyielding stone until his knuckles were raw and bloody. He felt as if his mind was descending into madness.

Rather than achieving his destiny, he had reached a dead end.

'Let there be light!'

Ghulam's pronouncement was so certain; so convincing.

But, of light, there came no sign. Instead, as they stood immured in a void as absent of radiance as the vacuum between galaxies, what suddenly assaulted their senses was an extended cacophony of sounds echoing from every direction, their cause inexplicable and their puzzling variety unnerving.

They could not know it, but the ledge on which they stood circuited the perimeter of a vast cavern, some thirty feet above its floor level. Evenly spaced along the ledge were large indents holding drums full of heavy fuel oil. From each drum, a sealed vent led down to a position just above a gully that also circuited the cavern. By pulling the boar's head lever, Kaye had set off a chain reaction - literally.

The motion of the lever applied power to a hidden gear system, which induced minor motion in a chain stretching between each drum and connected to each of the vent caps. The relatively small shift of the chain was sufficient to pull off the vent caps, releasing the fuel oil, which poured down into the gully below. From the perspective of the human listeners, this sequence of events translated into a series of metallic clicks, whirrs and rasping sounds; lots of simultaneous popping noises like bungs being drawn from ale casks and then a plethora of glugging sounds.

The distal end of the chain was connected to another ratchet system that, in response to the pull of the chain, caused the release of a heavy steel ball. That ball began to roll downwards, following the path of a long groove carved into the base of a small, cylindrical tunnel spiralling through the solid rock high above their heads, like the drain chute in a giant pinball machine. Even in the pitch black, the sound this made was recognisable as that of metal rolling over stone. As the glugging drew to a close, the rolling noise also ceased and there was a moment of utter silence during which everyone held their breath in fearful anticipation of what might come next.

His thoughts jumbled in crazed despair, at first Bashir thought he was hallucinating when the muffled sounds of human voices reached his ears. Yet how could he not listen? Encased, as he was, both physically and mentally, in the uttermost deeps, the sounds were a tantalising lifeline to a human world he had almost forgotten. The low murmurs grew clearer and then he distinctly heard a voice call out, 'Let there be light!'

It was not the figment of an unhinged mind - it was the English group! And close by! Could there be a route he had somehow missed? Struggling to his feet, Bashir retraced his steps, concentrating his attention - and his torchlight - on the walls he had lately ignored in his haste to reach his goal. Before he even reached the bend, he saw it: an insignificant patch of wooden boarding at ground level on the left side of the tunnel. Onto his knees he dropped, once more; this time to prise away the boards with the point of his swiftly drawn dagger and reveal the entrance to a tiny, roughly spherical crawl-space, hardly big enough for a man to enter. Yet what alternative did he have? His dagger back in its sheath, he placed the butt of his torch in his mouth, clamping his teeth down hard on it. He was going to need both hands for this.

Wriggling inside, his body stretched out at full length, he fitted the space like a worm in its hole. He could move only by pushing with his boot-tips and pulling with his fingers. Compressed between millions of tons of rock, claustrophobic fear combined with his unnatural bodily exertion to make sweat sluice down his panicked face. What if the hole got smaller and he became stuck, unable to move forwards or back? No; best not to imagine that.

To his incalculable relief, the passage did not diminish. If anything, it enlarged slightly. It also began to dip downhill, its inner surface becoming smoother at the same time. Soon, rather than pushing from the back, he had to brace at the front to save himself from sliding forwards. The incline grew ever steeper and, try as he might, he was soon in a helpless slide downwards, head first. The passage had transformed into a smooth chute and he was a human lozenge sliding down the long, stony throat of Golgotha.

Another chute-like conduit curved in from the left to join Bashir's and just as he approached the confluence, a large metallic ball catapulted out in front of him, missing his head by inches to tumble into a groove in the base of his chute and precede him as he continued downwards. Keep your eye on the ball, he thought wildly as his speeding body spun into a mad, disorientating spiral, heading only Ali knew where.

The chute ended with a slight up-curve and the metal ball launched from its lip, vanishing from sight.

The silence in the great cavern lasted only for as long as it took the steel ball, weighing several kilograms, to arc off the end of the spiral groove and impact with a broad glass tank full of water in which rested a large chunk of pure sodium, a highly flammable metal that, while immersed, as it had been for over fifty years, remained stable. Out of the dark came the crash of shattering glass.

Still, Richter and his captives had no idea what was happening.

With the tank in shards and the water spilt, the freed chunk of sodium began to fall towards the oil-filled gulley, the oxygen in the air immediately reacting with the volatile metal.

Bashir's rapidly moving body arced from the end of the chute just as the sodium spontaneously ignited in a brilliant, yellow-white flash that, happily for him, obscured the puny beam of light emanating from the battered torch he still held gripped between his teeth. Because he was heavier than the ball, his arc took him a little further and his hands, outstretched again, connected painfully with the rock lip of the oil-rich gulley, into which his body crumpled, despite the quasi-military training that had taught him how to roll on impact after a long fall.

Out of the endless darkness had burst the sodium's incendiary ball of light and, up on the ledge, all eyes were fastened on it in amazement, watching it drop like a miniature falling star.

Hearing their exclamations above him, the bruised Bashir instantly thumbed off his torch, but, in fact, no-one had seen him. The attention of the four above was directed solely at the light-extravaganza of the burning sodium. Ignoring his pain, he rolled over the outer lip of the gully to land, astonishingly, on a flat step, one of a set disappearing downwards in a zigzag. Bent double, he leapt down them and into cover at their base.

He had moved only just in time, for the incandescent sodium ball now ended its descent, hitting the gully precisely at the spot he had quit a moment earlier. It ignited the oil and, with a searing whoosh, tongues of flame flared dramatically into the air and spread rapidly in both directions. Within fifteen or twenty seconds, the entire gully system was ablaze and the uneven ring of devouring fire lining the circumference of its walls gave sufficient light to illuminate the immense cavern, highlighting its Hadean magnificence in a flickering, russet glow.

Buried deep under Golgotha, its roof at least eighty feet below the crowds who queued in line to touch the stone summit where it poked into the fabric of the Church of the Holy Sepulchre, the natural limestone cavern had been decorated far more elaborately by nature - and by former Keepers of the casket - than the church above had been adorned by Christian men of reverence. Even the soulless Richter was silent for a long moment, unable to remain unaffected by its megalithic grandeur.

The vaulting limestone roof arched thirty feet or more above their heads and at least two dozen stalactites had grown down from it, joining their cousin stalagmites rising from the floor, twenty feet below them, to form gargantuan white pillars, carved, in some past era, by the hand of man - like giant ivory tusks - to produce intricate designs of great beauty. Every pillar was a masterpiece, but the incredible labour had not stopped there. Large areas of the smooth, calcified walls had also been carved into fabulous bas-reliefs that told a progressive visual story, like a Bayeux tapestry set in stone.

But the story on these walls was not that of a single battle, but that of the casket of the Ancients; a tale spanning fifteen thousand years - the oldest story in the world.

'Oh my,' whispered Sam, 'See that?' and she pointed at a section of wall eighty feet away on the far side of the cavern, where men in beehive shaped headdresses rode in an imperious line on the backs of regally decorated mammoths towards a palace seven stories high. They were definitely mammoths - you only had to look at the length and curvature of their tusks to know that. Looking higher up the wall, she made out a fleet of strange, triangular shapes with what looked like jet trails shooting from funnels at their blunt ends. Her mouth dropping open, she pointed at them and said, in an awed voice, 'Oliver, look up there - I'd bet my last shekel on what those are meant to be!'

'The legendary vimana,' murmured Kaye, unable to take his eyes off them.

It was impossible to know whether the great frieze had been made by Keepers with too much spare time on their hands during the dark ages, when the casket lay behind bars in the kokh crypt, far above, or whether it dated from an even more ancient time. But of one thing Kaye was certain; the underground limestone cathedral they now gazed upon had been hidden from human knowledge for at least the better part of a thousand years and might never before have been seen by any man other than the chosen of the casket.

Cathedrals often had an inner sanctum somewhere, he thought. If this one did, perhaps that was where they would find the casket Sam's grandfather had hidden so well.

Pulling his eyes away from the view, Richter cast a malignant eye over the dishevelled group and, in particular, Samantha. Becoming aware of his malevolent gaze, she turned her head towards him and said, 'I know you'll want to hurry us on, but before we continue, I think we deserve some kind of explanation, don't you? I can see the hate in your eyes. Why do you hate us? What the hell is wrong with you, Raoul?'

'Your companions I merely suffer. My hatred I reserve for you,' he replied.

'What have I ever done to warrant it?'

'You'll know, before the end. Meanwhile, I will tell you one thing and you can think about that while you lead me to the casket.'

Everyone was looking at him, now.

'Your father didn't fall down those crypt steps all by himself. I gave him a bit of help.'

CHAPTER 24

THE CHAMBER OF THE CASKET

Beneath the Church of the Holy Sepulchre, Jerusalem, Israel, 22 June, 2016 AD

Kaye and Ghulam had to act fast to restrain Sam from launching herself forcibly at Richter. Struggling against their combined strength, Sam shrieked, 'Get off me, damn it! I'm going to kill the bastard! Let me go!'

'I know,' said Kaye through gritted teeth, gripping her arm as she fought to escape. 'Wouldn't mind having a go, myself - but he's got the gun. He'd shoot us dead before we could reach him. We can't have that, can we? So calm down. Take some deep breaths.' Dropping his voice to a faint whisper in her ear, he added, 'Bide your time, Sam.'

Slowly, her struggles subsided and then she turned her face into Kaye's shoulder and broke into deep, shaking sobs of grief and anger.

'Women's crocodile tears,' remarked Richter disparagingly. 'If you're finished, let's get on, shall we?'

Kaye clenched his jaw. It was clear they were in the presence of pure evil. Sam was not in a fit state to assert herself, so he said, on her behalf, 'That's enough, Richter. Just tell us what the map says next.'

'It calls this place the Hall of Flame. Apt, wouldn't you say? And the annotation - it's the last one, I might add - reads, 'Satisfy Eurystheus to reach the Atlantean treasure'. What's that all about?'

Kaye frowned. 'It's got to have something to do with one of the Greek myths. Was it one of the labours of Hercules to steal the cattle of the far west for Eurystheus? Yes, I believe it was... and to do that he had to pass through the Pillars of Hercules to reach the island of

Erythreia. Some six-limbed monster, there - can't remember its name - owned the cattle and Hercules shot him - with an arrow, I think.'

'Ah: a classics man. It never was my strong point,' spat Richter.

Pulling herself together, the red-eyed Sam looked up. Almost unconsciously, Kaye gave her a brief, supportive hug. Glancing at him gratefully, she took a deep breath and said, 'Wasn't Atlantis supposed to be beyond the Pillars of Hercules?'

'Yes,' agreed Kaye. 'Although some say it was the Greek island of Thira in the Aegean, which was virtually destroyed by a volcanic eruption three and a half thousand years ago. But regarding the reference to Atlantean treasure, I think Kai was probably just inferring that the casket comes from an ancient, lost civilisation - Atlantis being the catch-all name for that type of thing.'

Forcing herself to concentrate, Sam said, 'Okay, so to satisfy this Eurystheus we have to do what Hercules did, presumably; pass through the Pillars of Hercules... well, there are plenty of pillars around to choose from.'

'Facing due west,' broke in Kaye.

'How can we tell which way west is, down here?'

'That's easy. I can make a compass,' offered Ghulam, unexpectedly. He patted his pockets, pulled out a hotel sewing kit and extracted a small needle. Rifling another particularly heavily laden pocket, he picked through the odds and ends in his palm, plucking out a fridge magnet, which he used to magnetise the needle. Locating a saucer-sized hollow in the rock floor, he poured water into it from his water bottle. Finally he looked up and asked, 'Does anyone have a tissue?'

Wordlessly, Sam passed him one out of her own pocket.

He folded it carefully to make a tiny raft for his needle and, placing the needle on top of it, floated the raft delicately on the surface of the water. The water soaked through the tissue which, once saturated, sank away, leaving the needle floating almost magically on top of the water, borne up by surface tension. Slowly, the needle re-oriented itself to follow the line of the north-south magnetic poles. 'There we are,' he said in a matter-of-fact way, as if what he had just accomplished was an everyday event. Having calculated true north-south, he pointed across the expanse of the cavern. 'West must be that way,' he declared. 'It could possibly be east, but I think not, because, in that case, to go west would take us into the solid cliff at our backs.'

Kaye sighted along the exact direction in which Ghulam was pointing. Although carved pillars partially blocked his view, he found a good landmark in a section of the far wall frieze showing stylised figures of odd-looking creatures: multi-legged, multi-headed, winged and scaled. 'Well done, that man,' he said and then turned to their captor. 'All we can do is make our way over there and hope there are visible clues to help us onward.'

'For your sake, you'd better be right. Now, move,' ordered Richter, indicating the narrow flight of steps at their feet. No longer requiring his torch, he stashed it away, which enabled him to place a proprietorial hand on Sam's shoulder as they descended the switchback steps in single file. She shuddered at his murderer's touch, but bore it. *Oliver's right*, she thought grimly. *I'll bide my time.*

The floor of the gargantuan cavern had been chisel-worked and provided easy walking between the awe-inspiring calcified columns on which the intricately carved, writhing beasts and birds seemed almost alive in the florid, flickering glow cast by the encircling flames. Under other circumstances the walkers might have halted to appreciate the awesome splendours around them, but the gun at their backs kept them moving briskly. Behind them, a dark shape flitted silently from pillar to pillar, following closely in their wake. Bashir was also biding his time.

Approaching the far wall between two particularly stupendous pillars, Kaye looked up to check their position relative to the landmark portion of the frieze; he was sufficiently close, now, to observe that the strange figures represented on the bas-relief were all mythical creatures of some kind. The centrepiece of the panel was a six-armed, six-legged brute with three human heads, brandishing spears in all six of its meaty hands. The gaping mouth in its middle head was a round, black hole.

His worried eyes searching the base of the cavern wall in front of him for any sign of a doorway or tunnel entrance, Kaye was devastated to see nothing obvious. 'There has to be something we've missed,' he muttered aloud, thinking furiously. Mythical beasts... what was the connection there? Then it came to him. He had already given the answer in his earlier verbal description of the relevant labour of Hercules. The owner of the Erythreian cattle was a six-limbed monster - a giant fused triplet, just like the one on the frieze above their heads. And Hercules had killed him with...with...

'What's that?' asked Ghulam, diverting his steps curiously towards the gigantic pillar to their left.

'What's what?' queried Kaye, distractedly.

'Stop right there,' commanded Richter. 'What do you think you're up to?'

Ghulam halted and glanced round. 'I'm not trying to escape,' he said mildly. 'I just noticed something resting against the side of this pillar, over here - I thought it might be important.'

'Richter waved his pistol at the pillar in question. 'Fetch it, then, whatever it is: but be quick.'

Ghulam continued to the pillar, leaning round its bulk to reach whatever it was he had noticed. As he turned back, everyone saw what was grasped in his hand: an ash wood longbow, with two fletched arrows.

Everything suddenly made sense to Kaye. 'I know what has to be done!' he exclaimed. 'Hercules killed the six-legged giant with an arrow. We've got to do the same - metaphorically speaking. See that creature up there?' and he pointed at the bas-relief monster. 'I think we need to shoot an arrow into its open mouth.' He paused. 'Don't ask me to do it, though - I've never used a bow.'

'I have,' Sam said quietly. 'I took archery lessons for a while at school. It was that kind of school.' She shrugged. 'But I'm no expert.'

'You've got two tries,' pointed out Richter, acerbically. 'There are only two arrows.'

Sam sighed and took the proffered bow, along with one arrow, from Ghulam's outstretched hands. 'You can do it, Miss'm,' he

The Chamber of the Casket

encouraged her. 'You've always had good aim.' She might as well get on with it, she thought. The longer she deliberated, the more nervous she was going to become.

Nocking the arrow, she took up an archer's stance and drew the bowstring back, aiming at the monster's mouth and, in Kaye's eyes, looking rather more like Artemis the Huntress than Hercules.

Artemis let fly the arrow.

It did not have too far to travel and was very nearly on target, hitting the stone monster's broad lower lip. Unfortunately, the impact splintered the arrow point and the now useless shaft fell to the ground. Kaye groaned.

'Last chance,' warned Richter, his unnaturally pale, smoky eyes boring into Sam. She turned away from that compassionless stare, sure that if she missed, the next thing she would feel would be a bullet cleaving her spine. Ghulam passed her the second arrow and, again, she nocked it and drew the bow, swallowing her trepidation. Concentrating, she aimed infinitesimally higher and loosed the arrow, closing her eyes tight as soon as it had left the bow. Mindful of the price of failure, she could not bear to watch the arrow's flight.

This time, though, her aim proved true and the missile sped straight to its target, vanishing directly into the black hole of the monster's gaping mouth.

'Bullseye!' cried Kaye.

Sam's eyes blinked open and she threw the bow down. 'Good enough for you?' she enquired of Richter.

'We'll soon know,' he answered, summarily beckoning her to resume her position only inches from the muzzle of his gun.

What mechanism the arrow triggered they had no idea, but the result it delivered surpassed all expectations. With a low, gritty rumble, a small section of the cavern wall moved ponderously aside right in front of them, the Hall of Flame's dappled firelight reflecting off the walls of the narrow, straight passage beyond sufficiently well to show that it was little more than ten yards long. Gazing to its far end, they could just make out what looked like a doorway opening onto some kind of chamber.

Looking questioningly at Richter, who nodded, Kaye set off first, walking forwards into the ruddy, semi-dark.

Ghulam, Sam and, finally, Richter, followed.

Having observed the recent proceedings from behind an adjacent pillar, Bashir was convinced that his goal lay at the end of the tunnel his enemies had just managed to reveal. He could not afford to hesitate any longer. Drawing his Khangar dagger, he sprinted forwards, but the sound of his boots on the rock floor caught Richter's ears just as he was entering the tunnel. Reacting fast, Richter roughly pushed Sam forwards out of his way and spun round in the confined space, but had no time to shoot before the black-clad Syrian was upon him.

Automatically he parried the descent of Bashir's curved dagger by throwing up an arm to grab his attacker's knife wrist, only for Bashir to counter by gripping Richter's gun wrist in turn. Locked together chest to chest, they strained, testing each other's arm strength. Richter grimaced as Bashir viciously twisted his gun wrist, the pistol dropping from his suddenly nerveless fingers. Barrelling the Syrian against the tunnel wall, Richer pinned him there and repeatedly banged his knife hand against the rock until it, too, dropped to the ground. Well-trained in unarmed combat, Richter pressed home his advantage, brutally kneeing the other man in the gut. Bashir groaned in pain. 'I recognise you, you bastard,' snarled Richter. 'No windows to jump out of here, though, are there?'

Richter's push had made Sam stumble forwards. Recovering her balance, she distanced herself from the brawling antagonists, encouraged by Ghulam, who made way for her to pass him and run on into Kaye's waiting arms. 'Get behind me,' Kaye said. There was nowhere else to run to and the knife and pistol were well out of reach, so Kaye, Sam and Ghulam remained as unwilling voyeurs of the desperate battle going on a few yards away.

The veins standing out in his neck, Bashir forced back Richter's constraining arms and freed his own, making a grab for Richter's neck in an attempt to strangle him. Richter's eyes bulged under the choking pressure of Bashir's thumbs but he got in a couple of heavy gut punches, winding his attacker and making him loosen his grip and stagger backwards. Desperate now, Bashir suddenly thought of his crucifixion nail and grabbed it out of his pocket, raising it and dashing at Richter with a high-pitched scream. Again Richter grabbed his wrist, but, at the same time, twisted the Syrian's arm sharply back on itself and, turning with the man's momentum, dashed him against the tunnel wall, using Bashir's own pinioned arm and hand to ram the long, rusty nail deep into its owner's chest.

Bashir's dark, long-lashed eyes grew large as the nail thrust home, then a gasping sigh escaped his lips and he sagged, his back slowly sliding down the tunnel wall until he slumped at its base, his chin falling forwards onto his pierced chest.

'Should any man disturb your peace, let him be pierced with this nail, as you once were,' had been Balthazar's curse as he laid the Messiah to rest in the rock sepulchre high above Damascus. And so it had come to pass.

Having regained his breath and wiped his blood-spattered hands on Bashir's baggy black trousers, Richter moved and stooped again to retrieve his pistol, which had skittered to a spot just outside the tunnel entrance. As he was busy re-arming himself, Ghulam edged along the tunnel to the slumped form that was Bashir, his kindly nature intent on delivering a prayer.

Why did there have to be violence and killing? No-one should have to die for the sake of the casket, he thought - not for the sake of a power that is all about life-giving, not death-dealing. Kneeling to lay a hand gently on Bashir's still chest, he wondered why some men found it so much easier to break things than create them. If only he could mend what had been broken. He closed his eyes and began to pray, repeating soothing mantras that generated a sense of wellbeing and peace.

Incensed at having been surprised so easily and at having to fight so strenuously, Richter's mood was darkly psychotic as he re-entered the tunnel, clutching his gun. Finding Ghulam kneeling next to the man who had twice tried to kill him, his mercurial temper shot off the scale. 'How dare you pray for that murdering rag head? He tried to kill me!' he yelled. 'Let Allah take care of his own scum!' As Ghulam looked up, appalled, Richter lashed out in uncontrolled rage, pistol-whipping the side of the kneeling man's head with considerable force. Ghulam toppled sideways like a reed in the wind and lay unmoving.

Richter's act of violence was so sudden that neither Sam nor Kaye had time to cry out, much less intervene. Striding past Ghulam's sprawled form, Richter advanced on them, pointing his Beretta threateningly. 'And you can keep your mouths shut. There could be more of those swine about and I'm not your saviour. Get moving.'

Sam's face had changed to match the tunnel walls enclosing them - hard and sickly-white, with a fiery flush. Not knowing whether Ghulam was dead or alive, she and Kaye were forcibly herded to the end of the passage at the point of Richter's pistol.

Little light from the fires in the Hall of Flame penetrated this far. Ducking her head to pass under the thick, double lintel of the slender, smoothly finished, stone portal, Sam had time only for a scant glance around the chamber's dusky interior before Kaye ducked in behind her with the hateful gun jabbing his kidneys.

An oblong space, its only access route was the one by which they had just entered. The portal was positioned almost at the far left end of the long side of the chamber, the greatest part of which, consequently, lay to the right of the doorway. So it was that each of them, on entering, had to turn in order to look down its shadowed length, where each, in turn, saw, deep in the gloom, a centrally placed stone altar with torch-braziers of wrought iron at either side of it, bearing heavy wooden torches wound with pitch-soaked cloth, ready to be set alight.

The front of the altar was carved in a pattern of raised squares, each one decorated with a different letter of the Latin alphabet...and on top of it, a dim, indistinct object; box shaped, with cylindrical columns supporting its four corners and a lid that rose in bulbous, many layered, pyramidal tiers to a high, smoothly curved dome at its summit.

There it waited in the near-dark, timelessly patient, giving off a slight, soft glimmer that bewitched the eyes and mirrored its incalculable age - Balthazar's casket.

For perhaps a full minute, no-one spoke.

'Light the torches,' voiced Richter hoarsely, at last.

His eyes still on the casket, Kaye searched his pockets. He knew he had a card of matches somewhere, picked up in passing from a hotel lobby ashtray. Locating it, he pressed the card into Sam's palm, it seeming only fair to him that she should be the first to approach the altar. The casket was in her family's stewardship, after all - and was it too outlandish to hope that, as its designated Keeper, she might find in herself some key to its fabled magic that would counter Richter's malice?

Walking up to the braziers, Sam detached a match and struck it, holding the tiny flame to each of the pitch-impregnated torches in turn. They flared strongly, scenting the air with the redolence of exotic spices and revealing the casket, at last, in its full, golden glory. An object of more intricate complexity than she could possibly have imagined, every square inch was decorated with minute, perfectly executed, raised designs: tiny beehive temples; dancers with snake-entwined bodies; fabulous beasts; wheels within wheels... the variety was endless; but all fashioned with one end in mind - to draw the eye inescapably to the centre front, where the Mark of *The Power* stood proud of all other embellishments.

Richter stood transfixed by the glamour of the casket.

'*Fulfil your holy destiny,*' commanded the voice of the Lord God in the deeps of his mind. '*The time is nigh. Take up the mantle of your righteous supremacy over Earth and Heaven. Cast off your mortal coils - come, stand at the right hand of your Father!*'

'Bring it to me,' he commanded Sam harshly.

She had no choice, did she?

The moment she placed her hands on the golden treasure, Sam's *naevus* began to throb insistently, spreading a pool of pain across her chest and consuming every cell of her body in a sudden, fiery heat. She had always believed the casket still existed to be found and had, in the last few hours, achieved an uneasy peace with herself on the matter of her belief in *The Power*, but the revelation that her own body was responding directly to its physical connection with the casket still shocked her to the core.

It also bolstered her resolve.

Instead of lifting the golden treasure from the altar, she removed her hands again and said, quietly, 'It doesn't belong to you, Raoul. Why couldn't you just accept a finder's share like any decent man? There has to be some reason for all this anger; this hate. What is it? I'll bring you the casket, but first, I have to know.'

Her captor laughed. 'Then know that my real name isn't Raoul or Richter. It's Eloi Dexter, son of Seth, son of Cyrus, descendant of Grimbald, son of Simon, First Earl of Chaumont! Does *that* help you?'

It did. All at once, so many pieces of the puzzle fell into place for Sam.

'I'm your long lost distant cousin, Samantha. But we're not playing happy families, are we?' Eloi smirked.

'Obviously not,' answered Sam. 'Look, after Grimbald left Chaumont, your side of the family was unknown to us until the troubles between your grandfather and mine, so I still have no idea why the two halves of our line ever separated. Is the answer to that question the source of your hatred?'

Eloi's reply was richly laced with five hundred years of perceived familial injustice as he related the story of Simon Dexter's disinheritance of Grimbald, his true firstborn son.

'But Grimbald didn't bear the Mark, did he? Godwin did. I acknowledge the injustice, Eloi, truly I do - but I can also understand why Simon would feel an imperative to protect the casket - and he must have thought that the best way to do that was to keep it safely at Chaumont in the hands of its chosen Keeper.'

'No!' shouted Eloi. 'The inheritance was rightfully Grimbald's - it should be mine! I am the true Earl of Chaumont!'

'Then *be* the Earl,' cried Sam, emphatically. 'I'm barred from the title by my sex, anyway. We can share Chaumont - and you can have the damn title if it means that much to you! But you can't have the casket, because I'm the chosen Keeper, not you. It's that simple.'

'I *will* have the title - and Chaumont,' spat Eloi with venom in his tone, 'And I'll have the casket, too. You might bear the Mark, but that's irrelevant now.'

The Chamber of the Casket

'What do you mean?'

Eloi drew himself up, adopting an expression to suit the grandeur of the revelation he was about to impart. That look of haughty distain, Sam could not help noticing, was identical to the one on their joint ancestor's portrait - sneering Simon had come back to haunt her.

'You're not the only Keeper,' he informed her, to her astonishment and confusion. He wrenched his shirt up with his left hand to prove his claim. 'See! I bear the Mark too!'

Both Sam and Kaye stared in pity and horror at the inflamed wounds on Eloi's chest. It was quite obvious that the weals were self-inflicted - and that the mutilations had been repeated over and over to produce the raised, star-shaped scar. These were nasty discoveries in their own right, but far worse was the sudden, appalling realisation that the armed man facing them was utterly insane - and in the most dangerous way. They exchanged brief, grim glances, confirming their joint understanding of the situation.

Trembling in holy passion, Eloi continued, his voice rising to a crescendo; 'But my right to *The Power* goes far beyond that, for I am not only the chosen of the casket, I am the chosen of the Lord God Almighty, who has created, in me, the second Messiah - the *true* Messiah! Of the blood of the Ancients, I am he for whom the world has waited for so many eons - I am *The One!*'

At the far end of the tunnel leading to the chamber of the casket, Ghulam's eyelids fluttered as he roused, groggily, to consciousness. Wincing as he rubbed the tender lump where the pistol had connected with the side of his head, he sat up and blinked at the crumpled form of the young Syrian next to him. Everything began to come back to him. First priorities first, he thought, and, replacing his hand on the man's chest, he quickly finished the mantras that he had been murmuring. Then, avoiding the blunt head of the rusty nail, he put one ear over the man's heart to listen for any sign of a heartbeat.

As he did so, Bashir's lips parted and his chest rose in the slightest of breaths. The faint flutter that Ghulam's waiting ear heard grew steadier, moment by moment.

How could you reason with a madman? It was impossible, decided Sam. Not only was Eloi schizophrenic, but delusional enough to self-harm and without a vestige of conscience concerning others. Cross him and he would shoot without thinking twice. She wondered, in fact, why both she and Oliver were not already dead. Then she remembered that during the eighteenth century, George, the ninth Earl, in his extremis, had had no idea how to open the casket and access *The Power*, cursing his distant forebears for the fact. That knowledge must have been lost or forgotten at some point, perhaps even before the casket arrived in England. Sam didn't know the key and none of the diverse material she had read had hinted at it. Doubtless, Eloi also lacked the vital knowledge - but he might think *she* knew the all-important secret. Could that be why she was still alive?

Eloi had thrown his arms high at the climax of his revelation. Lowering them before Kaye could think of tackling him, he said, 'So you will obey me, just as, very soon, the whole world will obey me, for I shall have dominion over all! Now, bring me the casket!'

Sam acquiesced, slowly lifting the heavy golden object from its resting place.

A small stone plate that the casket's weight had held depressed was now free to rise and did so. Before Sam had taken a step, the two end walls of the chamber began to move, beginning to grind inwards with a menacing rumble. The wall nearest the portal had already advanced almost wholly across it before the three stunned occupants of the chamber realised the true extent of their danger. Now they were trapped, with no escape.

'Oh my God! We're going to be squashed!' Panicking, Sam couldn't help pointing out the obvious. 'There's got to be a way to stop this!' As if it had suddenly grown red hot and scalded her fingers, she dumped the casket back on the altar, but to no effect. The walls continued their ponderous ingress towards the centre of the chamber. Hurriedly, Sam fished the page of clue notes out of her zip pocket. She was sure she had jotted down something about walls closing in. Yes! - there it was - and it did seem pertinent. Speedily, she read it out aloud:

The Chamber of the Casket

'At the end, this letter alone will offer you one small element of hope when the walls close in around you, and all seems lost. To reverse the situation, you must know, to the very letter, the potent meaning of the spiral inscription that is written in the tongue of the Ancients on the Mark of The Power. Pray upon that element of hope and your prayers shall be answered.

'Well, we *do* know the meaning of the inscription. So, do I just say it out loud? Is that it?' Without waiting for a reply, she shouted out, '...The potency of the supreme cosmic force!'

The walls did not falter in their implacable progress. The remaining space was narrowing down fast.

'Say it in Sanskrit,' urged Kaye, wondering whether the stone altar would defeat the walls or be ground to powder between them. The latter, he decided.

'*Prakr Isvar!*' screamed Sam. '*Prakr Isvar!*' Her terrified eyes locked with Kaye's. 'It's not working. Did I say it wrong?'

'I don't think so...'

'Then we've missed something. Every word granddad wrote was important. What about the last sentence? What did he mean by telling us to 'pray on that element of hope'?'

Kaye racked his numb brain, trying to shut out the monstrous rumble of the approaching walls. All kinds of possible connections flashed across his beleaguered thoughts. *Pray* - church - altar! There was the altar in front of him. Casket - star - sun - potent cosmic force - *element* - hang on... what gave the sun its potent force? Where did its supreme energy derive from? And with that thought, he had the answer.

'Hydrogen!' he yelled. 'That's the potency of the supreme cosmic force - the element that gives the sun its energy; its life force, if you like.'

'How the hell does that help?' snarled Eloi, staring wildly around. The walls were almost upon them; only a yard away from each side of the altar, now.

Kaye winked reassuringly at Sam and said, 'This is how.' Dropping to his knees, he began to bring his hands together as if about to pray but, instead, placed their outer sides into the grooves making up the arms of the capital H carved on one of the alphabet squares in front of him. Then he pushed and the square obligingly gave to his pressure.

The wall behind him stopped an inch from his upturned heels and slowly went into reverse, as did its partner on the other side of the altar.

'Hydrogen,' repeated Kaye, momentarily closing his eyes in relief: 'It's the powerhouse that builds the universe, it's the first element of the periodic table - the smallest atom - and its symbol, of course, is the letter H.' He looked up and blinked. 'You could say the sun is God's version of a nuclear power plant - or a continuous, ten billion year long, hydrogen bomb explosion.'

'You're extraordinary,' breathed Sam, her heartbeat slowing as she adjusted to the idea of survival. 'But, I don't think this is the right moment for a lecture, if you take my point.'

The walls had almost completed their traverse back to their original positions, the portal was about to come into view and Eloi had recovered his composure. Turning his icily cold eyes - and his gun - on Kaye, he said, 'She's absolutely right. We owe you a debt of thanks for saving our lives. Unfortunately, you won't be around very long to enjoy our gratitude. You see, I only need Samantha's help to open the casket - and you're sure to attempt something stupidly heroic if I have to play rough to elicit that help, which, all in all, means you've outlived your usefulness, professor.'

'However much you hurt me,' interrupted Sam quickly, her heart speeding up again until it felt as though it was about to explode, 'I'll die before I utter a word if you don't let Oliver go - right now. Let him walk out of here and I'll explain all you need to know. He won't do anything silly - will you, Oliver?' She glared pleadingly at Kaye.

Kaye rose to his feet and put his hands up as if disowning his part in the proceedings. 'That's right,' he said. 'It's not my party. I only came along hoping to get a peer-reviewed paper out of it. Why should I care what you two get up to? The way I see it, it's a family matter, now.'

'Good try,' said Eloi, aiming at Kaye's heart. 'But I don't believe a word of it. Goodbye, professor.'

Out of alternatives, the despairing Sam swung her arm and hurled her torch, hard, at the pistol. The unexpected missile jolted Eloi's hand just as he pressed the trigger, deflecting his aim. The bullet spent itself harmlessly in the far wall of the chamber and at the same instant Kaye bravely launched himself at Eloi with the sole aim of disarming him before he could fire again. The two men struggled violently for a few seconds, eye to eye, the Beretta hidden between their bodies - and then came the muffled sound of a second shot.

At the far end of the tunnel, Ghulam heard the successive gun blasts. He scrambled to his feet at the first and had started towards the chamber when the second one sounded.

The brief battle had rotated its adversaries so that, as Sam heard the pistol fire, Kaye was directly facing her. She knew she would never forget the combination of yearning, sorrow and apology in the extraordinary blue eyes that locked unwaveringly with hers until the moment they slipped down, out of view, below Eloi's shoulders. Kaye's fingers grasped ineffectually at Eloi's jacket as his knees gave way beneath him and he slithered slowly to the ground.

Sam screamed in an agony of grief and lunged at Eloi, but, fast as a striking snake, he rounded on her and struck her on the jaw with enough force to send her flying backwards. She landed hard and, immediately, he was on top of her, pinning her splayed arms to the ground through the simple expedient of kneeling on them. Sam cried out again, this time in physical pain and desperately tried to knee him in the back. Eloi responded by using his body weight to squash her ribcage, leaving her barely able to breathe. Her heels drummed uselessly on the hard rock floor.

Placing the muzzle of his pistol to her gasping lips, he said, slowly and deliberately, savouring the moment, 'How I've waited for this! Death will be final - for both you and your lover-boy - unless you tell me what I want to know. If you tell me quickly enough, I might feel inclined to use *The Power* to bring him back to life. I can see from your eyes that you like that idea. So, talk. How do I open the casket?

And don't lie to me, because your precious Oliver is lying dead with a bullet through the heart and every second you waste reduces the chance that I will choose to revive him. Now, I'm going to relieve you of just enough weight that you can spill the beans, but please don't struggle or I'll really hurt you. Got that?'

Sam nodded helplessly, black spots beginning to dance across her vision.

Slipping off his polished, black leather shoes, Ghulam tiptoed silently through the chamber portal and took in the situation at a glance. Straddling Sam, Eloi presented his back to the new arrival, who knew that luck - and the stealth of a tiger - was all that was going to keep him from being shot. Creeping forward, he disengaged his torch from its belt loop. The bulb might be dead but the tool would make a perfectly serviceable blunt instrument for what he had in mind. Gripping it firmly, he crossed the last few feet and, with all his strength - while silently praying for forgiveness - brought the heavy rubber torch down onto the crown of Eloi's head. Sam's torturer gave a low grunt and fell forwards across his victim's windpipe.

'Technology is a marvellous thing,' muttered Ghulam softly, '... But sometimes the old-fashioned approach is the best.'

He heaved Eloi's inert form off Sam, who, by this time, was only semi-conscious. Relieved of the suffocating compression, she gasped and coughed; then coughed again, finally settling into regular, deep breaths.

'Ghulam! - thank God you're alright,' she croaked, struggling to a sitting position. She prodded the motionless form sprawled beside her. 'Did you kill him?'

'No, Miss'm - he's just out for the count. I was very careful.'

'Don't feel guilty, Ghulam. He deserves far worse,' whispered Sam, her desolate eyes turning to Kaye's body. She got to her feet, crossed the chamber and knelt to cradle his head in her hands. His beautiful blue eyes had dulled in the opacity of death and his tousled fair hair spread over her fingers to mingle with her tears.

She looked up at Ghulam, her eyes clouded with inconsolable longing. 'If *only* I knew how to open the casket... if *only* I could access

The Chamber of the Casket

The Power...' She returned her gaze to Kaye and smoothed his hair with one tender, trembling hand. 'But I don't know how. Nobody knows any more. So it's just a piece of golden junk, isn't it? No use at all.'

The slender Pakistani put a fist to his brow as a sudden thought struck him. 'Miss'm, do you remember my saying that I'd memorised something at Jesus' tomb - and you and the professor both thought I meant the tomb inscription?'

'I vaguely recollect,' said Sam, dully.

'You were mistaken, but I didn't want to explain in front of him,' continued Ghulam, indicating the unconscious Eloi. I'd noticed an inscription in Sanskrit, scratched on the roof of the sepulchre - and that was what I memorised. Now that I see the casket in front of me, I think it might be useful to you.'

'But I don't understand Sanskrit, Ghulam.'

'No, but - begging your pardon, Miss'm - I do. And here's the English translation:

'By the dip in the dome and the thumb of The One
May the blood of the Ancients bring life to those gone.'

Sam's chin rose sharply. 'The casket does have a domed lid,' she said, wonderingly. 'And I am of the blood of the Ancients - or so my father claimed. It's got to be worth a try!' Stripping off her jacket with a fresh sense of urgency, she cushioned Kaye's head with it and opened his shirt buttons to leave his chest - and the fatal bullet's entry point - exposed. Then she approached the casket, her heart in her mouth. There *was* an indent at the apex of its dome. Glancing at Ghulam, who nodded encouragement, she quickly pressed her thumb into the small hollow.

Although she never even felt it, the finest of needle points, sited at the centre of the hollow, pricked the base of her thumb upon contact. The necessary miniscule quotient of blood was extracted and drawn inside the lid of the casket. There, it was processed, in less than two seconds, by a lost technology from before recorded time, to determine whether its DNA was that of a Keeper. The result, being positive, was compared against its archive of known Keepers. There was no match, which meant that *this* Keeper was entitled to access *The Power* - this once only.

Consequently, the indent pushed itself upwards against Sam's thumb and, mistaking this for rejection, she removed the offending digit in despair, her heart once more shrinking into a hard pebble of grief.

Only then did the magic begin.

The lid of the casket sprang open and the conical tops of its cylindrical corner pillars began to fold away in segments. From the open pillars, beams of intensely bright light shot out, angled towards one another such that they converged in mid-air above the casket. As Sam and Ghulam watched, aghast, a globe of the brightest light imaginable formed at the point of their convergence, nourished by the beams. Terrifyingly beautiful, the incandescent, coruscating ball hung, spinning before their eyes like a mini-sun and bathing the chamber in a glorious, whiter-than-white radiance. Aside from its size, it differed from the sun in only one respect - it gave off not one calorie of heat.

Calm; unafraid - and never more certain that her impulse was right - Sam reached out her hand to the globe, which proved to be as insubstantial as sunlight. Her hand glided straight to its core, meeting no resistance and, immediately, she experienced a singular sensation flowing through her hand, up her arm and throughout her body, like an extended flash of painless lightning, transfiguring her into a creature brimming with sublime resplendence and suffused with a caressing glow of internal well-being. Although she did not know it, to Ghulam's eyes, at that instant she became a being of pure light, one with the sphere.

As *The Power* merged with Sam, a short-lived but blinding supernova overwhelmed the chamber, scoured the tunnel and enveloped the great cavern beyond in the perfect antithesis of the pitch black it had known for fifty million years. So intense was the surge that, finding a fissure in the ceiling of the chamber, it shot skywards through that gap, lancing up through a hundred and thirty feet of fissured rock, all the way to the stone paving inside the Holy Sepulchre, which, by chance or design, stood precisely overhead. Beaming through the cracks between the flags, it splintered and reflected off every surface, briefly anointing in a heavenly crown of light rays the small chapel housing the tomb where Christ was believed to have lain for three days after his crucifixion. The crowds filling the Rotunda gaped at the sudden phenomenon, shading their eyes against its impossible brightness and crying out in awe; some falling spontaneously to their knees in holy rapture. Never before had the Lord chosen to prove - and by such an unequivocal miracle - that the Holy Sepulchre truly was the site of resurrection of the King of kings.

Far below the clamour in the Church, Sam serenely withdrew her hand and, haloed like an angel, stepped over to Kaye, bending and placing her hand on his naked chest. Light flowed from her fingertips into his body, imbuing it with a shimmering aura identical to hers. But the brighter his aura waxed, the dimmer waned Sam's, until it winked out, leaving her human again, a wan creature, drooping with weariness. And, at the instant her aura vanished, so did the four converging beams and the brilliant sphere, the conical turret segments fanning out again to cover the summits of the four corner pillars and the lid of the casket dropping down with a deep, metallic clunk that lent an air of indisputable finality to the miracle that was *The Power*.

Kaye stirred, taking a shuddering gasp of air into his empty lungs. The light hovering in and around him faded, but not before both Sam and Ghulam witnessed the bullet hole in his chest close and heal over, leaving no scar. His bright blue eyes fluttered open and stared up, puzzled, at Sam, hovering over him like a guardian angel.

'What happened?' he asked weakly. He could not remember anything beyond charging at Eloi.

Sam cautioned Ghulam with a look that said *please collude in the little white lie I'm about to perpetrate* and then, burying her grief and exhaustion, she smiled down at Kaye. 'You did something stupidly heroic and got knocked unconscious, but Ghulam managed to knock out Eloi, so that's fine - and you're fine, too, aren't you, Oliver?'

Reaching up, Kaye put a hand behind Sam's stately neck and drew her gently but inexorably down, until their lips met. He kissed her - and it was anything but a peck this time - then looked into her searching emerald eyes and said, 'If I wasn't before, I am, now.'

Along the tunnel, Bashir blinked, invigorated by the brilliance of the light that had briefly flooded his world. His sole driving force was the imperative to act instantly - or lose the casket forever. Despite the excruciating pain in his chest, he forced himself to move. His Khangar dagger lay within arm's reach and, stretching painfully, he grasped its hilt and temporarily clamped the weapon between his teeth before placing his palms against the rock wall behind him and levering himself to his feet. Returning the dagger to his right hand, he blanked out his agony and staggered down the passage. The incredible light had vanished, but he could hear soft voices echoing from the chamber ahead. Breaking into a halting run, his eyes fixed on the portal, he prepared to exact ultimate vengeance.

Kaye had just risen to his feet when the wild-eyed, manic zealot appeared, the murderous nail still protruding, like a vampire's stake, from his bleeding torso. With a frenzied screech, he threw himself at the first infidel he saw - it was the English whore - his curved blade raised high to strike. Reacting instinctively, Kaye kicked out, his boot connecting with the groin of the would-be assassin. Protecting Sam was all that mattered now. Bashir doubled up, experiencing yet a further new world of pain, only for Kaye's boot to strike a second time, low under his descending chin, breaking his hyoid bone and fracturing his larynx. Unable to draw breath, Bashir collapsed, his body crashing forcefully into the base of the altar.

Dying of suffocation, his darkening eyes sought out the glittering casket above him and, in a last effort of will, he lifted one arm, his hand straining to reach the glorious prize right to the uttermost end. Then his arm dropped and his dead weight lolled against the altar.

By some quirk of fate, his head, coming to rest against one particular alphabet square, set into motion a final, unstoppable trap and, without warning, a previously concealed stone barrier began to grind down from a gap no-one had noticed between the double lintels of the portal.

Looking askance at the fast-disappearing doorway, Kaye took control. 'Everyone out: *right now!*'

Ghulam, already close to the portal, ducked easily under the descending barrier. Kaye grabbed Sam around the waist and began to propel her towards the lessening gap, meaning to help her through and follow on behind. But, as he crouched down to help her duck through, she abruptly pulled back, crying, 'Oh my God; the casket! Don't wait, Oliver - get out right now or I'll never forgive you - I swear it! The casket's my responsibility and, anyway, it'll only take me a moment.' And with that she quit the safety of his arms and ran back to the altar. Still feeling unaccountably weak, Kaye nevertheless protested volubly and was rising from his crouch to follow her when Ghulam reached through the gap and grabbed him by the lapels, summarily pulling him out of the chamber and onto his knees in the tunnel.

It was just then that Eloi, muzzy with concussion, regained consciousness. He raised his head, groaning, only to see his nemesis grab the casket and run past him to hunker down by the low gap that was the sole route out of the chamber.

'Back out on all fours; quick!' yelled the frantic Kaye, cursing her independent bloody-mindedness. If anyone had to risk their life, it should have been him. 'Come on. No arguments! Pull the casket out after you, if there's time. Hurry up!'

Sam's exhausted arms loosed their hold on the heavy golden casket and, letting it drop the last few inches to the floor of the chamber, she began shuffling backwards through the gap, pulling the weighty object with her as she went. It seemed terribly hard work. The casket was so heavy - and, inexplicably, she was so drained of strength...

His head ringing painfully, Eloi scrambled across the floor to regain what he saw as indisputably his.

The descending stone door was creeping oppressively close and Sam was relieved to feel someone grab her calves from behind and jerk backwards. Her legs flew out behind her and her belly hit the rock. Only her arms, at full stretch - and the casket onto which she still, somehow, clung - remained inside the chamber, but, lying prostrate and with both hands encumbered, she now had no choice but to rely on the men already in the tunnel to finish pulling her to safety.

Dropping flat, Eloi fastened his own hands on the far side of the casket. Her sinews already taxed to their limits, Sam whimpered in pain as she fought his protracted attempt to pull it away from her weakening grasp. Suddenly she'd become piggy-in-the-middle in an insane tug of war.

'Stop, Eloi!' she gasped. 'Grab my wrists instead. There's still time. Oliver and Ghulam can pull us both out together.'

Locked onto hers, Eloi's eyes were frigid whirlpools of obsession. In his madness, he refused to relinquish his ultimate desire. 'I am *The One*!' he shrieked. 'The casket is mine! *Mine*!'

'Please,' Sam begged in frantic despair. 'There's no more time!' Her head was directly under the grinding block. It was so close now that it was flattening her hair: in moments it would split her skull like a watermelon.

Squashed side by side in the narrow tunnel, Kaye and Ghulam finally succeeded in capturing her flailing legs and jointly gave them a mighty heave, falling backwards in the process.

Sam's scalp scraped the underside of the rock door as she shot backwards through the vanishing gap. At last! She was wholly inside the tunnel - and safe. She lay still, exhausted, while waves of agony passed through her almost dislocated shoulders. The stone barrier now had mere inches left to drop and, with her head angled sideways against the tunnel floor, Sam was the only one to see her distant cousin's eyes bulge in mortal terror as his crazed mind finally grasped the scope of his failure and its consequence.

The doomed Eloi drew himself up, threw back his head and began an endless scream. The horrific, spine-chilling sound split the air, its piercing discord abruptly cut short only when, with an abysmal thud that reverberated throughout the tunnel, the stone barrier completed its descent, sealing the chamber forever.

CHAPTER 25

TO THE MANOR BORN

Chaumont Hall, Derbyshire, England, 28 June, 2016 AD

Standing by the library desk, sipping Dom Perignon from a Waterford crystal flute, Kaye picked up Sam's unusual paper knife. Idly examining it, he noticed its boar's head insignia and the faded motto, '*Loyaulte me lie*', carved on the hilt. 'Where did you get this dagger?' he asked curiously. 'It must have cost some bundle, considering who its original owner was.'

'Oh, it's been in the family forever,' answered Sam, offhandedly, moving a stack of still-untouched paperwork so she could perch on the corner of the desk. 'Whose was it, then?'

Kaye looked up. 'The insignia and motto tell me it belonged to King Richard III - he of the infamous mystery of the vanishing Princes in the Tower.' With a wicked twinkle in his eye, he added, 'You never know; maybe he did away with them using this very dagger!'

Sam laughed disbelievingly. 'What a gory thought! If that were the case, how on earth did we Dexters end up with the murder weapon? Tell me that.'

'Ah,' replied Kaye, tapping his nose knowingly. 'I know your family, now, don't I? A devious, murdering bunch, if ever there was one. Your first Earl, Simon, was around at the time of Richard's accession, wasn't he? One has to wonder what services he performed for the monarchy in order to deserve an Earldom and all the property and lands that you've inherited.'

'You're not suggesting..?' Sam was mildly indignant.

'Anything's possible.' Kay looked around at the old books and manuscripts thickly packing the library shelves. 'You never know what truths may come to light if you let me investigate this lot.'

Sam swallowed a mouthful of champagne and wagged a finger at the man she was going to marry. 'Don't you think you'll have quite enough to do, what with publishing your discovery of a 'new' ancient language - that *proto*-Sanskrit - and running the estate once you're Lord Chaumont?'

Kaye put down Richard's royal dagger and gathered Sam up in his arms to kiss her, several times over. 'Don't worry,' he said between kisses, 'There'll be time. We've got all the time in the world, haven't we, now that the casket's safely back where it belongs?'

At those words, Sam could not help glancing across the library to the glass-fronted cabinet where Balthazar's casket now lay. How she had managed to wrest it from Eloi's clutches and hang onto it as she was bodily hauled out of the chamber she would never know, but here it was, back where it belonged at last, protected by a unique and sophisticated security system - devised by Ghulam, naturally. She had donned the mantle of Keeper, just as her father had predicted she would, but, in doing so, she had come to understand, far more than her new fiancé ever could, what a tremendous burden that was - a burden that was hers alone. So, he was never going to know that he had died that fateful day in the chamber at the base of Golgotha and that it was *The Power* that had brought him back to her.

It was best that way.

'Talking of my dubious family history,' she teased, returning her attention to Kaye, 'What about your own?'

'A blameless bunch of craftsmen and scholars, all,' replied Kaye airily. 'The earliest ancestor I ever managed to trace was one Lovell Caeg, carpenter in feu to Hoddington Hall in the Shire of Derby in the late fifteenth century. The surname Caeg, by the way, is an old English word meaning key-bearer; it's the origin of my own surname.'

'Hoddington?' exclaimed Sam. 'Did you know Hoddington was assimilated into the Chaumont estate when Simon became Earl? That means your ancestor was probably my ancestor's serf!'

Kaye pulled an exaggerated long-suffering face. '*Plus ça change; plus la même chose..*!'

The library door began to swing open. 'Quick, let go of me, you octopus,' remonstrated Sam, wriggling out of Kaye's embrace and hopping off the desk. 'This'll be Ghulam and I'm going to press him to a glass of bubbly, just this once. After all, we've got plenty to celebrate!'

'Don't I know it,' replied Kaye with a wide grin. 'If it hadn't been for Mister Superman personified tripping up over that fallen stalactite, back there in the maze, we'd never have noticed that little cleft in the rock with the chest of Ottoman gold wedged inside it.'

'Oh, you!' scolded Sam affectionately, pushing him away. 'Yes, I know that's going to solve all our worries about how to afford to run Chaumont properly, but what we're supposed to be celebrating, this particular minute, is our engagement!'

'Um... Shall I come back later, Miss'm?' enquired her factotum, catching his mistress and the professor just splitting from an embrace as he padded into the library.

'Not at all, old boy: come on in and welcome,' Kaye assured him. Sam knew that Ghulam did not normally touch alcohol, but on hearing the happy news, he gave in to tradition and accepted half a flute of champagne with which to toast their future nuptial bliss. He was sincerely glad for them and said so.

After a short interlude of happy chatter, Sam happened to catch sight of a photograph of her father on top one of the antique writing bureaus littered around. Her animated smile faded and she turned to Kaye with an appeal of the moment. 'Darling, would you mind walking out to the family crypt with me?'

Kaye, who was just explaining the origins of the interesting paper knife to the attentive Ghulam, glanced up and saw the sadness in Sam's lovely eyes; that old sadness that he hoped he would, one day, be able to banish for good. 'Not at all,' he replied, instantly. 'Let's do that.'

'Sorry, Ghulam,' said Sam. 'I hope you don't mind us deserting you.'

Considerate as always, Ghulam inclined his head and brought his palms together in his usual, inconspicuous obeisance. 'Don't mind me, Miss'm,' he said. 'I'll just clear up the glasses while you're out, shall I?'

'Thank you, Ghulam. Thank you so much - for everything,' said Sam.

The couple left the library and, as she went through the doorway, Ghulam heard Sam say, quietly, 'I know he killed Daddy and no excuses should be made for that, but his mind was deranged and... well, anyway, what I'm trying to say is that I've been thinking about it and I've decided that, whatever his crimes, Eloi was still a member of the Dexter family, so I'd like to have a simple memorial stone placed near the crypt, with his name on it - somewhere that's got a nice, *open* view. What do you think..?'

Ghulam nodded to himself. His mistress was going to make a fine Lady of the Manor, a very fine one indeed. He cleared the champagne bottle and glasses onto a tray, intending to take them to the kitchen and then retire to his quarters to brew a pot of good quality Indian tea before spending a quiet hour meditating; yet, on his way out, he hesitated in mid stride. It would be fitting to pay his respects to the casket first, he thought, turning on his heel.

Not wishing to risk the activation of a dozen warning sirens all over Chaumont, Ghulam did not approach the glass-fronted cabinet too closely. Prudently, he halted two yards away and fluidly sank into a humble, cross-legged pose on the Persian carpet, facing the object of his concern and delight. From the moment he had first seen it in the subterranean chamber he had been drawn to it with an inexplicable yearning that rose from the deepest core of his heart. Despite his mistrust of what he knew to be its sometimes deceitful and often dangerous glamour, still, the casket called to him.

Raising his gentle brown eyes, he stared at the intricate surface behind which lay a *Power* such as the world had never known. Well, no, he thought, that was not quite true, was it? Two men had once understood the potential of that *Power* in its entirety - the Ancients themselves: Ashar and Baal. The Keepers' line descending from Baal was, of course, of the line of the Ancients and there was no doubt in Ghulam's mind that Balthazar, Abdul Hamid, Simon

Dexter and ultimately his mistress, Lady Samantha Dexter, were all direct descendants of that line. There was sufficient historical documentation to support that conclusion, but the final proof had been given in the chamber hidden deep beneath the Holy Sepulchre.

Unfortunately, there were no known records of the descendants of Ashar, who, whilst not Keepers, were, nevertheless, also of the blood of the Ancients. The corners of Ghulam's lips curled into a barely discernible smile. He had not needed his mistress or the very fine Professor Oliver to tell him the legend of Ashar and Baal. Ghulam's own father had related their story to him, an ancestral history passed down from his father's father and all the great-great-grandfathers back through his family's generations for years beyond count, right back to the beginning - fifteen thousand years ago. It was a secret carried on the wings of time by word of mouth alone.

Ghulam rose effortlessly from his cross-legged pose, still gazing at the casket. Its finely wrought gold gave no hint that inside, it held, confined by unknowable means, the pulsing life force of a sun. Who could imagine that such a thing was possible? And who could imagine that some human being, of the blood of the Ancients, might be capable of controlling and utilising that extraordinary *Power* over and over again, as the Keepers' faith proclaimed? Who could imagine a veritable Day of Judgement?

The reflection of Balthazar's casket gleamed in his eyes.

I am Ghulam Gupta, he thought, born in a humble town in the North West of the United Kingdom, of Pakistani parentage. For thousands upon thousands of years, my ancestors farmed the fertile loam of that part of the Indian sub-continent that lately became Pakistan; the very area from which we understand Balthazar set out on his journey to Bethlehem; the very area from which the Vedic Sanskrit legends originate, concerning the time of the vimanas.

I am Ghulam and I am most assuredly a direct descendant of the Lord Ashar. So, like Miss'm', my blood, also, is the blood of the Ancients.

He shook his head in incredulity at the formidable array of coincidences that had brought him to this place, of all places, at this, of all times. Under the circumstances, how could he help wondering...?

'Surely not,' he whispered to himself. 'I should put such a crazy idea out of my head. After all, there must be thousands of living souls around the world who are descended from Baal or Ashar, most of whom don't even know it.

'Surely it would be one coincidence too many to suppose that, of all possible claimants, I, myself... might be... *The One?*'

EPILOGUE

Paris, France, 29 June, 2016 AD

'I've rung the carrier's freight handling service a dozen times today, already. They still haven't traced the crate. *Merde*! What a bunch of utter incompetents!' Desselle was beside himself.

Laurent paced the length of the university's forensic anthropology laboratory. 'We know the crate was loaded on that specific flight, because we watched them do it,' he said. 'And it was a direct flight to Charles de Gaulle Airport here in Paris, yes?'

Desselle nodded. 'Exactly; so how could such a large piece of freight go missing? It's inconceivable!'

Laurent shook his head, nonplussed at the triple dose of appalling misfortunes that had beset the Damascus expedition. First, Alain; horribly murdered - then that Cardinal shot dead at the dig site - and, now, not only were they were missing the vital samples that the postgraduates had somehow lost on their way back to France, but even the actual mummified remains from which the samples had been taken.

'I'm beginning to feel guilty for the hard time we gave Yves and Philippe,' he admitted. 'But the samples were in a well-labelled expedition attaché case and both the carriers swore there had been no handling errors. They seemed as surprised as we were that the attaché case had simply vanished somewhere between Cairo and Charles de Gaulle. I shouldn't have blamed the postgraduates. The case was checked in as hold baggage, not hand baggage, which, in retrospect, was an unfortunate choice, but the outcome really wasn't their fault.'

'No,' agreed Desselle. 'I think we should apologise to them, especially since it now appears that this kind of baggage disappearing act is a lot more common than we thought.' He paused, frowning. 'It's just that I was under the impression that ninety nine percent of lost luggage turned up within twenty four hours, but Yves and Philippe got back over a week ago and we've been back for four days - and there's still no news on either count.'

Laurent sighed. 'The samples we could live without, if we had the body. But without the body we can't take replacement samples, so we have no way to verify any of the locally conducted work we did.'

'I took a lot of photos, Henri.'

'Photos; yes,' replied Laurent, raising his arms in an expansive French shrug. 'Unfortunately, we can't publish on the basis of a few holiday snaps.' He sounded bitter, but Desselle did not take offence. It would be nothing less than a shattering blow for the team to lose the remains they had every reason to believe were those of Jesus Christ.

'I suppose all we can do is hope they turn up in a forgotten corner of some baggage store or lost luggage depot,' said Desselle, miserably.

His colleague had been pacing towards the far end of the laboratory, but abruptly turned to face him. 'And what if they don't, Jean? What if they never turn up?'

Desselle sighed. 'If they never turn up, then we have to face the facts. No-one is ever going to know whether Alain found the tomb of the real Jesus Christ, or not.'

Laurent's face took on a strange expression. 'You know,' he murmured, 'When I think about it, considering the tragic deaths that have already resulted from that discovery; the street violence that erupted between Christian and Muslim communities when the news of Cardinal Mercurio's assassination hit the headlines and the crisis of faith that so many people have been enduring, all because of a few dried-out bones entombed in a hillside above Damascus...'

Desselle completed Laurent's train of thought. '...Perhaps it's better if we never do establish the ultimate truth? Never know for sure?'

Laurent gazed heavenwards for a long moment before he replied. 'Perhaps we were never meant to.'

POSTSCRIPT

Having selected a vital *motif* at the start of writing my novel - a known, real, ancient sun symbol - in the case of my story, a symbol signifying the essence of that celestial body imprisoned within the casket - it was not until I reached the climax of the tale that I had cause to desk-research the interior of the Church of the Holy Sepulchre in Jerusalem, in order to make my written descriptions of it as true to life as possible.

When I examined photographs of that church's Greek Orthodox Chapel of the Crucifixion (in which the faithful kneel at the altar to reach down through a small gap in the floor and touch the bedrock of the hill of Golgotha, where it is thought Christ was crucified), imagine my astonishment and disbelief when these photographs revealed that the mediaeval stone flooring of that chapel is plain except for one large decorative embellishment built into it, directly facing the altar – yes, you've guessed it – the *motif* that actually exists in that real-life location turned out to be the self-same archaic sun symbol that had always rested at the core of my fictional story. Thus, an unexpected small slice of reality became woven into my fictional tale, providing one more elegant clue to the hiding place of a magical treasure far older than Christianity.

Wearing my scientist's white coat, I might call this a matter of fortuitous blind chance. Wearing my magician's pointy hat, I could term it fate, or perhaps even 'literary reverse engineering' (with my tongue in my cheek). But the truth is that the chances of picking a design at random from all the suitable solar symbols that exist in the real world, prior to the novel being written, and that symbol proving to be the very one that actually exists in precisely the most apt location imaginable for the fictional tale's purposes, namely, to act as a vital clue and guide to the treasure seekers at the culmination of the story, have got to be millions to one against.

Serendipity.

It's enough to make one wonder whether Someone up there might have played a part in the matter.

BIOGRAPHY

From childhood, I had always just wanted to write stories and paint pictures, but real life often forces sensible economic decisions upon us – such as the need to pay one's bills regularly. Consequently, after leaving university with a genetics degree, I joined an American pharmaceutical company as the sole female sales person on a team of a hundred men. That was quite an experience. I then expanded into international business development with a UK-based non-profit scientific publishing house, where there were lots of female employees, which was somewhat of a relief.

Next, I pioneered the role of Commercial Development Manager for Glasgow University's Institute of Biomedical and Life Sciences, where I developed a technology transfer and commercialisation programme and doubled faculty commercial income in two years. You can trust me when I say, with all due deference to their immense brainpower, that academic researchers are generally not commercially minded. I had to tread softly.

I managed to find some time to write alongside my developing commercial career, but my efforts were limited to poetry and short stories, some of which won competitions and were published. I had long been a member of one local writers' club or another, and relished the brief periods I was able to spend in the company of folk as passionate about creative writing as I have always been.

My next career step was to join the Hannah Research Institute as Commercial Development Manager, creating new high-tech companies based on research inventions. In 2002, I became Director of Research and Commercialisation for the then University of Paisley, restructuring internal business units to greater profitability, selling young business ventures into the private sector and directing the spin-out of several companies. I also managed the university's research grant income department.

Thankfully, becoming financially independent, at last I began to write seriously, with Balthazar's Casket being the first result of my determination to complete a magical mystery adventure novel. Friends who have read it tell me it's like a cross between Dan Brown's 'da Vinci Code' and an Indiana Jones adventure. I am now working on two further novels and divide my time between those, my husband, our pet Ragdoll cat Lotus Blossom and, occasionally, pet portrait painting. Some folk even pay real money for my art, these days.

Once you've read Balthazar's Casket, I'd be delighted to get your feedback to spur me on to create a sequel. I can be reached at my author website.

email:
cheryljwhite@hotmail.com